Since the days of Ann Radcliffe and Mary Shelley, women have produced many of the finest ghost stories ever written, bringing to their craft the qualities of their particular experience and their history of living on the margins. Yet before the arrival of the first *Virago Book of Ghost Stories* (1987), the contribution of women to the genre had been neglected in the countless anthologies published. This selection reaches back in time to the sublime terrors of the nineteenth century and presents tales by Charlotte Brontë, Elizabeth Gaskell, Mary Braddon and Willa Cather among many others. This is both an important addition to literary history and a thrilling, chilling read.

Richard Dalby is a literary researcher and bibliographer whose published works include *The Virago Book of Ghost Stories: The Twentieth Century* (1987), and *The Virago Book of Ghost Stories: The Twentieth Century II* (1991), plus several other anthologies of ghost stories. He lives in North Yorkshire.

Jennifer Uglow has published *George Eliot*, a study of the author's life and works (Virago 1987), and is currently editorial director of the Hogarth Press in London.

THE VIRAGO BOOK OF
VICTORIAN
GHOST
STORIES

EDITED BY RICHARD DALBY

Published by VIRAGO PRESS Limited, 1992
20-23 Mandela Street, Camden Town, London NW1 0HQ

Reprinted 1992

First published in hardback in Britain by Virago Press, 1988

A CIP catalogue record for this book is available from the British Library

Typeset by Goodfellow & Egan Ltd, Cambridge
Printed by Cox & Wyman Ltd, Reading, Berks.

CONTENTS

PREFACE

OVER the past 150 years Britain has led the world in the art of the classic ghost story, and it is no exaggeration to state that at least fifty per cent of quality examples in the genre were by women writers. This is especially true of the nineteenth century, which began with the classic Gothic novels of Ann Radcliffe, Clara Reeve and Mary Shelley.

The ghost story reached a high peak over a hundred years ago in magazines like Dickens' *Household Words* and *All the Year Round*, and became an essential annual ingredient of the best-selling Christmas numbers. Most of the greatest women writers of the Victorian era contributed marvellous tales to these magazines (often anonymously), and most of the leading names are represented in the present collection.

The definition of the Victorian Age is slightly extended at each end, from 1833 to 1903, to accommodate a very early pastiche by Charlotte Brontë, followed by an immortal tale by her friend and biographer Elizabeth Gaskell, and closing at the turn of the century with two American stories by Willa Cather and Mary E. Wilkins.

As with the companion volume (*The Virago Book of Ghost Stories, The Twentieth Century*), this anthology is arranged in strict chronological order. Again, due to limitation of space, a few notable names have had to be excluded, among them some pillars of children's literature: Juliana Horatia Ewing, Mary Louisa Molesworth, E. Nesbit and Dora Havers; Eliza Lynn Linton; William IV's granddaughter, the Countess of Munster; and George Eliot (whose supernatural novella, *The Lifted Veil*, has been published separately by Virago).

All kinds of ghosts are described here, malevolent as well as benevolent and sympathetic. In the opinion of one great practitioner of the ghost story, M. R. James:

There are but two really good ghost stories I know in the language wherein the elements of beauty and pity dominate horror. They are Lanoe Falconer's *Cecilia de Noël* and Mrs Oliphant's *The Open Door*. In both there are moments of horror; but in both we end by saying with Hamlet: 'Alas, poor ghost!' Perhaps my limit of two stories is overstrict: but that these two are by very much the best of their kind I do not doubt.

Both these stories appear in the present volume.

I have attempted to select the best example by each author, in some cases from a very wide choice, especially with Amelia Edwards, Mary E. Braddon, Margaret Oliphant, Mrs Henry Wood, and Vernon Lee, who each wrote more than enough fine supernatural tales to fill a large volume separately.

In this anthology, some acknowledged classics rub shoulders with several rare and unfamiliar tales, including those by Dinah Mulock, Amelia Edwards, Ella D'Arcy, and Willa Cather. I hope even the most avid collector of ghostly fiction will find something new here, alongside favourites worth savouring again.

Richard Dalby

INTRODUCTION

'OH the past, the past! Will it never leave us?'

Ghosts – and ghost stories – swim up out of history and pull us back, under the rim of the years, into their own time. The haunted victims may be full of terrors, as they pull the bedclothes over their heads or quake with guilt at past misdeeds, but modern readers, secure (or are we?) in our armchairs, look forward instead to an hour of marrow-chilling pleasure, satisfying a craving which persists from childhood, the fun of being safely scared.

This collection opens many doors into the past. It sweeps us from the 1830s to 1900, from Charlotte Brontë to Willa Cather, from Irish mountains to Mediterranean villas, London mansions to Boston backstreets. All the tales have their own individual shiver, special twist, powerful atmosphere, springing wit. They were written for entertainment, usually on the well-tried Wilkie Collins formula of 'make 'em laugh, make 'em cry, make 'em wait', and can still make us catch our breath and turn the page at double speed. Yet they offer more than that, for down their twisting corridors, or in that closed East Wing, are glimpses of the buried feelings, values, and sometimes the prejudices, of a hundred years ago which could not surface so readily in more 'respectable' works. And because these are women's stories, they grant an insight into women's longings, women's fears, suppressed resentments, buried angers and firmly held beliefs.

It also clears a path to the light for the shades of women writers. They step out, one by one, from the bulky shadow of the men who dominated ghost-story anthologies for so long: Scott and Le Fanu, Dickens and Wilkie Collins, Poe and Hawthorne, Stevenson, Kipling and Henry James. Some of these women, who may well be new to today's readers, were great favourites in their day: Rosa Mulholland, Charlotte Riddell, Louisa Baldwin (Kipling's aunt), the wayward, elegant Ella D'Arcy. To me the most striking discovery is Lanoe Falconer, who apparently had no formal education, yet whose famous story 'Cecilia de Noël' is so spontaneously funny, lively and moving, and so knowing about the foibles and philosophies of her age, that it seems extraordinary that she did not become a major writer – is there, in some dusty attic, a trunk of yellowing manuscripts waiting to be prised open?

Most of their stories appeared in the popular family journals which began their long run in the 1850s, expanded rapidly in the 1860s and flourished until the turn of the century, a few lingering on, like ghosts of their former selves, until the Second World War. Among the early leaders were Dickens' *Household Words*, founded in 1850, and his other journal *All The Year Round*, which followed nine years later. Others included the *Saturday Review*, the *Cornhill*, *St James' Magazine*, *Belgravia*, *Temple Bar*, *Argosy*, *Tinsleys*, *St Pauls* – their names are legion. Some appeared weekly, some monthly, all tapping a huge new readership avid for entertainment.

They provided much needed outlets for women writers, several of whom survived by their pens – I am always astounded by their courage, hard work and sticking-power. Several tackled the literary world on their own, like Dinah Mulock who came to London before she was twenty, determined to make a living as a writer. Many more were the chief support of their families and were often first pushed into 'professional' writing because the men in their lives were inadequate providers. Charlotte Riddell married a hopeless speculator and despite fifty successful books she died in poverty, still paying off his debts. Mary Braddon, who lived with the brilliant but feckless publisher John Maxwell, poured out novels and stories to support ten children (and Maxwell's wife, in a Dublin asylum). Mrs Oliphant's husband failed as a stained-glass artist and after he died in 1859 her writing was the only resource for herself and her children. (Her story, in touching contrast to her life, centres on a father who provides everything – money, security, strength and understanding). Some became editors themselves: Mary Braddon founded *Belgravia* in 1866 and also edited *Temple Bar*, while Mrs Henry Wood established the *Argosy* in 1867 and wrote much of its material, including the well-loved 'Johnny Ludlow' stories like 'Reality or Delusion?'

Ghost stories were a favourite feature of the bumper Christmas Annuals eagerly promoted by Dickens, taking pride of place among the charades, cartoons and adventure stories. When they were read aloud around a crackling fire, did they exorcise the cold and want without and, perhaps, the unnamed tensions within? Whatever the case, the yuletide tradition linked the bourgeoisie to an older world of demons and spirits which they thought they had left behind, the world which Henry Bourne had described in 1725:

Nothing is commoner in *Country Places*, than for a whole Family in a *Winter's Evening*, to sit around the fire, and tell stories of Apparitions and Ghosts. And no Question of it, but this adds to the natural Fearfulness of Men, and makes them many times imagine they see Things, which really are nothing but their own Fancy.

The rural past, which took for granted the spirits that rise from the graveyards on All Souls' Day, echoes in the stories themselves. You will find it is often the country people, the Irish peasants, the Scottish grooms, who open the eyes of the sceptical – or unsuspecting – middle classes to the secrets of the houses they live in and the past they would rather not recognise. This happens so often that it grows to feel like a kind of class conspiracy – the butcher knows, the grocer knows, the caretakers, nursemaids, cooks and servants certainly know, but the prosperous families who move into haunted spaces are kept in the dark until the crisis comes. In Mrs Gaskell's marvellous 'Old Nurse's Story' the lesson takes another form: the closer you are to those in power (in this case to old Miss Furnivall, last of a proud and cruel line), the closer you guard their secrets – the housekeeper won't talk but Bessy the kitchen maid will.

The result is the same: the pride of Gaskell's aristocrats, the confidence of Mrs Oliphant's businessman, the splendid nouveau-riche bumptiousness of Mary Wilkins' New Englanders – all are due for a tumble. In Rhoda Broughton's story two young society matrons are thrilled (like endless others – who clearly have *not* read their Christmas Annuals) when they find the perfect house for a peppercorn rent. They proceed to exchange their deliciously worldly letters: 'What a wealth of red hair she had last year! Well, that same wealth is black as the raven's wing this year! . . . Dresses are gored to as *indecent* an extent as ever; short skirts are rampant.' Alas, they learn to their cost what it is to look only at style and surfaces and not at the substance and depths beneath. The popular origins of ghost stories, their alliance to oral tradition, gave educated women one way of criticising and undermining the structures which constrained their lives. Allying themselves with the common people who know more than their 'betters', they can see their world from the outside, indeed from the 'other side'.

Literary traditions also gave writers ways of looking from a distance at contemporary society and prevailing attitudes. One influence was the Gothic novel, where women had also proved supreme, like Ann Radcliffe, whose *Mysteries of Udolpho*, published in 1794, set the tone for decades. Even reading her work could unleash a flood of stylised terrors.

In *Northanger Abbey* Catherine Morland, an eager devourer of Mrs Radcliffe, stands rooted to the spot, her candle flame hastily snuffed out:

Darkness impenetrable and immoveable filled the room. A violent gust of wind, rising with sudden fury, added fresh horror to the moment. Catherine trembled from head to foot. In the pause which succeeded, a sound like receding footsteps and the closing of a distant door struck on her affrighted ear. Human nature could support no more. A cold sweat stood on her forehead, the manuscript fell from her hand, and groping her way to the bed, she jumped hastily in, and sought some suspension of agony by creeping far underneath the clothes.

In daylight, of course, Catherine's manuscript turns out to be a laundry list, and she soon decides that 'charming as were all Mrs Radcliffe's works . . . it was not in them perhaps that human nature, at least in the midland counties of England, was to be looked for.' But as Austen slyly suggests, the Gothic does reveal some sides of human nature, if only our foolish longing for romance and excitement. At any rate the ghosts were not to be routed by common sense and still deeper aspects of humanity found expression in later women's fantasies – in the fearful images of birth and separation, eternal exile and cosmic loneliness of Mary Shelley's *Frankenstein* and *The Last Man*, and in Emily Brontë's Cathy, haunting the moors of Wuthering Heights. The Gothic lived on in the dreams and forebodings which form the darker underside of more 'realistic' women novelists, Charlotte Brontë, George Eliot and Mrs Gaskell.

Ghost-story writers also drew on Romantic writing, with its fondness for the picturesque, to place their characters on the edges of life, literally and metaphorically. Thus Gertrude Atherton's hero hangs perilously above a swirling pool below The Strid, the Yorkshire waterfall which had fascinated Wordsworth. (In true Romantic fashion her story finally came to her in a dream.) Sometimes the Romantic attraction to the exotic and the strange merge with a sympathy for outcast races or foreign cultures: when Amelia Edwards chooses Venice, the city rising from the water, meeting point of West and East, her hero thinks of the writers who have walked there before him: Goethe, Byron and Shelley. Although we may question her solution 'The Story of Salome' is a story of yearning, not only for love, but for understanding, the integration of a people who – like women – are at once at the heart of European culture and yet on the fringes, neglected and deprived of status. At sunset in the Jewish cemetery on the Lido, its graves encrusted by lichen, corroded with salt, half-buried and effaced, we are on the dissolving margins of the world, in more senses than one:

The *ghetto* of the dead! I remembered now to have read or heard long since how the

Venetian Jews, cut off in death as in life from the neighbourhood of their Christian rulers, had been buried from time immemorial upon this desolate waste.

From a different margin, the West of Ireland, Rosa Mulholland writes within another alien culture which intrigued and half-frightened the comfortable Protestant readers of the family magazines. Ireland, with its heavy brogue, bizarre folk customs and Catholic belief, was a place where passion and sin carried threats of hell-fire and the dread of body-snatchers denied the promise of resurrection. (The theft of corpses was a widespread fear, both a cause and symptom of distrust in medical advances. In Ireland this terror was so intense that graveyards had 'resurrection-lamps' where relatives could watch over the newly buried, and coffins were weighed down by iron bars, or encased in metal cages.) Yet however rich and rare its style might be, Rosa Mulholland's story is central to the experiences of Victorian women. For the beautiful independent daughter is a mere possession of her father, like his fine grand house, so that both form obvious targets for a disinherited man's revenge, while the fear which she feels is less supernatural than bodily, a sexual dread in which physical possession is synonymous with madness and death.

But women did not have to stand outside the society they addressed. Many of the writers in this book had quite different reputations, as social, domestic and sentimental novelists: Dinah Mulock (Mrs Craik) was the author of *John Halifax, Gentleman*; Charlotte Riddell, whose best-selling novel *George Geith of Fen Court* must surely be the first (of very few) to have an accountant as its hero, was known as 'the chronicler of business'; Mary Cholmondeley is better known as the author of *Red Pottage*. Their ghost stories bring out themes less openly expressed in their 'serious' work. For example in 'The Old Nurse's Story' Mrs Gaskell confronts the disruptive threat of sexuality and jealousy, the repressive power of the father, and stifling family pride. Both she and Mrs Oliphant use a familiar figure from sentimental fiction, the innocent child, as the catalyst of a crisis which forces adults either to acknowledge their own corruption, or to admit a sensitivity long buried under 'sensible' exteriors. Their stories bring out not only their belief in an inexorable law of consequences but also their faith in the power of compassion and protective love. And because these writers have such a gift for solid physical description and acute perception of character the sense of a rift in the real, a disruption of the normal, is all the more convincing and deeply disturbing.

On the other hand the 'sensation' writers of the 1860s, Mary Braddon and Mrs Henry Wood, had already unsettled Victorian complacency. In some ways the ghost story seems a natural extension of their novels, which brought dislocation and menace to the very heart of the family home. Desire, ambition, bigamy, adultery, even murder invade the sacred hearth; domestic angels turn out to be fiends. In the novels the wayward heroines are cruelly punished and order is restored, though the cracks in the structure remain. But in the stories the passionate women wreak vengeance on false, weak men, selfish betrayers of women's trust. The tables are suggestively turned.

Although – perhaps because – they were written as unpretentious entertainments, ghost stories seemed to give their writers a licence to experiment, to push the boundaries of fiction a little further. Mary Braddon's story is very much of its age, unashamedly theatrical (she was an actress before she became a writer), crying out to be read aloud. Yet it is also strikingly modern, for we suspect that the haunting takes place solely within the victim's mind. The cold embrace is a manifestation of guilt and remorse, unseen by others, which grips him whenever he is alone – and there are times, we realise, when everyone must be alone with their conscience. The image encapsulates Braddon's perception of the thin veneer of social life and sanity and of our vulnerability and isolation, and embodies the terrifying insight which comes to the hero of her most famous novel, *Lady Audley's Secret*:

There is nothing so delicate, so fragile, as that invisible balance upon which the mind is always trembling . . . Who has not been, or is not to be mad in some lonely hour of life? Who is quite safe from the trembling of the balance?

Again and again we find that the machinery of this most conventional genre frees, rather than restricts, the women who use it. The tricks of the unreal allow them to move into that deeper realm, where dream has greater clarity than daylight. Thus Charlotte Riddell, the most prosaic of writers, can produce a truly extraordinary effect in 'The Old House in Vauxhall Walk'. We feel no doubt here about the ghosts, who emerge from the hero's dreams into alarmingly violent activity. Instead all the gaps and silences cluster around the 'real' life of the young man whose predicament we will never fully understand. We do not need to – it is his inner experience which counts, and which counterbalances and corrects his understanding of the world of money, pride, ambition and family conflict from which he has fled.

Sometimes the short form sums up, in a startling way, the inner preoccupations of the writer. In Willa Cather's brilliant, horrifying tale, where the blanketing snow engulfs the prairies and the railway lines flee across the continent away from the enclosed glitter of the Inaugural Ball, we recognise her constant themes: the outsiders looking in on a forbidden world, the violence and fear which surround desire, the clash of cultures – ancient and modern, exotic and familiar, magical and material. But here they are drawn with heightened, graphic, disconcerting vividness. It is as if the form betrays her, catching her unawares, letting her speak out where she would usually be silent.

But how do these revealing stories relate to 'real' ghosts? In the later nineteenth century the spirit world certainly commanded a literal as well as fictional suspension of disbelief. When Mrs Crowe published *The Night Side of Nature* in 1848 she did so with a solemn purpose:

If I have done no more, I trust I shall at least have afforded some amusement; but I shall be better pleased to learn that I have induced any one, if it be *but* one, to look upon life and death, and the mysteries that attach to both, with a more curious and enquiring eye than they have hitherto done.

Catherine Crowe saw herself not as an imaginative writer but as a scientist. A disciple of the phrenologist George Combe, she was also interested in mesmerism, which was popular from the 1830s and suggested that spirits could communicate with sensitive souls, or mediums, through 'animal magnetism'. From the 1850s, after the celebrated 'Rochester knockings' in New York State, American mediums toured Europe as well as the USA. Seances flourished, as did table tapping, planchette writing, spirit photography and full-scale manifestations. When the Society for Psychical Research was founded in 1882 it was inundated with letters, which prompted long *Proceedings* and a gigantic census of reported apparitions.

Some of this hubbub is reflected in the fiction. Although Lanoe Falconer pokes fun at her Lucinda Molyneux, she does recognise that an addiction to the occult is a genuine expression of spiritual need. Both the reports and stories make good use of 'crisis apparitions' appearing at a moment of death and both remain fond of those very old-fashioned spirits who leave messages and warnings for the living, here to find their body. But most contemporary ghosts (unlike those of earlier eras) had, we are told, no obvious purpose at all but were just content to appear, rattle the wardrobe, scare the maid and vanish. You would think this wouldn't do at all in fiction where narratives turn on reason and revelation, but in fact some of the most unnerving ghosts in this book remain unexplained. Their stories are effective largely because the haunting *is* so random and unfathomable. As in 'The Villa Lucienne' ordinary people plunge from sunlight into darkness – and it is their reactions, not the motives of the ghost, which provide the real revelation.

The mass of recorded sightings and the popularity of the ghost story prompted the same questions. 'However we are to explain it,' wrote Andrew Lang, 'the ghosts have come forth again . . . Now this is a queer result of science, common-sense, cheap newspapers, popular education, and progress in general.' One answer is that it was precisely 'progress' – the revelations of geology, evolutionary theory, critical theology – which summoned up the spectres. As Julia Briggs explains it in *The Night Visitors: The Rise and Fall of the Ghost Story*, in an age where science has brought 'improving material circumstances and increasing spiritual discomfort' ghosts were an oddly reassuring, if uncomfortable, proof that there was something beyond: 'Man was not, as he had come to fear, alone in a universe infinitely older, larger, wilder and less anthropocentric than he had previously supposed.' The same presumably applies to 'woman'.

Certainly these stories tend to question 'science' and the search for rational knowledge. How often are men (and they inevitably are men) punished for thinking they can conquer the mysteries, for begging to stay the night in the haunted room? Many also have an implicit religious context. This is clear in a tale like 'The Open Door', with its references to purgatory and divine forgiveness, but more often, as in 'Cecilia de Noël', church institutions, individual priests and theological doctrines are shown to be hollow, while the concepts of pity and redeeming love remain, enduring apart from doctrine, in social and personal relationships.

One intriguing question remains. In all the collected 'evidence' women outnumber men – as reporters, seers and ghosts themselves. So why, in these stories, do male narrators, heroes and spirits outnumber women? A simple explanation lies in the demands of the form itself: to be believed ghost stories must be told by down-to-earth people whose reports we trust. The nineteenth century notoriously labelled women as 'nervous', 'hysterical', 'over-emotional' – hence the solid businessman, the London barrister, the paterfamilias. Sometimes the impersonation is acknowledged – Lanoe Falconer's narrator, emotionally wounded and physically disabled from manly pursuits, is clearly identified with the world of women and children. But elsewhere the male disguise works differently, allowing women authors access to 'unfeminine' freedoms – to stand on waterfalls, travel the world, take an active role in sexual conquest. In Vernon Lee's story, where the haunted becomes obsessed with his haunter one senses a double disguise: Winthrop's pursuit of the disturbingly feminine portrait of a dead man, a famous singer, may *reveal* an American expatriate's seduction by a European past, but it may also *conceal* a woman's desire for her own sex, and the anxiety this induces.

There may be more to it even than useful disguise. For note how the experience of seeing a ghost pushes men into conventional female roles: timid, nervous, helpless. At the very start of the book Charlotte Brontë's playfully vengeful ghost exposes poor Napoleon, putting him through a version of the humiliating dream, in which we find ourselves naked on stage in a crowded theatre. The Emperor has no clothes. From then on, in numerous ways, the men of authority and science – doctors, priests, fathers – lose their confidence, become oppressed, doubtful, unsure of their status, vulnerable to swings of emotion. They too are made to feel (as the women of their day so often did) that their destiny is out of their hands and their world is governed by uncontrollable, relentless, probably hostile, powers. To regain control and put the spirits to rest, as Mrs Oliphant's hero does, the father must shed his arrogance and knowledge and rely instead on humility, tolerance, love, care and forgiveness – all the virtues which the age prescribed to the feminine sphere, the realm of the mother.

Thus, even in its telling, the woman's supernatural tale can take its own, ghostly, revenge.

Jennifer Uglow, Canterbury, 1988

Charlotte Brontë

NAPOLEON AND THE SPECTRE

WELL, as I was saying, the Emperor got into bed.

'Chevalier,' says he to his valet, 'let down those window-curtains, and shut the casement before you leave the room.'

Chevalier did as he was told, and then, taking up his candlestick, departed.

In a few minutes the Emperor felt his pillow becoming rather hard, and he got up to shake it. As he did so a slight rustling noise was heard near the bed-head. His Majesty listened, but all was silent as he lay down again.

Scarcely had he settled into a peaceful attitude of repose, when he was disturbed by a sensation of thirst. Lifting himself on his elbow, he took a glass of lemonade from the small stand which was placed beside him. He refreshed himself by a deep draught. As he returned the goblet to its station a deep groan burst from a kind of closet in one corner of the apartment.

'Who's there?' cried the Emperor, seizing his pistols. 'Speak, or I'll blow your brains out.'

This threat produced no other effect than a short, sharp laugh, and a dead silence followed.

The Emperor started from his couch, and, hastily throwing on a *robe-de-chambre* which hung over the back of a chair, stepped courageously to the haunted closet. As he opened the door something rustled. He sprang forward sword in hand. No soul or even substance appeared, and the rustling, it was evident, proceeded from the falling of a cloak, which had been suspended by a peg from the door.

Half ashamed of himself he returned to bed.

Just as he was about once more to close his eyes, the light of the three wax tapers, which burned in a silver branch over the mantelpiece, was suddenly darkened. He looked up. A black, opaque shadow obscured it. Sweating with terror, the Emperor put out his hand to seize the bell-rope, but some invisible being snatched it rudely from his grasp, and at the same instant the ominous shade vanished.

'Pooh!' exclaimed Napoleon, 'it was but an ocular delusion.'

'Was it?' whispered a hollow voice, in deep mysterious tones, close to his ear. 'Was it a delusion, Emperor of France? No! all thou hast heard and seen is sad forewarning reality. Rise, lifter of the Eagle Standard! Awake, swayer of the Lily Sceptre! Follow me, Napoleon, and thou shalt see more.'

As the voice ceased, a form dawned on his astonished sight. It was that of a tall, thin man, dressed in a blue surtout edged with gold lace. It wore a black cravat very tightly round its neck, and confined by two little sticks placed behind each ear. The countenance was livid; the tongue protruded from between the teeth, and the eyes all glazed and bloodshot started with frightful prominence from their sockets.

'*Mon Dieu!*' exclaimed the Emperor, 'what do I see? Spectre, whence cometh thou?'

The apparition spoke not, but gliding forward beckoned Napoleon with uplifted finger to follow.

Controlled by a mysterious influence, which deprived him of the capability of either thinking or acting for himself, he obeyed in silence.

The solid wall of the apartment fell open as they approached, and, when both had passed through, it closed behind them with a noise like thunder.

They would now have been in total darkness had it not been for a dim light which shone round the ghost and revealed the damp walls of a long, vaulted passage. Down this they proceeded with mute rapidity. Ere long a cool, refreshing breeze, which rushed wailing up the vault and caused the Emperor to wrap his loose nightdress closer round, announced their approach to the open air.

This they soon reached, and Nap found himself in one of the principal streets of Paris.

'Worthy Spirit,' said he, shivering in the chill night air, 'permit me to return and put on some additional clothing. I will be with you again presently.'

'Forward,' replied his companion sternly.

He felt compelled, in spite of the rising indignation which almost choked him, to obey.

On they went through the deserted streets till they arrived at a lofty house built on the banks of the Seine. Here the Spectre stopped, the gates rolled back to receive them, and they entered a large marble hall which was partly concealed by a curtain drawn across, through the half transparent folds of which a bright light might be seen burning with dazzling lustre. A row of fine female figures, richly attired, stood before this screen. They wore on their heads garlands of the most beautiful flowers, but their faces were concealed by ghastly masks representing death's-heads.

'What is all this mummery?' cried the Emperor, making an effort to shake off the mental shackles by which he was so unwillingly restrained, 'Where am I, and why have I been brought here?'

'Silence,' said the guide, lolling out still further his black and bloody tongue. 'Silence, if thou wouldst escape instant death.'

The Emperor would have replied, his natural courage overcoming the temporary awe to which he had at first been subjected, but just then a strain of wild, supernatural music swelled behind the huge curtain, which waved to and fro, and bellied slowly out as if agitated by some internal commotion or battle of waving winds. At the same moment an over-powering mixture of the scents of mortal corruption, blent with the richest Eastern odours, stole through the haunted hall.

A murmur of many voices was now heard at a distance, and something grasped his arm eagerly from behind.

He turned hastily round. His eyes met the well-known countenance of Marie Louise.

'What! are you in this infernal place, too?' said he. 'What has brought you here?'

'Will your Majesty permit me to ask the same question of yourself?' said the Empress, smiling.

He made no reply; astonishment prevented him.

No curtain now intervened between him and the light. It had been removed as if by magic, and a splendid chandelier appeared suspended over his head. Throngs of ladies, richly dressed, but without death's-head masks, stood round, and a due proportion of gay cavaliers was mingled with them. Music was still sounding, but it was seen to proceed from a band of mortal musicians stationed in an orchestra near at hand. The air was yet redolent of incense, but it was incense unblended with stench.

'Mon Dieu!' cried the Emperor, 'how is all this come about? Where in the world is Piche?'

'Piche?' replied the Empress. 'What does your Majesty mean? Had you not better leave the apartment and retire to rest?'

'Leave the apartment? Why, where am I?'

'In my private drawing-room, surrounded by a few particular persons of the Court whom I had invited this evening to a ball. You entered a few minutes since in your nightdress with your eyes fixed and wide open. I suppose from the astonishment you now testify that you were walking in your sleep.'

The Emperor immediately fell into a fit of catalepsy, in which he continued during the whole of that night and the greater part of the next day.

Elizabeth Gaskell

THE OLD NURSE'S STORY

YOU know, my dears, that your mother was an orphan, and an only child; and I dare say you have heard that your grandfather was a clergyman up in Westmoreland, where I come from. I was just a girl in the village school, when, one day, your grandmother came in to ask the mistress if there was any scholar there who would do for a nurse-maid; and mighty proud I was, I can tell ye, when the mistress called me up, and spoke to my being a good girl at my needle, and a steady honest girl, and one whose parents were very respectable, though they might be poor. I thought I should like nothing better than to serve the pretty young lady, who was blushing as deep as I was, as she spoke of the coming baby, and what I should have to do with it. However, I see you don't care so much for this part of my story, as for what you think is to come, so I'll tell you at once. I was engaged and settled at the parsonage before Miss Rosamond (that was the baby, who is now your mother) was born. To be sure, I had little enough to do with her when she came, for she was never out of her mother's arms, and slept by her all night long; and proud enough was I sometimes when missis trusted her to me. There never was such a baby before or since, though you've all of you been fine enough in your turns; but for sweet, winning ways, you've none of you come up to your mother. She took after her mother, who was a real lady born; a Miss Furnivall, a granddaughter of Lord Furnivall's, in Northumberland. I believe she had neither brother nor sister, and had been brought up in my lord's family till she had married your grandfather, who was just a curate, son to a shopkeeper in Carlisle – but a clever, fine gentleman as ever was – and one who was a right-down hard worker in his parish, which was very wide, and scattered all abroad over the Westmoreland Fells. When your mother, little Miss Rosamond, was about four or five years old, both her parents died in a fortnight – one after the other. Ah! that was a sad time. My pretty young mistress and me was looking for another baby, when my master came home from one of his long rides, wet, and tired, and took the fever he died of; and then she never held up her head again, but just lived to see her dead baby, and have it laid on her breast before she sighed away her life. My mistress had asked me, on her death-bed, never to leave Miss Rosamond; but if she had never spoken a word, I would have gone with the little child to the end of the world.

The next thing, and before we had well stilled our sobs, the executors and guardians came to settle the affairs. They were my poor young mistress's own cousin, Lord Furnivall, and Mr Esthwaite, my master's brother, a shopkeeper in Manchester; not so well-to-do then as he was afterwards, and with a large family rising about him. Well! I don't know if it were their settling, or because of a letter my mistress wrote on her death-bed to her cousin, my lord; but somehow it was settled that Miss Rosamond and me were to go to Furnivall Manor House, in Northumberland, and my lord spoke as if it had been her mother's wish that she should live with his family, and as if he had no objections, for that one or two more or less could make no difference in so grand a household. So though that was not the way in which I should have wished the coming of my bright and pretty pet to have been looked at – who was like a sunbeam in any family, be it never so grand – I was well pleased that all the folks in the Dale should stare and admire, when they heard I was going to be young lady's maid at my Lord Furnivall's at Furnivall Manor.

But I made a mistake in thinking we were to go and live where my lord did. It turned out that the family had left Furnivall Manor House fifty years or more. I could not hear that my poor young mistress had ever been there, though she had been brought up in the family; and I was sorry for that, for I should have liked Miss Rosamond's youth to have passed where her mother's had been.

My lord's gentleman, from whom I asked so many questions as I durst, said that the Manor House was at the foot of the Cumberland Fells, and a very grand place; that an old Miss Furnivall, a great-aunt of my lord's, lived there, with only a few servants; but that it was a very healthy place, and my lord had thought that it would suit Miss Rosamond very well for a few years, and that her being there might perhaps amuse his old aunt.

I was bidden by my lord to have Miss Rosamond's things ready by a certain day. He was a stern proud man, as they say all the Lords Furnivall were; and he never spoke a word more than was necessary. Folk did say he had loved my young mistress; but that, because she knew that his father would object, she would never listen to him, and married Mr Esthwaite; but I don't know. He never married, at any rate. But he never took much notice of Miss Rosamond; which I thought he might have done if he had cared for her dead mother. He sent his gentleman with us to the Manor House, telling him to join him at Newcastle that same evening; so there was no great length of time for him to make us known to all the strangers before he, too, shook us off; and we were left, two lonely young things (I was not eighteen), in the great old Manor House. It seems like yesterday that we drove there. We had left our own dear parsonage very early, and we had both cried as if our hearts would break, though we were travelling in my lord's carriage, which I thought so much of once. And now it was long past noon on a September day, and we stopped to change horses for the last time at a little smoky town, all full of colliers and miners. Miss Rosamond had fallen asleep, but Mr Henry told me to waken her, that she might see the park and the Manor House as we drove up. I thought it rather a pity; but I did what he bade me, for fear he should complain of me to my lord. We had left all signs of a town, or even a village, and were then inside the gates of a large wild park – not like the parks here in the north, but with rocks, and the noise of running water, and gnarled thorn-trees, and old oaks, all white and peeled with age.

The road went up about two miles, and then we saw a great and stately house, with many trees close around it, so close that in some places their branches dragged against the walls when the wind blew; and some hung broken down; for no one seemed to take much charge of the place; – to lop the wood, or to keep the moss-covered carriageway in order. Only in front of the house all was clear. The great oval drive was without a weed; and neither tree nor creeper was allowed to grow over the long, many-windowed front; at both sides of which a wing projected, which were each the ends of other side fronts; for the house, although it was so desolate, was even grander than I expected. Behind it rose the Fells, which seemed unenclosed and bare enough; and on the left hand of the house, as you stood facing it, was a little, old-fashioned flower-garden, as I found out afterwards. A door opened out upon it from the west front; it had been scooped out of the thick dark wood for some old Lady Furnivall; but the branches of the great forest trees had grown and overshadowed it again, and there were very few flowers that would live there at that time.

When we drove up to the great front entrance, and went into the hall, I thought we should be lost – it was so large, and vast, and grand. There was a chandelier all of bronze, hung down from the middle of the ceiling; and I had never seen one before, and looked at it all in amaze. Then, at one end of the hall, was a great fireplace, as large as the sides of the houses in my country, with massy andirons and dogs to hold the wood; and by it were heavy old-fashioned sofas. At the opposite end of the hall, to the left as you went in – on the western side – was an organ built into the wall, and so large that it filled up the best part of that end.

Beyond it, on the same side, was a door; and opposite, on each side of the fireplace, were also doors leading to the east front; but those I never went through as long as I stayed in the house, so I can't tell you what lay beyond.

The afternoon was closing in, and the hall, which had no fire lighted in it, looked dark and gloomy, but we did not stay there a moment. The old servant, who had opened the door for us, bowed to Mr Henry, and took us in through the door at the further side of the great organ, and led us through several smaller halls and passages into the west drawing-room, where he said that Miss Furnivall was sitting. Poor little Miss Rosamond held very tight to me, as if she were scared and lost in that great place, and as for myself, I was not much better. The west drawing-room was very cheerful-looking, with a warm fire in it, and plenty of good, comfortable furniture about. Miss Furnivall was an old lady not far from eighty, I should think, but I do not know. She was thin and tall, and had a face as full of fine wrinkles as if they had been drawn all over it with a needle's point. Her eyes were very watchful, to make up, I suppose, for her being so deaf as to be obliged to use a trumpet. Sitting with her, working at the same great piece of tapestry, was Mrs Stark, her maid and companion, and almost as old as she was. She had lived with Miss Furnivall ever since they were both young, and now she seemed more like a friend than a servant; she looked so cold and grey, and stony as if she had never loved or cared for any one; and I don't suppose she did care for any one, except her mistress; and, owing to the great deafness of the latter, Mrs Stark treated her very much as if she were a child. Mr Henry gave some message from my lord, and then he bowed good-bye to us all, – taking no notice of my sweet little Miss Rosamond's outstretched hand – and left us standing there, being looked at by the two old ladies through their spectacles.

I was right glad when they rung for the old footman who had shown us in at first, and told him to take us to our rooms. So we went out of that great drawing-room, and into another sitting-room, and out of that, and then up a great flight of stairs, and along a broad gallery – which was something like a library, having books all down one side, and windows and writing-tables all down the other – till we came to our rooms, which I was not sorry to hear were just over the kitchens; for I began to think I should be lost in that wilderness of a house. There was an old nursery that had been used for all the little lords and ladies long ago, with a pleasant fire burning in the grate, and the kettle boiling on the hob, and tea-things spread out on the table; and out of that room was the night-nursery, with a little crib for Miss Rosamond close to my bed. And old James called up Dorothy, his wife, to bid us welcome; and both he and she were so hospitable and kind, that by and by Miss Rosamond and me felt quite at home; and by the time tea was over, she was sitting on Dorothy's knee, and chattering away as fast as her little tongue could go. I soon found out that Dorothy was from Westmoreland, and that bound her and me together, as it were; and I would never wish to meet with kinder people than were old James and his wife. James had lived pretty nearly all his life in my lord's family, and thought there was no one so grand as they. He even looked down a little on his wife; because, till he had married her, she had never lived in any but a farmer's household. But he was very fond of her, as well he might be. They had one servant under them, to do all the rough work. Agnes they called her; and she and me, and James and Dorothy, with Miss Furnivall and Mrs Stark, made up the family; always remembering my sweet little Miss Rosamond! I used to wonder what they had done before she came, they thought so much of her now. Kitchen and drawing-room, it was all the same. The hard, sad Miss Furnivall, and the cold Mrs Stark, looked pleased when she came fluttering in like a bird, playing and pranking hither and thither, with a continual murmur, and pretty prattle of gladness. I am sure, they were sorry many a time when she flitted away into the kitchen, though they were too proud to ask her to stay with them, and were a little surprised at her taste; though to be sure, as Mrs Stark said it was not to be wondered at, remembering what stock her father had come of. The great, old rambling house was a famous place for little Miss Rosamond. She made expeditions all over it, with me at her heels; all, except the east wing, which was never opened, and whither we never thought of going. But in the western and northern part was many a pleasant room; full of things that were curiosities to us, though they might not have been to people who had seen more. The windows were darkened by the sweeping boughs of the trees, and the ivy which had overgrown them: but, in the green gloom, we could manage to see old China jars and carved ivory boxes, and great heavy books, and, above all, the old pictures!

Once, I remember, my darling would have Dorothy go with us to tell us who they all were; for they were all portraits of some of my lord's family, though Dorothy could not tell us the names of every one. We had gone through most of the rooms, when we came to the old state drawing-room over the hall, and there was a picture of Miss Furnivall; or, as she was called in those days, Miss Grace, for she was the younger sister. Such a beauty she must have been! but with such a set, proud look, and such scorn looking out of her handsome eyes, with her eyebrows just a little raised, as if she were wondering how any one could have the impertinence to look at her; and her lip curled at us, as we stood there gazing. She had a dress on, the like of which I had never seen before, but it was all the fashion when she was young: a hat of some soft white stuff like beaver, pulled a little over her brows, and a beautiful plume of feathers sweeping round it on one side; and her gown of blue satin was open in front to a quilted white stomacher.

'Well, to be sure!' said I, when I had gazed my fill. 'Flesh is grass, they do say; but who would have thought that Miss Furnivall had been such an out-and-out beauty, to see her now?'

'Yes,' said Dorothy. 'Folks change sadly. But if what my master's father used to say was true, Miss Furnivall, the elder sister, was handsomer than Miss Grace. Her picture is here somewhere; but, if I show it you, you must never let on, even to James, that you have seen it. Can the little lady hold her tongue, think you?' asked she.

I was not so sure, for she was such a little sweet, bold, open-spoken child, so I set her to hide herself; and then I helped Dorothy to turn a great picture, that leaned with its face towards the wall, and was not hung up as the others were. To be sure, it beat Miss Grace for beauty; and, I think, for scornful pride, too, though in that matter it might be hard to choose. I could have looked at it an hour, but Dorothy seemed half frightened at having shown it to me, and hurried it back again, and bade me run and find Miss Rosamond, for that there were some ugly places about the house, where she should like ill for the child to go. I was a brave, high-spirited girl, and thought little of what the old woman said, for I liked hide-and-seek as well as any child in the parish; so off I ran to find my little one.

As winter drew on, and the days grew shorter, I was sometimes almost certain that I heard a noise as if some one was playing on the great organ in the hall. I did not hear it every evening; but, certainly, I did very often; usually when I was sitting with Miss Rosamond, after I had put her to bed, and keeping quite still and silent in the bedroom. Then I used to hear it booming and swelling away in the distance. The first night, when I went down to my supper, I asked Dorothy who had been playing music, and James said very shortly that I was a gowk to take the wind soughing among the trees for music: but I saw Dorothy look at him very fearfully, and Bessy, the kitchen-maid, said something beneath her breath, and went quite white. I saw they did not like my question, so I held my peace till I was with Dorothy alone, when I knew I could get a good deal out of her. So, the next day, I watched my time, and I coaxed and asked her who it was that played the organ; for I knew that it was the organ and not the wind well enough, for all I had kept silence before James. But Dorothy had had her lesson, I'll warrant, and never a word could I get from her. So then I tried Bessy, though I had always held my head rather above her, as I was evened to James and Dorothy, and she was little better than their servant. So she said I must never, never tell; and if I ever told, I was never to say *she* had told me; but it was a very strange noise, and she had heard it many a time, but most of all on winter nights, and before storms; and folks did say, it was the old lord playing on the great organ in the hall, just as he used to when he was alive; but who the old lord was, or why he played, and why he played on stormy winter evenings in particular, she either could not or would not tell me. Well! I told you I had a brave heart; and I thought it was rather pleasant to have that grand music rolling about the house, let who would be the player; for now it rose above the great gusts of wind, and wailed and triumphed just like a living creature, and then it fell to a softness most complete; only it was always music and tunes, so it was nonsense to call it the wind. I thought at first that it might be Miss Furnivall who played, unknown to Bessy; but one day when I was in the hall by myself, I opened the organ and peeped all about it and around it, as I had done to the organ in Crosthwaite Church once before, and I saw it was all broken and destroyed inside, though it looked so brave and fine; and then, though it was noonday, my flesh began to creep a little, and I shut it up, and run away pretty quickly to my own bright nursery; and I did not like hearing the music for some time after that, any more than James and Dorothy did. All this time Miss Rosamond was making herself more and more beloved. The old ladies liked her to dine with them at their early dinner; James stood behind Miss Furnivall's chair, and I behind Miss Rosamond's all in state; and, after dinner, she would play about in a corner of the great drawing-room, as still as any mouse, while Miss Furnivall slept, and I had my dinner in the kitchen. But she was glad enough to come to me in the nursery afterwards; for, as she said, Miss Furnivall was so sad, and Mrs Stark so dull; but she and I were merry enough; and, by-and-by, I got not to care for that weird rolling music, which did one no harm, if we did not know where it came from.

That winter was very cold. In the middle of October the frosts began, and lasted many, many weeks. I remember, one day at dinner, Miss Furnivall lifted up her sad, heavy eyes, and said to Mrs Stark, 'I am afraid we shall have a terrible winter,' in a strange kind of meaning way. But Mrs Stark pretended not to hear, and talked very loud of something else. My little lady and I did not care for the frost; not we! As long as it was dry we climbed up the steep brows, behind the house, and went up on the Fells, which were bleak, and bare enough, and there we ran races in the fresh, sharp air; and once we came down by a new path that took us past the two old gnarled holly-trees, which grew about half-way down by the east side of the house. But the days grew shorter and shorter; and the old lord, if it was he, played more and more stormily and sadly on the great organ. One Sunday afternoon – it must have been towards the end of November – I asked Dorothy to take charge of little Missey when she came out of the drawing-room, after Miss Furnivall had had her nap; for it was too cold to take her with me to church, and yet I wanted to go. And Dorothy was glad enough to promise, and was so fond of the child that all seemed well; Bessy and I set off very briskly, though the sky hung heavy and black over the white earth, as if the night had never fully gone away; and the air, though still, was very biting and keen.

'We shall have a fall of snow,' said Bessy to me. And sure enough, even while we were in church, it came down thick, in great large flakes, so thick it almost darkened the windows. It had stopped snowing before we came out, but it lay soft, thick and deep beneath our feet, as we tramped home. Before we got to the hall the moon rose, and I think it was lighter then, – what with the moon, and what with the white dazzling snow – than it had been when we went to church, between two and three o'clock. I have not told you that Miss Furnivall and Mrs Stark never went to church: they used to read the prayers together, in their quiet gloomy way; they seemed to feel the Sunday very long without their tapestry-work to be busy at. So when I went to Dorothy in the kitchen, to fetch Miss Rosamond and take her upstairs with me, I did not much wonder when the old woman told me that the ladies had kept the child with them, and that she had never come to the kitchen, as I had bidden her, when she was tired of behaving pretty in the drawing-room. So I took off my things and went to find her, and bring her to her supper in the nursery. But when I went into the best drawing-room there sat the two old ladies, very still and quiet, dropping out a word now and then but looking as if nothing so bright and merry as Miss Rosamond had ever been near them. Still I thought she might be hiding from me; it was one of her pretty ways; and that she had persuaded them to look as if they knew nothing about her; so I went softly peeping under this sofa, and behind that chair, making believe I was sadly frightened at not finding her.

'What's the matter, Hester?' said Mrs Stark, sharply. I don't know if Miss Furnivall had seen me, for, as I told you, she was very deaf, and she sat quite still, idly staring into the fire, with her hopeless face. 'I'm only looking for my little Rosy-Posy,' replied I, still thinking that the child was there, and near me, though I could not see her.

'Miss Rosamond is not here,' said Mrs Stark. 'She went away more than an hour ago to find Dorothy.' And she too turned and went on looking into the fire.

My heart sank at this, and I began to wish I had never left my darling. I went back to Dorothy and told her. James was gone out for the day, but she and me and Bessy took lights and went up into the nursery first, and then we roamed over the great large house, calling and entreating Miss Rosamond to come out of her hiding-place, and not frighten us to death in that way. But there was no answer; no sound.

'Oh!' said I at last, 'Can she have got into the east wing and hidden there?'

But Dorothy said it was not possible, for that she herself had never been there; that the doors were always locked, and my lord's steward had the keys, she believed; at any rate, neither she nor James had ever seen them: so I said I would go back, and see if, after all, she was not hidden in the drawing-room, unknown to the old ladies; and if I found her there, I said, I would whip her well for the fright she had given me; but I never meant to do it. Well, I went back to the west drawing-room, and I told Mrs Stark we could not find her anywhere, and asked for leave to look all about the furniture there, for I thought now, that she might have fallen asleep in some warm hidden corner; but no! we looked, Miss Furnivall got up and looked, trembling all over, and she was nowhere there; then we set off again, every one in the house, and looked in all the places we had searched before, but we could not find her. Miss Furnivall shivered and shook so much that Mrs Stark took her back into the warm drawing-room; but not before they had made me promise to bring her to them when she was found. Well-a-day! I began to think she never would be found, when I bethought me to look out into the great front court, all covered with snow. I was upstairs when I looked out; but it was such clear moonlight, I could see, quite plain, two little footprints, which might be traced from the hall door, and round the corner of the east wing. I don't know how I got down, but I tugged open the great, stiff hall door; and, throwing the skirt of my gown over my head for a cloak, I ran out. I turned the east corner, and there a black shadow fell on the snow; but when I came again into the moonlight, there were the little footmarks going up – up to the Fells. It was bitter cold; so cold that the air almost took the skin off my face as I ran, but I ran on, crying to think how my poor little darling must be perished, and frightened. I was within sight of the holly-trees when I saw a shepherd coming down the hill, bearing something in his arms wrapped in his maud. He shouted to me, and asked me if I had lost a bairn; and, when I could not speak for crying, he bore towards me, and I saw my wee bairnie lying still, and white, and stiff, in his arms, as if she had been dead. He told me he had been up the Fells to gather in his sheep, before the deep cold of night came on, and that under the holly-trees (black marks on the hillside, where no other bush was for miles around) he had found my little lady – my lamb – my queen – my darling – stiff and cold, in the terrible sleep which is frost-begotten. Oh! the joy, and the tears of having her in my arms once again! for I would not let him carry her; but took her, maud and all, into my own arms, and held her near my own warm neck and heart, and felt the life stealing slowly back again into her little gentle limbs. But she was still insensible when we reached the hall, and I had no breath for speech. We went in by the kitchen door.

'Bring the warming-pan,' said I; and I carried her upstairs and began undressing her by the nursery fire, which Bessy had kept up. I called my little lammie all the sweet and playful names I could think of – even while my eyes were blinded by my tears; and at last, oh! at length she opened her large blue eyes. Then I put her into her warm bed, and sent Dorothy down to tell Miss Furnivall that all was well; and I made up my mind to sit by my darling's bedside the live-long night. She fell away into a soft sleep as soon as her pretty head had touched the pillow, and I watched her until morning light; when she wakened up bright and clear – or so I thought at first – and, my dears, so I think now.

She said that she had fancied that she should like to go to Dorothy, for that both the old ladies were asleep, and it was very dull in the drawing-room; and that, as she was going through the west lobby, she saw the snow through the high window falling – falling – soft and steady; but she wanted to see it lying pretty and white on the ground; so she made her way into the great hall; and then, going to the window, she saw it bright and soft upon the drive; but while she stood there, she saw a little girl, not so old as she was, 'but so pretty,' said my darling, 'and this little girl beckoned to me to come out; and oh, she was so pretty and so sweet, I could not choose but to go.' And then this other little girl had taken her by the hand, and side by side the two had gone round the east corner.

'Now you are a naughty little girl, and telling stories,' said I. 'What would your good mamma, that is in heaven, and never told a story in her life, say to her little Rosamond, if she heard her – and I dare say she does – telling stories!'

'Indeed, Hester,' sobbed out my child, 'I'm telling you true. Indeed I am.'

'Don't tell me!' said I, very stern. 'I tracked you by your footmarks through the snow; there were only yours to be seen: and if you had had a little girl to go hand-in-hand with you up the hill, don't you think the footprints would have gone along with yours?'

'I can't help it, dear, dear Hester,' said she, crying, 'if they did not; I never looked at her feet, but she held my hand fast and tight in her little one, and it was very, very cold. She took me up the Fell-path, up to the holly-trees; and there I saw a lady weeping and crying; but when she saw me, she hushed her weeping, and smiled very proud and grand, and took me on her knee, and began to lull me to sleep; and that's all, Hester – but that is true; and my dear mamma knows it is,' said she, crying. So I thought the child was in a fever, and pretended to believe her, as she went over her story – over and over again, and always the same. At last Dorothy knocked at the door with Miss Rosamond's breakfast; and she told me the old ladies were down in the eating parlour, and that they wanted to speak to me. They had both been into the night-nursery the evening before, but it was after Miss Rosamond was asleep; so they had only looked at her – not asked me any questions.

'I shall catch it,' thought I to myself, as I went along the north gallery. 'And yet,' I thought, taking courage, 'it was in their charge I left her; and it's they that's to blame for letting her steal away unknown and unwatched.' So I went in boldly, and told my story. I told it all to Miss Furnivall, shouting close to her ear; but when I came to the mention of the other little girl out in the snow, coaxing and tempting her out, and willing her up to the grand and beautiful lady by the holly-tree, she threw her arms up – her old and withered arms – and cried aloud, 'Oh! Heaven, forgive! Have mercy!'

Mrs Stark took hold of her; roughly enough, I thought; but she was past Mrs Stark's management, and spoke to me, in a kind of wild warning and authority.

'Hester! keep her from that child! It will lure her to her death! That evil child! Tell her it is a wicked, naughty child.' Then Mrs Stark hurried me out of the room; where, indeed, I was glad enough to go; but Miss Furnivall kept shrieking out, 'Oh! have mercy! Wilt Thou never forgive! It is many a long year ago'—

I was very uneasy in my mind after that. I durst never leave Miss Rosamond, night or day, for fear lest she might slip off again, after some fancy or other; and all the more because I thought I could make out that Miss Furnivall was crazy, from their odd ways about her; and I was afraid lest something of the same kind (which might be in the family, you know) hung over my darling. And the great frost never ceased all this time; and whenever it was a more stormy night than usual, between the gusts, and through the wind, we heard the old lord playing on the great organ. But, old lord, or not, wherever Miss Rosamond went, there I followed; for my love for her, pretty helpless orphan, was stronger than my fear for the grand and terrible sound. Besides, it rested with me to keep her cheerful and merry, as beseemed her age. So we played together, and wandered together, here and there, and everywhere; for I never dared to lose sight of her again in that large and rambling house. And so it happened, that one afternoon, not long before Christmas Day, we were playing together on the billiard-table in the great hall (not that we knew the way of playing, but she liked to roll the smooth ivory balls with her pretty hands, and I liked to do whatever she did); and, by-and-by, without our noticing it, it grew dusk indoors, though it was still light in the open air, and I was thinking of taking her back into the nursery, when, all of a sudden, she cried out:

'Look, Hester! look! there is my poor little girl out in the snow!'

I turned towards the long narrow windows, and there, sure enough, I saw a little girl, less than my Miss Rosamond – dressed all unfit to be out-of-doors such a bitter night – crying, and beating against the window-panes, as if she wanted to be let in. She seemed to sob and wail, till Miss Rosamond could bear it no longer, and was flying to the door to open it, when, all of a sudden, and close up upon us, the great organ pealed out so loud and thundering, it fairly made me tremble; and all the more when I remembered me that, even in the stillness of that dead-cold weather, I had heard no sound of little battering hands upon the window-glass, although the Phantom Child had seemed to put forth all its force; and, although I had seen it wail and cry, no faintest touch of sound had fallen upon my ears. Whether I remembered all this at the very moment, I do not know; the great organ sound had so stunned me into terror; but this I know, I caught up Miss Rosamond before she got the hall door opened, and clutched her, and carried her away, kicking and screaming, into the large bright kitchen, where Dorothy and Agnes were busy with their mince-pies.

'What is the matter with my sweet one?' cried Dorothy, as I bore in Miss Rosamond, who was sobbing as if her heart would break.

'She won't let me open the door for my little girl to come in; and she'll die if she is out on the Fells all night. Cruel, naughty Hester,' she said, slapping me; but she might have struck harder, for I had seen a look of ghastly terror on Dorothy's face, which made my very blood run cold.

'Shut the back-kitchen door fast, and bolt it well,' said she to Agnes. She said no more; she gave me raisins and almonds to quiet Miss Rosamond: but she sobbed about the little girl in the snow, and would not touch any of the good things. I was thankful when she cried herself to sleep in bed. Then I stole down to the kitchen, and told Dorothy I had made up my mind. I would carry my darling back to my father's house in Applethwaite; where, if we lived humbly, we lived at peace. I said I had been frightened enough with the old lord's organ-playing; but now, that I had seen for myself this little moaning child, all decked out as no child in the neighbourhood could be, beating and battering to get in, yet always without any sound or noise – with the dark wound on its right shoulder; and that Miss Rosamond had known it again for the phantom that had nearly lured her to her death (which Dorothy knew was true); I would stand it no longer.

I saw Dorothy change colour once or twice. When I had done, she told me she did not think I could take Miss Rosamond with me, for that she was my lord's ward, and I had no right over her; and she asked me, would I leave the child that I was so fond of, just for sounds and sights that could do me no harm; and that they had all had to get used to in their turns? I was all in a hot, trembling passion; and I said it was very well for her to talk, that knew what these sights and noises betokened, and that had, perhaps, had something to do with the Spectre-Child while it was alive. And I taunted her so, that she told me all she knew, at last; and then I wished I had never been told, for it only made me afraid more than ever.

She said she had heard the tale from old neighbours, that were alive when she was first married; when folks used to come to the hall sometimes, before it had got such a bad name on the countryside: it might not be true, or it might, what she had been told.

The old lord was Miss Furnivall's father – Miss Grace as Dorothy called her, for Miss Maude was the elder, and Miss Furnivall by rights. The old lord was eaten up with pride. Such a proud man was never seen or heard of; and his daughters were like him. No one was good enough to wed them, although they had choice enough; for they were the great beauties of their day, as I had seen by their portraits, where they hung in the state drawing-room. But, as the old saying is, 'Pride will have a fall'; and these two haughty beauties fell in love with the same man, and he no better than a foreign musician, whom their father had down from London to play music with him at the Manor House. For, above all things, next to his pride, the old lord loved music. He could play on nearly every instrument that ever was heard of: and it was a strange thing it did not soften him; but he was a fierce dour old man, and had broken his poor wife's heart with his cruelty, they said. He was mad after music, and would pay any money for it. So he got this foreigner to come; who made such beautiful music, that they said the very birds on the trees stopped their singing to listen. And, by degrees, this foreign gentleman got such a hold over the old lord, that nothing would serve him but that he must come every year; and it was he that had the great organ brought from Holland, and built up in the hall, where it stood now. He taught the old lord to play on it; but many and many a time, when Lord Furnivall was thinking of nothing but his fine organ, and his finer music, the dark foreigner was walking abroad in the woods with one of the young ladies; now Miss Maude, and then Miss Grace.

Miss Maude won the day and carried off the prize, such as it was; and he and she were married, all unknown to any one; and before he made his next yearly visit, she had been confined of a little girl at a farm-house on the Moors, while her father and Miss Grace thought she was away at Doncaster Races. But though she was a wife and a mother, she was not a bit softened, but as haughty and as passionate as ever; and perhaps more so, for she was jealous of Miss Grace, to whom her foreign husband paid a deal of court – by way of blinding her – as he told his wife. But Miss Grace triumphed over Miss Maude, and Miss Maude grew fiercer and fiercer, both with her husband and with her sister; and the former – who could easily shake off what was disagreeable, and hide himself in foreign countries – went away a month before his usual time that summer, and half-threatened that he would never come back again. Meanwhile, the little girl was left at the farm-house, and her mother used to have her horse saddled and gallop wildly over the hills to see her once every week, at the very least – for where she loved, she loved; and where she hated, she hated. And the old lord went on playing – playing on his organ; and the servants thought the sweet music he made had soothed down his awful temper, of which (Dorothy said) some terrible tales could be told. He grew infirm too, and had to walk with a crutch; and his son – that was the present Lord Furnivall's father – was with the army in America, and the other son at sea; so Miss Maude had it pretty much her own way, and she and Miss Grace grew colder and bitterer to each other every day; till at last they hardly ever spoke, except when the old lord was by. The foreign musician came again the next summer, but it was for the last time; for they led him such a life with their jealousy and their passions, that he grew weary, and went away, and never was heard of again. And Miss Maude, who had always meant to have her marriage acknowledged when her father should be dead, was left now a deserted wife – whom nobody knew to have been married – with a child that she dared not own, although she loved it to distraction; living with a father whom she feared, and a sister whom she hated. When the next summer passed over and the dark foreigner never came, both Miss Maude and Miss Grace grew gloomy and sad; they had a haggard look about them, though they looked handsome as ever. But by-and-by Miss Maude brightened; for her father grew more and more infirm, and more than ever carried away by his music; and she and Miss Grace lived almost entirely apart, having separate rooms, the one on the west side, Miss Maude on the east – those very rooms which were now shut up. So she thought she might have her little girl with her, and no one need ever know except those who dared not speak about it, and were bound to believe that it was, as she said, a cottager's child she had taken a fancy to. All this, Dorothy said, was pretty well known; but what came afterwards no one knew, except Miss Grace, and Mrs Stark, who was even then her maid, and much more of a friend to her than ever her sister had been. But the servants supposed, from words that were dropped, that Miss Maude had triumphed over Miss Grace, and told her that all the time the dark foreigner had been mocking her with pretended love – he was her own husband; the colour left Miss Grace's cheek and lips that very day for ever, and she was heard to say many a time that sooner or later she would have her revenge; and Mrs Stark was for ever spying about the east rooms.

One fearful night, just after the New Year had come in, when the snow was lying thick and deep, and the flakes were still falling – fast enough to blind any one who might be out and abroad – there was a great and violent noise heard, and the old lord's voice above all, cursing and swearing awfully – and the cries of a little child – and the proud defiance of a fierce woman – and the sound of a blow – and a dead stillness – and moans and wailings dying away on the hill-side! Then the old lord summoned all his servants, and told them, with terrible oaths, and words more terrible, that his daughter had disgraced herself, and that he had turned her out of doors – her, and her child – and that if ever they gave her help – or food – or shelter – he prayed that they might never enter Heaven. And, all the while, Miss Grace stood by him, white and still as any stone; and when he had ended she heaved a great sigh, as much as to say her work was done, and her end was accomplished. But the old lord never touched his organ again, and died within the year; and no wonder! for, on the morrow of that wild and fearful night, the shepherds, coming down the Fell side, found Miss Maude sitting, all crazy and smiling, under the holly-trees, nursing a dead child – with a terrible mark on its right shoulder. 'But that was not what killed it,' said Dorothy; 'it was the frost and the cold; – every wild creature was in its hole, and every beast in its fold – while the child and its mother were turned out to wander on the Fells! And now you know all! and I wonder if you are less frightened now?'

I was more frightened than ever; but I said I was not. I wished Miss Rosamond and myself well out of that dreadful house for ever; but I would not leave her, and I dared not take her away. But oh! how I watched her, and guarded her! We bolted the doors and shut the window-shutters fast, an hour or more before dark, rather than leave them open five minutes too late. But my little lady still heard the weird child crying and mourning; and not all we could do or say could keep her from wanting to go to her, and let her in from the cruel wind and the snow. All this time, I kept away from Miss Furnivall and Mrs Stark, as much as ever I could; for I feared them – I knew no good could be about them, with their grey hard faces, and their dreamy eyes, looking back into the ghastly years that were gone. But, even in my fear, I had a kind of pity – for Miss Furnivall, at least. Those gone down to the pit can hardly have a more hopeless look than that which was ever on her face. At last I even got so sorry for her – who never said a word but what was quite forced from her – that I prayed for her; and I taught Miss Rosamond to pray for one who had done a deadly sin; but often when she came to those words, she would listen, and start up from her knees, and say, 'I hear my little girl plaining and crying very sad – Oh! let her in, or she will die!'

One night – just after New Year's Day had come at last, and the long winter had taken a turn, as I hoped – I heard the west drawing-room bell ring three times, which was a signal for me. I would not leave Miss Rosamond alone, for all she was asleep – for the old lord had been playing wilder than ever – and I feared lest my darling should waken to hear the Spectre-Child; see her I knew she could not. I had fastened the windows too well for that. So I took her out of her bed and wrapped her up in such outer clothes as were most handy, and carried her down to the drawing-room, where the old ladies sat at their tapestry-work as usual. They looked up when I came in, and Mrs Stark asked, quite astounded, 'Why did I bring Miss Rosamond there, out of her warm bed?' I had begun to whisper, 'Because I was afraid of her being tempted out while I was away, by the wild child in the snow,' when she stopped me short (with a glance at Miss Furnivall), and said Miss Furnivall wanted me to undo some work she had done wrong, and which neither of them could see to unpick. So I laid my pretty dear on the sofa, and sat down on a stool by them, and hardened my heart against them, as I heard the wind rising and howling.

Miss Rosamond slept on sound, for all the wind blew so; and Miss Furnivall said never a word, nor looked round when the gusts shook the windows. All at once she started up to her full height, and put up one hand, as if to bid us listen.

'I hear voices!' said she, 'I hear terrible screams – I hear my father's voice!'

Just at that moment my darling wakened with a sudden start: 'My little girl is crying, oh, how she is crying!' and she tried to get up and go to her, but she got her feet entangled in the blanket, and I caught her up; for my flesh had begun to creep at these noises, which they heard while we could catch no sound. In a minute or two the noises came, and gathered fast, and filled our ears; we, too, heard voices and screams, and no longer heard the winter's wind that raged abroad. Mrs Stark looked at me, and I at her, but we dared not speak. Suddenly Miss Furnivall went towards the door, out into the ante-room, through the west lobby, and opened the door into the great hall. Mrs Stark followed, and I durst not be left, though my heart almost stopped beating for fear. I wrapped my darling tight in my arms, and went out with them. In the hall the screams were louder than ever; they sounded to come from the east wing – nearer and nearer – close on the other side of the locked-up doors – close behind them. Then I noticed that the great bronze chandelier seemed all alight, though the hall was dim, and that a fire was blazing in the vast hearth-place, though it gave no heat; and I shuddered up with terror, and folded my darling closer to me. But as I did so, the east door shook, and she, suddenly struggling to get free from me, cried, 'Hester, I must go! My little girl is there; I hear her; she is coming! Hester, I must go!'

I held her tight with all my strength; with a set will, I held her. If I had died, my hands would have grasped her still, I was so resolved in my mind. Miss Furnivall stood listening, and paid no regard to my darling, who had got down to the ground, and whom I, upon my knees now, was holding with both my arms clasped round her neck; she still striving and crying to get free.

All at once the east door gave way with a thundering crash, as if torn open in a violent passion, and there came into that broad and mysterious light, the figure of a tall old man, with grey hair and gleaming eyes. He drove before him, with many a relentless gesture of abhorrence, a stern and beautiful woman, with a little child clinging to her dress.

'O Hester! Hester!' cried Miss Rosamond. 'It's the lady! the lady below the holly-trees; and my little girl is with her. Hester! Hester! let me go to her; they are drawing me to them. I feel them – I feel them. I must go!'

Again she was almost convulsed by her efforts to get away; but I held her tighter and tighter, till I feared I should do her a hurt; but rather that than let her go towards those terrible phantoms. They passed along towards the great hall-door, where the winds howled and ravened for their prey; but before they reached that, the lady turned; and I could see that she defied the old man with a fierce and proud defiance; but then she quailed – and then she threw up her arms wildly and piteously to save her child – her little child – from a blow from his uplifted crutch.

And Miss Rosamond was torn as if by a power stronger than mine, and writhed in my arms, and sobbed (for by this time the poor darling was growing faint).

'They want me to go with them on to the Fells – they are drawing me to them. Oh, my little girl! I would come, but cruel, wicked Hester holds me very tight.' But when she saw the uplifted crutch she swooned away, and I thanked God for it. Just at this moment – when the tall old man, his hair streaming as in the blast of a furnace, was going to strike the little shrinking child – Miss Furnivall, the old woman by my side, cried out, 'Oh, father! father! spare the little innocent child!' But just then I saw – we all saw – another phantom shape itself, and grow clear out of the blue and misty light that filled the hall; we had not seen her till now, for it was another lady who stood by the old man, with a look of relentless hate and triumphant scorn. That figure was very beautiful to look upon, with a soft white hat drawn down over the proud brows and a red and curling lip. It was dressed in an open robe of blue satin. I had seen that figure before. It was the likeness of Miss Furnivall in her youth; and the terrible phantoms moved on, regardless of old Miss Furnivall's wild entreaty – and the uplifted crutch fell on the right shoulder of the little child, and the younger sister looked on, stony and deadly serene. But at that moment the dim lights, and the fire that gave no heat, went out of themselves, and Miss Furnivall lay at our feet stricken down by the palsy – death-stricken.

Yes! she was carried to her bed that night never to rise again. She lay with her face to the wall muttering low but muttering alway: 'Alas! alas! what is done in youth can never be undone in age! What is done in youth can never be undone in age!'

Dinah M. Mulock

THE LAST HOUSE IN C——STREET

I AM not a believer in ghosts in general; I see no good in them. They come – that is, are reported to come – so irrelevantly, purposelessly – so ridiculously, in short – that one's common sense as regards this world, one's supernatural sense of the other, are alike revolted. Then nine out of ten 'capital ghost stories' are so easily accounted for; and in the tenth, when all natural explanation fails, one who has discovered the extraordinary difficulty there is in all society in getting hold of that very slippery article called a *fact*, is strongly inclined to shake a dubious head, ejaculating, 'Evidence! it is all a question of evidence!'

But my unbelief springs from no dogged or contemptuous scepticism as to the possibility – however great the improbability – of that strange impression upon, or communication to, spirit in matter, from spirit wholly immaterialised, which is vulgarly called 'a ghost'. There is no credulity more blind, no ignorance more childish, that that of the sage who tries to measure 'heaven and earth and the things under the earth', with the small two-foot rule of his own brains. The presumption of mere folly alone would argue concerning any mystery of the universe, 'It is inexplicable, and therefore impossible.'

Premising these opinions, though simply as opinions, I am about to relate what I must confess seems to me a thorough ghost story; its external and circumstantial evidence being indisputable, while its psychological causes and results, though not easy of explanation, are still more difficult to be explained away. The ghost, like Hamlet's, was 'an honest ghost'. From her daughter – an old lady, who, bless her good and gentle memory! has since learned the secrets of all things – I heard this veritable tale.

'My dear,' said Mrs MacArthur to me – it was in the early days of table-moving, when young folk ridiculed and elder folk were shocked at the notion of calling up one's departed ancestors into one's dinner-table, and learning the wonders of the angelic world by the bobbings of a hat or the twirlings of a plate; – 'My dear,' continued the old lady, 'I do not like trifling with spirits.'

'Why not? Do you believe in them?'

'A little.'

'Did you ever see one?'

'Never. But once, I heard one.'

She looked serious, as if she hardly liked to speak about it, either from a sense of awe or from fear of ridicule. But it was impossible to laugh at any illusions of the gentle old lady, who never uttered a harsh or satirical word to a living soul. Likewise the evident awe with which she mentioned the circumstance was rather remarkable in one who had a large stock of common sense, little wonder, and no ideality.

I was very curious to hear Mrs MacArthur's ghost story.

'My dear, it was a long time ago, so long that you may fancy I forget and confuse the circumstances. But I do not. Sometimes I think one recollects more clearly things that happened in one's teens – I was eighteen that year – than a great many nearer events. And besides, I had other reasons for remembering vividly everything belonging to this time, – for I was in love, you must know.'

She looked at me with a mild deprecating smile, as if hoping my youthfulness would not consider the thing so very impossible or ridiculous. No; I was all interest at once.

'In love with Mr MacArthur,' I said, scarcely as a question, being at that Arcadian time of life when one takes as a natural necessity, and believes in as an undoubted truth, that all people, that is, good people, marry their first love.

'No, my dear; not with Mr MacArthur.'

I was so astonished, so completely dumbfounded – for I had woven a sort of ideal round my good old friend – that I suffered Mrs MacArthur to knit in silence for full five minutes. My surprise was not lessened when she said, with a gratified little smile –

'He was a young gentleman of good parts; and he was very fond of me. Proud, too, rather. For though you might not think it, my dear, I was actually a beauty in those days.'

I had very little doubt of it. The slight lithe figure, the tiny hands and feet, – if you had walked behind Mrs MacArthur down the street you might have taken her for a young woman still. Certainly, people lived slower and easier in the last generation than in ours.

'Yes, I was the beauty of Bath. Mr Everest fell in love with me there. I was much gratified; for I had just been reading Miss Burney's *Cecilia*, and I thought him exactly like Mortimer Delvil. A very pretty story, *Cecilia*; did you ever read it?'

'No.' And, to arrive quicker at her tale, I leaped to the only conclusion which could reconcile the two facts of my good old friend having had a lover named Everest, and being now Mrs MacArthur. 'Was it *his* ghost you saw?'

'No, my dear, no; thank goodness, he is alive still. He calls here sometimes; he has been a faithful friend to our family. Ah!' with a slow shake of the head, half pleased, half pensive, 'you would hardly believe, my dear, what a very pretty fellow he was.'

One could scarcely smile at the odd phrase, pertaining to last-century novels and to the loves of our great-grandmothers. I listened patiently to the wandering reminiscences which still further delayed the ghost story.

'But, Mrs MacArthur, was it in Bath that you saw or heard what I think you were going to tell me? The ghost, you know?'

'Don't call it *that*; it sounds as if you were laughing at it. And you must not, for it is really true; as true as that I sit here, an old lady of seventy-five, and that then I was a young gentlewoman of eighteen. Nay, my dear, I will tell you all about it.

'We had been staying in London, my father and mother, Mr Everest, and I. He had persuaded them to take me; he wanted to show me a little of the world, though even his world was but a narrow one, my dear, – for he was a law student, living poorly and working hard.

'He took lodgings for us near the Temple; in C— street, the last house there, looking on to the river. He was very fond of the river; and often of evenings, when his work was too heavy to let him take us to Ranelagh or to the play, he used to walk with my father and mother and me up and down the Temple Gardens. Were you ever in the Temple Gardens? It is a pretty place now – a quiet, grey nook in the midst of noise and bustle; the stars look wonderful through those great trees; but still it is not like what it was then, when I was a girl.'

Ah! no; impossible.

'It was in the Temple Gardens, my dear, that I remember we took our last walk – my mother, Mr Everest, and I – before she went home to Bath. She was very anxious and restless to go, being too delicate for London gaieties. Besides, she had a large family at home, of which I was the eldest; and we were anxiously expecting another baby in a month or two. Nevertheless, my dear mother had gone about with me, taken me to all the shows and sights that I, a hearty and happy girl, longed to see, and entered into them with almost as great enjoyment as my own.

'But tonight she was pale, rather grave, and steadfastly bent on returning home.

'We did all we could to persuade her to the contrary, for on the next night but one was to have been the crowning treat of all our London pleasures: we were to see *Hamlet* at Drury-lane, with John Kemble and

Sarah Siddons! Think of that, my dear. Ah! you have no such sights now. Even my grave father longed to go, and urged in his mild way that we should put off our departure. But my mother was determined.

'At last Mr Everest said – I could show you the very spot where he stood, with the river – it was high water – lapping against the wall, and the evening sun shining on the Southwark houses opposite. He said – it was very wrong, of course, my dear; but then he was in love, and might be excused –

'"Madam," said he, "it is the first time I ever knew you think of yourself alone."

'"Myself, Edmond?"

'"Pardon me, but would it not be possible for you to return home, leaving behind, for two days only, Dr Thwaite and Mistress Dorothy?"

'"Leave them behind – leave them behind!" She mused over the words. "What say you, Dorothy?"

'I was silent. In very truth, I had never been parted from her in all my life. It had never crossed my mind to wish to part from her, or to enjoy any pleasure without her, till – till within the last three months. "Mother, don't suppose I—"

'But here I caught sight of Mr Everest and stopped.

'"Pray continue, Mistress Dorothy."

'No, I could not. He looked so vexed, so hurt; and we had been so happy together. Also, we might not meet again for years, for the journey between London and Bath was then a serious one, even to lovers; and he worked very hard – had few pleasures in his life. It did indeed seem almost selfish of my mother.

'Though my lips said nothing, perhaps my sad eyes said only too much, and my mother felt it.

'She walked with us a few yards, slowly and thoughtfully. I could see her now, with her pale, tired face, under the cherry-coloured ribbons of her hood. She had been very handsome as a young woman, and was most sweet-looking still – my dear, good mother!

'"Dorothy, we will discuss this no more. I am very sorry, but I must go home. However, I will persuade your father to remain with you till the week's end. Are you satisfied?'

'"No," was the first filial impulse of my heart; but Edmund pressed my arm with such an entreating look, that almost against my will I answered "Yes."

'Mr Everest overwhelmed my mother with his delight and gratitude. She walked up and down for some time longer, leaning on his arm – she was very fond of him; then stood looking on the river, upwards and downwards.

'"I suppose this is my last walk in London. Thank you for all the care you have taken of me. And when I am gone home – mind, oh, mind, Edmond, that you take special care of Dorothy."

'These words, and the tone in which they were spoken, fixed themselves on my mind – first, from gratitude, not unmingled with regret, as if I had not been so considerate to her as she to me; *afterwards*— But we often err, my dear, in dwelling too much on that word. We finite creatures have only to deal with "now" – nothing whatever to do with "afterwards". In this case, I have ceased to blame myself or others. Whatever was, being past, was right to be, and could not have been otherwise.

'My mother went home next morning, alone. We were to follow in a few days, though she would not allow us to fix any time. Her departure was so hurried that I remember nothing about it, save her answer to my father's urgent desire – almost command – that if anything went amiss she would immediately let him know.

'"Under all circumstances, wife," he reiterated, "this you promise?"

'"I promise."

'Though when she was gone he declared she need not have said it so earnestly, since we should be at home almost as soon as the slow Bath coach could take her there and bring us back a letter. And besides, there was nothing likely to happen. But he fidgeted a good deal, being unused to her absence in their happy wedded life. He was, like most men, glad to blame anybody but himself, and the whole day, and the next, was cross at intervals with both Edmond and me; but we bore it – and patiently.

'"It will be all right when we get him to the theatre. He has no real cause for anxiety about her. What a dear woman she is, and a precious – your mother, Dorothy!"

'I rejoiced to hear my lover speak thus, and thought there hardly ever was young gentlewoman so blessed as I.

'We went to the play. Ah, you know nothing of what a play is, nowadays. You never saw John Kemble and Mrs Siddons. Though in dresses and shows it was far inferior to the *Hamlet* you took me to see last week, my dear – and though I perfectly well remember being on the point of laughing when in the most solemn scene, it became clearly evident that the Ghost had been drinking. Strangely enough, no after events connected therewith ever were able to drive from my mind the vivid impression of this my first play. Strange, also, that the play should have been *Hamlet*. Do you think that Shakespeare believed in – in what people call "ghosts?"'

I could not say; but I thought Mrs MacArthur's ghost very long in coming.

'Don't, my dear – don't; do anything but laugh at it.'

She was visibly affected, and it was not without an effort that she proceeded in her story.

'I wish you to understand exactly my position that night – a young girl, her head full of the enchantment of the stage – her heart of something not less engrossing. Mr Everest had supped with us, leaving us both in the best of spirits; indeed my father had gone to bed, laughing heartily at the remembrance of the antics of Mr Grimaldi, which had almost obliterated the Queen and Hamlet from his memory, on which the ridiculous always took a far stronger hold than the awful or sublime.

'I was sitting – let me see – at the window, chatting with my maid Patty, who was brushing the powder out of my hair. The window was open half-way, and looking out on the Thames; and the summer night being very warm and starry, made it almost like sitting out of doors. There was none of the awe given by the solitude of a closed room, when every sound is magnified, and every shadow seems alive.

'As I said, we had been chatting and laughing; for Patty and I were both very young, and she had a sweetheart, too. She, like every one of our household, was a warm admirer of Mr Everest. I had just been half scolding, half smiling at her praises of him, when St Paul's great clock came booming over the silent river.

'"Eleven," counted Patty. "Terrible late we be, Mistress Dorothy: not like Bath hours, I reckon."

'"Mother will have been in bed an hour ago," said I, with a little self-reproach at not having thought of her till now.

'The next minute my maid and I both started up with a simultaneous exclamation.

'"Did you hear that?"

'"Yes, a bat flying against the window."

'"But the lattices are open, Mistress Dorothy."

'So they were; and there was no bird or bat or living thing about – only the quiet summer night, the river, and the stars.

'"I be certain sure I heard it. And I think it was like – just a bit like – somebody tapping."

'"Nonsense, Patty!" But it *had* struck me thus – though I said it was a bat. It was exactly like the sound of fingers against a pane – very soft, gentle fingers, such as, in passing into her flower-garden, my mother used often to tap outside the school-room casement at home.

'"I wonder, did father hear anything. It – the bird, you know, Patty – might have flown at his window, too?"

'"Oh, Mistress Dorothy!" Patty would not be deceived. I gave her the brush to finish my hair, but her hand shook too much. I shut the window, and we both sat down facing it.

'At that minute, distinct, clear, and unmistakeable, like a person giving a summons in passing by, we heard once more the tapping on the pane. But nothing was seen; not a single shadow came between us and the open air; the bright starlight.

'Startled I was, and awed, but I was not frightened. The sound gave me even an inexplicable delight. But I had hardly time to recognise my feelings, still less to analyse them, when a loud cry came from my father's room.

'"Dolly, – Dolly!"

'Now my mother and I had both one name, but he always gave her the old-fashioned pet name, – I was invariably Dorothy. Still I did not pause to think, but ran to his locked door and answered.

'It was a long time before he took any notice, though I heard him talking to himself, and moaning. He was subject to bad dreams, especially before his attacks of gout. So my first alarm lightened. I stood listening, knocking at intervals, until at last he replied.

'"What do 'ee want, child?"

'"Is anything the matter, father?"

'"Nothing. Go to thy bed, Dorothy."

'"Did you not call? Do you want any one?"

'"Not thee. O Dolly, my poor Dolly," – and he seemed to be almost sobbing, "why did I let thee leave me?"

'"Father, you are not going to be ill? It is not the gout, is it? (for that was the time when he wanted my mother most, and, indeed, when he was wholly unmanageable by any one but her.)

'"Go away. Get to thy bed, girl; I don't want 'ee."

'I thought he was angry with me for having been in some sort the cause of our delay, and retired very miserable. Patty and I sat up a good while longer, discussing the dreary prospect of my father's having a fit of the gout here in London lodgings, with only us to nurse him, and my mother away. Our alarm was so great that we quite forgot the curious circumstance which had first attracted us, till Patty spoke up from her bed on the floor.

'"I hope master beant going to be very ill, and that noise – you know – came for a warning. Do 'ee think it *was* a bird, Mistress Dorothy?"

'"Very likely. Now, Patty, let us go to sleep."

'But I did not, for all night I heard my father groaning at intervals. I was certain it was the gout, and wished from the bottom of my heart that we had gone home with mother.

'What was my surprise when, quite early, I heard him rise and go down, just as if nothing was ailing him! I found him sitting at the breakfast-table in his travelling coat, looking very haggard and miserable, but evidently bent on a journey.

'"Father, you are not going to Bath?"

'"Yes, I be."

'"Not till the evening coach starts," I cried, alarmed. "We can't, you know?"

'"I'll take a post-chaise, then. We must be off in an hour."

'An hour! The cruel pain of parting – (my dear, I believe I used to feel things keenly when I was young) – shot through me – through and through. A single hour, and I should have said good-bye to Edmond – one of those heart-breaking farewells when we seem to leave half of our poor young life behind us, forgetting that the only real parting is when there is no love left to part from. A few years, and I wondered how I could have crept away and wept in such intolerable agony at the mere bidding good-bye to Edmond – Edmond, who loved me!

'Every minute seemed a day till he came in, as usual, to breakfast. My red eyes and my father's corded trunk explained all.

'"Dr Thwaite, you are not going?"

'"Yes, I am," repeated my father. He sat moodily leaning on the table – would not taste his breakfast.

'"Not till the night coach, surely? I was to take you and Mistress Dorothy to see Mr Benjamin West, the king's painter."

'"Let king and painters alone, lad; I am going home to my Dolly."

'Mr Everest used many arguments, gay and grave, upon which I hung with earnest conviction and hope. He made things so clear always; he was a man of much brighter parts than my father, and had great influence over him.

'"Dorothy," he whispered, "help me to persuade the Doctor. It is so little time I beg for, only a few hours; and before so long a parting." – Ay, longer than he thought, or I.

'"Children," cried my father at last, "you are a couple of fools. Wait till you have been married twenty years. I must go to my Dolly. I know there is something amiss at home."

'I should have felt alarmed, but I saw Mr Everest smile; and besides, I was yet glowing under his fond look, as my father spoke of our being "married twenty years".

'"Father, you have surely no reason for thinking this? If you have, tell us."

'My father just lifted his head, and looked at me woefully in the face.

'"Dorothy, last night, as sure as I see you now, I saw your mother."

'"Is that all?" cried Mr Everest, laughing: "why, my good sir, very likely you did; you were dreaming about her."

'"I had not gone to sleep."

'"How did you see her?"

'"Coming into my room, just as she used to do in our bedroom at home, with the candle in her hand and the baby asleep on her arm."

'"Did she speak?" asked Mr Everest, with another and rather satirical smile; "remember, you saw *Hamlet* last night. Indeed, sir – indeed, Dorothy – it was a mere dream. I do not believe in ghosts; it would be an insult to common sense, to human wisdom – nay, even to Divinity itself."

'Edmond spoke so earnestly, justly, and withal so affectionately, that perforce I agreed; and even my father began to feel rather ashamed of his own weakness. He, a sensible man and the head of a family, to yield to a mere superstitious fancy, springing probably from a hot supper and an over-excited brain! To the same cause Mr Everest attributed the other incident, which somewhat hesitatingly I told him.

'"Dear, it was a bird; nothing but a bird. One flew in at my window last spring; it had hurt itself, and I kept it, and nursed it, and petted it. It was such a pretty gentle little thing, it put me in mind of Dorothy."

'"Did it?" said I.

'"And at last it got well and flew away."

'"Ah! that was not like Dorothy."

'Thus, my father being persuaded, it was not hard to persuade me. We settled to remain till evening. Edmond and I, with my maid Patty, went about together chiefly in Mr West's Gallery, and in the quiet shade of our favourite Temple Gardens. And if for those four stolen hours, and the sweetness in them, I afterwards suffered untold remorse and bitterness, I have entirely forgiven myself, as I know my dear mother would have forgiven me, long ago.'

Mrs MacArthur stopped, wiped her eyes, and then continued – speaking more in the matter-of-fact way that old people speak in, than she had been lately doing.

'Well, my dear, where was I?'

'In the Temple Gardens.'

'Yes, yes. Then we came home to dinner. My father always enjoyed his dinner, and his nap afterwards; he had nearly recovered himself now: only looked tired from loss of rest. Edmond and I sat in the window, watching the barges and wherries down the Thames; there were no steam-boats then, you know.

'Some one knocked at the door with a message for my father, but he slept so heavily he did not hear. Mr Everest went to see what it was; I stood at the window. I remember mechanically watching the red sail of a Margate hoy that was going down the river, and thinking with a sharp pang how dark the room seemed to grow, in a moment, with Edmond not there.

'Re-entering, after a somewhat long absence, he never looked at me, but went straight to my father.

'"Sir, it is almost time for you to start; (oh! Edmond). "There is a coach at the door; and, pardon me, but I think you should travel quickly."

'My father sprang to his feet.

'"Dear sir, wait one moment; I have received news from Bath. You have another little daughter, sir, and—"

'"Dolly, my Dolly!" Without another word my father rushed away, leaped into the post-chaise that was waiting and drove off.

'"Edmond!" I gasped.

'"My poor little girl – my own Dorothy!"

'By the tenderness of his embrace, less lover-like than brother-like – by his tears, for I could feel them on my neck – I knew, as well as if he had told me, that I should never see my dear mother any more. –

'She had died in childbirth,' continued the old lady after a long pause – 'died at night, at the same hour and minute that I had heard the tapping on the window-pane, and my father had thought he saw her coming into his room with a baby on her arm.'

'Was the baby dead, too?'

'They thought so then, but it afterwards revived.'

'What a strange story!'

'I do not ask you to believe in it. How and why and what it was I cannot tell; I only know that it assuredly was as I have told it.'

'And Mr Everest?' I inquired, after some hesitation.

The old lady shook her head. 'Ah, my dear, you may perhaps learn – though I hope you will not – how very, very seldom things turn out as one expects when one is young. After that day I did not see Mr Everest for twenty years.'

'How wrong of him – how—'

'Don't blame him; it was not his fault. You see, after that time my father took a prejudice against him – not unnatural, perhaps; and *she* was not there to make things straight. Besides, my own conscience was very sore, and there were the six children at home, and the little baby had no mother: so at last I made up my mind. I should have loved him just the same if we had waited twenty years. I told him so: but he could not see things in that light. Don't blame him, my dear, don't blame him. It was as well, perhaps, as it happened.'

'Did he marry?'

'Yes, after a few years; and loved his wife dearly. When I was about one-and-thirty, I married Mr MacArthur. So neither of us was unhappy, you see – at least, not more so than most people; and we became sincere friends afterwards. Mr and Mrs Everest come to see me still, almost every Sunday. Why, you foolish child, you are not crying?'

Ay, I was – but scarcely at the ghost story.

Catherine Crowe

ROUND THE FIRE

'MY story will be a very short one,' said Mrs M.; 'for I must tell you that though, like everybody else, I have heard a great many ghost stories, and have met people who assured me they had seen such things, I cannot, for my own part, bring myself to believe in them; but a circumstance occurred when I was abroad that you may perhaps consider of a ghostly nature, though I cannot.

'I was travelling through Germany, with no one but my maid – it was before the time of railways, and on my road from Leipsic to Dresden I stopped at an inn that appeared to have been long ago part of an aristocratic residence – a castle, in short; for there was a stone wall and battlements, and a tower at one side; while the other was a prosaic-looking square building that had evidently been added in modern times. The inn stood at one end of a small village, in which some of the houses looked so antique that they might, I thought, be coeval with the castle itself. There were a good many travellers, but the host said he could accommodate me; and when I asked to see my room, he led me up to the towers, and showed me a tolerably comfortable one. There were only two apartments on each floor; so I asked him if I could have the other for my maid, and he said yes, if no other traveller arrived. None came, and she slept there.

'I supped at the *table d'hôte*, and retired to bed early, as I had an excursion to make on the following day; and I was sufficiently tired with my journey to fall asleep directly.

'I don't know how long I had slept – but I think some hours, when I awoke quite suddenly, almost with a start, and beheld near the foot of the bed the most hideous, dreadful-looking old woman, in an antique dress, that imagination can conceive. She seemed to be approaching me – not as if walking, but gliding, with her left arm and hand extended towards me.

'"Merciful God, deliver me!" I exclaimed under my first impulse of amazement; and as I said the words she disappeared.'

'Then, though you don't believe in ghosts, you thought it was one when you saw it,' said I.

'I don't know what I thought – I admit I was a good deal frightened, and it was a long time before I fell asleep again.

'In the morning,' continued Mrs M., 'my maid knocked, and I told her to come in; but the door was locked, and I had to get out of bed to admit her – I thought I might have forgotten to fasten it. As soon as I was up I examined every part of the room, but I could find nothing to account for this intrusion. There was neither trap nor moving panel, nor door that I could see, except the one I had locked. However, I made up my mind not to speak of the circumstance, for I fancied I must have been deceived in supposing myself awake, and that it was only a dream; more particularly as there was no light in my room, and I could not comprehend how I could have seen this woman.

'I went out early, and was away the greater part of the day. When I returned I found more travellers had arrived, and that they had given the room next mine to a German lady and her daughter, who were at the *table d'hôte*. I therefore had a bed made up in my room for my maid; and before I lay down, I searched thoroughly, that I might be sure nobody was concealed there.

'In the middle of the night – I suppose about the same time I had been disturbed on the preceding one – I and my maid were awakened by a piercing scream; and I heard the voice of the German girl in the adjoining room, exclaiming, "Ach! *meine mutter! meine mutter!*"

'For some time afterwards I heard them talking, and then I fell asleep – wondering, I confess, whether they had had a visit from the frightful old woman. They left me in no doubt the next morning. They came down to breakfast greatly excited – told everybody the cause – described the old woman exactly as I had seen her, and departed from the house incontently, declaring they would not stay there another hour.'

'What did the host say to it?' we asked.

'Nothing; he said we must have dreamed it – and I suppose we did.'

'Your story,' said I, 'reminds me of a very interesting letter which I received soon after the publication of *The Night Side of Nature*. It was from a clergyman who gave his name, and said he was chaplain to a nobleman. He related that in a house he inhabited, or had inhabited, a lady had one evening gone upstairs and seen, to her amazement, in a room, the door of which was open, a lady in an antique dress standing before a chest of drawers and apparently examining their contents. She stood still, wondering who this stranger could be, when the figure turned her face towards her and, to her horror, she saw there were no eyes. Other members of the family saw the same apparition also. I believe there were further particulars; but I unfortunately lost this letter, with some others, in the confusion of changing my residence.

'The absence of eyes I take to be emblematical of moral blindness; for in the world of spirits there is no deceiving each other by false seemings; as we are, so we appear.'

'Then,' said Mrs W.C., 'the apparition – if it was an apparition – that two of my servants saw lately, must be in a very degraded state.

'There is a road, and on one side of it a path, just beyond my garden wall. Not long ago two of my servants were in the dusk of the evening walking up this path, when they saw a large, dark object coming towards them. At first they thought it was an animal; and when it got close one of them stretched out her hand to touch it; but she could feel nothing, and it passed on between her and the garden wall, although there was *no space*, the path being only wide enough for two; and on looking back, they saw it walking down the hill behind them. Three men were coming up on the path, and as the thing approached they jumped off into the road.

'"Good heavens, what is that!" cried the women.

'"I don't know," replied the men; "I never saw such a thing as that before."

'The women came home greatly agitated; and we have since heard there is a tradition that the spot is haunted by the ghost of a man who was killed in a quarry close by.'

'I have travelled a great deal,' said our next speaker, the Chevalier de La C.G.; 'and, certainly, I have never been in any country where instances of these spiritual appearances were not adduced on apparently credible authority. I have heard numerous stories of the sort, but the one that most readily occurs to me at present was told to me not long ago, in Paris, by Count P. – the nephew of the celebrated Count P. whose name occurs in the history of the remarkable incidents connected with the death of the Emperor Paul.

'Count P., my authority for the following story, was attached to the Russian embassy; and he told me, one evening, when the conversation turned on the inconveniences of travelling in the East of Europe, that on one occasion, when in Poland, he found himself about seven o'clock in an autumn evening on a forest road, where there was no possibility of finding a house of public entertainment within many miles. There was a frightful storm; the road, not good at the best, was almost impracticable from the weather, and his horses were completely knocked up. On consulting his people what was best to be done, they said that to go back was as impossible as to go forward; but that by turning a little out of the main road, they should soon reach a castle where possibly shelter might be procured for the night. The count gladly consented, and it was not long before they found themselves at the gate of what appeared a building on a very splendid scale. The courier quickly alighted and rang at the bell, and while waiting for admission he inquired who the castle belonged to, and was told that it was Count X's.

'It was some time before the bell was answered, but at length an elderly man appeared at a wicket, with a lantern, and peeped out. On perceiving the equipage, he came forward and stepped up to the carriage, holding the light aloft to discover who was inside. Count P. handed him his card, and explained his distress.

'"There is no one here, my lord," replied the man, "but myself and my family; the castle is not inhabited."

'"That's bad news," said the count; "but nevertheless, you can give me what I am most in need of, and that is – shelter for the night."

'"Willingly," said the man, "if your lordship will put up with such accommodation as we can hastily prepare."

'"So," said the count, "I alighted and walked in; and the old man unbarred the great gates to admit my carriages and people. We found ourselves in an immense *cour*, with the castle *en face*, and stables and offices on each side. As we had a *fourgon* with us, with provender for the cattle and provisions for ourselves, we wanted nothing but beds and a good fire; and as the only one lighted was in the old man's apartments, he first took us there. They consisted of a suite of small rooms in the left wing, that had probably been formerly occupied by the upper servants. They were comfortably furnished, and he and his large family appeared to be very well lodged. Besides the wife, there were three sons, with their wives and children, and two nieces; and in a part of the offices, where I saw a light, I was told there were labourers and women servants, for it was a valuable estate, with a fine forest, and the sons acted as *gardes chasse*.

'"Is there much game in the forest?" I asked.

'"A great deal of all sorts," they answered.

'"Then I suppose during the season the family live here?"

'"Never," they replied. "None of the family ever reside here."

'"Indeed!" I said; "how is that? It seems a very fine place."

'"Superb," answered the wife of the custodian; "but the castle is haunted."

'She said this with a simple gravity that made me laugh; upon which they all stared at me with the most edifying amazement.

'"I beg your pardon," I said; "but you know, perhaps, in great cities, such as I usually inhabit, there are no ghosts."

'"Indeed!" said they. "No ghosts!"

'"At least," I said, "I never heard of any; and we don't believe in such things."

'They looked at each other with surprise, but said nothing; not appearing to have any desire to convince me. "But do you mean to say," said I, "that that is the reason the family don't live here, and that the castle is abandoned on that account?"

'"Yes," they replied, "that is the reason nobody has resided here for many years."

'"But how can you live here then?"

'"We are never troubled in this part of the building," said she. "We hear noises, but we are used to that."

'"Well, if there is a ghost, I hope I shall see it," said I.

'"God forbid!" said the woman, crossing herself. "But we shall guard against that; your seigneurie will sleep not far from this, where you will be quite safe."

'"Oh! but," said I, "I am quite serious: if there is a ghost I should particularly like to see him, and I should be much obliged to you to put me in the apartments he most frequents."

'They opposed this proposition earnestly, and begged me not to think of it; besides, they said if anything was to happen to my lord, how should they answer for it; but as I insisted, the women went to call the members of the family who were lighting fires and preparing beds in some rooms on the same floor as they occupied themselves. When they came they were as earnest against the indulgence of my wishes as the women had been. Still I insisted.

'"Are you afraid," I said, "to go yourselves in the haunted chambers?"

'"No," they answered. "We are the custodians of the castle and have to keep the rooms clean and well aired lest the furniture be spoiled – my lord talks always of removing it, but it has never been removed yet – but we would not sleep up there for all the world."

'"Then it is the upper floors that are haunted?"

'"Yes, especially the long room, no one could pass a night there; the last that did is in a lunatic asylum now at Warsaw," said the custodian.

'"What happened to him?"

'"I don't know," said the man; "he was never able to tell."

'"Who was he?" I asked.

'"He was a lawyer. My lord did business with him; and one day he was speaking of this place, and saying that it was a pity he was not at liberty to pull it down and sell the materials; but he cannot, because it is family property and goes with the title; and the lawyer said he wished it was his, and that no ghost should keep him out of it. My lord said that it was easy for any one to say that who knew nothing about it, and that he must suppose the family had not abandoned such a fine place without good reasons. But the lawyer said it was some trick, and that it was coiners, or robbers, who had got a footing in the castle, and contrived to frighten people away that they might keep it to themselves; so my lord said if he could prove that he should be very much obliged to him, and more than that, he would give him a great sum – I don't know how much. So the lawyer said he would; and my lord wrote to me that he was coming to inspect the property, and I was to let him do anything he liked.

'"Well, he came, and with him his son, a fine young man and a soldier. They asked me all sorts of questions, and went over the castle and examined every part of it. From what they said, I could see that they thought the ghost was all nonsense, and that I and my family were in collusion with the robbers or coiners. However, I did not care for that; my lord knew that the castle had been haunted before I was born.

'"I had prepared rooms on this floor for them – the same I am preparing for your lordship, and they slept there, keeping the keys of the upper rooms to themselves, so I did not interfere with them. But one morning, very early, we were awakened by someone knocking at our bedroom door, and when we opened it we saw Mr Thaddeus – that was the lawyer's son – standing there half-dressed and as pale as a ghost; and he said his father was very ill and he begged us to go to him; to our surprise he led us upstairs to the haunted chamber, and there we found the poor gentleman speechless, and we thought they had gone up there early and that he had had a stroke. But it was not so; Mr Thaddeus said that after we were all in bed they had gone up there to pass the night. I know they thought that there was no ghost but us, and that's why they would not let us know their intention. They laid down upon some sofas, wrapt up in their fur cloaks, and resolved to keep awake, and they did so for some time, but at last the young man was overcome by drowsiness; he struggled against it, but could not conquer it, and the last thing he recollects was his father shaking him and saying, 'Thaddeus, Thaddeus, for God's sake keep awake!' But he could not, and he knew no more till he woke and saw that day was breaking, and found his father sitting in a corner of the room speechless, and looking like a corpse; and there he was when we went up. The young man thought he'd been taken ill or had a stroke, as we supposed at first; but when we found they had passed the night in the haunted chambers, we had no doubt what had happened – he had seen some terrible sight and so lost his senses."

'"He lost his senses, I should say, from terror when his son fell asleep," said I, "and he felt himself alone. He could have been a man of no nerve. At all events, what you tell me raises my curiosity. Will you take me upstairs and shew me these rooms?"

'"Willingly," said the man, and fetching a bunch of keys and a light, and calling one of his sons to follow him with another, he led the way up the great staircase to a suite of apartments on the first floor. The rooms were lofty and large, and the man said the furniture was very handsome, but old. Being all covered with canvas cases, I could not judge of it. "Which is the long room?" I said.

'Upon which he led me into a long narrow room that might rather have been called a gallery. There were sofas along each side, something like a dais at the upper end; and several large pictures hanging on the walls.

'I had with me a bull dog, of a very fine breed, that had been given me in England by Lord F. She had followed me upstairs – indeed, she followed me everywhere – and I watched her narrowly as she went smelling about, but there were no indications of her perceiving anything extraordinary. Beyond this gallery there was only a small octagon room, with a door that led out upon another staircase. When I had examined it all thoroughly, I returned to the long room and told the man as that was the place especially frequented by the ghost, I should feel much obliged if he would allow me to pass the night there. I could take upon myself to say that Count X. would have no objection.

'"It is not that," replied the man; "but the danger to your lordship," and he conjured me not to insist on such a perilous experiment.

'When he found I was resolved, he gave way, but on condition that I signed a paper, stating that in spite of his representations I had determined to sleep in the long room.

'I confess the more anxious these people seemed to prevent my sleeping there, the more curious I was; not that I believed in the ghost the least in the world. I thought that the lawyer had been right in his conjecture, but that he hadn't nerve enough to investigate whatever he saw or heard; and that they had succeeded in frightening him out of his senses. I saw what an excellent place these people had got, and how much it was their interest to maintain the idea that the castle was uninhabitable. Now, I have pretty good nerves – I have been in situations that have tried them severely – and I did not believe that any ghost, if there was such a thing, or any jugglery by which a semblance of one might be contrived, would shake them. As for any real danger, I did not apprehend it; the people knew who I was, and any mischief happening to me would have led to consequences they well understood. So they lighted fires in both the grates of the gallery and as they had abundance of dry wood they soon blazed up. I was determined not to leave the room after I was once in it, lest, if my suspicions were correct, they might have time to make their arrangements; so I desired my people to bring up my supper, and I ate it there.

'My courier said he had always heard the castle was haunted, but he dare say there was no ghost but the people below, who had a very comfortable berth of it; and he offered to pass the night with me, but I declined any companion and preferred trusting to myself and my dog. My valet, on the contrary, strongly advised me against the enterprise, assuring me that he had lived with a family in France whose château was haunted, and had left his place in consequence.

'By the time I had finished my supper it was ten o'clock, and everything was prepared for the night. My bed, though an impromptu, was very comfortable, made of amply stuffed cushions and thick coverlets, placed in front of the fire. I was provided with light and plenty of wood; and I had my regimental cutlass, and a case of excellent pistols, which I carefully primed and loaded in presence of the custodian, saying, "You see I am determined to fire at the ghost, so if he cannot stand a bullet he had better not pay me a visit."

'The old man shook his head calmly, but made no answer. Having desired the courier, who said he should not go to bed, to come upstairs immediately if he heard the report of firearms, I dismissed my people and locked the doors, barricading each with a heavy ottoman besides. There was no arras or hangings of any sort behind which a door could be concealed; and I went round the room, the walls of which were panelled with white and gold, knocking every part, but neither the sound, nor Dido, the dog, gave any indications of there being anything unusual. Then I undressed and lay down with my sword and my pistols beside me; and Dido at the foot of my bed, where she always slept.

'I confess I was in a state of pleasing excitement; my curiosity and my love of adventure were roused; and whether it was ghost, or robber, or coiner, I was to have a visit from, the interview was likely to be equally interesting. It was half-past ten when I lay down; my expectations were too vivid to admit of sleep; and after an attempt at a French novel, I was obliged to give it up; I could not fix my attention to it. Besides, my chief care was not to be surprised. I could not help thinking the custodian and his family had some secret way of getting into the room, and I hoped to detect them in the act; so I lay with my eyes and ears open in a position that gave me a view of every part of it, till my travelling clock struck twelve, which being pre-eminently the ghostly hour, I thought the critical moment was arrived. But no, no sound, no interruption of any sort to the silence and solitude of the night occurred. When half-past twelve and one struck, I pretty well made up my mind that I should be disappointed in my expectations, and that the ghost, whoever he was, knew better than to encounter Dido and a brace of well charged pistols; but just as I arrived at this conclusion an unaccountable *frisson* came over me, and I saw Dido, who tired with her day's journey had lain till now quietly curled up asleep, begin to move, and slowly get upon her feet. I thought she was only going to turn, but, instead of lying down, she stood still with her ears erect and her head towards the dais, uttering a low growl.

'The dais, I should mention, was but the skeleton of a dais, for the draperies were taken off. There was only remaining a canopy covered with crimson velvet, and an arm-chair covered with velvet too, but cased in canvas like the rest of the furniture. I had examined this part of the room thoroughly, and had moved the chair aside to ascertain that there was nothing under it.

'Well, I sat up in bed and looked steadily in the same direction as the dog, but I could see nothing at first, though it appeared that she did; but as I looked I began to perceive something like a cloud in the chair, while at the same time a chill which seemed to pervade the very marrow in my bones crept through me, yet the fire was good; and it was not the chill of fear, for I cocked my pistols with perfect self-possession and abstained from giving Dido the signal to advance, because I wished eagerly to see the dénouement of the adventure.

'Gradually this cloud took a form, and assumed the shape of a tall white figure that reached from the ceiling to the floor of the dais, which was raised by two steps. "At him, Dido! At him!" I said, and away she dashed to the steps, but instantly turned and crept back completely cowed. As her courage was undoubted, I own this astonished me, and I should have fired, but that I was perfectly satisfied that what I saw was not a substantial human form, for I had seen it grow into its present shape and height from the undefined cloud that first appeared in the chair. I laid my hand on the dog, who had crept up to my side, and I felt her shaking in her skin. I was about to rise myself and approach the figure, though I confess I was a good deal awestruck, when it stepped majestically from the dais, and seemed to be advancing. "At him!" I said, "At him, Dido!" and I gave the dog every encouragement to go forward; she made a sorry attempt, but returned when she had got half-way and crouched beside me whining with terror. The figure advanced upon me; the cold became icy; the dog crouched and trembled; and I, as it approached, honestly confess,' said Count P., 'that I hid my head under the bedclothes and did not venture to look up till morning. I know not what it was – as it passed over me I felt a sensation of undefinable horror, that no words can describe – and I can only say that nothing on earth would tempt me to pass another night in that room, and I am sure if Dido could speak you'd find her of the same opinion.

'I had desired to be called at seven o'clock, and when the custodian, who accompanied my valet, found me safe and in my perfect senses, I must say the poor man appeared greatly relieved; and when I descended the whole family seemed to look upon me as a hero. I thought it only just to them to admit that something had happened in the night that I felt impossible to account for, and that I should not recommend anybody who was not very sure of their nerves to repeat the experiment.'

When the Chevalier had concluded this extraordinary story, I suggested that the apparition of the castle very much resembled that mentioned by the late Professor Gregory, in his letters on mesmerism, as having appeared in the Tower of London some years ago, and, from the alarm it created, having occasioned the death of a lady, the wife of an officer quartered there, and one of the sentries. Every one who had read that very interesting publication was struck by the resemblance.

Mary E. Braddon

THE COLD EMBRACE

HE was an artist – such things as happened to him happen sometimes to artists.

He was a German – such things as happened to him happen sometimes to Germans.

He was young, handsome, studious, enthusiastic, metaphysical, reckless, unbelieving, heartless.

And being young, handsome and eloquent, he was beloved.

He was an orphan, under the guardianship of his dead father's brother, his uncle Wilhelm, in whose house he had been brought up from a little child; and she who loved him was his cousin – his cousin Gertrude, whom he swore he loved in return.

Did he love her? Yes, when he first swore it. It soon wore out, this passionate love; how threadbare and wretched a sentiment it became at last in the selfish heart of the student! But in its first golden dawn, when he was only nineteen, and had just returned from his apprenticeship to a great painter at Antwerp, and they wandered together in the most romantic outskirts of the city at rosy sunset, by holy moonlight, or bright and joyous morning, how beautiful a dream!

They keep it a secret from Wilhelm, as he has the father's ambition of a wealthy suitor for his only child – a cold and dreary vision beside the lover's dream.

So they are betrothed; and standing side by side when the dying sun and the pale rising moon divide the heavens, he puts the betrothal ring upon her finger, the white and taper finger whose slender shape he knows so well. This ring is a peculiar one, a massive golden serpent, its tail in its mouth, the symbol of eternity; it had been his mother's, and he would know it amongst a thousand. If he were to become blind tomorrow, he could select it from amongst a thousand by the touch alone.

He places it on her finger, and they swear to be true to each other for ever and ever – through trouble and danger – sorrow and change – in wealth or poverty. Her father must needs be won to consent to their union by-and-by, for they were now betrothed, and death alone could part them.

But the young student, the scoffer at revelation, yet the enthusiastic adorer of the mystical asks:

'Can death part us? I would return to you from the grave, Gertrude. My soul would come back to be near my love. And you – you, if you died before me – the cold earth would not hold you from me; if you loved me, you would return, and again these fair arms would be clasped round my neck as they are now.'

But she told him, with a holier light in her deep-blue eyes than had ever shone in his – she told him that the dead who die at peace with God are happy in heaven, and cannot return to the troubled earth; and that it is only the suicide – the lost wretch on whom sorrowful angels shut the door of Paradise – whose unholy spirit haunts the footsteps of the living.

The first year of their betrothal is passed, and she is alone, for he has gone to Italy, on a commission for some rich man, to copy Raphaels, Titians, Guidos, in a gallery at Florence. He has gone to win fame, perhaps; but it is not the less bitter – he is gone!

Of course her father misses his young nephew, who has been as a son to him; and he thinks his daughter's sadness no more than a cousin should feel for a cousin's absence.

In the meantime, the weeks and months pass. The lover writes – often at first, then seldom – at last, not at all.

How many excuses she invents for him! How many times she goes to the distant little post-office, to which he is to address his letters! How many times she hopes, only to be disappointed! How many times she despairs, only to hope again!

But real despair comes at last, and will not be put off any more. The rich suitor appears on the scene, and her father is determined. She is to marry at once. The wedding-day is fixed – the fifteenth of June.

The date seems burnt into her brain.

The date, written in fire, dances for ever before her eyes.

The date, shrieked by the Furies, sounds continually in her ears.

But there is time yet – it is the middle of May – there is time for a letter to reach him at Florence; there is time for him to come to Brunswick, to take her away and marry her, in spite of her father – in spite of the whole world.

But the days and weeks fly by, and he does not write – he does not come. This is indeed despair which usurps her heart, and will not be put away.

It is the fourteenth of June. For the last time she goes to the little post-office; for the last time she asks the old question, and they give her for the last time the dreary answer, 'No; no letter.'

For the last time – for tomorrow is the day appointed for her bridal. Her father will hear no entreaties; her rich suitor will not listen to her prayers. They will not be put off a day – an hour; tonight alone is hers – this night, which she may employ as she will.

She takes another path than that which leads home; she hurries through some by-streets of the city, out on to a lonely bridge, where he and she had stood so often in the sunset, watching the rose-coloured light glow, fade, and die upon the river.

* * *

He returns from Florence. He had received her letter. That letter, blotted with tears, entreating, despairing – he had received it, but he loved her no longer. A young Florentine, who has sat to him for a model, had bewitched his fancy – that fancy which with him stood in place of a heart – and Gertrude had been half-forgotten. If she had a rich suitor, good; let her marry him; better for her, better far for himself. He had no wish to fetter himself with a wife. Had he not his art always? – his eternal bride, his unchanging mistress.

Thus he thought it wiser to delay his journey to Brunswick, so that he should arrive when the wedding was over – arrive in time to salute the bride.

And the vows – the mystical fancies – the belief in his return, even after death, to the embrace of his beloved? O, gone out of his life; melted away for ever, those foolish dreams of his boyhood.

So on the fifteenth of June he enters Brunswick, by that very bridge on which she stood, the stars looking down on her, the night before. He strolls across the bridge and down by the water's edge, a great rough dog at his heels, and the smoke from his short meerschaum-pipe curling in blue wreaths fantastically in the pure morning air. He has his sketch-book under his arm, and attracted now and then by some object that catches his artist's eye, stops to draw: a few weeds and pebbles on the river's brink – a crag on the opposite shore – a group of pollard willows in the distance. When he has done, he admires his drawing, shuts his sketch-book, empties the ashes from his pipe, refills from his tobacco-pouch, sings the refrain of a gay drinking-song, calls to his dog, smokes again, and walks on. Suddenly he opens his sketch-book again; this time that which attracts him is a group of figures: but what is it?

It is not a funeral, for there are no mourners.

It is not a funeral, but a corpse lying on a rough bier, covered with an old sail, carried between two bearers.

It is not a funeral, for the bearers are fishermen – fishermen in their everyday garb.

About a hundred yards from him they rest their burden on a bank – one stands at the head of the bier, the other throws himself down at the foot of it.

And thus they form a perfect group; he walks back two or three paces, selects his point of sight, and begins to sketch a hurried outline. He has finished it before they move; he hears their voices, though he cannot hear their words, and wonders what they can be talking of. Presently he walks on and joins them.

'You have a corpse there, my friends?' he says.

'Yes; a corpse washed ashore an hour ago.'

'Drowned?'

'Yes, drowned. A young girl, very handsome.'

'Suicides are always handsome,' says the painter; and then he stands for a little while idly smoking and meditating, looking at the sharp outline of the corpse and the stiff folds of the rough canvas covering.

Life is such a golden holiday for him – young, ambitious, clever – that it seems as though sorrow and death could have no part in his destiny.

At last he says that, as this poor suicide is so handsome, he should like to make a sketch of her.

He gives the fishermen some money, and they offer to remove the sailcloth that covers her features.

No; he will do it himself. He lifts the rough, coarse, wet canvas from her face. What face?

The face that shone on the dreams of his foolish boyhood; the face which once was the light of his uncle's home. His cousin Gertrude – his betrothed!

He sees, as in one glance, while he draws one breath, the rigid features – the marble arms – the hands crossed on the cold bosom; and, on the third finger of the left hand, the ring which had been his mother's – the golden serpent; the ring which, if he were to become blind, he could select from a thousand others by the touch alone.

But he is a genius and a metaphysician – grief, true grief, is not for such as he. His first thought is flight – flight anywhere out of that accursed city – anywhere far from the brink of that hideous river – anywhere away from remorse – anywhere to forget.

* * *

He is miles on the road that leads away from Brunswick before he knows that he has walked a step.

It is only when his dog lies down panting at his feet than he feels how exhausted he is himself, and sits down upon a bank to rest. How the landscape spins round and round before his dazzled eyes, while his morning's sketch of the two fishermen and the canvas-covered bier glares redly at him out of the twilight!

At last, after sitting a long time by the roadside, idly playing with his dog, idly smoking, idly lounging, looking as any idle, light-hearted travelling student might look, yet all the while acting over that morning's scene in his burning brain a hundred times a minute; at last he grows a little more composed, and tries presently to think of himself as he is, apart from his cousin's suicide. Apart from that, he was no worse off than he was yesterday. His genius was not gone; the money he had earned at Florence still lined his pocket-book; he was his own master, free to go whither he would.

And while he sits on the roadside, trying to separate himself from the scene of that morning – trying to put away the image of the corpse covered with the damp canvas sail – trying to think of what he should do next, where he should go, to be farthest away from Brunswick and remorse, the old diligence comes rumbling and jingling along. He remembers it; it goes from Brunswick to Aix-la-Chapelle.

He whistles to his dog, shouts to the postillion to stop, and springs into the *coupé*.

During the whole evening, through the long night, though he does not once close his eyes, he never speaks a word; but when morning dawns, and the other passengers awake and begin to talk to each other, he joins in the conversation. He tells them that he is an artist, that he is going to Cologne and to Antwerp to copy Rubenses, and the great picture by Quentin Matsys, in the museum. He remembered afterwards that he talked and laughed boisterously, and that when he was talking and laughing loudest, a passenger, older and graver than the rest, opened the window near him, and told him to put his head out. He remembered the fresh air blowing in his face, the singing of the birds in his ears, and the flat fields and roadside reeling before his eyes. He remembered this, and then falling in a lifeless heap on the floor of the diligence.

It is a fever that keeps him for six long weeks on a bed at a hotel in Aix-la-Chapelle.

He gets well, and, accompanied by his dog, starts on foot for Cologne. By this time he is his former self once more. Again the blue smoke from his short meerschaum curls upwards in the morning air – again he sings some old university drinking-song – again stops here and there, meditating and sketching.

He is happy, and has forgotten his cousin – and so on to Cologne.

It is by the great cathedral he is standing, with his dog at his side. It is night, the bells have just chimed the hour, and the clocks are striking eleven; the moonlight shines full upon the magnificent pile, over which the artist's eye wanders, absorbed in the beauty of form.

He is not thinking of his drowned cousin, for he has forgotten her and is happy.

Suddenly some one, something from behind him, puts two cold arms round his neck, and clasps its hands on his breast.

And yet there is no one behind him, for on the flags bathed in the broad moonlight there are only two shadows, his own and his dog's. He turns quickly round – there is no one – nothing to be seen in the broad square but himself and his dog; and though he feels, he cannot see the cold arms clasped round his neck.

It is not ghostly, this embrace, for it is palpable to the touch – it cannot be real, for it is invisible.

He tries to throw off the cold caress. He clasps the hands in his own to tear them asunder, and to cast them off his neck. He can feel the long delicate fingers cold and wet beneath his touch, and on the third finger of the left hand he can feel the ring which was his mother's – the golden serpent – the ring which he has always said he would know among a thousand by the touch alone. He knows it now!

His dead cousin's cold arms are round his neck – his dead cousin's wet hands are clasped upon his breast. He asks himself if he is mad. 'Up, Leo!' he shouts. 'Up, up, boy!' and the Newfoundland leaps to his shoulders – the dog's paws are on the dead hands, and the animal utters a terrific howl, and springs away from his master.

The student stands in the moonlight, the dead arms around his neck, and the dog at a little distance moaning piteously.

Presently a watchman, alarmed by the howling of the dog, comes into the square to see what is wrong.

In a breath the cold arms are gone.

He takes the watchman home to the hotel with him and gives him money; in his gratitude he could have given that man half his little fortune.

Will it ever come to him again, this embrace of the dead?

He tries never to be alone; he makes a hundred acquaintances, and shares the chamber of another student. He starts up if he is left by himself in the public room at the inn where he is staying, and runs into the street. People notice his strange actions, and begin to think that he is mad.

But, in spite of all, he is alone once more; for one night the public room being empty for a moment, when on some idle pretence he strolls into the street, the street is empty too, and for the second time he feels the cold arms round his neck, and for the second time, when he calls his dog, the animal slinks away from him with a piteous howl.

After this he leaves Cologne, still travelling on foot – of necessity now, for his money is getting low. He joins travelling hawkers, he walks side by side with labourers, he talks to every foot-passenger he falls in with, and tries from morning till night to get company on the road.

At night he sleeps by the fire in the kitchen of the inn at which he stops; but do what he will, he is often alone, and it is now a common thing for him to feel the cold arms around his neck.

Many months have passed since his cousin's death – autumn, winter, early spring. His money is nearly gone, his health is utterly broken, he is the shadow of his former self, and he is getting near to Paris. He will reach that city at the time of the Carnival. To this he looks forward. In Paris, in Carnival time, he need never, surely, be alone, never feel that deadly caress; he may even recover his lost gaiety, his lost health, once more resume his profession, once more earn fame and money by his art.

How hard he tries to get over the distance that divides him from Paris, while day by day he grows weaker, and his step slower and more heavy!

But there is an end at last; the long dreary roads are passed. This is Paris, which he enters for the first time – Paris, of which he has dreamed so much – Paris, whose million voices are to exorcise his phantom.

To him tonight Paris seems one vast chaos of lights, music, and confusion – lights which dance before his eyes and will not be still – music that rings in his ears and deafens him – confusion which makes his head whirl round and round.

But, in spite of all, he finds the opera-house, where there is a masked ball. He has enough money left to buy a ticket of admission, and to hire a domino to throw over his shabby dress. It seems only a moment after his entering the gates of Paris that he is in the very midst of all the wild gaiety of the opera-house ball.

No more darkness, no more loneliness, but a mad crowd, shouting and dancing, and a lovely Débardeuse hanging on his arm.

The boisterous gaiety he feels surely is his old light-heartedness come back. He hears the people round him talking of the outrageous conduct of some drunken student, and it is to him they point when they say this – to him, who has not moistened his lips since yesterday at noon, for even now he will not drink; though his lips are parched, and his throat burning, he cannot drink. His voice is thick and hoarse, and his utterance indistinct; but still this must be his old light-heartedness come back that makes him so wildly gay.

The little Débardeuse is wearied out – her arm rests on his shoulder heavier than lead – the other dancers one by one drop off.

The lights in the chandeliers one by one die out.

The decorations look pale and shadowy in that dim light which is neither night nor day.

A faint glimmer from the dying lamps, a pale streak of cold grey light from the new-born day, creeping in through half-opened shutters.

And by this light the bright-eyed Débardeuse fades sadly. He looks her in the face. How the brightness of her eyes dies out! Again he looks her in the face. How white that face has grown! Again – and now it is the shadow of a face alone that looks in his.

Again – and they are gone – the bright eyes, the face, the shadow of the face. He is alone; alone in that vast saloon.

Alone, and, in the terrible silence, he hears the echoes of his own footsteps in that dismal dance which has no music.

No music but the beating of his breast. For the cold arms are round his neck – they whirl him round, they will not be flung off, or cast away; he can no more escape from their icy grasp than he can escape from death. He looks behind him – there is nothing but himself in the great empty *salle*; but he can feel – cold, deathlike, but O, how palpable! – the long slender fingers, and the ring which was his mother's.

He tries to shout, but he has no power in his burning throat. The silence of the place is only broken by the echoes of his own footsteps in the dance from which he cannot extricate himself. Who says he has no partner? The cold hands are clasped on his breast, and now he does not shun their caress. No! One more polka, if he drops down dead.

The lights are all out, and, half an hour after, the *gendarmes* come in with a lantern to see that the house is empty; they are followed by a great dog that they have found seated howling on the steps of the theatre. Near the principal entrance they stumble over—

The body of a student, who has died from want of food, exhaustion, and the breaking of a blood-vessel.

Rosa Mulholland

✾

NOT TO BE TAKEN AT BED-TIME

THIS is the legend of a house called the Devil's Inn, standing in the heather on the top of the Connemara mountains, in a shallow valley hollowed between five peaks. Tourists sometimes come in sight of it on September evenings; a crazy and weather-stained apparition, with the sun glaring at it angrily between the hills, and striking its shattered window-panes. Guides are known to shun it, however.

The house was built by a stranger, who came no one knew whence, and whom the people nicknamed Coll Dhu (Black-Coll), because of his sullen bearing and solitary habits. His dwelling they called the Devil's Inn, because no tired traveller had ever been asked to rest under its roof, nor friend known to cross its threshold. No one bore him company in his retreat but a wizen-faced old man, who shunned the good-morrow of the trudging peasant when he made occasional excursions to the nearest village for provisions for himself and master, and who was as secret as a stone concerning all the antecedents of both.

For the first year of their residence in the country, there had been much speculation as to who they were, and what they did with themselves up there among the clouds and eagles. Some said that Coll Dhu was a scion of the old family from whose hands the surrounding lands had passed; and that, embittered by poverty and pride, he had come to bury himself in solitude, and brood over his misfortunes. Others hinted of crime, and flight from another country; others again whispered of those who were cursed from their birth, and could never smile, nor yet make friends with a fellow-creature till the day of their death. But when two years had passed, the wonder had somewhat died out, and Coll Dhu was little thought of, except when a herd looking for sheep crossed the track of a big dark man walking the mountains gun in hand, to whom he did not dare say 'Lord save you!' or when a housewife rocking the cradle of a winter's night, crossed herself as a gust of storm thundered over her cabin-roof, with the exclamation, 'Oh, then, its Coll Dhu that has enough o' the fresh air about his head up there this night, the crature!'

Coll Dhu had lived thus in his solitude for some years, when it became known that Colonel Blake, the new lord of the soil, was coming to visit the country. By climbing one of the peaks encircling his eyrie, Coll could look sheer down a mountain-side, and see in miniature beneath him, a grey old dwelling with ivied chimneys and weather-slated walls, standing amongst straggling trees and grim warlike rocks, that gave it the look of a fortress, gazing out to the Atlantic for ever with the eager eyes of all its windows, as if demanding perpetually, 'What tidings from the New World?'

He could see now masons and carpenters crawling about below, like ants in the sun, over-running the old house from base to chimney, daubing here and knocking there, tumbling down walls that looked to Coll, up among the clouds, like a handful of jack-stones, and building up others that looked like the toy fences in a child's Farm. Throughout several months he must have watched the busy ants at their task of breaking and mending again, disfiguring and beautifying; but when all was done he had not the curiosity to stride down and admire the handsome panelling of the new billiard-room, nor yet the fine view which the enlarged bay-window in the drawing-room commanded of the watery highway to Newfoundland.

Deep summer was melting into autumn, and the amber streaks of decay were beginning to creep out and trail over the ripe purple of moor and mountain, when Colonel Blake, his only daughter, and a party of friends, arrived in the country. The grey house below was alive with gaiety, but Coll Dhu no longer found an interest in observing it from his eyrie. When he watched the sun rise or set, he chose to ascend some crag that looked on no human habitation. When he sailed forth on his excursions, gun in hand, he set his face towards the most isolated wastes, dipping into the loneliest valleys, and scaling the nakedest ridges. When he came by chance within call of other excursionists, gun in hand he plunged into the shade of some hollow, and avoided an encounter. Yet it was fated, for all that, that he and Colonel Blake should meet.

Towards the evening of one bright September day, the wind changed, and in half an hour the mountains were wrapped in a thick blinding mist. Coll Dhu was far from his den, but so well had he searched these mountains, and inured himself to their climate, that neither storm, rain, nor fog, had power to disturb him. But while he stalked on his way, a faint and agonised cry from a human voice reached him through the smothering mist. He quickly tracked the sound, and gained the side of a man who was stumbling along in danger of death at every step.

'Follow me!' said Coll Dhu to this man, and, in an hour's time, brought him safely to the lowlands, and up to the walls of the eager-eyed mansion.

'I am Colonel Blake,' said the frank soldier, when, having left the fog behind them, they stood in the starlight under the lighted windows. 'Pray tell me quickly to whom I owe my life.'

As he spoke, he glanced up at his benefactor, a large man with a sombre sun-burned face.

'Colonel Blake,' said Coll Dhu, after a strange pause, 'your father suggested to my father to stake his estates at the gaming-table. They were staked, and the tempter won. Both are dead; but you and I live, and I have sworn to injure you.'

The colonel laughed good humouredly at the uneasy face above him.

'And you began to keep your oath tonight by saving my life?' said he. 'Come! I am a soldier, and know how to meet an enemy; but I had far rather meet a friend. I shall not be happy till you have eaten my salt. We have merrymaking tonight in honour of my daughter's birthday. Come in and join us?'

Coll Dhu looked at the earth doggedly.

'I have told you,' he said, 'who and what I am, and I will not cross your threshold.'

But at this moment (so runs the story) a French window opened among the flower-beds by which they were standing, and a vision appeared which stayed the words on Coll's tongue. A stately girl, clad in white satin, stood framed in the ivied window, with the warm light from within streaming around her richly-moulded figure into the night. Her face was as pale as her gown, her eyes were swimming in tears, but a firm smile sat on her lips as she held out both hands to her father. The light behind her touched the glistening folds of her dress – the lustrous pearls round her throat – the coronet of blood-red roses which encircled the knotted braids at the back of her head. Satin, pearls, and roses – had Coll Dhu, of the Devil's Inn, never set eyes upon such things before?

Evleen Blake was no nervous tearful miss. A few quick words – 'Thank God! you're safe; the rest have been home an hour' – and a tight pressure of her father's fingers between her own jewelled hands, were all that betrayed the uneasiness she had suffered.

'Faith, my love, I owe my life to this brave gentleman!' said the blithe colonel. 'Press him to come in and be our guest, Evleen. He wants to retreat to his mountains, and lose himself again in the fog where I found him; or, rather, where he found me! Come, sir' (to Coll), 'you must surrender to this fair besieger.'

An introduction followed. 'Coll Dhu!' murmured Evleen Blake, for she had heard the common tales of him; but with a frank welcome she invited her father's preserver to taste the hospitality of that father's house.

'I beg you to come in, sir,' she said; 'but for you our gaiety must have been turned into mourning. A shadow will be upon our mirth if our benefactor disdains to join in it.'

With a sweet grace, mingled with a certain hauteur from which she was never free, she extended her white hand to the tall looming figure outside the window; to have it grasped and wrung in a way that made the proud girl's eyes flash their amazement, and the same little hand clench itself in displeasure, when it had hid itself like an outraged thing among the shining folds of her gown. Was this Coll Dhu mad, or rude?

The guest no longer refused to enter, but followed the white figure into a little study where a lamp burned; and the gloomy stranger, the bluff colonel, and the young mistress of the house, were fully discovered to each other's eyes. Evleen glanced at the newcomer's dark face, and shuddered with a feeling of indescribable dread and dislike; then, to her father, accounted for the shudder after a popular fashion, saying lightly: 'There is someone walking over my grave.'

So Coll Dhu was present at Evleen Blake's birthday ball. Here he was, under a roof which ought to have been his own, a stranger, known only by a nickname, shunned and solitary. Here he was, who had lived among the eagles and foxes, lying in wait with a fell purpose, to be revenged on the son of his father's foe for poverty and disgrace, for the broken heart of a dead mother, for the loss of a self-slaughtered father, for the dreary scattering of brothers and sisters. Here he stood, a Samson shorn of his strength; and all because a haughty girl had melting eyes, a winning mouth, and looked radiant in satin and roses.

Peerless where many were lovely, she moved among her friends, trying to be unconscious of the gloomy fire of those strange eyes which followed her unweariedly wherever she went. And when her father begged her to be gracious to the unsocial guest whom he would fain conciliate, she courteously conducted him to see the new picture-gallery adjoining the drawing-rooms; explained under what odd circumstances the colonel had picked up this little painting or that; using every delicate art her pride would allow to achieve her father's purpose, whilst maintaining at the same time her own personal reserve; trying to divert the guest's oppressive attention from herself to the objects for which she claimed his notice. Coll Dhu followed his conductress and listened to her voice, but what she said mattered nothing; nor did she wring many words of comment or reply from his lips, until they paused in a retired corner where the light was dim, before a window from which the curtain was withdrawn. The sashes were open, and nothing was visible but water; the night Atlantic, with the full moon riding high above a bank of clouds, making silvery tracks outward towards the distance of infinite mystery dividing two worlds. Here the following little scene is said to have been enacted.

'This window of my father's own planning, is it not creditable to his taste?' said the young hostess, as she stood, herself glittering like a dream of beauty, looking on the moonlight.

Coll Dhu made no answer; but suddenly, it is said, asked her for a rose from a cluster of flowers that nestled in the lace on her bosom.

For the second time that night Evleen Blake's eyes flashed with no gentle light. But this man was the saviour of her father. She broke off a blossom, and with such good grace, and also with such queen-like dignity as she might assume, presented it to him. Whereupon, not only was the rose seized, but also the hand that gave it, which was hastily covered with kisses.

Then her anger burst upon him.

'Sir,' she cried, 'if you are a gentleman you must be mad! If you are not mad, then you are not a gentleman!'

'Be merciful,' said Coll Dhu; 'I love you. My God, I never loved a woman before! Ah!' he cried, as a look of disgust crept over her face, 'you hate me. You shuddered the first time your eyes met mine. I love you, and you hate me!'

'I do,' cried Evleen, vehemently, forgetting everything but her indigna-tion. 'Your presence is like something evil to me. Love me? – your looks poison me. Pray, sir, talk no more to me in this strain.'

'I will trouble you no longer,' said Coll Dhu. And, stalking to the window, he placed one powerful hand upon the sash, and vaulted from it out of her sight.

Bare-headed as he was, Coll Dhu strode off to the mountains, but not towards his own home. All the remaining dark hours of that night he is believed to have walked the labyrinths of the hills, until dawn began to scatter the clouds with a high wind. Fasting, and on foot from sunrise the morning before, he was then glad enough to see a cabin right in his way. Walking in, he asked for water to drink, and a corner where he might throw himself to rest.

There was a wake in the house, and the kitchen was full of people, all wearied out with the night's watch; old men were dozing over their pipes in the chimney-corner, and here and there a woman was fast asleep with her head on a neighbour's knee. All who were awake crossed themselves when Coll Dhu's figure darkened the door, because of his evil name; but an old man of the house invited him in, and offering him milk, and promising him a roasted potato by-and-by, conducted him to a small room off the kitchen, one end of which was strewed with heather, and where there were only two women sitting gossiping over a fire.

'A thraveller,' said the old man, nodding his head at the women, who nodded back, as if to say 'he has the traveller's right.' And Coll Dhu flung himself on the heather, in the furthest corner of the narrow room.

The women suspended their talk for a while; but presently, guessing the intruder to be asleep, resumed it in voices above a whisper. There was but a patch of window with the grey dawn behind it, but Coll could see the figures by the firelight over which they bent: an old woman sitting forward with her withered hands extended to the embers, and a girl reclining against the hearth wall, with her healthy face, bright eyes, and crimson draperies, glowing by turns in the flickering blaze.

'I do' know,' said the girl, 'but it's the quarest marriage iver I h'ard of. Sure, it's not three weeks since he tould right an' left that he hated her like poison!'

'Whist, asthoreen!' said the colliagh, bending forward confidentially; 'throth an' we all know that o' him. But what could he do, the crature! When she put the burragh-bos on him!'

'The *what*?' asked the girl.

'Then the burragh-bos machree-o? That's the spanchel o' death, avourneen; an' well she has him tethered to her now, bad luck to her!'

The old woman rocked herself and stifled the Irish cry breaking from her wrinkled lips by burying her face in her cloak.

'But what is it?' asked the girl, eagerly. 'What's the burragh-bos, anyways, an' where did she get it?'

'Och, och! it's not fit for comin' over to young ears, but cuggir (whisper), acushla! It's a sthrip o' the skin o' a corpse, peeled from the crown o' the head to the heel, without crack or split, or the charm's broke; an' that, rowled up, and put on a sthring roun' the neck o' the wan that's cowld by the wan that wants to be loved. An' sure enough it puts the fire in their hearts, hot an' sthrong, afore twenty-four hours is gone.'

The girl had started from her lazy attitude, and gazed at her companion with eyes dilated by horror.

'Marciful Saviour!' she cried. 'Not a sowl on airth would bring the curse out o' heaven by sich a black doin'!'

'Aisy, Biddeen alanna! an' there's wan that does it, an' isn't the divil. Arrah, asthoreen, did ye niver hear tell o' Pexie na Pishrogie, that lives betune two hills o' Maam Turk?'

'I h'ard o' her,' said the girl, breathlessly.

'Well, sorra bit lie, but it's hersel' that does it. She'll do it for money any day. Sure they hunted her from the graveyard o' Salruck, where she had the dead raised; an' glory be to God! they would ha' murthered her, only they missed her thracks, an' couldn't bring it home to her afther.'

'Whist, a-wauher' (my mother), said the girl; 'here's the thraveller gettin' up to set off on his road again! Och, then, it's the short rest he tuk, the sowl!'

It was enough for Coll, however. He had got up, and now went back to the kitchen, where the old man had caused a dish of potatoes to be roasted, and earnestly pressed his visitor to sit down and eat of them. This Coll did readily; having recruited his strength by a meal, he betook himself to the mountains again, just as the rising sun was flashing among the waterfalls, and sending the night mists drifting down the glens. By sundown the same evening he was striding over the hills of Maam Turk, asking of herds his way to the cabin of one Pexie na Pishrogie.

In a hovel on a brown desolate heath, with scared-looking hills flying off into the distance on every side, he found Pexie: a yellow-faced hag, dressed in a dark-red blanket, with elf-locks of coarse black hair protruding from under an orange kerchief swathed round her wrinkled jaws. She was bending over a pot upon her fire, where herbs were simmering, and she looked up with an evil glance when Coll Dhu darkened her door.

'The burragh-bos is it her honour wants?' she asked, when he had made known his errand. 'Ay, ay; but the arighad, the arighad (money) for Pexie. The burragh-bos is ill to get.'

'I will pay,' said Coll Dhu, laying a sovereign on the bench before her.

The witch sprang upon it, and chuckling, bestowed on her visitor a glance which made even Coll Dhu shudder.

'Her honour is a fine king,' she said, 'an' her is fit to get the burragh-bos. Ha! ha! her sall get the burragh-bos from Pexie. But the arighad is not enough. More, more!'

She stretched out her claw-like hand, and Coll dropped another sovereign into it. Whereupon she fell into more horrible convulsions of delight.

'Hark ye!' cried Coll. 'I have paid you well, but if your infernal charm does not work, I will have you hunted for a witch!'

'Work!' cried Pexie, rolling up her eyes. 'If Pexie's charrm not work, then her honour come back here an' carry these bits o' mountain away on her back. Ay, her will work. If the colleen hate her honour like the old diaoul hersel', still an' withal her love will love her honour like her own white sowl afore the sun sets or rises. That, (with a furtive leer,) or the colleen dhas go wild mad afore wan hour.'

'Hag!' returned Coll Dhu; 'the last part is a hellish invention of your own. I heard nothing of madness. If you want more money, speak out, but play none of your hideous tricks on me.'

The witch fixed her cunning eyes on him, and took her cue at once from his passion.

'Her honour guess thrue,' she simpered; 'it is only the little bit more arighad poor Pexie want.'

Again the skinny hand was extended. Coll Dhu shrank from touching it, and threw his gold coin upon the table.

'King, king!' chuckled Pexie. 'Her honour is a grand king. Her honour is fit to get the burragh-bos. The colleen dhas sall love her like her own white sowl. Ha, ha!'

'When shall I get it?' asked Coll Dhu, impatiently.

'Her honour sall come back to Pexie in so many days, do-deag (twelve), so many days, fur that the burragh-bos is hard to get. The lonely graveyard is far away, an' the dead man is hard to raise—'

'Silence!' cried Coll Dhu; 'not a word more. I will have your hideous charm, but what it is, or where you get it, I will not know.'

Then, promising to come back in twelve days, he took his departure. Turning to look back when a little way across the heath, he saw Pexie gazing after him, standing on her black hill in relief against the lurid flames of the dawn, seeming to his dark imagination like a fury with all hell at her back.

At the appointed time Coll Dhu got the promised charm. He sewed it with perfumes into a cover of cloth of gold, and slung it to a fine-wrought chain. Lying in a casket which had once held the jewels of Coll's broken-hearted mother, it looked a glittering bauble enough. Meantime the people of the mountains were cursing over their cabin fires, because there had been another unholy raid upon their graveyard, and were banding themselves to hunt the criminal down.

A fortnight passed. How or where could Coll Dhu find an opportunity to put the charm round the neck of the colonel's proud daughter? More gold was dropped into Pexie's greedy claw, and then she promised to assist him in his dilemma.

Next morning the witch dressed herself in decent garb, smoothed her elf-locks under a snowy cap, smoothed the wrinkles out of her face, and with a basket on her arm locked the door of the hovel, and took her way to the lowlands. Pexie seemed to have given up her disreputable calling for that of a simple mushroom-gatherer. The housekeeper at the grey house bought poor Muireade's mushrooms of her every morning. Every morning she left unfailingly a nosegay of wild flowers for Miss Evleen Blake, 'God bless her! She had never seen the darling young lady with her own two longing eyes, but sure hadn't she heard tell of her sweet purty face, miles away!' And at last, one morning, whom should she meet but Miss Evleen herself returning alone from a ramble. Whereupon poor Muireade 'made bold' to present her flowers in person.

'Ah,' said Evleen, 'it is you who leave me the flowers every morning? They are very sweet.'

Muireade had sought her only for a look at her beautiful face. And now that she had seen it, as bright as the sun, and as fair as the lily, she would take up her basket and go away contented. Yet she lingered a little longer.

'My lady never walk up big mountain?' said Pexie.

'No,' said Evleen, laughing; she feared she could not walk up a mountain.

'Ah yes; my lady ought to go, with more gran' ladies an' gentlemen, ridin' on purty little donkeys, up the big mountains. Oh, gran' things up big mountains for my lady to see!'

Thus she set to work, and kept her listener enchained for an hour, while she related wonderful stories of those upper regions. And as Evleen looked up to the burly crowns of the hills, perhaps she thought there might be sense in this wild old woman's suggestion. It ought to be a grand world up yonder.

Be that as it may, it was not long after this when Coll Dhu got notice that a party from the grey house would explore the mountains next day; that Evleen Blake would be one of the number; and that he, Coll, must prepare to house and refresh a crowd of weary people, who in the evening should be brought, hungry and faint, to his door. The simple mushroom-gatherer should be discovered laying in her humble stock among the green places between the hills, should volunteer to act as guide to the party, should lead them far out of their way through the mountains and up and down the most toilsome ascents and across dangerous places; to escape safely from which, the servants should be told to throw away the baskets of provisions which they carried.

Coll Dhu was not idle. Such a feast was set forth, as had never been spread so near the clouds before. We are told of wonderful dishes furnished by unwholesome agency, and from a place believed much hotter than is necessary for purposes of cookery. We are told also how Coll Dhu's barren chambers were suddenly hung with curtains of velvet, and with fringes of gold; how the blank white walls glowed with delicate colours and gilding; how gems of pictures sprang into sight between the panels; how the tables blazed with plate and gold, and glittered with the rarest glass; how such wines flowed, as the guests had never tasted; how servants in the richest livery, amongst whom the wizen-faced old man was a mere nonentity, appeared, and stood ready to carry in the wonderful dishes, at whose extraordinary fragrance the eagles came pecking to the windows, and the foxes drew near the walls, snuffing. Sure enough, in all good time, the weary party came within sight of the Devil's Inn, and Coll Dhu sallied forth to invite them across his lonely threshold. Colonel Blake (to whom Evleen, in her delicacy, had said no word of the solitary's strange behaviour to herself) hailed his appearance with delight, and the whole party sat down to Coll's banquet in high good humour. Also, it is said, in much amazement at the magnificence of the mountain rescue.

All went in to Coll's feast, save Evleen Blake, who remained standing on the threshold of the outer door; weary, but unwilling to rest there; hungry, but unwilling to eat there. Her white cambric dress was gathered on her arms, crushed and sullied with the toils of the day; her bright cheek was a little sun-burned; her small dark head with its braids a little tossed, was bared to the mountain air and the glory of the sinking sun; her hands were loosely tangled in the strings of her hat; and her foot sometimes tapped the threshold-stone. So she was seen.

The peasants tell that Coll Dhu and her father came praying her to enter, and that the magnificent servants brought viands to the threshold; but no step would she move inward, no morsel would she taste.

'Poison, poison!' she murmured, and threw the food in handfuls to the foxes, who were snuffing on the heath.

But it was different when Muireade, the kindly old woman, the simple mushroom-gatherer, with all the wicked wrinkles smoothed out of her face, came to the side of the hungry girl, and coaxingly presented a savoury mess of her own sweet mushrooms, served on a common earthen platter.

'An' darlin', my lady, poor Muireade her cook them hersel', an' no thing o' this house touch them or look at poor Muireade's mushrooms.'

Then Evleen took the platter and ate a delicious meal. Scarcely was it finished when a heavy drowsiness fell upon her, and, unable to sustain herself on her feet, she presently sat down upon the door-stone. Leaning her head against the framework of the door, she was soon in a deep sleep, or trance. So she was found.

'Whimsical, obstinate little girl!' said the colonel, putting his hand on the beautiful slumbering head. And taking her in his arms he carried her into a chamber which had been (say the story-tellers) nothing but a bare and sorry closet in the morning but which was now fitted up with Oriental splendour. And here on a luxurious couch she was laid, with a crimson coverlet wrapping her feet. And here in the tempered light coming through jewelled glass, where yesterday had been a coarse rough-hung window, her father looked his last upon her lovely face.

The colonel returned to his host and friends, and by-and-by the whole party sallied forth to see the after-glare of a fierce sunset swathing the hills in flames. It was not until they had gone some distance that Coll Dhu remembered to go back and fetch his telescope. He was not long absent. But he was absent long enough to enter that glowing chamber with a stealthy step, to throw a light chain around the neck of the sleeping girl, and to slip among the folds of her dress the hideous glittering burragh-bos.

After he had gone away again, Pexie came stealing to the door, and, opening it a little, sat down on the mat outside, with her cloak wrapped round her. An hour passed, and Evleen Blake still slept, her breathing scarcely stirring the deadly bauble on her breast. After that, she began to murmur and moan, and Pexie pricked up her ears. Presently a sound in the room told her that the victim was awake and had risen. Then Pexie put her face to the aperture of the door and looked in, gave a howl of dismay, and fled from the house, to be seen in that country no more.

The light was fading among the hills, and the ramblers were returning towards the Devil's Inn, when a group of ladies who were considerably in advance of the rest, met Evleen Blake advancing towards them on the heath, with her hair disordered as by sleep, and no covering on her head. They noticed something bright, like gold, shifting and glancing with the motion of her figure. There had been some jesting among them about Evleen's fancy for falling asleep on the door-step instead of coming in to dinner, and they advanced laughing, to rally her on the subject. But she stared at them in a strange way, as if she did not know them, and passed on. Her friends were rather offended, and commented on her fantastic humour; only one looked after her, and got laughed at by her companions for expressing uneasiness on the wilful young lady's account.

So they kept their way, and the solitary figure went fluttering on, the white robe blushing, and the fatal burragh-bos glittering in the reflection from the sky. A hare crossed her path, and she laughed out loudly, and clapping her hands, sprang after it. Then she stopped and asked questions of the stones, striking them with her open palm because they would not answer. (An amazed little herd sitting behind a rock, witnessed these strange proceedings.) By-and-by she began to call after the birds, in a wild shrill way startling the echoes of the hills as she went along. A party of gentlemen returning by a dangerous path, heard the unusual sound and stopped to listen.

'What is that?' asked one.

'A young eagle,' said Coll Dhu, whose face had become livid; 'they often give such cries.'

'It was uncommonly like a woman's voice!' was the reply; and immediately another wild note rang towards them from the rocks above; a bare saw-like ridge, shelving away to some distance ahead, and projecting one hungry tooth over an abyss. A few more moments and they saw Evleen Blake's light figure fluttering out towards this dizzy point.

'My Evleen!' cried the colonel, recognising his daughter, 'she is mad to venture on such a spot!'

'Mad!' repeated Coll Dhu. And then dashed off to the rescue with all the might and swiftness of his powerful limbs.

When he drew near her, Evleen had almost reached the verge of the terrible rock. Very cautiously he approached her, his object being to seize her in his strong arms before she was aware of his presence, and carry her many yards away from the spot of danger. But in a fatal moment Evleen turned her head and saw him. One wild ringing cry of hate and horror, which startled the very eagles and scattered a flight of curlews above her head, broke from her lips. A step backward brought her within a foot of death.

One desperate though wary stride, and she was struggling in Coll's embrace. One glance in her eyes, and he saw that he was striving with a mad woman. Back, back, she dragged him, and he had nothing to grasp by. The rock was slippery and his shod feet would not cling to it. Back, back! A hoarse panting, a dire swinging to and fro; and then the rock was standing naked against the sky, no one was there, and Coll Dhu and Evleen Blake lay shattered far below.

Amelia B. Edwards

THE STORY OF SALOME

A FEW years ago, no matter how many, I, Harcourt Blunt, was travelling with my friend Coventry Turnour, and it was on the steps of our hotel that I received from him the announcement – he sent one to me – that he was again in love.

'I tell you, Blunt,' said my fellow-traveller, 'she's the loveliest creature I ever beheld in my life.'

I laughed outright.

'My dear fellow,' I replied, 'you've so often seen the loveliest creature you ever beheld in your life.'

'Ay, but I am in earnest now for the first time.'

'And you have so often been in earnest for the first time! Remember the innkeeper's daughter at Cologne.'

'A pretty housemaid, whom no training could have made presentable.'

'Then there was the beautiful American at Interlachen.'

'Yes; but—'

'And the Bella Marchesa at Prince Torlonia's ball.'

'Not one of them worthy to be named in the same breath with my imperial Venetian. Come with me to the Merceria and be convinced. By taking a gondola to St Mark's Place we shall be there in a quarter of an hour.'

I went, and he raved of his new flame all the way. She was a Jewess – he would convert her. Her father kept a shop in the Merceria – what of that? He dealt only in costliest Oriental merchandise, and was as rich as a Rothschild. As for any probable injury to his own prospects, why need he hesitate on that account? What were 'prospects' when weighed against the happiness of one's whole life? Besides, he was not ambitious. He didn't care to go into Parliament. If his uncle Sir Geoffrey cut him off with a shilling, what then? He had a moderate independence of which no one living could deprive him, and what more could any reasonable man desire?

I listened, smiled, and was silent. I knew Coventry Turnour too well to attach the smallest degree of importance to anything that he might say or do in a matter of this kind. To be distractedly in love was his normal condition. We had been friends from boyhood; and since the time when he used to cherish a hopeless attachment to the young lady behind the counter of the tart-shop at Harrow, I had never known him 'fancy-free' for more than a few weeks at a time. He had gone through every phase of no less than three *grandes passions* during the five months that we had now been travelling together; and having left Rome about eleven weeks before with every hope laid waste, and a heart so broken that it could never by any possibility be put together again, he was now, according to the natural course of events, just ready to fall in love again.

We landed at the traghetto San Marco. It was a cloudless morning towards the middle of April, just ten years ago. The ducal palace glowed in the hot sunshine; the boatmen were clustered, gossiping, about the Molo; the orange-vendors were busy under the arches of the piazzetta; the flâneurs were already eating ices and smoking cigarettes outside the cafés. There was an Austrian military band, strapped, buckled, moustachioed, and white-coated, playing just in front of St Mark's; and the shadow of the great bell-tower slept all across the square.

Passing under the low round archway leading to the Merceria, we plunged at once into that cool labyrinth of narrow, intricate, and picturesque streets, where the sun never penetrates – where no wheels are heard, and no beast of burden is seen – where every house is a shop, and every shop-front is open to the ground, as in an Oriental bazaar – where the upper balconies seem almost to meet overhead, and are separated by only a strip of burning sky – and where more than three people cannot march abreast in any part. Pushing our way as best we might through the motley crowd that here chatters, cheapens, buys, sells, and perpetually bustles to and fro, we came presently to a shop for the sale of Eastern goods. A few glass jars filled with spices, and some pieces of stuff, untidily strewed the counter next the street; but within, dark and narrow though it seemed, the place was crammed with costliest merchandise. Cases of gorgeous Oriental jewellery, embroideries and fringes of massive gold and silver bullion, precious drugs and spices, exquisite toys in filigree, miracles of carving in ivory, sandal-wood, and amber, jewelled yataghans, scimitars of state rich with 'barbaric pearl and gold', bales of Cashmere shawls, China silks, India muslins, gauzes, and the like, filled every inch of available space from floor to ceiling, leaving only a narrow lane from the door to the counter, and a still narrower passage to the rooms beyond the shop.

We went in. A young woman, who was sitting reading on a low seat behind the counter, laid aside her book, and rose slowly. She was dressed wholly in black. I cannot describe the fashion of her garments. I only know that they fell about her in long, soft, trailing folds, leaving a narrow band of fine cambric visible at the throat and wrists; and that, however graceful and unusual this dress may have been, I scarcely observed it, so entirely was I taken up with admiration of her beauty.

For she was indeed very beautiful – beautiful in a way that I had not anticipated. Coventry Turnour, with all his enthusiasm, had failed to do her justice. He had raved of her eyes – her large, lustrous, melancholy eyes – of the transparent paleness of her complexion, of the faultless delicacy of her features; but he had not prepared me for the unconscious dignity, the perfect nobleness and refinement, that informed her every look and gesture. My friend requested to see a bracelet at which he had been looking the day before. Proud, stately, silent, she unlocked the case in which it was kept, and laid it before him on the counter. He asked permission to take it over to the light. She bent her head, but answered not a word. It was like being waited upon by a young empress.

Turnour took the bracelet to the door and affected to examine it. It consisted of a double row of gold coins linked together at intervals by a bean-shaped ornament, studded with pink coral and diamonds. Coming back into the shop he asked me if I thought it would please his sister, to whom he had promised a remembrance of Venice.

'It is a pretty trifle,' I replied; 'but surely a remembrance of Venice should be of Venetian manufacture. This, I suppose, is Turkish.'

The beautiful Jewess looked up. We spoke in English; but she understood and replied:

'E Greco, signore,' she said coldly.

At this moment an old man came suddenly forward from some dark counting-house at the back – a grizzled, bearded, eager-eyed Shylock, with a pen behind his ear.

'Go in, Salome – go in, my daughter,' he said hurriedly. 'I will serve these gentlemen.'

She lifted her eyes to his for one moment – then moved silently away, and vanished in the gloom of the room beyond.

We saw her no more. We lingered awhile, looking over the contents of the jewel-cases; but in vain. Then Turnour bought his bracelet, and we went out again into the narrow streets, and back to the open daylight of the Gran' Piazza.

'Well,' he said breathlessly, 'what do you think of her?'

'She is very lovely.'

'Lovelier than you expected?'

'Much lovelier. But—'

'But what?'

'The sooner you succeed in forgetting her, the better.'

He vowed, of course, that he never would and never could forget her. He would hear of no incompatibilities, listen to no objections, believe in no obstacles. That the beautiful Salome was herself not only unconscious of his passion and indifferent to his person, but ignorant of his very name and station, were facts not even to be admitted on the list of difficulties. Finding him thus deaf to reason, I said no more.

It was all over, however, before the week was out.

'Look here, Blunt,' he said, coming up to me one morning in the coffee-room of our hotel just as I was sitting down to answer a pile of home-letters; 'would you like to go on to Trieste tomorrow? There, don't look at me like that – you can guess how it is with me. I was a fool ever to suppose she would care for me – a stranger, a foreigner, a Christian. Well, I'm horribly out of sorts anyhow – and – and I wish I was a thousand miles off at this moment!'

We travelled on together to Athens, and there parted, Turnour being bound for England, and I for the EaSt My own tour lasted many months longer. I went first to Egypt and the Holy Land; then joined an exploring party on the Euphrates; and at length, after just twelve months of Oriental life, found myself back again at Trieste about the middle of April in the year following that during which occurred the events I have just narrated. There I found that batch of letters and papers to which I had been looking forward for many weeks past; and amongst the former, one from Coventry Turnour. This time he was not only irrecoverably in love, but on the eve of matrimony. The letter was rapturous and extravagant enough. The writer was the happiest of men; his destined bride the loveliest and most amiable of her sex; the future a paradise; the past a melancholy series of mistakes. As for love, he had never, of course, known what it was till now.

And what of the beautiful Salome?

Not one word of her from beginning to end. He had forgotten her as utterly as if she had never existed. And yet how desperately in love and how desperately in despair he was 'one little year ago'! Ah, yes; but then it *was* 'one little year ago'; and who that had ever known Coventry Turnour would expect him to remember *la plus grande des grandes passions* for even half that time?

I slept that night at Trieste, and went on next day to Venice. Somehow, I could not get Turnour and his love affairs out of my head. I remembered our visit to the Merceria. I was haunted by the image of the beautiful Jewess. Was she still so lovely? Did she still sit reading in her wonted seat by the open counter, with the gloomy shop reaching away behind, and the cases of rich robes and jewels all around?

An irresistible impulse prompted me to go to the Merceria and see her once again. I went. It had been a busy morning with me, and I did not get there till between three and four o'clock in the afternoon. The place was crowded. I passed up the well-remembered street, looking out on both sides for the gloomy little shop with its unattractive counter; but in vain. When I had gone so far that I thought I must have passed it, I turned back. House by house I retraced my steps to the very entrance, and still could not find it. Then, concluding that I had not gone far enough at first, I turned back again till I reached a spot where several streets diverged. Here I came to a standstill, for beyond this point I knew I had not passed before.

It was now only too evident that the Jew no longer occupied his former shop in the Merceria, and that my chance of discovering his whereabouts was exceedingly slender. I could not inquire of his successor, because I could not identify the house. I found it impossible even to remember what trades were carried on by his neighbours on either side. I was ignorant of his very name. Convinced, therefore, of the inutility of making any further effort, I gave up the search, and comforted myself by reflecting that my own heart was not made of adamant, and that it was, perhaps, better for my peace not to see the beautiful Salome again. I was destined to see her again, however, and that ere many days had passed over my head.

A year of more than ordinarily fatiguing Eastern travel had left me in need of rest, and I had resolved to allow myself a month's sketching in Venice and its neighbourhood before turning my face homewards. As, therefore, it is manifestly the first object of a sketcher to select his points of view, and as no more luxurious machine than a Venetian gondola was ever invented for the use of man, I proceeded to employ the first days of my stay in endless boatings to and fro: now exploring all manner of canals and canaletti; rowing out in the direction of Murano; now making for the islands beyond San Pietro Castello, and in the course of these pilgrimages noting down an infinite number of picturesque sites, and smoking an infinite number of cigarettes. It was, I think, about the fourth or fifth day of this pleasant work, when my gondolier proposed to take me as far as the Lido. It wanted about two hours to sunset, and the great sandbank lay not more than three or four miles away; so I gave the word, and in another moment we had changed our route and were gliding farther and farther from Venice at each dip of the oar. Then the long dull distant ridge that had all day bounded the shallow horizon rose gradually above the placid level of the Lagune, assumed a more broken outline, resolved itself into hillocks and hollows of tawny sand, showed here and there a patch of parched grass and tangled brake, and looked like the coasts of some inhospitable desert beyond which no traveller might penetrate. My boatman made straight for a spot where some stakes at the water's edge gave token of a landing-place; and here, though with some difficulty, for the tide was low, ran the gondola aground. I landed. My first step was among graves.

'E'l cimeterio giudaico, signore,' said my gondolier, with a touch of his cap.

The Jewish cemetery! The *ghetto* of the dead! I remembered now to have read or heard long since how the Venetian Jews, cut off in death as in life from the neighbourhood of their Christian rulers, had been buried from immemorial time upon this desolate waste. I stooped to examine the headstone at my feet. It was but a shattered fragment, crusted over with yellow lichens, and eaten away by the salt sea air. I passed on to the next, and the next. Some were completely matted over with weeds and brambles; some were half-buried in the drifting sand; of some, only a corner remained above the surface. Here and there a name, a date, a fragment of heraldic carving, or part of a Hebrew inscription, was yet legible; but all were more or less broken and effaced.

Wandering on thus among graves and hillocks, ascending at every step, and passing some three or four glassy pools overgrown with gaunt-looking reeds, I presently found that I had reached the central and most elevated part of the Lido, and that I commanded an uninterrupted view on every side. On the one hand lay the broad, silent Lagune bounded by Venice and the Euganean hills – on the other, stealing up in long, lazy folds, and breaking noiselessly against the endless shore, the blue Adriatic. An old man gathering shells on the seaward side, a distant gondola on the Lagune, were the only signs of life for miles around.

Standing on the upper ridge of this narrow barrier, looking upon both waters, and watching the gradual approach of what promised to be a gorgeous sunset, I fell into one of those wandering trains of thought in which the real and unreal succeed each other as capriciously as in a dream. I remembered how Goethe here conceived his vertebral theory of the skull – how Byron, too lame to walk, kept his horse on the Lido, and here rode daily to and fro – how Shelley loved the wild solitude of the place, wrote of it in *Julian and Maddalo*, listened, perhaps from this very spot, to the mad-house bell on the island of San Giorgio. Then I wondered if Titian had ever come hither from his gloomy house on the other side of Venice, to study the gold and purple of these western skies

– if Othello had walked here with Desdemona – if Shylock was buried yonder, and Leah whom he loved 'when he was a bachelor'.

And then in the midst of my reverie, I came suddenly upon another Jewish cemetery.

Was it indeed another, or but an outlying portion of the first? It was evidently another, and a more modern one. The ground was better kept. The monuments were newer. Such dates as I had succeeded in deciphering on the broken sepulchres lower down were all of the fourteenth and fifteenth centuries; but the inscriptions upon these bore reference to quite recent interments.

I went on a few steps farther. I stopped to copy a quaint Italian couplet on one tomb – to gather a wild forget-me-not from the foot of another – to put aside a bramble that trailed across a third – and then I became aware for the first time of a lady sitting beside a grave not a dozen yards from the spot on which I stood.

I had believed myself so utterly alone, and was so taken by surprise, that for the first moment I could almost have persuaded myself that she also was 'of the stuff that dreams are made of'. She was dressed from head to foot in the deepest mourning; her face turned from me, looking towards the sunset; her cheek resting in the palm of her hand. The grave by which she sat was obviously recent. The scant herbage round about had been lately disturbed, and the marble headstone looked as if it had not yet undergone a week's exposure to wind and weather.

Persuaded that she had not observed me, I lingered for an instant looking at her. Something in the grace and sorrow of her attitude, something in the turn of her head and the flow of her sable draperies, arrested my attention. Was she young? I fancied so. Did she mourn a husband? – a lover? – a parent? I glanced towards the headstone. It was covered with Hebrew characters; so that, had I even been nearer, it could have told me nothing.

But I felt that I had no right to stand there, a spectator of her sorrow, an intruder on his privacy. I proceeded to move noiselessly away. At that moment she turned and looked at me.

It was Salome.

Salome, pale and worn as from some deep and wasting grief, but more beautiful, if that could be, than ever. Beautiful, with a still more spiritual beauty than of old; with cheeks so wan and eyes so unutterably bright and solemn, that my very heart seemed to stand still as I looked upon them. For one second I paused, half fancying, half hoping that there was recognition in her glance; then, not daring to look or linger longer, turned away. When I had gone far enough to do so without discourtesy, I stopped and gazed back. She had resumed her former attitude, and was looking over towards Venice and the setting sun. The stone by which she watched was not more motionless.

The sun went down in glory. The last flush faded from the domes and bell-towers of Venice; the western peaks changed from rose to purple, from gold to grey; a scarcely perceptible film of mist became all at once visible upon the surface of the Lagune; and overhead, the first star trembled into light. I waited and watched till the shadows had so deepened that I could no longer distinguish one distant object from another. Was that the spot? Was she still there? Was she moving? Was she gone? I could not tell. The more I looked, the more uncertain I became. Then, fearing to miss my way in the fast-gathering twilight, I struck down towards the water's edge, and made for the point at which I had landed.

I found my gondolier fast asleep, with his head on a cushion, and his bit of gondola-carpet thrown over him for a counterpane. I asked if he had seen any other boat put off from the Lido since I left? He rubbed his eyes, started up, and was awake in a moment.

'Per Bacco, signore, I have been asleep,' he said apologetically: 'I have seen nothing.'

'Did you observe any other boat moored hereabouts when we landed?'

'None, signore.'

'And you have seen nothing of a lady in black?'

He laughed and shook his head.

'Consolatevi, signore,' he said archly. 'She will come tomorrow.'

Then, finding that I looked grave, he touched his cap, and with a gentle, 'Scusate, signore,' took his place at the stern, and there waited. I bade him row to my hotel; and then, leaning dreamily back in my little dark cabin, I folded my arms, closed my eyes, and thought of Salome.

How lovely she was! How infinitely more lovely than even my first remembrance of her! How was it that I had not admired her more that day in the Merceria? Was I blind, or had she become indeed more beautiful? It was a sad and strange place in which to meet her again. By whose grave was she watching? By her father's? Yes, surely by her father's. He was an old man when I saw him, and in the course of nature had not long to live. He was dead: hence my unavailing search in the Merceria. He was dead. His shop was let to another occupant. His stock-in-trade was sold and dispersed. And Salome – was she left alone? Had she no mother? no brother? – no lover? Would her eyes have had that look of speechless woe in them if she had any very near or dear tie left on earth? Then I thought of Coventry Turnour, and his approaching marriage. Did he ever really love her? I doubted it. 'True love,' saith an old song, 'can ne'er forget'; but he had forgotten, as though the past had been a dream. And yet he was in earnest while it lasted – would have risked all for her sake, if she would have listened to him. Ah, if she *had* listened to him! And then I remembered that he had never told me the particulars of that affair. Did she herself reject him, or did he lay his suit before her father? And was he rejected only because he was a Christian? I had never cared to ask these things while we were together; but now I would have given the best hunter in my stables to know every minute detail connected with the matter.

Pondering thus, travelling over the same ground again and again, wondering whether she remembered me, whether she was poor, whether she was indeed alone in the world, how long the old man had been dead, and a hundred other things of the same kind – I scarcely noticed how the watery miles glided past, or how the night closed in. One question, however, recurred oftener than any other: How was I to see her again?

I arrived at my hotel; I dined at the *table d'hôte*; I strolled out, after dinner, to my favourite café in the piazza; I dropped in for half an hour at the Fenice, and heard one act of an extremely poor opera; I came home restless, uneasy, wakeful; and sitting for hours before my bedroom fire, asked myself the same perpetual question, How was I to see her again?

Fairly tired out at last, I fell asleep in my chair, and when I awoke the sun was shining upon my window.

I started to my feet. I had it now. It flashed upon me, as if it came with the sunlight. I had but to go again to the cemetery, copy the inscription upon the old man's tomb, ask my learned friend Professor Nicolai, of Padua, to translate it for me, and then, once in possession of names and dates, the rest would be easy.

In less than an hour, I was once more on my way to the Lido.

I took a rubbing of the stone. It was the quickest way, and the surest; for I knew that in Hebrew everything depended on the pointing of the characters, and I feared to trust my own untutored skill. This done, I hastened back, wrote my letter to the professor, and dispatched both letter and rubbing by the midday train.

The professor was not a prompt man. On the contrary he was a pre-eminently slow man; dreamy, indolent, buried in Oriental lore. From any other correspondent one might have looked for a reply in the course of the morrow; but from Nicolai of Padua it would have been folly to expect one under two or three days. And in the meanwhile? Well, in the meanwhile there were churches and palaces to be seen, sketches to be made, letters of introduction to be delivered. It was, at all events, of no use to be impatient.

And yet I was impatient – so impatient that I could neither sketch, nor read, nor sit still for ten minutes together. Possessed by an uncontrollable restlessness, I wandered from gallery to gallery, from palace to palace, from church to church. The imprisonment of even a gondola was irksome to me. I was, as it were, impelled to be moving and doing; and even so, the day seemed endless.

The next was even worse. There was just the possibility of a reply from Padua, and the knowledge of that possibility unsettled me for the day. Having watched and waited for every post from eight to four, I went down to the traghetto of St Mark's, and was there hailed by my accustomed gondolier.

He touched his cap and waited for orders.

'Where to, *signore*?' he asked, finding that I remained silent.

'To the Lido.'

It was an irresistible temptation, and I yielded to it; but I yielded in opposition to my judgment. I knew that I ought not to haunt the place. I had resolved that I would not. And yet I went.

Going along, I told myself that I had only come to reconnoitre. It was not unlikely that she might be going to the same spot about the same hour as before; and in that case I might overtake her gondola by the way, or find it moored somewhere along the shore. At all events, I was determined not to land. But we met no gondola beyond San Pietro Castello; saw no sign of one along the shore. The afternoon was far advanced; the sun was near going down; we had the Lagune and the Lido to ourselves.

My boatman made for the same landing-place, and moored his gondola to the same stake as before. He took it for granted that I meant to land; and I landed. After all, however, it was evident that Salome could not be there, in which case I was guilty of no intrusion. I might stroll in the direction of the cemetery, taking care to avoid her, if she were anywhere about, and keeping well away from that part where I had last seen her. So I broke another resolve, and went up towards the top of the Lido. Again I came to the salt pools and the reeds; again stood with the sea upon my left hand and the Lagune upon my right, and the endless sandbank reaching on for miles between the two. Yonder lay the new cemetery. Standing thus I overlooked every foot of the ground. I could even distinguish the headstone of which I had taken the rubbing the morning before. There was no living thing in sight. I was, to all appearance, as utterly alone as Enoch Arden on his desert island.

Then I strolled on, a little nearer, and a little nearer still; and then, contrary to all my determinations, I found myself standing upon the very spot, beside the very grave, which I had made my mind on no account to approach.

The sun was now just going down – had gone down, indeed, behind a bank of golden-edged cumuli – and was flooding earth, sea, and sky with crimson. It was at this hour that I saw her. It was upon this spot that she was sitting. A few scant blades of grass had sprung up here and there upon the grave. Her dress must have touched them as she sat there – her dress; perhaps her hand. I gathered one, and laid it carefully between the leaves of my note-book.

At last I turned to go, and, turning, met her face to face!

She was distant about six yards, and advancing slowly towards the spot on which I was standing. Her head drooped slightly forward; her hands were clasped together; her eyes were fixed upon the ground. It was the attitude of a nun. Startled, confused, scarcely knowing what I did, I took off my hat, and drew aside to let her pass.

She looked up – hesitated – stood still – gazed at me with a strange, steadfast, mournful expression – then dropped her eyes again, passed me without another glance, and resumed her former place and attitude beside her father's grave.

I turned away. I would have given worlds to speak to her; but I had not dared, and the opportunity was gone. Yet I might have spoken! She looked at me – looked at me with so strange and piteous an expression in her eyes – continued looking at me as long as one might have counted five . . . I might have spoken. I surely might have spoken! And now – ah! now it was impossible. She had fallen into the old thoughtful attitude with her cheek resting on her hand. Her thoughts were far away. She had forgotten my very presence.

I went back to the shore, more disturbed and uneasy than ever. I spent all the remaining daylight in rowing up and down the margin of the Lido, looking for her gondola – hoping, at all events, to see her put off – to follow her, perhaps, across the waste of waters. But the dusk came quickly on, and then darkness, and I left at last without having seen any further sign or token of her presence.

Lying awake that night, tossing uneasily upon my bed, and thinking over the incidents of the last few days, I found myself perpetually recurring to that long, steady, sorrowful gaze which she fixed upon me in the cemetery. The more I thought of it, the more I seemed to feel that there was in it some deeper meaning than I, in my confusion, had observed at the time. It was such a strange look – a look almost of entreaty, of asking for help or sympathy; like the dumb appeal in the eyes of a sick animal. Could this really be? What, after all, more possible than that, left alone in the world – with, perhaps, not a single male relation to advise her – she found herself in some position of present difficulty, and knew not where to turn for help? All this might well be. She had even, perhaps, some instinctive feeling that she might trust me. Ah! if she would indeed trust me . . .

I had hoped to receive my Paduan letter by the morning delivery; but morning and afternoon went by as before, and still no letter came. As the day began to decline, I was again on my way to the Lido; this time for the purpose, and with the intention, of speaking to her. I landed, and went direct to the cemetery. It had been a dull day. Lagune and sky were both one leaden uniform grey, and a mist hung over Venice.

I saw her from the moment I reached the upper ridge. She was walking slowly to and fro among the graves, like a stately shadow. I had felt confident, somehow, that she would be there; and now, for some reason that I could not have defined for my life, I felt equally confident that she expected me.

Trembling and eager, yet half dreading the moment when she should discover my presence, I hastened on, printing the loose sand at every noiseless step. A few moments more, and I should overtake her, speak to her, hear the music of her voice – that music which I remembered so well, though a year had gone by since I last heard it. But how should I address her? What had I to say? I knew not. I had no time to think. I could only hurry on till within some ten feet of her trailing garments; stand still when she turned, and uncover before her as if she were a queen.

She paused and looked at me, just as she had paused and looked at me the evening before. With the same sorrowful meaning in her eyes; with even more than the same entreating expression. But she waited for me to speak.

I did speak. I cannot recall what I said; I only know that I faltered something of an apology – mentioned that I had had the honour of meeting her before, many months ago; and, trying to say more – trying to express how thankfully and proudly I would devote myself to any service, however humble, however laborious, I failed both in voice and words, and broke down utterly.

Having come to a stop, I looked up, and found her eyes still fixed upon me.

'You are a Christian,' she said.

A trembling came upon me at the first sound of her voice. It was the same voice; distinct, melodious, scarce louder than a whisper – and yet it was not quite the same. There was a melancholy in the music, and, if I may use a word which, after all, fails to express my meaning, a *remoteness*, that fell upon my ear like the plaintive cadence in an autumnal wind.

I bent my head, and answered that I was.

She pointed to the headstone of which I had taken a rubbing a day or two before.

'A Christian soul lies there,' she said, 'laid in earth without one Christian prayer – with Hebrew rites – in a Hebrew sanctuary. Will you, stranger, perform an act of piety towards the dead?'

'The Signora has but to speak,' I said. 'All that she wishes shall be done.'

'Read one prayer over this grave; trace a cross upon this stone.'

'I will.'

She thanked me with a gesture, slightly bowed her head, drew her outer garment more closely round her, and moved away to a rising ground at some little distance. I was dismissed. I had no excuse for lingering – no right to prolong the interview – no business to remain there one moment longer. So I left her there, nor once looked back till I reached the last point from which I knew I should be able to see her. But when I turned for that last look she was no longer in sight.

I had resolved to speak to her, and this was the result. A stranger interview never, surely, fell to the lot of man! I had said nothing that I meant to say – had learnt nothing that I sought to know. With regard to her circumstances, her place of residence, her very name, I was no wiser than before. And yet I had, perhaps, no reason to be dissatisfied. She had honoured me with her confidence, and entrusted to me a task of some difficulty and importance. It now only remained for me to execute that task as thoroughly and as quickly as possible. That done, I might fairly hope to win some place in her remembrance – by and by, perhaps, in her esteem.

Meanwhile, the old question rose again – whose grave could it be? I had settled this matter so conclusively in my own mind from the first, that I could scarcely believe even now that it was not her father's. Yet that he should have died a secret convert to Christianity was incredible. Whose grave could it be? A lover's? a Christian lover's? Alas! it might be. Or a sister's? In either of these cases it was more than probable that Salome was herself a convert. But I had no time to waste in conjecture. I must act, and act promptly.

I hastened back to Venice as fast as my gondolier could row me; and as we went along I promised myself that all her wishes should be carried out before she visited the spot again. To at once secure the services of a clergyman who would go with me to the Lido at early dawn, and there read some portion, at least, of the burial-service! and at the same time to engage a stonemason to cut the cross – to have all done before she, or anyone, should have approached the place next day, was my especial object. And that object I was resolved to carry out, though I had to search Venice through before I laid my head upon the pillow.

I found my clergyman without difficulty. He was a young man occupying rooms in the same hotel, and on the same floor as myself. I had met him each day at the *table d'hôte*, and conversed with him once or twice in the reading-room. He was a North countryman, had not long since taken orders, and was both gentlemanly and obliging. He promised in the readiest manner to do all that I required, and to breakfast with me at six the next morning, in order that we might reach the cemetery by eight.

To find my stonemason, however, was not so easy; and yet I went to work methodically enough. I began with the Venetian Directory; then copied a list of stonemasons' names and addresses; then took a gondola *a due rame*, and started upon my voyage of discovery.

But a night's voyage of discovery among the intricate back canaletti of Venice is no very easy and no very safe enterprise. Narrow, tortuous, densely populated, often blocked by huge hay, wood, and provision barges, almost wholly unlighted, and so perplexingly alike that no mere novice in Venetian topography need ever hope to distinguish one from another, they baffle the very gondoliers, and are a terra incognita to all but the dwellers therein.

I succeeded, however, in finding three of the places entered on my list. At the first I was told that the workman of whom I was in quest was working by the week somewhere over by Murano, and would not be back again till Saturday night. At the second and third, I found the men at home, supping with their wives and children at the end of the day's work; but neither would consent to undertake my commission. One, after a whispered consultation with his son, declined reluctantly. The other told me plainly that he dared not do it, and that he did not believe I should find a stonemason in Venice who would be bolder than himself.

The Jews, he said, were rich and powerful; no longer an oppressed people; no longer to be insulted even in Venice with impunity. To cut a Christian cross upon a Jewish headstone in the Jewish cemetery, would be 'a sort of sacrilege', and punishable, no doubt, by the law. This sounded like truth; so finding that my rowers were by no means confident of their way, and that the canaletti were dark as the catacombs, I prevailed upon the stonemason to sell me a small mallet and a couple of chisels, and made up my mind to commit the sacrilege myself.

With this single exception, all was done next morning as I had planned to do. My new acquaintance breakfasted with me, accompanied me to the Lido, read such portions of the burial-service as seemed proper to him, and then, having business in Venice, left me to my task. It was by no means an easy one. To a skilled hand it would have been, perhaps, the work of half an hour; but it was my first effort, and rude as the thing was – a mere grooved attempt at a Latin cross, about two inches and a half in length, cut close at the bottom of the stone, where it could be easily concealed by a little piling of the sand – it took me nearly four hours to complete. While I was at work, the dull grey morning grew duller and greyer; a thick sea fog drove up from the Adriatic, and a low moaning wind came and went like the echo of a distant requiem. More than once I started, believing that she had surprised me there – fancying I saw the passing of a shadow – heard the rustling of a garment – the breathing of a sigh. But no. The mists and the moaning wind deceived me. I was alone.

When at length I got back to my hotel, it was just two o'clock. The hall-porter put a letter into my hand as I passed through. One glance at that crabbed superscription was enough. It was from Padua. I hastened to my room, tore open the envelope, and read these words:

'CARO SIGNORE, – The rubbing you send is neither ancient nor curious, as I fear you suppose it to be. *Altro*; it is of yesterday. It merely records that one Salome, the only and beloved child of a certain Isaac da Costa, died last autumn on the eighteenth of October, aged twenty-one years, and that by the said Isaac da Costa this monument is erected to the memory of her virtues and his grief.

'I pray you *caro signore*, to receive the assurance of my sincere esteem.

NICOLO NICOLAI.

'Padua, April 27th, 1857.'

The letter dropped from my hand. I seemed to have read without understanding it. I picked it up; went through it again, word by word; sat down; rose up; took a turn across the room; felt confused, bewildered, incredulous.

Could there, then, be two Salomes? or was there some radical and extraordinary mistake?

I hesitated; I knew not what to do. Should I go down to the Merceria, and see whether the name of da Costa was known in the *quartier*? Or find out the registrar of births and deaths for the Jewish district? Or call upon the principal rabbi, and learn from him who this second Salome had been, and in what degree of relationship she stood towards the Salome whom I knew? I decided upon the last course. The chief rabbi's address was easily obtained. He lived in an ancient house on the Giudecca, and there I found him – a grave, stately old man, with a grizzled beard reaching nearly to his waist.

I introduced myself, and stated my business. I came to ask if he could give me any information respecting the late Salome da Costa, who died on the 18th of October last, and was buried on the Lido.

The rabbi replied that he had no doubt he could give me any information I desired, as he had known the lady personally, and was the intimate friend of her father.

'Can you tell me,' I asked, 'whether she had any dear friend or female relative of the same name – Salome?' The rabbi shook his head. 'I think not,' he said. 'I remember no other maiden of that name.'

'Pardon me, but I know there was another,' I replied. 'There was a very beautiful Salome living in the Merceria when I was last in Venice, just this time last year.'

'Salome da Costa was very fair,' said the rabbi; 'and she dwelt with her father in the Merceria. Since her death, he hath removed to the neighbourhood of the Rialto.'

'This Salome's father was a dealer in Oriental goods,' I said, hastily.

'Isaac da Costa is a dealer in Oriental goods,' replied the old man very gently. 'We are speaking, my son, of the same persons.'

'Impossible!'

He shook his head again.

'But she lives!' I exclaimed, becoming greatly agitated. 'She lives. I have seen her. I have spoken to her. I saw her only last evening.'

'Nay,' he said compassionately, 'this is some dream. She of whom you speak is indeed no more.'

'I saw her only last evening,' I repeated.

'Where did you suppose you beheld her?'

'On the Lido.'

'On the Lido?'

'And she spoke to me. I heard her voice – heard it as distinctly as I hear my own at this moment.'

The rabbi stroked his beard thoughtfully, and looked at me. 'You think you heard her voice!' he ejaculated. 'That is strange. What said she?'

I was about to answer. I checked myself – a sudden thought flashed upon me – I trembled from head to foot. 'Have you – have you any reason for supposing that she died a Christian?' I faltered.

The old man started, and changed colour.

'I – I – that is a strange question,' he stammered. 'Why do you ask it?'

'Yes or no?' I cried wildly. 'Yes or no?'

He frowned, looked down, hesitated. 'I admit,' he said, after a moment or two – 'I admit that I may have heard something tending that way. It may be that the maiden cherished some secret doubt. Yet she was no professed Christian.'

'*Laid in earth without one Christian prayer; with Hebrew rites; in a Hebrew sanctuary!*' I repeated to myself.

'But I marvel how you come to have heard of this,' continued the rabbi. 'It was known only to her father and myself.'

'Sir,' I said solemnly, 'I know now that Salome da Costa is dead; I have seen her spirit thrice, haunting the spot where—'

My voice broke. I could not utter the words.

'Last evening, at sunset,' I resumed, 'was the third time. Never doubting that – that I indeed beheld her in the flesh, I spoke to her. She answered me. She – she told me this.'

The rabbi covered his face with his hands, and so remained for some time, lost in meditation. 'Young man,' he said at length, 'your story is strange, and you bring strange evidence to bear upon it. It may be as you say; it may be that you are the dupe of some waking dream – I know not.'

He knew not; but I – ah! I knew, only too well. I knew now why she had appeared to me clothed with such unearthly beauty. I understood now that look of dumb entreaty in her eyes – that tone of strange remoteness in her voice. The sweet soul could not rest amid the dust of its kinsfolk, 'unhousel'd, unanointed, unaneal'd', lacking even 'one Christian prayer' above its grave. And now – was it all over? Should I never see her more?

Never – ah! never. How I haunted the Lido at sunset for many a month, till spring had blossomed into autumn, and autumn had ripened into summer; how I wandered back to Venice year after year, at the same season, while yet any vestige of that wild hope remained alive; how my heart has never throbbed, my pulse never leaped, for love of mortal woman since that time – are details into which I need not enter here. Enough that I watched and waited but that her gracious spirit appeared to me no more. I wait still, but I watch no longer. I know now that our place of meeting will not be here.

Rhoda Broughton

THE TRUTH, THE WHOLE TRUTH, AND NOTHING BUT THE TRUTH

MRS DE WYNT TO MRS MONTRESOR.

18, Eccleston Square,
May 5th.

My dearest Cecilia,

Talk of the friendships of Orestes and Pylades, of Julie and Claire, what are they to ours? Did Pylades ever go *ventre à terre*, half over London on a day more broiling than any but an *âme damnée* could even imagine, in order that Orestes might be comfortably housed for the season? Did Claire ever hold sweet converse with from fifty to one hundred house agents, in order that Julie might have three windows to her drawing-room and a pretty *portière*? You see I am determined not to be done out of my full meed of gratitude.

Well, my friend, I had no idea till yesterday how closely we were packed in this great smoky beehive, as tightly as herrings in a barrel. Don't be frightened, however. By dint of squeezing and crowding, we have managed to make room for two more herrings in our barrel, and those two are yourself and your other self, *i.e.* your husband. Let me begin at the beginning. After having looked over, I verily believe, every undesirable residence in West London; after having seen nothing intermediate between what was suited to the means of a duke, and what was suited to the needs of a chimney-sweep; after having felt bed-ticking, and explored kitchen-ranges till my brain reeled under my accumulated experience, I arrived at about half-past five yesterday afternoon at 32, — Street, May Fair.

'Failure No. 253, I don't doubt,' I said to myself, as I toiled up the steps with my soul athirst for afternoon tea, and feeling as ill-tempered as you please. So much for my spirit of prophecy. Fate, I have noticed, is often fond of contradicting us flat, and giving the lie to our little predictions. Once inside, I thought I had got into a small compartment of Heaven by mistake. Fresh as a daisy, clean as a cherry, bright as a seraph's face, it is all these, and a hundred more, only that my limited stock of similes is exhausted. Two drawing-rooms as pretty as ever woman crammed with people she did not care two straws about; white curtains with rose-coloured ones underneath, festooned in the sweetest way; marvellously, *immorally* becoming, my dear, as I ascertained entirely for your benefit, in the mirrors, of which there are about a dozen and a half; Persian mats, easy chairs, and lounges suited to every possible physical conformation, from the Apollo Belvedere to Miss Biffin; and a thousand of the important little trivialities that make up the sum of a woman's life: peacock fans, Japanese screens, naked boys and *décolletée* shepherdesses; not to speak of a family of china pugs, with blue ribbons round their necks, which ought of themselves to have added fifty pounds a year to the rent. Apropos, I asked, in fear and trembling, what the rent might be – 'Three hundred pounds a year.' A feather would have knocked me down. I could hardly believe my ears, and made the woman repeat it several times, that there might be no mistake. To this hour it is a mystery to me.

With that suspiciousness which is so characteristic of you, you will immediately begin to hint that there must be some terrible unaccountable smell, or some odious inexplicable noise haunting the reception-rooms. Nothing of the kind, the woman assured me, and she did not look as if she were telling stories. You will next suggest – remembering the rose-coloured curtains – that its last occupant was a member of the demi-monde. Wrong again. Its last occupant was an elderly and unexceptionable Indian officer, without a liver, and with a most lawful wife. They did not stay long, it is true, but then, as the housekeeper told me, he was a deplorable old hypochondriac, who never could bear to stay a fortnight in any one place. So lay aside that scepticism, which is your besetting sin, and give unfeigned thanks to St Brigitta, or St Gengulpha, or St Catherine of Siena, or whoever is your tutelar saint, for having provided you with a palace at the cost of a hovel, and for having sent you such an invaluable friend as

Your attached

ELIZABETH DE WYNT.

P.S. – I am so sorry I shall not be in town to witness your first raptures, but dear Artie looks so pale and thin and tall after the whooping-cough, that I am sending him off at once to the sea, and as I cannot bear the child out of my sight, I am going into banishment likewise.

———

MRS MONTRESOR TO MRS DE WYNT.

32, — Street, May Fair,
May 14th.

Dearest Bessy,

Why did not dear little Artie defer his whooping-cough convalescence &c., till August? It is very odd, to me, the perverse way in which children always fix upon the most inconvenient times and seasons for their diseases. Here we are installed in our Paradise, and have searched high and low, in every hole and corner, for the serpent, without succeeding in catching a glimpse of his spotted tail. Most things in this world are disappointing, but 32, — Street, May Fair, is not. The mystery of the rent is still a mystery. I have been for my first ride in the Row this morning; my horse was a little fidgety; I am half afraid that my nerve is not what it was. I saw heaps of people I knew. Do you recollect Florence Watson? What a wealth of red hair she had last year! Well, that same wealth is black as the raven's wing this year! I wonder how people can make such walking impositions of themselves, don't you? Adela comes to us next week; I am so glad. It is dull driving by oneself of an afternoon; and I always think that one young woman alone in a brougham, or with only a dog beside her, does not look *good*. We sent round our cards a fortnight before we came up, and have been already deluged with callers. Considering that we have been two years exiled from civilised life, and that London memories are not generally of the longest, we shall do pretty well, I think. Ralph Gordon came to see me on Sunday; he is in the —th Hussars now. He has grown up such a *dear* fellow, and so good-looking! Just my style, large and fair and whiskerless! Most men nowadays make themselves as like monkeys, or Scotch terriers, as they possibly can. I intend to be quite a *mother* to him. Dresses are gored to as *indecent* an extent as ever; short skirts are rampant. I am sorry; I hate them. They make tall women look *lank*, and short ones insignificant. A knock! Peace is a word that might as well be expunged from one's London dictionary.

Yours affectionately,

CECILIA MONTRESOR.

MRS DE WYNT TO MRS MONTRESOR.

The Lord Warden, Dover,
May 18th.

Dearest Cecilia,

You will perceive that I am about to devote only one small sheet of note-paper to you. This is from no dearth of time, Heaven knows! time is a drug in the market here, but from a total dearth of ideas. Any ideas that I ever have, come to me from without, from external objects; I am not clever enough to generate any within myself. My life here is not an eminently suggestive one. It is spent digging with a wooden spade, and eating prawns. Those are my employments at least; my relaxation is going down to the Pier, to see the Calais boat come in. When one is miserable oneself, it is decidedly consolatory to see someone more miserable still; and wretched and bored, and reluctant vegetable as I am, I am not *sea-sick*. I always feel my spirits rise after having seen that peevish, draggled procession of blue, green and yellow fellow-Christians file past me. There is a wind here *always*, in comparison of which the wind that behaved so violently to the corners of Job's house was a mere zephyr. There are heights to climb which require more daring perseverance than ever Wolfe displayed, with his paltry heights of Abraham. There are glaring white houses, glaring white roads, glaring white cliffs. If any one knew how unpatriotically I detest the chalk-cliffs of Albion! Having grumbled through my two little pages – I have actually been reduced to writing very large in order to fill even them – I will send off my dreary little billet. How I wish I could get into the envelope myself too, and whirl up with it to dear, beautiful, filthy London. Not more heavily could Madame de Staël have sighed for Paris from among the shades of Coppet.

Your disconsolate,

BESSY.

MRS MONTRESOR TO MRS DE WYNT.

32, — Street, May Fair,
May 27th.

Oh, my dearest Bessy, how I wish we were out of this dreadful, dreadful house! Please don't think me very ungrateful for saying this, after your taking such pains to provide us with a Heaven upon earth, as you thought.

What has happened could, of course, have been neither foretold, nor guarded against, by any human being. About ten days ago, Benson (my maid) came to me with a very long face, and said, 'If you please, 'm, did you know that this house was *haunted*?' I was so startled: you know what a coward I am. I said, 'Good Heavens! No! is it?' 'Well, 'm, I'm pretty nigh sure it is,' she said, and the expression of her countenance was about as lively as an undertaker's; and then she told me that cook had been that morning to order groceries from a shop in the neighbourhood, and on her giving the man the direction where to send the things to, he had said, with a very peculiar smile, 'No. 32, — Street, eh? h'm? I wonder how long *you'll* stand it; last lot held out just a fortnight.' He looked so odd that she asked him what he meant, but he only said, 'Oh! nothing! only that parties never *do* stay long at 32.' He had known parties go in one day, and out the next, and during the last four years he had never known any remain over the month. Feeling a good deal alarmed by this information, she naturally inquired the reason; but he declined to give it, saying that if she had not found it out for herself, she had much better leave it alone, as it would only frighten her out of her wits; and on her insisting and urging him, she could only extract from him, that the house had such a villainously bad name, that the owners were glad to let it for a mere song. You know how firmly I believe in apparitions, and what an unutterable fear I have of them: anything material, tangible, that I can lay hold of – anything of the same fibre, blood, and bone as myself, I could, I think, confront bravely enough; but the mere thought of being brought face to face with the 'bodiless dead', makes my brain unsteady. The moment Henry came in, I ran to him, and told him; but he pooh-poohed the whole story, laughed at me, and asked whether we should turn out of the prettiest house in London, at the very height of the season, because a grocer said it had a bad name. Most good things that had ever been in the world had had a bad name in their day; and, moreover, the man had probably a motive for taking away the house's character, some friend for whom he coveted the charming situation and the low rent. He derided my 'babyish fears', as he called them, to such an extent that I felt half ashamed, and yet not quite comfortable either; and then came the usual rush of London engagements, during which one has no time to think of anything but how to speak, and act, and look for the moment then present. Adela was to arrive yesterday, and in the morning our weekly hamper of flowers, fruit, and vegetables arrived from home. I always dress the flower vases myself, servants are so tasteless; and as I was arranging them, it occurred to me – you know Adela's passion for flowers – to carry up one particular cornucopia of roses and mignonette and set it on her toilet-table, as a pleasant surprise for her. As I came downstairs, I had seen the housemaid – a fresh, round-faced country girl – go into the room, which was being prepared for Adela, with a pair of sheets that had been airing over her arm. I went upstairs very slowly, as my cornucopia was full of water, and I was afraid of spilling some. I turned the handle of the bedroom-door and entered, keeping my eyes fixed on my flowers, to see how they bore the transit, and whether any of them had fallen out. Suddenly a sort of shiver passed over me; and feeling frightened – I did not know why – I looked up quickly. The girl was standing by the bed, leaning forward a little with her hands clenched in each other, rigid, every nerve tense; her eyes, wide open, starting out of her head, and a look of unutterable stony horror in them; her cheeks and mouth not pale, but livid as those of one that died awhile ago in mortal pain. As I looked at her, her lips moved a little, and an awful hoarse voice, not like hers in the least, said, 'Oh! my God, I have seen it!' and then she fell down suddenly, like a log, with a heavy noise. Hearing the noise, loudly audible all through the thin walls and floors of a London house, Benson came running in, and between us we managed to lift her on to the bed, and tried to bring her to herself by rubbing her feet and hands, and holding strong salts to her nostrils. And all the while we kept glancing over our shoulders, in a vague cold terror of seeing some awful, shapeless apparition. Two long hours she lay in a state of utter unconsciousness. Meanwhile Harry, who had been down to his club, returned. At the end of two hours we succeeded in bringing her back to sensation and life, but only to make the awful discovery that she was raving mad. She became so violent that it required all the combined strength of Harry and Phillips (our butler) to hold her down in the bed. Of course, we sent off instantly for a doctor, who on her growing a little calmer towards evening, removed her in a cab to his own house. He has just been here to tell me that she is now pretty quiet, not from any return to sanity, but from sheer exhaustion. We are, of course, utterly in the dark as to *what* she saw, and her ravings are far too disconnected and unintelligible to afford us the slightest clue. I feel so completely shattered and upset by this awful occurrence, that you will excuse me, dear, I'm sure, if I write incoherently. One thing I need hardly tell you, and that is, that no earthly consideration would induce me to allow Adela to occupy that terrible room. I shudder and run by quickly as I pass the door.

Yours, in great agitation,
CECILIA.

MRS DE WYNT TO MRS MONTRESOR.

The Lord Warden, Dover,
May 28th.

Dearest Cecilia,

Yours just come; how very dreadful! But I am still unconvinced as to the house being in fault. You know I feel a sort of godmother to it, and responsible for its good behaviour. Don't you think that what the girl had might have been a fit? Why not? I myself have a cousin who is subject to seizures of the kind, and immediately on being attacked his whole body becomes rigid, his eyes glassy and staring, his complexion livid, exactly as in the case you describe. Or, if not a fit, are you sure that she has not been subject to fits of madness? *Please* be sure and ascertain whether there is not insanity in her family. It is so common nowadays, and so much on the increase, that nothing is more likely. You know my utter disbelief in ghosts. I am convinced that most of them, if run to earth, would turn out about as genuine as the famed Cock Lane one. But even allowing the possibility, nay, the actual unquestioned existence of ghosts in the abstract, is it likely that there should be anything to be seen so horribly fear-inspiring, as to send a perfectly sane person *in one instant* raving mad, which you, after three weeks' residence in the house, have never caught a glimpse of? According to your hypothesis, your whole household ought, by this time, to be stark staring mad. Let me implore you not to give way to a panic which may, possibly, probably prove utterly groundless. Oh, how I wish I were with you, to make you listen to reason! Artie ought to be the best prop ever woman's old age was furnished with, to indemnify me for all he and his whooping-cough have made me suffer. Write immediately, please, and tell me how the poor patient progresses. Oh, had I the wings of a dove! I shall be on wires till I hear again.

Yours,

BESSY.

MRS MONTRESOR TO MRS DE WYNT.

No. 5, Bolton Street, Piccadilly,

June 12th.

Dearest Bessy,

You will see that we have left that terrible, hateful, fatal house. How I wish we had escaped from it sooner! Oh, my dear Bessy, I shall never be the same woman again if I live to be a hundred. Let me try to be coherent, and to tell you connectedly what has happened. And first, as to the housemaid, she has been removed to a lunatic asylum, where she remains in much the same state. She has had several lucid intervals, and during them has been closely, pressingly questioned as to what it was she saw; but she has maintained an absolute, hopeless silence, and only shudders, moans, and hides her face in her hands when the subject is broached. Three days ago I went to see her, and on my return was sitting resting in the drawing-room, before going to dress for dinner, talking to Adela about my visit, when Ralph Gordon walked in. He has always been walking in the last ten days, and Adela has always flushed up and looked very happy, poor little cat, whenever he made his appearance. He looked very handsome, dear fellow, just come in from the park; seemed in tremendous spirits, and was as sceptical as even you could be, as to the ghostly origin of Sarah's seizure. 'Let me come here tonight and sleep in that room; *do*, Mrs Montresor,' he said, looking very eager and excited. 'With the gas lit and a poker, I'll engage to exorcise every demon that shows his ugly nose; even if I should find – .

Seven white ghostisses
Sitting on seven white postisses.'

'You don't mean really?' I asked, incredulously. 'Don't I? that's all,' he answered emphatically. 'I should like nothing better. Well, is it a bargain?' Adela turned quite pale. 'Oh, don't,' she said, hurriedly, '*please*, don't! why should you run such a risk? How do you know that you might not be sent mad too?' He laughed very heartily, and coloured a little with pleasure at seeing the interest she took in his safety. 'Never fear,' he said, 'it would take more than a whole squadron of departed ones, with the old gentleman at their head, to send me crazy.' He was so eager, so persistent, so thoroughly in earnest, that I yielded at last, though with a certain strong reluctance, to his entreaties. Adela's blue eyes filled with tears, and she walked away hastily to the conservatory, and stood picking bits of heliotrope to hide them. Nevertheless, Ralph got his own way; it was so difficult to refuse him anything. We gave up all our engagements for the evening, and he did the same with his. At about ten o'clock he arrived, accompanied by a friend and brother officer, Captain Burton, who was anxious to see the result of the experiment. 'Let me go up at once,' he said, looking very happy and animated. 'I don't know when I have felt in such good tune; a new sensation is a luxury not to be had every day of one's life; turn the gas up as high as it will go; provide a good stout poker, and leave the issue to Providence and me.' We did as he bid. 'It's all ready now,' Henry said, coming downstairs after having obeyed his orders; 'the room is nearly as light as day. Well, good luck to you, old fellow!' 'Good-bye, Miss Bruce,' Ralph said, going over to Adela, and taking her hand with a look, half laughing, half sentimental –

> 'Fare thee well, and if for ever
> Then for ever, fare thee well,

that is my last dying speech and confession. Now mind,' he went on, standing by the table, and addressing us all; 'if I ring once, *don't* come. I may be flurried, and lay hold of the bell without thinking; if I ring twice, *come.*' Then he went, jumping up the stairs three steps at a time, and humming a tune. As for us, we sat in different attitudes of expectation and listening about the drawing-room. At first we tried to talk a little, but it would not do; our whole souls seemed to have passed into our ears. The clock's ticking sounded as loud as a great church bell close to one's ear. Addy lay on the sofa, with her dear little white face hidden in the cushions. So we sat for exactly an hour; but it seemed like two years, and just as the clock began to strike eleven, a sharp ting, ting, ting, rang clear and shrill through the house. 'Let us go,' said Addy, starting up and running to the door. 'Let us go,' I cried too, following her. But Captain Burton stood in the way, and intercepted our progress. 'No,' he said, decisively, 'you must not go; remember Gordon told us distinctly, if he rang once *not* to come. I know the sort of fellow he is, and that nothing would annoy him more than having his directions disregarded.'

'Oh, nonsense!' Addy cried passionately, 'he would never have rung if he had not seen something dreadful; do, *do* let us go!' she ended, clasping her hands. But she was overruled, and we all went back to our seats. Ten minutes more of suspense, next door to unendurable; I felt a lump in my throat, a gasping for breath; – ten minutes on the clock, but a thousand centuries on our hearts. Then again, loud, sudden, violent, the bell rang! We made a simultaneous rush to the door. I don't think we were one second flying upstairs. Addy was first. Almost simultaneously she and I burst into the room. There he was, standing in the middle of the floor, rigid, petrified, with that same look – that look that is burnt into my heart in letters of fire – of awful, unspeakable, stony fear on his brave young face. For one instant he stood thus; then stretching out his arms stiffly before him, he groaned in a terrible, husky voice, 'Oh, my God! I have seen it!' and fell down *dead*. Yes, *dead*. Not in a swoon or in a fit, but *dead*. Vainly we tried to bring back the life to that strong young heart; it will never come back again till that day when the earth and the sea give up the dead that are therein. I cannot see the page for the tears that are blinding me; he was such a dear fellow! I can't write any more today.

Your broken-hearted
CECILIA.

This is a true story.

Mrs Henry Wood

REALITY OR DELUSION?

THIS is a ghost story. Every word of it is true. And I don't mind confessing that for ages afterwards some of us did not care to pass the spot alone at night. Some people do not care to pass it yet.

It was autumn, and we were at Crabb Cot. Lena had been ailing; and in October Mrs Todhetley proposed to the Squire that they should remove with her there, to see if the change would do her good.

We Worcestershire people call North Crabb a village; but one might count the houses in it, little and great, and not find four-and-twenty. South Crabb, half a mile off, is ever so much larger; but the church and school are at North Crabb.

John Ferrar had been employed by Squire Todhetley as a sort of overlooker on the estate, or working bailiff. He had died the previous winter; leaving nothing behind him except some debts; for he was not provident; and his handsome son Daniel. Daniel Ferrar, who was rather superior as far as education went, disliked work: he would make a show of helping his father, but it came to little. Old Ferrar had not put him to any particular trade or occupation, and Daniel, who was as proud as Lucifer, would not turn to it himself. He liked to be a gentleman. All he did now was to work in his garden, and feed his fowls, ducks, rabbits, and pigeons, of which he kept a great quantity, selling them to the houses around and sending them to market.

But, as every one said, poultry would not maintain him. Mrs Lease, in the pretty cottage hard by Ferrar's, grew tired of saying it. This Mrs Lease and her daughter, Maria, must not be confounded with Lease the pointsman: they were in a better condition of life, and not related to him. Daniel Ferrar used to run in and out of their house at will when a boy, and he was now engaged to be married to Maria. She would have a little money, and the Leases were respected in North Crabb. People began to whisper a query as to how Ferrar got his corn for the poultry: he was not known to buy much: and he would have to go out of his house at Christmas, for its owner, Mr Coney, had given him notice. Mrs Lease, anxious about Maria's prospects, asked Daniel what he intended to do then, and he answered, 'Make his fortune: he should begin to do it as soon as he could turn himself round.' But the time was going on, and the turning round seemed to be as far off as ever.

After Midsummer, a niece of the schoolmistress's, Miss Timmens, had come to the school to stay: her name was Harriet Roe. The father, Humphrey Roe, was half-brother to Miss Timmens. He had married a Frenchwoman, and lived more in France than in England until his death. The girl had been christened Henriette; but North Crabb, not understanding much French, converted it into Harriet. She was a showy, free-mannered, good-looking girl, and made speedy acquaintance with Daniel Ferrar; or he with her. They improved upon it so rapidly that Maria Lease grew jealous, and North Crabb began to say he cared for Harriet more than for Maria. When Tod and I got home the latter end of October, to spend the Squire's birthday, things were in this state. James Hill, the bailiff who had been taken on by the Squire in John Ferrar's place (but a far inferior man to Ferrar; not much better, in fact, than a common workman, and of whose doings you will hear soon in regard to his little step-son, David Garth) gave us an account of matters in general. Daniel Ferrar had been drinking lately, Hill added, and his head was not strong enough to stand it; and he was also beginning to look as if he had some care upon him.

'A nice lot, he, for them two women to be fighting for,' cried Hill, who was no friend to Ferrar. 'There'll be mischief between 'em if they don't draw in a bit. Maria Lease is next door to mad over it, I know; and t'other, finding herself the best liked, crows over her. It's something like the Bible story of Leah and Rachel, young gents, Dan Ferrar likes the one, and he's bound by promise to the t'other. As to the French jade,' concluded Hill, giving his head a toss, 'she'd make a show of liking any man that followed her, she would; a dozen of 'em on a string.'

It was all very well for surly Hill to call Daniel Ferrar a 'nice lot', but he was the best-looking fellow in the church on Sunday morning – well-dressed too. But his colour seemed brighter; and his hands shook as they were raised, often, to push back his hair, that the sun shone upon through the south-window, turning it to gold. He scarcely looked up, not even at Harriet Roe, with her dark eyes roving everywhere, and her streaming pink ribbons. Maria Lease was pale, quiet, and nice, as usual; she had no beauty, but her face was sensible, and her deep grey eyes had a strange and curious earnestness. The new parson preached, a young man just appointed to the parish of Crabb. He went in for great observances of Saints' days, and told his congregation that he should expect to see them at church on the morrow, which would be the Feast of All Saints.

Daniel Ferrar walked home with Mrs Lease and Maria after service, and was invited to dinner. I ran across to shake hands with the old dame, who had once nursed me through an illness, and promised to look in and see her later. We were going back to school on the morrow. As I turned away, Harriet Roe passed, her pink ribbons and her cheap gay silk dress gleaming in the sunlight. She stared at me, and I stared back again. And now, the explanation of matters being over, the real story begins. But I shall have to tell some of it as it was told by others.

The tea-things waited on Mrs Lease's table in the afternoon; waited for Daniel Ferrar. He had left them shortly before to go and attend to his poultry. Nothing had been said about his coming back for tea: that he would do so had been looked upon as a matter of course. But he did not make his appearance, and the tea was taken without him. At half-past five the church-bell rang out for evening service, and Maria put her things on. Mrs Lease did not go out at night.

'You are starting early, Maria. You'll be in church before other people.'

'That won't matter, mother.'

A jealous suspicion lay on Maria – that the secret of Daniel Ferrar's absence was his having fallen in with Harriet Roe: perhaps he had gone of his own accord to seek her. She walked slowly along. The gloom of dusk, and a deep dusk, had stolen over the evening, but the moon would be up later. As Maria passed the school-house, she halted to glance in at the little sitting-room window: the shutters were not closed yet, and the room was lighted by the blazing fire. Harriet was not there. She only saw Miss Timmens, the mistress, who was putting on her bonnet before a hand-glass propped upright on the mantelpiece. Without warning, Miss Timmens turned and threw open the window. It was only for the purpose of pulling-to the shutters, but Maria thought she must have been observed, and spoke.

'Good evening, Miss Timmens.'

'Who is it?' cried out Miss Timmens, in answer, peering into the dusk. 'Oh, it's you, Maria Lease! Have you seen anything of Harriet? She went off somewhere this afternoon, and never came in to tea.'

'I have not seen her.'

'She's gone to the Batleys', I'll be bound. She knows I don't like her to be with the Batley girls: they make her ten times flightier than she would otherwise be.'

Miss Timmens drew in her shutters with a jerk, without which they would not close, and Maria Lease turned away.

'Not at the Batleys', not at the Batleys', but with *him*,' she cried, in bitter rebellion, as she turned away from the church. From the church, not to it. Was Maria to blame for wishing to see whether she was right or not? – for walking about a little in the thought of meeting them? At any rate it is what she did. And had her reward; such as it was.

As she was passing the top of the withy walk, their voices reached her ear. People often walked there, and it was one of the ways to South Crabb. Maria drew back amidst the trees, and they came on: Harriet Roe and Daniel Ferrar, walking arm-in-arm.

'I think I had better take it off,' Harriet was saying. 'No need to invoke a storm upon my head. And that would come in a shower of hail from stiff old Aunt Timmens.'

The answer seemed one of quick accent, but Ferrar spoke low. Maria Lease had hard work to control herself: anger, passion, jealousy, all blazed up. With her arms stretched out to a friendly tree on either side, – with her heart beating, – with her pulses coursing on to fever-heat, she watched them across the bit of common to the road. Harriet went one way then; he another, in the direction of Mrs Lease's cottage. No doubt to fetch her – Maria – to church, with a plausible excuse of having been detained. Until now she had had no proof of his falseness; had never perfectly believed in it.

She took her arms from the trees and went forward, a sharp faint cry of despair breaking forth on the night air. Maria Lease was one of those silent-natured girls who can never speak of a wrong like this. She had to bury it within her; down, down, out of sight and show; and she went into church with her usual quiet step. Harriet Roe with Miss Timmens came next, quite demure, as if she had been singing some of the infant scholars to sleep at their own homes. Daniel Ferrar did not go to church at all: he stayed, as was found afterwards, with Mrs Lease.

Maria might as well have been at home as at church: better perhaps that she had been. Not a syllable of the service did she hear: her brain was a sea of confusion; the tumult within it rising higher and higher. She did not hear even the text, 'Peace, be still', or the sermon; both so singularly appropriate. The passions in men's minds, the preacher said, raged and foamed just like the angry waves of the sea in a storm, until Jesus came to still them.

I ran after Maria when church was over, and went in to pay the promised visit to old Mother Lease. Daniel Ferrar was sitting in the parlour. He got up and offered Maria a chair at the fire, but she turned her back and stood at the table under the window, taking off her gloves. An open Bible was before Mrs Lease: I wondered whether she had been reading aloud to Daniel.

'What was the text, child?' asked the old lady.

No answer.

'Do you hear, Maria! What was the text?'

Maria turned at that, as if suddenly awakened. Her face was white; her eyes had in them an uncertain terror.

'The text?' she stammered. 'I – I forget it, mother. It was from Genesis, I think.'

'Was it, Master Johnny?'

'It was from the fourth chapter of St Mark, "Peace, be still."'

Mrs Lease stared at me. 'Why, that is the very chapter I've been reading. Well now, that's curious. But there's never a better in the Bible, and never a better text was taken from it than those three words. I have been telling Daniel here, Master Johnny, that when once that peace, Christ's peace, is got into the heart, storms can't hurt us much. And you are going away again tomorrow, sir?' she added, after a pause. 'It's a short stay?'

I was not going away on the morrow. Tod and I, taking the Squire in a genial moment after dinner, had pressed to be let stay until Tuesday, Tod using the argument, and laughing while he did it, that it must be wrong to travel on All Saints' Day, when the parson had specially enjoined us to be at church. The Squire told us we were a couple of encroaching rascals, and if he did let us stay it should be upon condition that we did go to church. This I said to them.

'He may send you all the same, sir, when the morning comes,' remarked Daniel Ferrar.

'Knowing Mr Todhetley as you do Ferrar, you may remember that he never breaks his promises.'

Daniel laughed. 'He grumbles over them, though, Master Johnny.'

'Well, he may grumble tomorrow about our staying, say it is wasting time that ought to be spent in study, but he will not send us back until Tuesday.'

Until Tuesday! If I could have foreseen then what would have happened before Tuesday! If all of us could have foreseen! Seen the few hours between now and then depicted, as in a mirror, event by event! Would it have saved the calamity, the dreadful sin that could never be redeemed? Why, yes; surely it would. Daniel Ferrar turned and looked at Maria.

'Why don't you come to the fire?'

'I am very well here, thank you.'

She had sat down where she was, her bonnet touching the curtain. Mrs Lease, not noticing that anything was wrong, had begun talking about

Lena, whose illness was turning to low fever, when the house door opened and Harriet Roe came in.

'What a lovely night it is!' she said, taking of own accord the chair I had not cared to take, for I kept saying I must go. 'Maria, what went with you after church? I hunted for you everywhere.'

Maria gave no answer. She looked black and angry; and her bosom heaved as if a storm were brewing. Harriet Roe slightly laughed.

'Do you intend to take holiday tomorrow, Mrs Lease?'

'Me take holiday! what is there in tomorrow to take holiday for?' returned Mrs Lease.

'I shall,' continued Harriet, not answering the question: 'I have been used to it in France. All Saints' Day is a grand holiday there; we go to church in our best clothes, and pay visits afterwards. Following it, like a dark shadow, comes the gloomy Jour des Morts.'

'The what?' cried Mrs Lease, bending her ear.

'The day of the dead. All Souls' Day. But you English don't go to the cemeteries to pray.'

Mrs Lease put on her spectacles, which lay upon the open pages of the Bible, and stared at Harriet. Perhaps she thought they might help her to understand. The girl laughed.

'On All Souls' Day, whether it be wet or dry, the French cemeteries are full of kneeling women draped in black; all praying for the repose of their dead relatives, after the manner of the Roman Catholics.'

Daniel Ferrar, who had not spoken a word since she came in, but sat with his face to the fire, turned and looked at her. Upon which she tossed back her head and her pink ribbons, and smiled till all her teeth were seen. Good teeth they were. As to reverence in her tone, there was none.

'I have seen them kneeling when the slosh and wet have been ankle-deep. Did you ever see a ghost?' added she, with energy. 'The French believe that the spirits of the dead come abroad on the night of All Saints' Day. You'd scarcely get a French woman to go out of her house after dark. It is their chief superstition.'

'What *is* the superstition?' questioned Mrs Lease.

'Why, *that*,' said Harriet. 'They believe that the dead are allowed to revisit the world after dark on the Eve of All Souls; that they hover in the air, waiting to appear to any of their living relatives, who may venture out, lest they should forget to pray on the morrow for the rest of their souls.'[*]

'Well, I never!' cried Mrs Lease, staring excessively. 'Did you ever hear the like of that, sir?' turning to me.

[*] A superstition obtaining amongst some of the lower orders in France.

'Yes; I have heard of it.'

Harriet Roe looked up at me; I was standing at the corner of the mantelpiece. She laughed a free laugh.

'I say, wouldn't it be fun to go out tomorrow night, and meet the ghosts? Only, perhaps they don't visit this country, as it is not under Rome.'

'Now just you behave yourself before your betters, Harriet Roe,' put in Mrs Lease, sharply. 'That gentleman is young Mr Ludlow of Crabb Cot.'

'And very happy I am to make young Mr Ludlow's acquaintance,' returned easy Harriet, flinging back her mantle from her shoulders. 'How hot your parlour is, Mrs Lease.'

The hook of the cloak had caught in a thin chain of twisted gold that she wore round her neck, displaying it to view. She hurriedly folded her cloak together, as if wishing to conceal the chain. But Mrs Lease's spectacles had seen it.

'What's that you've got on, Harriet? A gold chain?'

A moment's pause, and then Harriet Roe flung back her mantle again, defiance upon her face, and touched the chain with her hand.

'That's what it is, Mrs Lease: a gold chain. And a very pretty one, too.'

'Was it your mother's?'

'It was never anybody's but mine. I had it made a present to me this afternoon; for a keepsake.'

Happening to look at Maria, I was startled at her face, it was so white and dark: white with emotion, dark with an angry despair that I for one did not comprehend. Harriet Roe, throwing at her a look of saucy triumph, went out with as little ceremony as she had come in, just calling back a general good night; and we heard her footsteps outside getting gradually fainter in the distance. Daniel Ferrar rose.

'I'll take my departure too, I think. You are very unsociable tonight, Maria.'

'Perhaps I am. Perhaps I have cause to be.'

She flung his hand back when he held it out; and in another moment, as if a thought struck her, ran after him into the passage to speak. I, standing near the door in the small room, caught the words.

'I must have an explanation with you, Daniel Ferrar. Now. Tonight. We cannot go on thus for a single hour longer.'

'Not tonight, Maria; I have no time to spare. And I don't know what you mean.'

'You do know. Listen. I will not go to my rest, no, though it were for twenty nights to come, until we have had it out. I *vow* I will not. There. You are playing with me. Others have long said so, and I know it now.'

He seemed to speak some quieting words to her, for the tone was low and soothing; and then went out, closing the door behind him. Maria came back and stood with her face and its ghastliness turned from us. And still the old mother noticed nothing.

'Why don't you take your things off, Maria?' she asked.

'Presently,' was the answer.

I said good night in my turn, and went away. Half-way home I met Tod with the two young Lexoms. The Lexoms made us go in and stay to supper, and it was ten o'clock before we left them.

'We shall catch it,' said Tod, setting off at a run. They never let us stay out late on a Sunday evening, on account of the reading.

But, as it happened, we escaped scot-free this time, for the house was in a commotion about Lena. She had been better in the afternoon, but at nine o'clock the fever returned worse than ever. Her little cheeks and lips were scarlet as she lay on the bed, her wide-open eyes were bright and glistening. The Squire had gone up to look at her, and was fuming and fretting in his usual fashion.

'The doctor has never sent the medicine,' said patient Mrs Todhetley, who must have been worn out with nursing. 'She ought to take it; I am sure she ought.'

'These boys are good to run over to Cole's for that,' cried the Squire. 'It won't hurt them; it's a fine night.'

Of course we were good for it. And we got our caps again; being charged to enjoin Mr Cole to come over the first thing in the morning.

'Do you care much about my going with you, Johnny?' Tod asked as we were turning out at the door. 'I am awfully tired.'

'Not a bit. I'd as soon go alone as not. You'll see me back in half-an-hour.'

I took the nearest way; flying across the fields at a canter, and startling the hares. Mr Cole lived near South Crabb, and I don't believe more than ten minutes had gone by when I knocked at his door. But to get back as quickly was another thing. The doctor was not at home. He had been called out to a patient at eight o'clock, and had not yet returned.

I went in to wait: the servant said he might be expected to come in from minute to minute. It was of no use to go away without the medicine; and I sat down in the surgery in front of the shelves, and fell asleep counting the white jars and physic bottles. The doctor's entrance awoke me.

'I am sorry you should have had to come over and to wait,' he said. 'When my other patient, with whom I was detained a considerable time, was done with, I went on to Crabb Cot with the child's medicine, which I had in my pocket.'

'They think her very ill tonight, sir.'

'I left her better, and going quietly to sleep. She will soon be well again, I hope.'

'Why! is that the time?' I exclaimed, happening to catch sight of the clock as I was crossing the hall. It was nearly twelve. Mr Cole laughed, saying time passed quickly when folk were asleep.

I went back slowly. The sleep, or the canter before it, had made me feel as tired as Tod had said he was. It was a night to be abroad in and to enjoy; calm, warm, light. The moon, high in the sky, illumined every blade of grass; sparkled on the water of the little rivulet; brought out the moss on the grey walls of the old church; played on its round-faced clock, then striking twelve.

Twelve o'clock at night at North Crabb answers to about three in the morning in London, for country people are mostly in bed and asleep at ten. Therefore, when loud and angry voices struck up in dispute, just as the last stroke of the hour was dying away on the midnight air, I stood still and doubted my ears.

I was getting near home then. The sounds came from the back of a building standing alone in a solitary place on the left-hand side of the road. It belonged to the Squire, and was called the yellow barn, its walls being covered with a yellow wash; but it was in fact used as a storehouse for corn. I was passing in front of it when the voices rose upon the air. Round the building I ran, and saw – Maria Lease: and something else that I could not at first comprehend. In the pursuit of her vow, not to go to rest until she had 'had it out' with Daniel Ferrar, Maria had been abroad searching for him. What ill fate brought her looking for him up near our barn? – perhaps because she had fruitlessly searched in every other spot.

At the back of this barn, up some steps, was an unused door. Unused partly because it was not required, the principal entrance being in front; partly because the key of it had been for a long time missing. Stealing out at this door, a bag of corn upon his shoulders, had come Daniel Ferrar in a smock-frock. Maria saw him, and stood back in the shade. She watched him lock the door and put the key in his pocket; she watched him give the heavy bag a jerk as he turned to come down the steps. Then she burst out. Her loud reproaches petrified him, and he stood there as one suddenly turned to stone. It was at that moment that I appeared.

I understood it all soon; it needed not Maria's words to enlighten me. Daniel Ferrar possessed the lost key and could come in and out at will in the midnight hours when the world was sleeping, and help himself to the corn. No wonder his poultry throve; no wonder there had been grumblings at Crabb Cot at the mysterious disappearance of the good grain.

Maria Lease was decidedly mad in those few first moments. Stealing is looked upon in an honest village as an awful thing; a disgrace, a crime; and there was the night's earlier misery besides. Daniel Ferrar was a thief! Daniel Ferrar was false to her! A storm of words and reproaches poured forth from her in confusion, none of it very distinct. 'Living upon theft! Convicted felon! Transportation for life! Squire Todhetley's corn! Fattening poultry on stolen goods! Buying gold chains with the profits for that bold, flaunting French girl, Harriet Roe! Taking his stealthy walks with her!'

My going up to them stopped the charge. There was a pause; and then Maria, in her mad passion, denounced him to me, as representative (so she put it) of the Squire – the breaker-in upon our premises! the robber of our stored corn!

Daniel Ferrar came down the steps; he had remained there still as a statue, immovable; and turned his white face to me. Never a word in defence said he: the blow had crushed him; he was a proud man (if any one can understand that), and to be discovered in this ill-doing was worse than death to him.

'Don't think of me more hardly than you can help, Master Johnny,' he said in a quiet tone. 'I have been almost tired of my life this long while.'

Putting down the bag of corn near the steps, he took the key from his pocket and handed it to me. The man's aspect had so changed; there was something so grievously subdued and sad about him altogether, that I felt as sorry for him as if he had not been guilty. Maria Lease went on in her fiery passion.

'You'll be more tired of it tomorrow when the police are taking you to Worcester gaol. Squire Todhetley will not spare you, though your father was his many-years bailiff. He could not, you know, if he wished; Master Ludlow has seen you in the act.'

'Let me have the key again for a minute, sir,' he said, as quietly as though he had not heard a word. And I gave it to him. I'm not sure but I should have given him my head had he asked for it.

He swung the bag on his shoulders, unlocked the granary door, and put the bag beside the other sacks. The bag was his own, as we found afterwards, but he left it there. Locking the door again, he gave me the key, and went away with a weary step.

'Good-bye, Master Johnny.'

I answered back good night civilly, though he had been stealing. When he was out of sight, Maria Lease, her passion full upon her still, dashed off towards her mother's cottage, a strange cry of despair breaking from her lips.

'Where have you been lingering, Johnny?' roared the Squire, who was sitting up for me. 'You have been throwing at the owls, sir, that's what you've been at; you have been scudding after the hares.'

I said I had waited for Mr Cole, and had come back slower than I went; but I said no more, and went up to my room at once. And the Squire went to his.

I know I am only a muff; people tell me so, often: but I can't help it; I did not make myself. I lay awake till nearly daylight, first wishing Daniel Ferrar could be screened, and then thinking it might perhaps be done. If he would only take the lesson to heart and go straight for the future, what a capital thing it would be. We had liked old Ferrar; he had done me and Tod many a good turn: and, for the matter of that, we liked Daniel. So I never said a word when morning came of the past night's work.

'Is Daniel at home?' I asked, going to Ferrar's the first thing before breakfast. I meant to tell him that if he would keep right, I would keep counsel.

'He went out at dawn, sir,' answered the old woman who did for him, and sold his poultry at market. 'He'll be in presently: he have had no breakfast yet.'

'Then tell him when he comes, to wait in, and see me: tell him it's all right. Can you remember, Goody? "It is all right."'

'I'll remember, safe enough, Master Ludlow.'

Tod and I, being on our honour, went to church, and found about ten people in the pews. Harriet Roe was one, with her pink ribbons, the twisted gold chain showing outside a short-cut velvet jacket.

'No, sir; he has not been home yet; I can't think where he can have got to,' was the old Goody's reply when I went again to Ferrar's. And so I wrote a word in pencil, and told her to give it him when he came in, for I could not go dodging there every hour of the day.

After luncheon, strolling by the back of the barn: a certain reminiscence I suppose taking me there, for it was not a frequented spot: I saw Maria Lease coming along.

Well, it was a change! The passionate woman of the previous night had subsided into a poor, wild-looking, sorrow-stricken thing, ready to die of remorse. Excessive passion had wrought its usual consequences; a reaction: a reaction in favour of Daniel Ferrar. She came up to me, clasping her hands in agony – beseeching that I would spare him; that I would not tell of him; that I would give him a chance for the future: and her lips quivered and trembled, and there were dark circles round her hollow eyes.

I said that I had not told and did not intend to tell. Upon which she was going to fall down on her knees, but I rushed off.

'Do you know where he is?' I asked, when she came to her sober senses.

'Oh, I wish I did know! Master Johnny, he is just the man to go and do something desperate. He would never face shame; and I was a mad, hard-hearted, wicked girl to do what I did last night. He might run away to sea; he might go and enlist for a soldier.'

'I dare say he is at home by this time. I have left a word for him there, and promised to go in and see him tonight. If he will undertake not to be up to wrong things again, no one shall ever know of this from me.'

She went away easier, and I sauntered on towards South Crabb. Eager as Tod and I had been for the day's holiday, it did not seem to be turning out much of a boon. In going home again – there was nothing worth staying out for – I had come to the spot by the three-cornered grove where I saw Maria, when a galloping policeman overtook me. My heart stood still; for I thought he must have come after Daniel Ferrar.

'Can you tell me if I am near to Crabb Cot – Squire Todhetley's?' he asked, reining-in his horse.

'You will reach it in a minute or two. I live there. Squire Todhetley is not at home. What do you want with him?'

'It's only to give in an official paper, sir. I have to leave one personally upon all the county magistrates.'

He rode on. When I got in I saw the folded paper upon the hall-table; the man and horse had already gone onwards. It was worse indoors than out; less to be done. Tod had disappeared after church; the Squire was abroad; Mrs Todhetley sat upstairs with Lena: and I strolled out again. It was only three o'clock then.

An hour, or more, was got through somehow; meeting one, talking to another, throwing at the ducks and geese; anything. Mrs Lease had her head, smothered in a yellow shawl, stretched out over the palings as I passed her cottage.

'Don't catch cold, mother.'

'I am looking for Maria, sir. I can't think what has come to her today, Master Johnny,' she added, dropping her voice to a confidential tone. 'The girl seems demented: she has been going in and out ever since daylight like a dog in a fair.'

'If I meet her I will send her home.'

And in another minute I did meet her. For she was coming out of Daniel Ferrar's yard. I supposed he was at home again.

'No,' she said looking more wild, worn, haggard than before; 'that's what I have been to ask. I am just out of my senses, sir. He has gone for certain. Gone!'

I did not think it. He would not be likely to go away without clothes.

'Well, I know he is, Master Johnny; something tells me. I've been all about everywhere. There's a great dread upon me, sir; I never felt anything like it.'

'Wait until night, Maria; I dare say he will go home then. Your mother is looking out for you; I said if I met you I'd send you in.'

Mechanically she turned towards the cottage, and I went on. Presently, as I was sitting on a gate watching the sunset, Harriet Roe passed towards the withy walk, and gave me a nod in her free but good-natured way.

'Are you going there to look out for the ghosts this evening?' I asked: and I wished not long afterwards I had not said it. 'It will soon be dark.'

'So it will,' she said, turning to the red sky in the west. 'But I have no time to give to the ghosts tonight.'

'Have you seen Ferrar today?' I cried, an idea occurring to me.

'No. And I can't think where he has got to; unless he is off to Worcester. He told me he should have to go there some day this week.'

She evidently knew nothing about him, and went on her way with another free-and-easy nod. I sat on the gate till the sun had gone down, and then thought it was time to be getting homewards.

Close against the yellow barn, the scene of last night's trouble, whom should I come upon but Maria Lease. She was standing still, and turned quickly at the sound of my footsteps. Her face was bright again, but had a puzzled look upon it.

'I have just seen him: he has not gone,' she said in a happy whisper. 'You were right, Master Johnny, and I was wrong.'

'Where did you see him?'

'Here; not a minute ago. I saw him twice. He is angry, very, and will not let me speak to him; both times he got away before I could reach him. He is close by somewhere.'

I looked round, naturally; but Ferrar was nowhere to be seen. There was nothing to conceal him except the barn, and that was locked up. The account she gave was this – and her face grew puzzled again as she related it.

Unable to rest indoors, she had wandered up here again, and saw Ferrar standing at the corner of the barn, looking very hard at her. She thought he was waiting for her to come up, but before she got close to him he had disappeared, and she did not see which way. She hastened past the front of the barn, ran round to the back, and there he was. He stood near the steps looking out for her; waiting for her, as it again seemed; and was gazing at her with the same fixed stare. But again she missed him before she could get quite up; and it was at that moment that I arrived on the scene.

I went all round the barn, but could see nothing of Ferrar. It was an extraordinary thing where he could have got to. Inside the barn he could not be: it was securely locked; and there was no appearance of him in the open country. It was, so to say, broad daylight yet, or at least not far short of it; the red light was still in the west. Beyond the field at the back of the barn, was a grove of trees in the form of a triangle; and this grove was flanked by Crabb Ravine, which ran right and left. Crabb Ravine had the reputation of being haunted; for a light was sometimes seen dodging about its deep descending banks at night that no one could account for. A lively spot altogether for those who liked gloom.

'Are you sure it was Ferrar, Maria?'

'Sure!' she returned in surprise. 'You don't think I could mistake him, Master Johnny, do you? He wore that ugly seal-skin winter-cap of his tied over his ears, and his thick grey coat. The coat was buttoned closely round him. I have not seen him wear either since last winter.'

That Ferrar must have gone into hiding somewhere seemed quite evident; and yet there was nothing but the ground to receive him. Maria said she lost sight of him the last time in a moment; both times in fact; and it was absolutely impossible that he could have made off to the triangle or elsewhere, as she must have seen him cross the open land. For that matter I must have seen him also.

On the whole, not two minutes had elapsed since I came up, though it seems to have been longer in telling it: when, before we could look further, voices were heard approaching from the direction of Crabb Cot; and Maria, not caring to be seen, went away quickly. I was still puzzling about Ferrar's hiding-place, when they reached me – the Squire, Tod, and two or three men. Tod came slowly up, his face dark and grave.

'I say, Johnny, what a shocking thing this is!'

'What is a shocking thing?'

'You have not heard of it? – But I don't see how you could hear it.'

I had heard nothing. I did not know what there was to hear. Tod told me in a whisper.

'Daniel Ferrar's dead, lad.'

'What?'

'He has destroyed himself. Not more than half-an-hour ago. Hung himself in the grove.'

I turned sick, taking one thing with another, comparing this recollection with that; which I dare say you will think no one but a muff would do.

Ferrar was indeed dead. He had been hiding all day in the three-cornered grove: perhaps waiting for night to get away – perhaps only waiting for night to go home again. Who can tell? About half-past two,

Luke Macintosh, a man who sometimes worked for us, sometimes for old Coney, happening to go through the grove, saw him there, and talked with him. The same man, passing back a little before sunset, found him hanging from a tree, dead. Macintosh ran with the news to Crabb Cot, and they were now flocking to the scene. When facts came to be examined there appeared only too much reason to think that the unfortunate appearance of the galloping policeman had terrified Ferrar into the act; perhaps – we all hoped it! – had scared his senses quite away. Look at it as we would, it was very dreadful.

But what of the appearance Maria Lease saw? At that time, Ferrar had been dead at least half-an-hour. Was it reality or delusion? That is (as the Squire put it), did her eyes see a real, spectral Daniel Ferrar; or were they deceived by some imagination of the brain? Opinions were divided. Nothing can shake her own steadfast belief in its reality; to her it remains an awful certainty, true and sure as heaven.

If I say that I believe in it too, I shall be called a muff and a double muff. But there is no stumbling-block difficult to be got over. Ferrar, when found, was wearing the seal-skin cap tied over the ears and the thick grey coat buttoned up round him, just as Maria Lease had described to me; and he had never worn them since the previous winter, or taken them out of the chest where they were kept. The old woman at his home did not know he had done it then. When told that he had died in these things, she protested that they were in the chest, and ran up to look for them. But the things were gone.

Vernon Lee

WINTHROP'S ADVENTURE

I

ALL the intimates at the villa S— knew Julian Winthrop to be an odd sort of creature, but I am sure no one ever expected from him such an eccentric scene as that which took place on the first Wednesday of last September.

Winthrop had been a constant visitor at the Countess S—'s villa ever since his arrival in Florence, and the better we knew, the more we liked, his fantastic character. Although quite young, he had shown very considerable talent for painting, but every one seemed to agree that this talent would never come to anything. His nature was too impressionable, too mobile, for steady work; and he cared too much for all kinds of art to devote himself exclusively to any one; above all, he had too ungovernable a fancy, and too uncontrollable a love of detail, to fix and complete any impression in an artistic shape; his ideas and fancies were constantly shifting and changing like the shapes in a kaleidoscope, and their instability and variety were the chief sources of his pleasure. All that he did and thought and said had an irresistible tendency to become arabesque, feelings and moods gliding strangely into each other, thoughts and images growing into inextricable tangles, just as when he played he passed insensibly from one fragment to another totally incongruous, and when he drew one form merged into another beneath his pencil. His head was like his sketch-book – full of delightful scraps of colour and quaint, graceful forms, none finished, one on the top of the other: leaves growing out of heads, houses astride on animals, scraps of melodies noted down across scraps of verse, gleanings from all quarters – all pleasing, and all jumbled into a fantastic, useless, but very delightful whole. In short, Winthrop's artistic talent was frittered away by his love of the picturesque, and his career was spoilt by his love of adventure; but such as he was, he was almost a work of art, a living arabesque himself.

On this particular Wednesday we were all seated out on the terrace of the villa S— at Bellosguardo, enjoying the beautiful serene yellow moonlight and the delightful coolness after an intensely hot day. The Countess S—, who was a great musician, was trying over a violin sonata with one of her friends in the drawing-room, of which the doors opened on to the terrace. Winthrop, who had been particularly gay all the evening, had cleared away the plates and cups from the tea-table, had pulled out his sketch-book and begun drawing in his drowsy, irrelevant fashion – acanthus leaves uncurling into sirens' tails, satyrs growing out of passion flowers, little Dutch manikins in tail coats and pigtails peeping out of tulip leaves under his whimsical pencil, while he listened partly to the music within, partly to the conversation without.

When the violin sonata had been tried over, passage by passage, sufficiently often, the Countess, instead of returning to us on the terrace, addressed us from the drawing-room –

'Remain where you are,' she said; 'I want you to hear an old air which I discovered last week among a heap of rubbish in my father-in-law's lumber room. I think it quite a treasure, as good as a wrought-iron ornament found among a heap of old rusty nails, or a piece of Gubbio majolica found among cracked coffee cups. It is very beautiful to my mind. Just listen.'

The Countess was an uncommonly fine singer, without much voice, and not at all emotional, but highly delicate and refined in execution, and with a great knowledge of music. The air which she deemed beautiful could not fail to really be so; but it was so totally different from all we moderns are accustomed to, that it seemed, with its exquisitely-finished phrases, its delicate vocal twirls and spirals, its symmetrically ordered ornaments, to take one into quite another world of musical feeling, of feeling too subdued and artistic, too subtly and cunningly balanced, to move us more than superficially – indeed, it could not move at all, for it expressed no particular state of feeling; it was difficult to say whether it was sad or cheerful; all that could be said was that it was singularly graceful and delicate.

This is how the piece affected me, and I believe, in less degree, all the rest of our party; but, turning towards Winthrop, I was surprised at seeing how very strong an impression its very first bars had made on him. He was seated at the table, his back turned towards me, but I could see that he had suddenly stopped drawing and was listening with intense eagerness. At one moment I almost fancied I saw his hand tremble as it lay on his sketch-book, as if he were breathing spasmodically. I pulled my chair near his; there could be no doubt, his whole frame was quivering.

'Winthrop,' I whispered.

He paid no attention to me, but continued listening intently, and his hand unconsciously crumpled up the sheet he had drawn on.

'Winthrop,' I repeated, touching his shoulder.

'Be quiet,' he answered quickly, as if shaking me off; 'let me listen.'

There was something almost fierce in his manner; and this intense emotion caused by a piece which did not move any of the rest of us, struck me as being very odd.

He remained with his head between his hands till the end. The piece concluded with a very intricate and beautiful passage of execution, and with a curious sort of sighing fall from a high note on to a lower one, short and repeated at various intervals, with lovely effect.

'Bravo! beautiful!' cried every one. 'A real treasure; so quaint and so elegant, and so admirably sung!'

I looked at Winthrop. He had turned round; his face was flushed, and he leaned against his chair as if oppressed by emotion.

The Countess returned to the terrace. 'I am glad you like the piece,' she said; 'it is a graceful thing. Good heavens! Mr Winthrop!' she suddenly interrupted herself; 'what is the matter? are you ill?'

For ill he certainly did look.

He rose and, making an effort, answered in a husky, uncertain voice –

'It's nothing; I suddenly felt cold. I think I'll go in – or rather, no, I'll stay. What is – what is that air you have just sung?'

'That air?' she answered absently, for the sudden change in Winthrop's manner put everything else out of her thoughts. 'That air? Oh! it is by a very forgotten composer of the name of Barbella, who lived somewhere about the year 1780.' It was evident that she considered this question as a sort of mask to his sudden emotion.

'Would you let me see the score?' he asked quickly.

'Certainly. Will you come into the drawing-room? I left it on the piano.'

The piano candles were still lit; and as they stood there she watched his face with as much curiosity as myself. But Winthrop took no notice of either of us; he had eagerly snatched the score, and was looking at it in a fixed, vacant way. When he looked up his face was ashy; he handed me the score mechanically. It was an old yellow, blurred manuscript, in some now disused clef, and the initial words, written in a grand, florid style, were: 'Sei Regina, io son pastore'. The Countess was still under the impression that Winthrop was trying to hide his agitation by pretending great interest in the song; but I, having seen his extraordinary emotion during its performance, could not doubt of the connection between them.

'You say the piece is very rare,' said Winthrop; 'do you – do you then think that no one besides yourself is acquainted with it at present?'

'Of course I can't affirm that,' answered the Countess, 'but this much I know, that Professor G—, who is one of the most learned of musical authorities, and to whom I showed the piece, had heard neither of it nor of its composer, and that he positively says it exists in no musical archives in Italy or in Paris.'

'Then how,' I asked, 'do you know that it is of about the year 1780?'

'By the style; Professor G— compared it at my request with some compositions of that day, and the style perfectly coincides.'

'You think, then,' continued Winthrop slowly, but eagerly – 'you think, then, that no one else sings it at present?'

'I should say not; at least it seems highly unlikely.'

Winthrop was silent, and continued looking at the score, but, as it seemed to me, mechanically.

Some of the rest of the party had meanwhile entered the drawing-room.

'Did you notice Mr Winthrop's extraordinary behaviour?' whispered a lady to the Countess. 'What *has* happened to him?'

'I can't conceive. He is excessively impressionable, but I don't see how that piece could impress him at all; it is a sweet thing, but so unemotional,' I answered.

'That piece!' replied the Countess: 'you don't suppose that piece has anything to do with it?'

'Indeed I do; it has everything to do with it. In short, I noticed that from the very first notes it violently affected him.'

'Then all these inquiries about it?'

'Are perfectly genuine.'

'It cannot be the piece itself which has moved him, and he can scarcely have heard it before. It's very odd. There certainly is something the matter with him.'

There certainly was; Winthrop was excessively pale and agitated, all the more so as he perceived that he had become an object of universal curiosity. He evidently wished to make his escape, but was afraid of doing so too suddenly. He was standing behind the piano, looking mechanically at the old score.

'Have you ever heard that piece before, Mr Winthrop?' asked the Countess, unable to restrain her curiosity.

He looked up, much discomposed, and answered after a moment's hesitation: 'How can I have heard it, since you are the sole possessor of it?'

'The sole possessor? Oh! I never said that. I thought it unlikely, but perhaps there is some other. Tell me, is there another? Where did you hear that piece before?'

'I did not say I had heard it before,' he rejoined hurriedly.

'But have you, or have you not?' persisted the Countess.

'I never have,' he answered decidedly, but immediately reddened as if conscious of prevarication. 'Don't ask me any questions,' he added quickly; 'it worries me,' and in a minute he was off.

We looked at each other in mute astonishment. This astonishing behaviour, this mixture of concealment and rudeness, above all, the violent excitement in which Winthrop had evidently been, and his unaccountable eagerness respecting the piece which the Countess had sung, all this entirely baffled our efforts at discovery.

'There is some mystery at the bottom of it,' we said, and further we could not get.

Next evening, as we were seated once more in the Countess's drawing-room, we of course reverted to Winthrop's extraordinary behaviour.

'Do you think he will return soon?' asked one of us.

'I should think he would rather let the matter blow over, and wait till we had forgotten his absurdity,' answered the Countess.

At that moment the door opened, and Winthrop entered.

He seemed confused and at a loss what to say; he did not answer our trivial remarks, but suddenly burst out, as if with a great effort:

'I have come to beg you to forgive my last night's behaviour. Forgive my rudeness and my want of openness; but I could not have explained anything then: that piece, you must know, had given me a great shock.'

'A great shock? And how could it give you a shock?' we all exclaimed.

'You surely don't mean that so prim a piece as that could have affected you?' asked the Countess's sister.

'If it did,' added the Countess, 'it is the greatest miracle music ever worked.'

'It is difficult to explain the matter,' hesitated Winthrop; 'but – in short – that piece gave me a shock because as soon as I heard the first bars I recognised it.'

'And you told me you had never heard it before!' exclaimed the Countess indignantly.

'I know I did; it was not true, but neither was it quite false. All I can say is that I knew the piece; whether I had heard it before, or not, I knew it – in fact,' he dashed out, 'you will think me mad, but I had long doubted whether the piece existed at all, and I was so moved just because your performance proved that it *did* exist. Look here,' and pulling a sketch-book from his pocket he was just about to open it when he stopped – 'Have you got the notes of that piece?' he asked hurriedly.

'Here they are,' and the Countess handed him the old roll of music.

He did not look at it, but turned over the leaves of his sketch-book.

'See,' he said after a minute; 'look at this,' and he pushed the open sketch-book across the table to us. On it, among a lot of sketches, were some roughly ruled lines, with some notes scrawled in pencil, and the words 'Sei Regina, io Pastor sono'.

'Why, this is the beginning of the very air!' exclaimed the Countess. 'How did you get this?'

We compared the notes in the sketch-book with those on the score; they were the same, but in another clef and tone.

Winthrop sat opposite, looking doggedly at us. After a moment he remarked –

'They are the same notes, are they not? Well, this pencil scrawl was done in July of last year, while the ink of this score has been dry ninety years; yet when I wrote down these notes, I swear I did not know that any such score existed, and until yesterday I disbelieved it.'

'Then,' remarked one of the party, 'there are only two explanations: either you composed this melody yourself, not knowing that some one else had done so ninety years ago; or, you heard that piece without knowing what it was.'

'Explanation!' cried Winthrop contemptuously; 'why, don't you see, that it is just what needs explaining! Of course, I either composed it myself or heard it, but which of the two was it?'

We remained much humbled and silenced.

'This is a very astonishing puzzle,' remarked the Countess, 'and I think it useless to rack our brains about it since Mr Winthrop is the only person who can explain it. We don't and can't understand; he can and must explain it himself. I don't know,' she added, 'whether there is any reason for not explaining the mystery to us; but if not, I wish you would.'

'There is no reason,' he answered, 'except that you would set me down as a maniac. The story is so absurd a one – you will never believe me – and yet . . .'

'Then there is a story at the bottom of it!' exclaimed the Countess. 'What is it? Can't you tell it us?'

Winthrop gave a sort of deprecatory shrug, and trifled with the paper cutters and dogseared the books on the table. 'Well,' he said at last, 'if you really wish to know – why – perhaps I might as well tell it you; only don't tell me afterwards that I am mad. Nothing can alter the fact of the real existence of that piece; and, as long as you continue to regard it as unique, I cannot but regard my adventure as being true.'

We were afraid lest he might slip away through all these deprecatory premisings, and that after all we might hear no story whatever; so we summoned him to begin at once, and he, keeping his head well in the shadow of the lampshade, and scribbling as usual on his sketch-book, began his narrative, at first slowly and hesitatingly, with plentiful interruptions, but, as he grew more interested in it, becoming extremely rapid and dramatic, and exceedingly minute in details.

II

You must know (said Winthrop), that about a year and a half ago I spent the autumn with some cousins of mine, rambling about Lombardy. In poking into all sorts of odd nooks and corners, we made the acquaintance at M— of a highly learned and highly snuffy old gentleman (I believe he was a count or a marchese), who went by the nickname of Maestro Fa Diesis (Master F-Sharp), and who possessed a very fine collection of things musical, a perfect museum. He had a handsome old palace, which was literally tumbling to pieces, and of which the whole first floor was taken up by his collections. His old MSS., his precious missals, his papyri, his autographs, his black-letter books, his prints and pictures, his innumerable ivory inlaid harpsichords and ebony fretted lutes and viols, lived in fine, spacious rooms, with carved oaken ceilings and painted window frames, while he lived in some miserable little garret to the back, on what I can't say, but I should judge, by the spectral appearance of his old woman servant and of a half-imbecile boy who served him, on nothing more substantial than bean husks and warm water. They seemed to suffer from this diet; but I suspect that their master must have absorbed some mysterious vivifying fluid from his MSS. and old instruments, for he seemed to be made of steel, and was the most provokingly active old fellow, keeping one's nerves in perpetual irritation by his friskiness and volubility. He cared for nothing in the wide world save his collections; he had cut down tree after tree, he had sold field after field and farm after farm; he had sold his furniture, his tapestries, his plate, his family papers, his own clothes. He would have taken the tiles off his roof and the glass out of his windows to buy some score of the sixteenth century, some illuminated mass book or some Cremonese fiddle. For music itself I firmly believe he cared not a jot, and regarded it as useful only inasmuch as it had produced the objects of his passion, the things which he could spend all his life in dusting, labelling, counting, and cataloguing, for not a chord, not a note was ever heard in his house, and he would have died rather than spend a soldino on going to the opera.

My cousin, who is music mad after a fashion, quickly secured the old gentleman's good will by accepting a hundred commissions for the obtaining of catalogues and the attending of sales, and we were consequently permitted daily to enter that strange, silent house full of musical things, and to examine its contents at our leisure; always, however, under old Fa Diesis's vigilant supervision. The house, its contents, and proprietor formed a grotesque whole, which had a certain charm for me. I used often to fancy that the silence could be only apparent; that, as soon as the master had drawn his bolts and gone off to bed, all this slumbering music would awake, that the pictures of dead musicians would slip out of their frames, the glass cases fly open, the big paunched inlaid lutes turn into stately Flemish burghers, with brocaded doublets; the yellow, faded sides of the Cremonese bass viols expand into the stiff satin hoops of powdered ladies; and the little ribbed mandolins put forth a parti-coloured leg and a bushy-haired head, and hop about as Provençal Court dwarfs or Renaissance pages, while the Egyptian sistrum and fife players would slip from off the hieroglyphics of the papyrus, and all the parchment palimpsests of Greek musicians turn into chlamys-robed auletes, and citharœdi; then the kettledrums and tamtams would strike up, the organ tubes would suddenly be filled with sound, the old gilded harpsichords would jingle like fury, the old chapel-master yonder, in his peruke and furred robe, would beat time on his picture frame, and the whole motley company set to dancing; until all of a sudden old Fa Diesis, awakened by the noise, and suspecting thieves, would rush in wildly in his dressing-gown, a three-wicked kitchen lamp in one hand and his great-grandfather's court sword in the other, when all the dancers and players would start and slide back into their frames and cases. I should not, however, have gone so often to the old gentleman's museum had not my cousin extorted from me the promise of a water-colour sketch of a picture of Palestrina, which, for some reason or other, she (for the cousin was a lady, which explains my docility) chose to consider as particularly authentic. It was a monster, a daub, which I shuddered at, and my admiration for Palestrina would have rather induced me to burn the hideous, blear-eyed, shoulderless thing; but musical folk have their whims, and hers was to hang a copy of this monstrosity over her grand piano. So I acceded, took my drawing block and easel, and set off for Fa Diesis's palace. This palace was a queer old place, full of ups and downs and twistings and turnings, and in going to the only tolerably lighted room of the house, whither the delightful subject for my brush had been transported for my convenience, we had to pass through a narrow and wriggling corridor somewhere in the heart of the building. In doing so we passed by a door up some steps.

'By the way,' exclaimed old Fa Diesis, 'have I shown you this? 'Tis of no great value, but still, as a painter, it may interest you.' He mounted the steps, pushed open the door, which was ajar, and ushered me into a small, bleak, whitewashed lumber-room, peopled with broken book-shelves, crazy music desks, and unsteady chairs and tables, the whole covered by a goodly layer of dust. On the walls were a few time-stained portraits in corslets and bobwigs, the senatorial ancestors of Fa Diesis, who had had to make room for the bookshelves and instrument-cases filling the state rooms. The old gentleman opened a shutter, and threw the full light upon another old picture, from whose cracked surface he deliberately swept away the dust with the rusty sleeve of his fur-lined coat.

I approached it. 'This is not a bad picture,' I said at once; 'by no means a bad picture.'

'Indeed,' exclaimed Fa Diesis. 'Oh, then, perhaps, I may sell it. What do you think? Is it worth much?'

I smiled, 'Well, it is not a Raphael,' I answered; 'but, considering its date and the way people then smeared, it is quite creditable.'

'Ah!' sighed the old fellow, much disappointed.

It was a half-length, life-size portrait of a man in the costume of the latter part of the last century – a pale lilac silk coat, a pale pea-green satin waistcoat, both extremely delicate in tint, and a deep warm-tinted amber cloak; the voluminous cravat was loosened, the large collar flapped back, the body slightly turned, and the head somewhat looking over the shoulder, Cenci fashion.

The painting was uncommonly good for an Italian portrait of the eighteenth century, and had much that reminded me, though of course vastly inferior technically, of Greuze – a painter I detest, and who yet fascinates me. The features were irregular and small, with intensely red lips and a crimson flush beneath the transparent bronzed skin; the eyes were slightly upturned and looking sideways, in harmony with the turn of the head and the parted lips, and they were beautiful, brown, soft, like those of some animals, with a vague, wistful depth of look. The whole had the clear greyness, the hazy, downy touch of Greuze, and left that strange mixed impression which all the portraits of his school do. The face was not beautiful; it had something at once sullen and effeminate, something odd and not entirely agreeable; yet it attracted and riveted your attention with its dark, warm colour, rendered all the more striking for the light, pearly, powdered locks, and the general lightness and haziness of touch.

'It is a very good portrait in its way,' I said, 'though not of the sort that people buy. There are faults of drawing here and there, but the colour and touch are good. By whom is it?'

Old Fa Diesis, whose vision of heaps of banknotes to be obtained in exchange for the picture had been rudely cut short, seemed rather sulky.

'I don't know by whom it is,' he grumbled. 'If it's bad it's bad, and may remain here.'

'And whom does it represent?'

'A singer. You see he has got a score in his hand. A certain Rinaldi, who lived about a hundred years ago.'

Fa Diesis had rather a contempt for singers, regarding them as poor creatures, who were of no good, since they left nothing behind them that could be collected, except indeed in the case of Madame Banti, one of whose lungs he possessed in spirits of wine.

We went out of the room, and I set about my copy of that abominable old portrait of Palestrina. At dinner that day I mentioned the portrait of the singer to my cousins, and somehow or other I caught myself using expressions about it which I should not have used in the morning. In trying to describe the picture my recollection of it seemed to differ from the original impression. It returned to my mind as something strange and striking. My cousin wished to see it, so the next morning she accompanied me to old Fa Diesis's palace. How it affected her I don't know; but for me it had a queer sort of interest, quite apart from that in the technical execution. There was something peculiar and unaccountable in the look of that face, a yearning, half-pained look, which I could not well define to myself. I became gradually aware that the portrait was, so to speak, haunting me. Those strange red lips and wistful eyes rose up in my mind. I instinctively and without well knowing why reverted to it in our conversation.

'I wonder who he was,' I said, as we sat in the square behind the cathedral apse, eating our ices in the cool autumn evening.

'Who?' asked my cousin.

'Why, the original of that portrait at old Fa Diesis's; such a weird face. I wonder who he was?'

My cousins paid no attention to my speech, for they did not share that vague, unaccountable feeling with which the picture had inspired me, but as we walked along the silent porticoed streets, where only the illuminated sign of an inn or the chestnut-roasting brazier of a fruit stall flickered in the gloom, and crossed the vast desolate square, surrounded by Oriental-like cupolas and minarets, where the green bronze condottiere rode on his green bronze charger – during our evening ramble through the quaint Lombard city my thoughts kept reverting to the picture, with its hazy, downy colour and curious, unfathomed expression.

The next day was the last of our stay at M—, and I went to Fa Diesis's palace to finish my sketch, to take leave, present thanks for his civility towards us, and inquire whether we could execute any commission for him. In going to the room where I had left my easel and painting things, I passed through the dark, wriggling lobby and by the door up the three steps. The door was ajar, and I entered the room where the portrait was. I approached and examined it carefully. The man was apparently singing, or rather about to sing, for the red, well-cut lips were parted; and in his hand – a beautiful plump, white, blue-veined hand, strangely out of keeping with the brown, irregular face – he held an open roll of notes. The notes were mere unintelligible blotches, but I made out, written on the score, the name – Ferdinando Rinaldi, 1782; and above, the words – 'Sei Regina, io pastor sono'. The face had a beauty, a curious, irregular beauty, and in those deep, soft eyes there was something like a magnetic power, which I felt, and which others must have felt before me. I finished my sketch, strapped up my easel and paint-box, gave a parting snarl at the horrible blear-eyed, shoulderless Palestrina, and prepared to leave. Fa Diesis, who, in his snuffy fur-lined coat, the tassel of his tarnished blue skull-cap bobbing over his formidable nose, was seated at a desk hard by, rose also, and politely escorted me through the passage.

'By the way,' I asked, 'do you know an air called, "Sei Regina, io Pastor sono"?'

'"Sei Regina, io Pastor sono?" No, such an air doesn't exist.' All airs not in his library had no business to exist, even if they did.

'It must exist,' I persisted; 'those words are written on the score held by the singer on that picture of yours.'

'That's no proof,' he cried peevishly; 'it may be merely some fancy title, or else – or else it may be some rubbishy *trunk air* (aria di baule).'

'What is a *trunk air*?' I asked in amazement.

'A *trunk air*,' he explained, 'was a wretched air – merely a few trumpery notes and lots of pauses, on to which great singers used formerly to make their own variations. They used to insert them in every opera they sang in, and drag them all over the world; that was why they were called trunk airs. They had no merit of their own – no one ever cared to sing them except the singer to whom they belonged – no one ever kept such rubbish as that! It all went to wrap up sausages or make curl-papers.' And old Fa Diesis laughed his grim little cackling laugh.

He then dropped the subject, and said –

'If I had an opportunity, or one of my illustrious family, of obtaining any catalogues of musical curiosities or attending any sales' – he was still searching for the first printed copy of Guido of Arezzo's 'Micrologus' – he had copies of all the other editions, a unique collection; there was also one specimen wanting to complete his set of Amati's fiddles, one with *fleurs-de-lys* on the sounding board, constructed for Charles IX of France – alas! he had spent years looking for that instrument – he would pay – yes, he, as I saw him there, he standing before me, would pay five hundred golden *marenghi** for that violin with the *fleurs-de-lys* . . .

'Pardon me,' I interrupted rather rudely; 'may I see this picture again?'

We had come to the door up the three steps.

'Certainly,' he answered, and continued his speech about the Amati violin with the *fleurs-de-lys*, getting more and more frisky and skippery every moment.

That strange face with its weird, yearning look! I remained motionless before it while the old fellow jabbered and gesticulated like a maniac. What a deep incomprehensible look in those eyes!

'Was he a very famous singer?' I asked, by way of saying something.

'He? *Eh altro!* I should think so! Do you think perhaps the singers of that day were like ours? Pooh! Look at all they did in that day. Their paper made of linen rag, no tearing *that*; and how they built their violins! Oh, what times those were!'

'Do you know anything about this man?' I asked.

'About this singer, this Rinaldi? Oh, yes; he was a very great singer, but he ended badly.'

'Badly? in what way?'

'Why – you know what such people are, and then youth! we have all been young, all young!' and old Fa Diesis shrugged his shrivelled person.

'What happened to him?' I persisted, continuing to look at the portrait; it seemed as if there were life in those soft, velvety eyes, and as if those red lips were parting in a sigh – a long, weary sigh.

'Well,' answered Fa Diesis, 'this Ferdinando Rinaldi was a very great singer. About the year 1780 he took service with the Court of Parma. There, it is said, he obtained too great notice from a lady in high favour at Court, and was consequently dismissed. Instead of going to a distance, he kept hanging about the frontier of Parma, now here, now there, for he had many friends among the nobility. Whether he was suspected of attempting to return to Parma, or whether he spoke with less reserve than he should, I don't know. *Basta!* one fine morning he was found lying on the staircase landing of our Senator Negri's house, stabbed.'

Old Fa Diesis pulled out his horn snuff-box.

'Who had done it, no one ever knew or cared to know. A packet of letters, which his valet said he always carried on his person, was all that was found missing. The lady left Parma and entered the Convent of the Clarisse here; she was my father's aunt, and this portrait belonged to her. A common story, a common story in those days.'

And the old gentleman rammed his long nose with snuff.

---

* A Lombard coin struck by Napoleon after the battle of Marengo, and by which elderly people still occasionally count.

'You really don't think I could sell the picture?' he asked.

'No!' I answered very decidedly, for I felt a sort of shudder. I took leave, and that evening we set off for Rome.

Winthrop paused, and asked for a cup of tea. He was flushed and seemed excited, but at the same time anxious to end his story. When he had taken his tea, he pushed back his irregular hair with both hands, gave a little sigh of recollection, and began again as follows:—

III

I returned to M— the next year, on my way to Venice, and stopped a couple of days in the old place, having to bargain for certain Renaissance carved work, which a friend wished to buy. It was midsummer; the fields which I had left planted with cabbages and covered with white frost were tawny with ripe corn, and the vine garlands drooped down to kiss the tall, compact green hemp; the dark streets were reeking with heat, the people were all sprawling about under colonnade and awning; it was the end of June in Lombardy, God's own orchard on earth. I went to old Fa Diesis's palace to ask whether he had any commissions for Venice; he might, indeed, be in the country, but the picture, *the* portrait was at his palace, and that was enough for me. I had often thought of it in the winter, and I wondered whether now, with the sun blazing through every chink, I should still be impressed by it as I had been in the gloomy autumn. Fa Diesis was at home, and overjoyed to see me; he jumped and frisked about like a figure in the Dance of Death, in intense excitement about certain MSS. he had lately seen. He narrated, or rather acted, for it was all in the present tense and accompanied by appropriate gestures, a journey he had recently made to Guastalla to see a psaltery at a monastery; how he had bargained for a post-chaise; how the post-chaise had upset half-way; how he had sworn at the driver; how he had rung – drling, drling – at the monastery door; how he cunningly pretended to be in quest of an old, valueless crucifix; how the monks had had the impudence to ask a hundred and fifty francs for it. How he had hummed and hah'd, and, pretending suddenly to notice the psaltery, had asked what it was, etc., as if he did not know; and finally struck the bargain for both crucifix and psaltery for a hundred and fifty francs – a psaltery of the year 1310 for a hundred and fifty francs! And those idiots of monks were quite overjoyed! They thought they had cheated me – cheated me! And he frisked about in an ecstasy of pride and triumph. We had got to the well-known door; it was open; I could see the portrait. The sun streamed brightly on the brown face and light powdered locks. I know not how; I felt a momentary giddiness and sickness, as if of long desired, unexpected pleasure; it lasted but an instant, and I was ashamed of myself.

Fa Diesis was in splendid spirits.

'Do you see that?' he said, forgetting all he had previously told me – 'that is a certain Ferdinando Rinaldi, a singer, who was assassinated for making love to my great-aunt'; and he stalked about in great glee, thinking of the psaltery at Guastalla, and fanning himself complacently with a large green fan.

A thought suddenly struck me –

'It happened here at M—, did it not?'

'To be sure.'

And Fa Diesis continued shuffling to and fro in his old red and blue dressing-gown, with parrots and cherry branches on it.

'Did you never know anyone who had seen him – heard him?'

'I? Never. How could I? He was killed ninety-four years ago.'

Ninety-four years ago! I looked up at the portrait; ninety-four years ago! and yet – the eyes seemed to me to have a strange, fixed, intent look.

'And where—' I hesitated despite myself, 'where did it happen?'

'That few people know; no one, probably, except me, nowadays,' he answered with satisfaction. 'But my father pointed out the house to me when I was little; it had belonged to a Marchese Negri, but somehow or other, after that affair, no one would live there any longer, and it was left to rot; already, when I was a child, it was all deserted and falling to pieces. A fine house, though! A fine house! and one which ought to have been worth something. I saw it again some years ago – I rarely go outside the gates now – outside Porta San Vitale – about a mile.'

'Outside Porta San Vitale? the house where this Rinaldi was – it is still there?'

Fa Diesis looked at me with intense contempt.

'*Bagatella!*' (fiddlestick) he exclaimed. 'Do you think a villa flies away like that?'

'You are sure?'

'*Per Bacco!* as sure as that I see you – outside Porta San Vitale, an old tumbledown place with obelisks and vases, and that sort of thing.'

We had come to the head of the staircase. 'Good-bye', I said; 'I'll return tomorrow for your parcels for Venice,' and I ran down the stair. 'Outside Porta San Vitale!' I said to myself; 'outside Porta San Vitale!' It was six in the afternoon and the heat still intense; I hailed a crazy old cab, a sky-blue carriage of the year '20, with a cracked hood and emblazoned panels. '*Dove commanda?*' (whither do you command?) asked the sleepy driver.

'Outside Porta San Vitale,' I cried. He touched his bony, long-maned white horse, and off we jolted over the uneven pavement, past the red Lombard cathedral and baptistery, through the long, dark Via San Vitale, with its grand old palaces; under the red gate with the old word 'Libertas' still on it, along a dusty road bordered by acacias out into the rich Lombard plain. On we rattled through the fields of corn, hemp, and glossy dark maize, ripening under the rich evening sun. In the distance the purple walls and belfries and shining cupolas gleaming in the light; beyond, the vast blue and gold and hazy plain, bounded by the far-off Alps. The air was warm and serene, everything quiet and solemn. But I was excited. I sought out every large country house; I went wherever a tall belvedere tower peeped from behind the elms and poplars; I crossed and recrossed the plain, taking one lane after another, as far as where the road branched off to Crevalcuore; passed villa after villa, but found none with vases and obelisks, none crumbling and falling, none that could have been *the* villa. What wonder, indeed? Fa Diesis had seen it, but Fa Diesis was seventy, and that – that had happened ninety-four years ago! Still I might be mistaken; I might have gone too far or not far enough – there was lane within lane and road within road. Perhaps the house was screened by trees, or perhaps it lay towards the next gate. So I went again, through the cyclamen-lined lanes, overhung by gnarled mulberries and oaks; I looked up at one house after another: all were old, many dilapidated, some seeming old churches with walled-up colonnades, others built up against old watch-towers; but of what old Fa Diesis had described I could see nothing. I asked the driver, and the driver asked the old women and the fair-haired children who crowded out of the little farms. Did anyone know of a large deserted house with obelisks and vases – a house that had once belonged to a Marchese Negri? Not in that neighbourhood; there was the Villa Montecasignoli with the tower and the sundial, which was dilapidated enough, and the Casino Fava crumbling in yonder cabbage-field, but neither had vases nor obelisks, neither had ever belonged to a Marchese Negri.

At last I gave it up in despair. Ninety-four years ago! The house no longer existed; so I returned to my inn, where the three jolly mediaeval pilgrims swung over the door lamp; took my supper and tried to forget the whole matter.

Next day I went and finally settled with the owner of the carved work I had been commissioned to buy, and then I sauntered lazily about the old town. The day after there was to be a great fair, and preparations were being made for it; baskets and hampers being unloaded, and stalls put up everywhere in the great square; festoons of tinware and garlands of onions were slung across the Gothic arches of the Town Hall and to its massive bronze torch-holders; there was a quack already holding forth on the top of his stage coach, with a skull and many bottles before him, and a little bespangled page handing about his bills; there was a puppet-show at a corner, with a circle of empty chairs round it, just under the stone pulpit where the monks of the Middle Ages has once exhorted the Montagus and Capulets of M— to make peace and embrace. I sauntered about among the crockery and glassware, picking my way among the packing-cases and hay, and among the vociferating peasants and townsfolk. I looked at the figs and cherries and red peppers in the baskets, at the old ironwork, rusty keys, nails, chains, bits of ornament on the stalls; at the vast blue and green glazed umbrellas, at the old prints and images of saints tied against the church bench, at the whole moving, quarrelling, gesticulating crowd. I bought an old silver death's-head trinket at the table of a perambulating watch-maker, and some fresh sweet peas and roses from a peasant woman selling fowls and turkeys; then I turned into the maze of quaint little paved streets, protected by chains from carts and carriages, and named after mediæval hostelries and labelled on little slabs, 'Scimmia' (monkey), 'Alemagna' (Germany), 'Venetia', and, most singular of all, 'Brocca in dosso' (Jug on the Back). Behind the great, red, time-stained, castle-like Town Hall were a number of tinkers' dens; and beneath its arches hung caldrons, pitchers, saucepans, and immense pudding moulds with the imperial eagle of Austria on them, capacious and ancient enough to have contained the puddings of generations of German Cæsars. Then I poked into some of those wondrous curiosity-shops of M—, little black dens, where oaken presses contain heaps and heaps of brocaded dresses and embroidered waistcoats, and yards of lace, and splendid chasubles, the spoils of centuries of magnificence. I walked down the main street and saw a crowd collected round a man with an immense white crested owl; the creature was such a splendid one, I determined to buy him and keep him in my studio at Venice, but when I approached him he flew at me, shaking his wings and screeching so that I beat an ignominious retreat. At length I returned to the square and sat down beneath an awning, where two bare-legged urchins served me excellent snow and lemon juice, at the price of a sou the glass. In short, I enjoyed my last day at M— amazingly; and, in this bright, sunny square, with all the bustle about me, I wondered whether the person who the previous evening had scoured the country in search of a crazy villa where a man had been assassinated ninety-four years ago, could really and truly have been myself.

So I spent the morning; and the afternoon I passed indoors, packing up the delicate carved work with my own hands, although the perspiration ran down my face, and I gasped for air. At length, when evening and coolness were approaching, I took my hat and went once more to Fa Diesis's palace.

I found the old fellow in his many-coloured dressing-gown, seated in his cool, dusky room, among his inlaid lutes and Cremonese viols, carefully mending the torn pages of an illuminated missal, while his old, witchlike housekeeper was cutting out and pasting labels on to a heap of manuscript scores on the table. Fa Diesis got up, jumped about ecstatically, made magnificent speeches, and said that since I insisted on being of use to him, he had prepared half a dozen letters, which I might kindly leave on various correspondents of his at Venice, in order to save the twopenny stamp for each. The grim, lank, old fellow, with his astounding dressing-gown and cap, his lantern-jawed housekeeper, his old, morose grey cat, and his splendid harpsichords and lutes and missals, amused me more than usual. I sat with him for some time while he patched away at his missal. Mechanically I turned over the yellow pages of a music book that lay, waiting for a label, under my hand, and mechanically my eye fell on the words, in faded, yellow ink, at the top of one of the pieces, the indication of its performer:–

Rondò di Cajo Gracco, 'Mille pene mio tesoro', per il Signor Ferdinando Rinaldi. Parma, 1782.

I positively started, for somehow that whole business had gone out of my mind.

'What have you got there?' asked Fa Diesis, perhaps a little suspic-iously, and leaning across the table, he twitched the notes towards him –

'Oh, only that old opera of Cimarosa's – Ah, by the way, *per Bacco*, how could I have made such a mistake yesterday? Didn't I tell you that Rinaldi had been stabbed in a villa outside Porta San Vitale?'

'Yes,' I cried eagerly. 'Why?'

'Why, I can't conceive how, but I must have been thinking about that blessed psaltery at San Vitale, at Guastalla. The villa where Rinaldi was killed is outside Porta San Zaccaria, in the direction of the river, near that old monastery where there are those frescoes by – I forget the fellow's name, that all the foreigners go to see. Don't you know?'

'Ah,' I exclaimed, 'I understand.' And I did understand, for Porta San Zaccaria happens to be at exactly the opposite end of the town to Porta San Vitale, and here was the explanation of my unsuccessful search of the previous evening. So after all the house might still be standing; and the desire to see it again seized hold of me. I rose, took the letters, which I strongly suspected contained other letters whose postage was to be saved in the same way, by being delivered by the original correspondent, and prepared to depart.

'Good-bye, good-bye,' said old Fa Diesis, with effusion, as we passed through the dark passage in order to get to the staircase. 'Continue, my dear friend, in those paths of wisdom and culture which the youth of our days has so miserably abandoned, in order that the sweet promise of your happy silver youth be worthily accomplished in your riper— Ah, by the way,' he interrupted himself, 'I have forgotten to give you a little pamphlet of mine on the manufacture of violin strings which I wish to send as an act of reverence to my old friend the Commander of the garrison of Venice'; and off he scuddled. I was near the door up the three steps and could not resist the temptation of seeing the picture once more. I pushed open the door and entered; a long ray of declining sunlight, reflected from the neighbouring red church tower, fell across the face of the portrait, playing in the light, powdered hair and on the downy, well-cut lips, and ending in a tremulous crimson stain on the boarded floor. I went close up to the picture; there was the name 'Ferdinando Rinaldi, 1782', on the roll of music he was holding; but the notes themselves were mere imitative, meaningless smears and blotches, although the title of the piece stood distinct and legible – 'Sei Regina, io Pastor sono'.

'Why, where is he?' cried Fa Diesis's shrill voice in the passage. 'Ah, here you are'; and he handed me the pamphlet, pompously addressed to the illustrious General S—, at Venice. I put it in my pocket.

'You won't forget to deliver it?' he asked, and then went on with the speech he had before begun: 'Let the promise of your happy silver youth be fulfilled in a golden manhood, in order that the world may mark down your name *albo lapillo*. Ah,' he continued, 'perhaps we shall never meet again. I am old, my dear friend, I am old!' and he smacked his lips. 'Perhaps, when you return to M—, I may have gone to rest with my immortal ancestors, who, as you know, intermarried with the Ducal family of Sforza, A.D. 1490!'

The last time! This might be the last time I saw the picture! What would become of it after old Fa Diesis's death? I turned once more towards it, in leaving the room; the last flicker of light fell on the dark, yearning face, and it seemed, in the trembling sunbeam, as if the head turned and looked towards me. I never saw the portrait again.

I walked along quickly through the darkening streets, on through the crowd of loiterers and pleasure seekers, on towards Porta San Zaccaria. It was late, but if I hastened, I might still have an hour of twilight; and next morning I had to leave M—. This was my last opportunity, I could not relinquish it; so on I went, heedless of the ominous puffs of warm, damp air, and of the rapidly clouding sky.

It was St John's Eve, and bonfires began to appear on the little hills round the town; fire-balloons were sent up, and the great bell of the cathedral boomed out in honour of the coming holiday. I threaded my way through the dusty streets and out by Porta San Zaccaria. I walked smartly along the avenues of poplars along the walls, and then cut across into the fields by a lane leading towards the river. Behind me were the city walls, all crenellated and jagged; in front the tall belfry and cypresses of the Carthusian monastery; above, the starless, moonless sky, overhung by heavy clouds. The air was mild and relaxing; every now and then there came a gust of hot, damp wind, making a shudder run across the silver poplars and trailed vines; a few heavy drops fell, admonishing me of the coming storm, and every moment some of the light faded away. But I was determined; was not this my last opportunity? So on I stumbled through the rough lane, on through the fields of corn and sweet, fresh-scented hemp, the fireflies dancing in fantastic spirals before me. Something dark wriggled across my path; I caught it on my stick: it was a long, slimy snake which slipped quickly off. The frogs roared for rain, the crickets sawed with ominous loudness, the fireflies crossed and recrossed before me; yet on I went, quicker and quicker in the fast increasing darkness. A broad sheet of pink lightning and a distant rumble: more drops fell; the frogs roared louder, the crickets sawed faster and faster, the air got heavier and the sky yellow and lurid where the sun had set; yet on I went towards the river. Suddenly down came a tremendous stream of rain, as if the heavens had opened, and with it down came the darkness, complete though sudden; the storm had changed evening into the deepest night. What should I do? Return? How? I saw a light glimmering behind a dark mass of trees; I would go on; there must be a house out there, where I could take shelter till the storm was over; I was too far to get back to the town. So on I went in the pelting rain. The lane made a sudden bend, and I found myself in an open space in the midst of the fields, before an iron gate, behind which, surrounded by trees, rose a dark, vast mass; a rent in the clouds permitted me to distinguish a gaunt, grey villa, with broken obelisks on its triangular front. My heart gave a great thump; I stopped, the rain continuing to stream down. A dog began to bark furiously from a little peasant's house on the other side of road, whence issued the light I had perceived. The door opened and a man appeared holding a lamp.

'Who's there?' he cried.

I went up to him. He held up the light and surveyed me.

'Ah!' he said immediately, 'a stranger – a foreigner. Pray enter, *illustrissimo.'* My dress and my sketch-book had immediately revealed what I was; he took me for an artist, one of the many who visited the neighbouring Carthusian Abbey, who had lost his way in the maze of little lanes.

I shook the rain off me and entered the low room, whose whitewashed walls were lit yellow by the kitchen fire. A picturesque group of peasants stood out in black outline on the luminous background: an old woman was spinning on her classic distaff, a young one was unravelling skeins of thread on a sort of rotating star; another was cracking pea pods; an old, close-shaven man sat smoking with his elbows on the table, and opposite to him sat a portly priest in three-cornered hat, knee-breeches, and short coat. They rose and looked at me, and welcomed me with the familiar courtesy of their class; the priest offered me his seat, the girl took my soaking coat and hat, and hung them over the fire, the young man brought an immense hempen towel, and proceeded to dry me, much to the general hilarity. They had been reading their usual stories of Charlemagne in their well-thumbed 'Reali di Francia', that encyclopædia of Italian peasants; but they put by their books on my entrance and began talking, questioning me on every possible and impossible subject. Was it true that it always rained in England? (at that rate, remarked the old man shrewdly, how could the English grow grapes; and if they did not make wine, what could they live on?) Was it true that one could pick up lumps of gold somewhere in England? Was there any town as large as M— in that country? etc., etc. The priest thought these questions foolish, and inquired with much gravity after the health of Milord Vellingtone, who, he understood, had been seriously unwell of late. I scarcely listened; I was absent and preoccupied. I gave the women my sketch-book to look over; they were delighted with its contents; mistook all the horses for oxen and all the men for women, and exclaimed and tittered with much glee. The priest, who prided himself on superior education, gave me the blandest encouragement; asked me whether I had been to the picture gallery, whether I had been to the neighbouring Bologna (he was very proud of having been there last St Petronius's day); informed me that the city was the mother of all art, and that the Caracci especially were her most glorious sons, etc., etc. Meanwhile, the rain continued coming down in a steady pour.

'I don't think I shall be able to get home tonight,' said the priest, looking through the window into the darkness. 'My donkey is the most wonderful donkey in the world – quite a human being. When you say "Leone, Leone" to him, he kicks up his heels and stands on his hind legs like an acrobat; indeed he does, upon my honour; but I don't believe even he could find his way through this darkness, and the wheels of my gig would infallibly stick in some rut, and where should I be then? I must stay here overnight, no help for that; but I'm sorry for the Signore here, who will find these very poor quarters.'

'Indeed,' I said, 'I shall be but too happy to stay, if I be sure that I shall be in no one's way.'

'In our way! What a notion!' they all cried.

'That's it,' said the priest, particularly proud of the little vehicle he drove, after the droll fashion of Lombard clergymen. 'And I'll drive the Signore into town tomorrow morning, and you can bring your cart with the vegetables for the fair.'

I paid but little attention to all this; I felt sure I had at length found the object of my search; there, over the way, was the villa; but I seemed almost as far from it as ever, seated in this bright, whitewashed kitchen, among these country folk. The young man asked me timidly, and as a special favour, to make a picture of the girl who was his bride, and very pretty, with laughing, irregular features, and curly crisp golden hair. I took out my pencil and began, I fear not as conscientiously as these good people deserved; but they were enchanted, and stood in a circle round me, exchanging whispered remarks, while the girl sat all giggling and restless on the large wooden settle.

'What a night!' exclaimed the old man. 'What a bad night, and St John's Eve too!'

'What has that to do with it?' I asked.

'Why,' he answered, 'they say that on St John's night they permit dead people to walk about.'

'What rubbish!' cried the priest indignantly; 'who ever told you that? What is there about ghosts in the mass book, or in the Archbishop's pastorals, or in the Holy Fathers of the Church?' and he raised his voice to inquisitorial dignity.

'You may say what you like,' answered the old man doggedly; 'it's true none the less. I've never seen anything myself, and perhaps the Archbishop hasn't either, but I know people who have.'

The priest was about to fall upon him with a deluge of arguments in dialect, when I interrupted.

'To whom does that large house over the way belong?' I waited with anxiety for an answer.

'It belongs to the Avvocato Bargellini,' said the woman with great deference, and they proceeded to inform me that they were his tenants, his *contadini* having charge of all the property belonging to the house; that the Avvocato Bargellini was immensely rich and immensely learned.

'An encyclopædic man!' burst out the priest; 'he knows everything, law, art, geography, mathematics, numismatics, gymnastics!' And he waved his hand between each branch of knowledge. I was disappointed.

'Is it inhabited?' I asked.

'No,' they answered, no one has ever lived in it. 'The Avvocato bought it twenty years ago from the heir of a certain Marchese Negri who died very poor.'

'A Marchese Negri?' I exclaimed; then, after all, I was right.

'But why is it not inhabited, and since when?'

'Oh, since – since always – no one has ever lived in it since the Marchese Negri's grandfather. It is all going to pieces; we keep our garden tools and a few sacks there, but there is no living there – there are no windows or shutters.'

'But why doesn't the Avvocato patch it up?' I persisted. 'It seems a very fine house.'

The old man was going to answer, but the priest glanced at him and answered quickly –

'The position in these fields is unhealthy.'

'Unhealthy!' cried the old man angrily, much annoyed at the priest's interference. 'Unhealthy! why, haven't I lived here these sixty years, and not one of us has had a headache? Unhealthy, indeed! No, the house is a bad house to live in, that's what it is!'

'This is very odd,' I said, 'surely there must be ghosts?' and I tried to laugh.

The word *ghosts* acted like magic; like all Italian peasants, they loudly disclaimed such a thing when questioned, although they would accidentally refer to it themselves.

'Ghosts! Ghosts!' they cried, 'surely the Signore does not believe in such trash? Rats there are and in plenty. Do ghosts gnaw the chestnuts, and steal the Indian corn?'

Even the old man, who had seemed inclined to be ghostly from rebellion to the priest, was now thoroughly on his guard, and not a word on the subject could be extracted from him. They did not wish to talk about ghosts, and I for my part did not want to hear about them; for in my present highly wrought, imaginative mood, an apparition in a winding sheet, a clanking of chains, and all the authorised ghostly manifestations seemed in the highest degree disgusting; my mind was too much haunted to be intruded on by vulgar spectres, and as I mechanically sketched the giggling, blushing little peasant girl, and looked up in her healthy, rosy, sunburnt face, peeping from beneath a gaudy silk kerchief, my mental eyes were fixed on a very different face, which I saw as distinctly as hers –

that dark yearning face with the strange red lips and the lightly powdered locks. The peasants and the priest went on chattering gaily, running from one topic to another – the harvest, the vines, the next day's fair; politics the most fantastic, scraps of historical lore even more astounding, rattling on unceasingly, with much good humour, the most astonishing ignorance of facts, infantile absurdity, perfect seriousness, and much shrewd sceptical humour. I did my best to join in this conversation, and laughed and joked to the best of my power. The fact is I felt quite happy and serene, for I had little by little made up my mind to an absurd step, either babyish in the extreme or foolhardy to the utmost, but which I contemplated with perfect coolness and assurance, as one sometimes does hazardous or foolish courses which gratify a momentary whim. I had at length found the house; I would pass the night there.

I must have been in violent mental excitement, but the excitement was so uniform and unimpeded as to seem almost regular; I felt as if it were quite natural to live in an atmosphere of weirdness and adventure, and I was firm in my purpose. At length came the moment for action: the women put by their work, the old man shook the ashes out of his pipe; they looked at each other as if not knowing how to begin. The priest, who had just re-entered from giving his wondrous donkey some hay, made himself their spokesman –

'Ahem!' he cleared his throat; 'the Signore must excuse the extreme simplicity of these uneducated rustics, and bear in mind that as they are unaccustomed to the luxuries of cities, and have, moreover, to be up by daybreak in order to attend to their agricultural—'

'Yes, yes,' I answered, smiling; 'I understand. They want to go to bed, and they are quite right. I must beg you all to forgive my having thoughtlessly kept you up so late.' How was I now to proceed? I scarcely understood.

'Keep them up late? Oh, not at all; they had been but too much honoured,' they cried.

'Well,' said the priest, who was growing sleepy, 'of course there is no returning through this rain; the lanes are too unsafe; besides, the city gates are locked. Come, what can we do for the Signore? Can we make him up a bed here? I will go and sleep with our old Maso,' and he tapped the young man's shoulder.

The women were already starting off for pillows, and mattresses, and what not; but I stopped them.

'On no account,' I said. 'I will not encroach upon your hospitality. I can sleep quite comfortably over the way – in the large house.'

'Over the way? In the big house?' they cried, all together. 'The Signore sleep in the big house? Oh, never, never! Impossible.'

'Rather than that, I'll harness my donkey and drive the Signore through the mud and rain and darkness; that I will, *corpo di Bacco*,' cried the little, red-faced priest.

'But why not?' I answered, determined not to be baulked. 'I can get a splendid night's rest over the way. Why shouldn't I?'

'Never, never!' they answered in a chorus of expostulation.

'But since there are no ghosts there,' I protested, trying to laugh, 'what reason is there against it?'

'Oh, as to ghosts,' put in the priest, 'I promise you there are none. I snap my fingers at ghosts!'

'Well,' I persisted, 'you won't tell me that the rats will mistake me for a sack of chestnuts and eat me up, will you? Come, give me the key.' I was beginning to believe in the use of a little violence. 'Which is it?' I asked, seeing a bunch hanging on a nail; 'is it this one? – or this one? V*ia*! tell me which it is.'

The old man seized hold of the keys. 'You must not sleep there,' he said, very positively. 'It's no use trying to hide it. That house is no house for a Christian to sleep in. A bad thing happened there once – some one was murdered; that is why no one will live in it. It's no use to say No, Abate,' and he turned contemptuously towards the priest. 'There are evil things in that house.'

'Ghosts?' I cried, laughing, and trying to force the keys from him.

'Not exactly ghosts,' he answered; 'but – the devil is sometimes in that house.'

'Indeed!' I exclaimed, quite desperate. 'That is just what I want. I have to paint a picture of him fighting with a saint of ours who once pulled his nose with a pair of tongs, and I am overjoyed to do his portrait from the life.'

They did not well understand; they suspected I was mad, and so, truly, I was.

'Let him have his way,' grumbled the old man; 'he is a headstrong boy – let him go and see and hear all he will.'

'For heaven's sake, Signore!' entreated the women.

'Is it possible, Signore Forestiere, that you can be serious?' protested the priest, with his hand on my arm.

'Indeed I am,' I answered; 'you shall hear all I have seen tomorrow morning. I'll throw my black paint at the devil if he won't sit still while I paint him.'

'Paint the devil! is he mad?' whispered the women, aghast.

I had got hold of the keys. 'Is this it?' I asked, pointed to a heavy, handsomely-wrought, but very rusty key.

The old man nodded.

I took it off the ring. The women, although extremely terrified by my daring, were secretly delighted at the prospect of a good story the next morning. One of them gave me a large, two-wicked kitchen lamp, with snuffers and tweezers chained to its tall stand; another brought an immense rose-coloured umbrella; the young man produced a large mantle lined with green and a thick horsecloth; they would have brought a mattress and blankets if I had let them.

'You insist on going?' asked the priest. 'Think how wretchedly cold and damp it must be over there!'

'Do, pray, reflect, Signore!' entreated the young woman.

'Haven't I told you I am engaged to paint the devil's portrait?' I answered, and, drawing the bolt, and opening the umbrella, I dashed out of the cottage.

'*Gesù Maria!*' cried the women; 'to go there on such a night as this!'

'To sleep on the floor!' exclaimed the priest; 'what a man, what a man!'

'*È matto, è matto!* he is mad!' they all joined, and shut the door.

I dashed across the flood before the door, unlocked the iron gate, walked quickly through the dark and went up the avenue of moaning poplars. A sudden flash of lightning, broad, pink, and enduring, permitted me to see the house, like an immense stranded ship or huge grim skeleton, looming in the darkness.

I ran up the steps, unlocked the door, and gave it a violent shake.

IV

I gave a vigorous push to the old, rotten door; it opened, creaking, and I entered a vast, lofty hall, the entrance saloon of the noble old villa. As I stepped forward cautiously, I heard a cutting, hissing sound, and something soft and velvety brushed against my cheek. I stepped backwards and held up the lamp: it was only an owl whom the light had scared; it hooted dismally as it regained its perch. The rain fell sullen and monotonous; the only other sound was that of my footsteps waking the echoes of the huge room. I looked about as much as the uncertain light of my two-wicked lamp permitted; the shiny marble pavement was visible only in a few places; dust had formed a thick crust over it, and everywhere yellow maize seed was strewn about. In the middle were some broken chairs – tall, gaunt chairs, with remains of gilding and brocade, and some small wooden ones with their ragged straw half pushed out. Against a large oaken table rested some sacks of corn; in the corners were heaps of chestnuts and of green and yellow silkworm cocoons, hoes, spades, and other garden implements; roots and bulbs strewed the floor; the whole place was full of a vague, musty smell of decaying wood and plaster, of earth, of drying fruit and silkworms. I looked up; the rain battered in through the unglazed windows and poured in a stream over some remains of tracery and fresco; I looked higher, at the bare mouldering rafters. Thus I stood while the rain fell heavy and sullen, and the water splashed down outside from the roof; there I stood in the desolate room, in a stupid, unthinking condition. All this solemn, silent decay impressed me deeply, far more than I had expected; all my excitement seemed over, all my whims seemed to have fled.

I almost forgot why I had wished to be here; indeed, why had I? That mad infatuation seemed wholly aimless and inexplicable; this strange, solemn scene was enough in itself. I felt at a loss what to do, or even how to feel; I had the object of my wish, all was over. I was in the house; further I neither ventured to go nor dared to think of; all the dare-devil courting of the picturesque and the supernatural which had hitherto filled me was gone; I felt like an intruder, timid and humble – an intruder on solitude and ruin.

I spread the horsecloth on the floor, placed the lamp by my side, wrapped myself in the peasant's cloak, leaned my head on a broken chair and looked up listlessly at the bare rafters, listening to the dull falling rain and to the water splashing from the roof; thoughts or feelings I appeared to have none.

How long I remained thus I cannot tell; the minutes seemed hours in this vigil, with nothing but the spluttering and flickering of the lamp within, the monotonous splash without; lying all alone, awake but vacant, in the vast crumbling hall.

I can scarcely tell whether suddenly or gradually I began to perceive, or thought I perceived, faint and confused sounds issuing I knew not whence. What they were I could not distinguish; all I knew was that they were distinct from the drop and splash of the rain. I raised myself on my elbow and listened; I took out my watch and pressed the repeater to assure myself I was awake: one, two, three, four, five, six, seven, eight, nine, ten, eleven, twelve tremulous ticks. I sat up and listened more intently, trying to separate the sounds from those of the rain outside. The sounds – silvery, sharp, but faint – seemed to become more distinct. Were they approaching, or was I awaking? I rose and listened, holding my breath. I trembled; I took up the lamp and stepped forward; I waited a moment, listening again. There could be no doubt the light, metallic sounds proceeded from the interior of the house; they were notes, the notes of some instrument. I went on cautiously. At the end of the hall was a crazy, gilded, battered door up some steps; I hesitated before opening it, for I had a vague, horrible fear of what might be behind it. I pushed it open gently and by degrees, and stood on the threshold, trembling and breathless. There was nothing save a dark, empty room, and then another; they had the cold, damp feeling and smell of a crypt. I passed through them slowly, startling the bats with my light; and the sounds, the sharp, metallic chords became more and more distinct; and as they did so, the vague, numbing terror seemed to gain more and more hold on me. I came to a broad spiral staircase, of which the top was lost in the darkness, my lamp shedding a flickering light on the lower steps. The sounds were now quite distinct, the light, sharp, silvery sounds of a harpsichord or spinet; they fell clear and vibrating into the silence of the crypt-like house. A cold perspiration covered my forehead; I seized hold of the banisters of the stairs, and little by little dragged myself up them like an inert mass. There came a chord, and delicately, insensibly there glided into the modulations of the instrument the notes of a strange, exquisite voice. It was of a wondrous sweet, thick, downy quality, neither limpid nor penetrating, but with a vague, drowsy charm, that seemed to steep the soul in enervating bliss; but, together with this charm, a terrible cold seemed to sink into my heart. I crept up the stairs, listening and panting. On the broad landing was a folding, gilded door, through whose interstices issued a faint glimmer of light, and from behind it proceeded the sounds. By the side of the door, but higher up, was one of those oval, ornamental windows called in French *œil de bœuf*; an old broken table stood beneath it. I summoned up my courage and, clambering on to the unsteady table, raised myself on tiptoe to the level of the window and, trembling, peeped though its dust-dimmed glass. I saw into a large, lofty room, the greater part of which was hidden in darkness, so that I could distinguish only the outline of the heavily-curtained windows, and of a screen, and of one or two ponderous chairs. In the middle was a small, inlaid harpsichord, on which stood two wax lights, shedding a bright reflection on the shining marble floor, and forming a pale, yellowish mass of light in the dark room. At the harpsichord, turned slightly away from me, sat a figure in the dress of the end of the last century – a long, pale lilac coat, and pale green waistcoat, and lightly-powdered hair gathered into a black silk bag; a deep amber-coloured silk cloak was thrown over the chairback. He was singing intently, and accompanying himself on the harpsichord, his back turned towards the window at which I was. I stood spellbound, incapable of moving, as if all my blood were frozen and my limbs paralysed, almost insensible, save that I saw and I heard, saw and heard him alone. The wonderful sweet, downy voice glided lightly and dexterously through the complicated mazes of the song; it rounded off ornament after ornament, it swelled imperceptibly into glorious, hazy magnitude, and diminished, dying gently away from a high note to a lower one, like a weird, mysterious sigh; then it leaped into a high, clear, triumphant note, and burst out into a rapid, luminous shake.

For a moment he took his hands off the keys, and turned partially round. My eyes caught his: they were the deep, soft, yearning eyes of the portrait at Fa Diesis's.

At that moment a shadow was interposed between me and the lights, and instantly, by whom or how I know not, they were extinguished, and the room left in complete darkness; at the same instant the modulation was broken off unfinished; the last notes of the piece changed into a long, shrill, quivering cry; there was a sound of scuffling and suppressed voices, the heavy dead thud of a falling body, a tremendous crash, and another long, vibrating, terrible cry. The spell was broken, I started up, leaped from the table, and rushed to the closed door of the room; I shook its gilded panels twice and thrice in vain; I wrenched them asunder with a tremendous effort, and entered.

The moonlight fell in a broad, white sheet through a hole in the broken roof, filling the desolate room with a vague, greenish light. It was empty. Heaps of broken tiles and plaster lay on the floor; the water trickled down the stained wall and stagnated on the pavement; a broken fallen beam lay across the middle; and there, solitary and abandoned in the midst of the room, stood an open harpsichord, its cover encrusted with dust and split from end to end, its strings rusty and broken, its yellow keyboard thick with cobweb; the greenish-white light falling straight upon it.

I was seized with an irresistible panic; I rushed out, caught up the lamp which I had left on the landing, and dashed down the staircase, never daring to look behind me, nor to the right or the left, as if something horrible and undefinable were pursuing me, that long, agonised cry continually ringing in my ears. I rushed on through the empty, echoing rooms and tore open the door of the large entrance hall – there, at least, I might be safe – when, just as I entered it, I slipped, my lamp fell and was extinguished, and I fell down, down, I knew not where, and lost consciousness.

When I came to my senses, gradually and vaguely, I was lying at the extremity of the vast entrance hall of the crumbling villa, at the foot of some steps, the fallen lamp by my side. I looked round all dazed and astonished; the white morning light was streaming into the hall. How had I come there? what had happened to me? Little by little I recollected, and as the recollection returned, so also returned my fear, and I rose quickly. I pressed my hand to my aching head, and drew it back stained with a little blood. I must, in my panic, have forgotten the steps and fallen, so that my head had struck against the sharp base of a column. I wiped off the blood, took the lamp and the cloak and horsecloth, which lay where I had left them, spread on the dust-encrusted marble floor, amidst the sacks of flour and the heaps of chestnuts, and staggered through the room, not well aware whether I was really awake. At the doorway I paused and looked back once more on the great bare hall, with its mouldering rafters and decaying frescoes, the heaps of rubbish and garden implements, its sad, solemn ruin. I opened the door and went out on to the long flight of steps before the house, and looked wonderingly at the serenely lovely scene. The storm had passed away, leaving only a few hazy white clouds in the blue sky; the soaking earth steamed beneath the already strong sun; the yellow corn was beaten down and drenched, the maize and vine leaves sparkled with rain drops, the tall green hemp gave out its sweet, fresh scent. Before me lay the broken-up garden, with its overgrown box hedges, its immense decorated lemon vases, its spread out silkworm mats, its tangle of weeds and vegetables and flowers; further, the waving green plain with its avenues of tall poplars stretching in all directions, and from its midst rose the purple and grey walls and roofs and towers of the old town; hens were cackling about in search of worms in the soft moist earth, and the deep, clear sounds of the great cathedral bell floated across the fields. Looking down on all this fresh, lovely scene, it struck me, more vividly than ever before, how terrible it must be to be cut off for ever from all this, to lie blind and deaf and motionless mouldering underground. The idea made me shudder and shrink from the decaying house; I ran down to the road; the peasants were there, dressed in their gayest clothes, red, blue, cinnamon, and pea-green, busy piling vegetables into a light cart, painted with vine wreaths and souls in the flames of purgatory. A little further, at the door of the white, arcaded farmhouse, with its sundial and vine trellis, the jolly little priest was buckling the harness of his wonderful donkey, while one of the girls, mounted on a chair, was placing a fresh wreath of berries and a fresh dripping nosegay before the little faded Madonna shrine. When they saw me, they all cried out and came eagerly to meet me.

'Well!' asked the priest, 'did you see any ghosts?'

'Did you do the devil's picture?' laughed the girl.

I shook my head with a forced smile.

'Why!' exclaimed the lad, 'the Signore has hurt his forehead. How could that have happened?'

'The lamp went out and I stumbled against a sharp corner,' I answered hastily.

They noticed that I seemed pale and ill, and attributed it to my fall. One of the women ran into the house and returned with a tiny, bulb-shaped glass bottle, filled with some greenish fluid.

'Rub some of this into the cut,' she directed; 'this is infallible, it will cure any wound. It is some holy oil more than a hundred years old, left us by our grandmother.'

I shook my head, but obeyed and rubbed some of the queer smelling green stuff on to the cut, without noticing any particularly miraculous effect.

They were going to the fair; when the cart was well stocked, they all mounted on to its benches, till it tilted upwards with the weight; the lad touched the shaggy old horse and off they rattled, waving their hats and handkerchiefs at me. The priest courteously offered me a seat beside him in his gig; I accepted mechanically, and off we went, behind the jingling cart of the peasants, through the muddy lanes, where the wet boughs bent over us, and we brushed the drops off the green hedges. The priest was highly talkative, but I scarcely heard what he said, for my head ached and reeled. I looked back at the deserted villa, a huge dark mass in the shining green fields of hemp and maize, and shuddered.

'You are unwell,' said the priest; 'you must have taken cold in that confounded damp old hole.'

We entered the town, crowded with carts and peasants, passed through the market place, with its grand old buildings all festooned with tin ware and onions and coloured stuffs, and what not; and he set me down at my inn, where the sign of the three pilgrims swings over the door.

'Good-bye, good-bye!' *a rivederci!* to our next meeting!' he cried.

'A *rivederci!*' I answered faintly. I felt numb and sick; I paid my bill and sent off my luggage at once. I longed to be out of M—; I knew instinctively that I was on the eve of a bad illness, and my only thought was to reach Venice while I yet could.

I proved right; the day after my arrival at Venice the fever seized me and kept fast hold of me many a week.

'That's what comes of remaining in Rome until July!' cried all my friends, and I let them continue in their opinion.

Winthrop paused, and remained for a moment with his head between his hands; none of us made any remark, for we were at a loss what to say.

'That air – the one I had heard that night,' he added after a moment, 'and its opening words, those on the portrait, "Sei Regina, io Pastor sono", remained deep in my memory. I took every opportunity of discovering whether such an air really existed; I asked lots of people, and ransacked half a dozen musical archives. I did find an air, even more than one, with those words, which appear to have been set by several composers; but on trying them over at the piano they proved totally different from the one in my mind. The consequence naturally was that, as the impression of the adventure grew fainter, I began to doubt whether it had not been all a delusion, a nightmare phantasm, due to over-excitement and fever, due to the morbid, vague desire for something strange and supernatural. Little by little I settled down in this idea, regarding the whole story as an hallucination. As to the air, I couldn't explain that, I shuffled it off half unexplained and tried to forget it. But now, on suddenly hearing that very same air from you – on being assured of its existence outside my imagination – the whole scene has returned to me in all its vividness, and I feel compelled to believe. Can I do otherwise? Tell me! Is it reality or fiction? At any rate,' he added, rising and taking his hat, and trying to speak more lightly, 'will you forgive my begging you never to let me hear that piece again?'

'Be assured you shall not,' answered the Countess, pressing his hand; 'it makes even me feel a little uncomfortable now; besides, the comparison would be too much to my disadvantage. Ah! my dear Mr Winthrop, do you know, I think I would almost spend a night in the Villa Negri in order to hear a song of Cimarosa's time sung by a singer of the last century.'

'I knew you wouldn't believe a word of it,' was Winthrop's only reply.

Charlotte Riddell

THE OLD HOUSE IN
VAUXHALL WALK

CHAPTER ONE

'HOUSELESS – homeless – hopeless!'

Many a one who had before him trodden that same street must have uttered the same words – the weary, the desolate, the hungry, the forsaken, the waifs and strays of struggling humanity that are always coming and going, cold, starving and miserable, over the pavements of Lambeth Parish; but it is open to question whether they were ever previously spoken with a more thorough conviction of their truth, or with a feeling of keener self-pity, than by the young man who hurried along Vauxhall Walk one rainy winter's night, with no overcoat on his shoulders and no hat on his head.

A strange sentence for one-and-twenty to give expression to – and it was stranger still to come from the lips of a person who looked like and who was a gentleman. He did not appear either to have sunk very far down in the good graces of Fortune. There was no sign or token which would have induced a passer-by to imagine he had been worsted after a long fight with calamity. His boots were not worn down at the heels or broken at the toes, as many, many boots were which dragged and shuffled and scraped along the pavement. His clothes were good and fashionably cut, and innocent of the rents and patches and tatters that slunk wretchedly by, crouched in doorways, and held out a hand mutely appealing for charity. His face was not pinched with famine or lined with wicked wrinkles, or brutalised by drink and debauchery, and yet he said and thought he was hopeless, and almost in his young despair spoke the words aloud.

It was a bad night to be about with such a feeling in one's heart. The rain was cold, pitiless and increasing. A damp, keen wind blew down the cross streets leading from the river. The fumes of the gas works seemed to fall with the rain. The roadway was muddy; the pavement greasy; the lamps burned dimly; and that dreary district of London looked its very gloomiest and worst.

Certainly not an evening to be abroad without a home to go to, or a sixpence in one's pocket, yet this was the position of the young gentleman who, without a hat, strode along Vauxhall Walk, the rain beating on his unprotected head.

Upon the houses, so large and good – once inhabited by well-to-do citizens, now let out for the most part in floors to weekly tenants – he looked enviously. He would have given much to have had a room, or even part of one. He had been walking for a long time, ever since dark in fact, and dark falls soon in December. He was tired and cold and hungry, and he saw no prospect save of pacing the streets all night.

As he passed one of the lamps, the light falling on his face revealed handsome young features, a mobile, sensitive mouth, and that particular formation of the eyebrows – not a frown exactly, but a certain draw of the brows – often considered to bespeak genius, but which more surely accompanies an impulsive organisation easily pleased, easily depressed, capable of suffering very keenly or of enjoying fully. In his short life he had not enjoyed much, and he had suffered a good deal. That night, when he walked bareheaded through the rain, affairs had come to a crisis. So far as he in his despair felt able to see or reason, the best thing he could do was to die. The world did not want him; he would be better out of it.

The door of one of the houses stood open, and he could see in the dimly lighted hall some few articles of furniture waiting to be removed. A van stood beside the curb, and two men were lifting a table into it as he, for a second, paused.

'Ah,' he thought, 'even those poor people have some place to go to, some shelter provided, while I have not a roof to cover my head, or a shilling to get a night's lodging.' And he went on fast, as if memory were spurring him, so fast that a man running after had some trouble to overtake him.

'Master Graham! Master Graham!' this man exclaimed, breathlessly; and, thus addressed, the young fellow stopped as if he had been shot.

'Who are you that know me?' he asked, facing round.

'I'm William; don't you remember William, Master Graham? And, Lord's sake, sir, what are you doing out a night like this without your hat?'

'I forgot it,' was the answer; 'and I did not care to go back and fetch it.'

'Then why don't you buy another, sir? You'll catch your death of cold; and besides, you'll excuse me, sir, but it does look odd.'

'I know that,' said Master Graham grimly; 'but I haven't a halfpenny in the world.'

'Have you and the master, then—' began the man, but there he hesitated and stopped.

'Had a quarrel? Yes, and one that will last us our lives,' finished the other, with a bitter laugh.

'And where are you going now?'

'Going! Nowhere, except to seek out the softest paving stone, or the shelter of an arch.'

'You are joking, sir.'

'I don't feel much in a mood for jesting either.'

'Will you come back with me, Master Graham? We are just at the last of our moving, but there is a spark of fire still in the grate, and it would be better talking out of this rain. Will you come, sir?'

'Come! Of course I will come,' said the young fellow, and, turning, they retraced their steps to the house he had looked into as he passed along.

An old, old house, with long, wide hall, stairs low, easy of ascent, with deep cornices to the ceilings, and oak floorings, and mahogany doors, which still spoke mutely of the wealth and stability of the original owner, who lived before the Tradescants and Ashmoles were thought of, and had been sleeping far longer than they, in St Mary's churchyard, hard by the archbishop's palace.

'Step upstairs, sir,' entreated the departing tenant; 'it's cold down here, with the door standing wide.'

'Had you the whole house, then, William?' asked Graham Coulton, in some surprise.

'The whole of it, and right sorry I, for one, am to leave it; but nothing else would serve my wife. This room, sir,' and with a little conscious pride, William, doing the honours of his late residence, asked his guest into a spacious apartment occupying the full width of the house on the first floor.

Tired though he was, the young man could not repress an exclamation of astonishment.

'Why, we have nothing so large as this at home, William,' he said.

'It's a fine house,' answered William, raking the embers together as he spoke and throwing some wood upon them; 'but, like many a good family, it has come down in the world.'

There were four windows in the room, shuttered close; they had deep, low seats, suggestive of pleasant days gone by; when, well-curtained and well-cushioned, they formed snug retreats for the children, and some-times for adults also; there was no furniture left, unless an oaken settle beside the hearth, and a large mirror let into the panelling at the opposite end of the apartment, with a black marble console table beneath it, could be so considered; but the very absence of chairs and tables enabled the magnificent proportions of the chamber to be seen to full advantage, and there was nothing to distract the attention from the ornamented ceiling, the panelled walls, the old-world chimney-piece so quaintly carved, and the fireplace lined with tiles, each one of which contained a picture of some scriptural or allegorical subject.

'Had you been staying on here, William,' said Coulton, flinging himself wearily on the settle, 'I'd have asked you to let me stop where I am for the night.'

'If you can make shift, sir, there is nothing as I am aware of to prevent you stopping,' answered the man, fanning the wood into a flame. 'I shan't take the key back to the landlord till tomorrow, and this would be better for you than the cold streets at any rate.'

'Do you really mean what you say?' asked the other eagerly. 'I should be thankful to lie here; I feel dead beat.'

'Then stay, Master Graham, and welcome. I'll fetch a basket of coals I was going to put in the van, and make up a good fire, so that you can warm yourself; then I must run round to the other house for a minute or two, but it's not far, and I'll be back as soon as ever I can.'

'Thank you, William; you were always good to me,' said the young man gratefully. 'This is delightful,' and he stretched his numbed hands over the blazing wood, and looked round the room with a satisfied smile.

'I did not expect to get into such quarters,' he remarked, as his friend in need reappeared, carrying a half-bushel basket full of coals, with which he proceeded to make up a roaring fire. 'I am sure the last thing I could have imagined was meeting with anyone I knew in Vauxhall Walk.'

'Where were you coming from, Master Graham?' asked William curiously.

'From old Melfield's. I was at his school once, you know, and he has now retired, and is living upon the proceeds of years of robbery in Kennington Oval. I thought, perhaps he would lend me a pound, or offer me a night's lodging, or even a glass of wine; but, oh dear, no. He took the moral tone, and observed he could have nothing to say to a son who defied his father's authority. He gave me plenty of advice, but nothing else, and showed me out into the rain with a bland courtesy, for which I could have struck him.'

William muttered something under his breath which was not a blessing, and added aloud:

'You are better here, sir, I think, at any rate. I'll be back in less than half an hour.'

Left to himself, young Coulton took off his coat, and shifting the settle a little, hung it over the end to dry. With his handkerchief he rubbed some of the wet out of his hair; then, perfectly exhausted, he lay down before the fire and, pillowing his head on his arm, fell fast asleep.

He was awakened nearly an hour afterwards by the sound of someone gently stirring the fire and moving quietly about the room. Starting into a sitting posture, he looked around him, bewildered for a moment, and then, recognising his humble friend, said laughingly:

'I had lost myself; I could not imagine where I was.'

'I am sorry to see you here, sir,' was the reply; 'but still this is better than being out of doors. It has come on a nasty night. I brought a rug round with me that, perhaps, you would wrap yourself in.'

'I wish, at the same time, you had brought me something to eat,' said the young man, laughing.

'Are you hungry, then, sir?' asked William, in a tone of concern.

'Yes; I have had nothing to eat since breakfast. The governor and I commenced rowing the minute we sat down to luncheon, and I rose and left the table. But hunger does not signify; I am dry and warm, and can forget the other matter in sleep.'

'And it's too late now to buy anything,' soliloquised the man; 'the shops are all shut long ago. Do you think, sir,' he added, brightening, 'you could manage some bread and cheese?'

'Do I think – I should call it a perfect feast,' answered Graham Coulton. 'But never mind about food tonight, William; you have had trouble enough, and to spare, already.'

William's only answer was to dart to the door and run downstairs. Presently he reappeared, carrying in one hand bread and cheese wrapped up in paper, and in the other a pewter measure full of beer.

'It's the best I could do, sir,' he said apologetically. 'I had to beg this from the landlady.'

'Here's to her good health!' exclaimed the young fellow gaily, taking a long pull at the tankard. 'That tastes better than champagne in my father's house.'

'Won't he be uneasy about you?' ventured William, who, having by this time emptied the coals, was now seated on the inverted basket, looking wistfully at the relish with which the son of the former master was eating his bread and cheese.

'No,' was the decided answer. 'When he hears it pouring cats and dogs he will only hope I am out in the deluge, and say a good drenching will cool my pride.'

'I do not think you are right there,' remarked the man.

'But I am sure I am. My father always hated me, as he hated my mother.'

'Begging your pardon, sir; he was over fond of your mother.'

'If you had heard what he said about her today, you might find reason to alter your opinion. He told me I resembled her in mind as well as body; that I was a coward, a simpleton, and a hypocrite.'

'He did not mean it, sir.'

'He did, every word. He does think I am a coward, because I– I—' And the young fellow broke into a passion of hysterical tears.

'I don't half like leaving you here alone,' said William, glancing round the room with a quick trouble in his eyes; 'but I have no place fit to ask you to stop, and I am forced to go myself, because I am night watchman, and must be on at twelve o'clock.'

'I shall be right enough,' was the answer. 'Only I mustn't talk any more of my father. Tell me about yourself, William. How did you manage to get such a big house, and why are you leaving it?'

'The landlord put me in charge, sir; and it was my wife's fancy not to like it.'

'Why did she not like it?'

'She felt desolate alone with the children at night,' answered William, turning away his head; then added, next minute: 'Now, sir, if you think I can do no more for you, I had best be off. Time's getting on. I'll look round tomorrow morning.'

'Good night,' said the young fellow, stretching out his hand, which the other took as freely and frankly as it was offered. 'What should I have done this evening if I had not chanced to meet you?'

'I don't think there is much chance in the world, Master Graham,' was the quiet answer. 'I do hope you will rest well, and not be the worse for your wetting.'

'No fear of that,' was the rejoinder, and the next minute the young man found himself all alone in the Old House in Vauxhall Walk.

CHAPTER TWO

LYING on the settle, with the fire burnt out, and the room in total darkness, Graham Coulton dreamed a curious dream. He thought he awoke from deep slumber to find a log smouldering away upon the hearth, and the mirror at the end of the apartment reflecting fitful gleams of light. He could not understand how it came to pass that, far away as he was from the glass, he was able to see everything in it; but he resigned himself to the difficulty without astonishment, as people generally do in dreams.

Neither did he feel surprised when he beheld the outline of a female figure seated beside the fire, engaged in picking something out of her lap and dropping it with a despairing gesture.

He heard the mellow sound of gold, and knew she was lifting and dropping sovereigns. He turned a little so as to see the person engaged in such a singular and meaningless manner, and found that, where there had been no chair on the previous night, there was a chair now, on which was seated an old, wrinkled hag, her clothes poor and ragged, a mob cap barely covering her scant white hair, her cheeks sunken, her nose hooked, her fingers more like talons than aught else as they dived down into the heap of gold, portions of which they lifted but to scatter mournfully.

'Oh! my lost life,' she moaned, in a voice of the bitterest anguish. 'Oh! my lost life – for one day, for one hour of it again!'

Out of the darkness – out of the corner of the room where the shadows lay deepest – out from the gloom abiding near the door – out from the dreary night, with their sodden feet and wet dripping from their heads, came the old men and the young children, the worn women and the weary hearts, whose misery that gold might have relieved, but whose wretchedness it mocked.

Round that miser, who once sat gloating as she now sat lamenting, they crowded – all those pale, sad shapes – the aged of days, the infant of hours, the sobbing outcast, honest poverty, repentant vice; but one low cry proceeded from those pale lips – a cry for help she might have given, but which she withheld.

They closed about her, all together, as they had done singly in life; they prayed, they sobbed, they entreated; with haggard eyes the figure regarded the poor she had repulsed, the children against whose cry she had closed her ears, the old people she had suffered to starve and die for want of what would have been the merest trifle to her; then, with a terrible scream, she raised her lean arms above her head, and sank down – down – the gold scattering as it fell out of her lap, and rolling along the floor, till its gleam was lost in the outer darkness beyond.

Then Graham Coulton awoke in good earnest, with the perspiration oozing from every pore, with a fear and an agony upon him such as he had never before felt in all his existence, and with the sound of the heart-rending cry – 'Oh! my lost life' – still ringing in his ears.

Mingled with all, too, there seemed to have been some lesson for him which he had forgotten, that, try as he would, eluded his memory, and which, in the very act of waking, glided away.

He lay for a little thinking about all this, and then, still heavy with sleep, retraced his way into dreamland once more.

It was natural, perhaps, that, mingling with the strange fantasies which follow in the train of night and darkness, the former vision should recur, and the young man ere long found himself toiling through scene after scene wherein the figure of the woman he had seen seated beside a dying fire held principal place.

He saw her walking slowly across the floor munching a dry crust – she who could have purchased all the luxuries wealth can command; on the hearth, contemplating her, stood a man of commanding presence, dressed in the fashion of long ago. In his eyes there was a dark look of anger, on his lips a curling smile of disgust, and somehow, even in his sleep, the dreamer understood it was the ancestor to the descendant he beheld – that the house put to mean uses in which he lay had never so far descended from its high estate, as the woman possessed of so pitiful a soul, contaminated with the most despicable and insidious vice poor humanity knows, for all other vices seem to have connection with the flesh, but the greed of the miser eats into the very soul.

Filthy of person, repulsive to look at, hard of heart as she was, he yet beheld another phantom, which, coming into the room, met her almost on the threshold, taking her by the hand, and pleading, as it seemed, for assistance. He could not hear all that passed, but a word now and then fell upon his ear. Some talk of former days; some mention of a fair young mother – an appeal, as it seemed, to a time when they were tiny brother and sister, and the accursed greed for gold had not divided them. All in vain; the hag only answered him as she had answered the children, and the young girls, and the old people in his former vision. Her heart was as invulnerable to natural affection as it had proved to human sympathy. He begged, as it appeared, for aid to avert some bitter misfortune or terrible disgrace, and adamant might have been found more yielding to his prayer. Then the figure standing on the hearth changed to an angel, which folded its wings mournfully over its face, and the man, with bowed head, slowly left the room.

Even as he did so the scene changed again; it was night once more, and the miser wended her way upstairs. From below, Graham Coulton fancied he watched her toiling wearily from step to step. She had aged strangely since the previous scenes. She moved with difficulty; it seemed the greatest exertion for her to creep from step to step, her skinny hand traversing the balusters with slow and painful deliberateness. Fascinated, the young man's eyes followed the progress of that feeble, decrepit woman. She was solitary in a desolate house, with a deeper blackness than the darkness of night waiting to engulf her.

It seemed to Graham Coulton that after that he lay for a time in a still, dreamless sleep, upon awaking from which he found himself entering a chamber as sordid and unclean in its appointments as the woman of his previous vision had been in her person. The poorest labourer's wife would have gathered more comforts around her than that room contained. A four-poster bedstead without hangings of any kind – a blind drawn up awry – an old carpet covered with dust, and dirt on the floor – a rickety washstand with all the paint worn off it – an ancient mahogany dressing-table, and a cracked glass spotted all over – were all the objects he could at first discern, looking at the room through that dim light which oftentimes obtains in dreams.

By degrees, however, he perceived the outline of someone lying huddled on the bed. Drawing nearer, he found it was that of the person whose dreadful presence seemed to pervade the house. What a terrible sight she looked, with her thin white locks scattered over the pillow, with what were mere remnants of blankets gathered about her shoulders, with her claw-like fingers clutching the clothes, as though even in sleep she was guarding her gold!

An awful and a repulsive spectacle, but not with half the terror in it of that which followed. Even as the young man looked he heard stealthy footsteps on the stairs. Then he saw first one man and then his fellow steal cautiously into the room. Another second, and the pair stood beside the bed, murder in their eyes.

Graham Coulton tried to shout – tried to move, but the deterrent power which exists in dreams only tied his tongue and paralysed his limbs. He could but hear and look, and what he heard and saw was this: aroused suddenly from sleep, the woman started, only to receive a blow from one of the ruffians, whose fellow followed his lead by plunging a knife into her breast.

Then, with a gurgling scream, she fell back on the bed, and at the same moment, with a cry, Graham Coulton again awoke, to thank heaven it was but an illusion.

CHAPTER THREE

'I HOPE you slept well, sir.' It was William, who, coming into the hall with the sunlight of a fine bright morning streaming after him, asked this question: 'Had you a good night's rest?'

Graham Coulton laughed, and answered:

'Why, faith, I was somewhat in the case of Paddy, "who could not slape for dhraming". I slept well enough, I suppose, but whether it was in consequence of the row with my dad, or the hard bed, or the cheese – most likely the bread and cheese so late at night – I dreamt all the night long, the most extraordinary dreams. Some old woman kept cropping up, and I saw her murdered.'

'You don't say that, sir?' said William nervously.

'I do, indeed,' was the reply. 'However, that is all gone and past. I have been down in the kitchen and had a good wash, and I am as fresh as a daisy, and as hungry as a hunter; and, oh, William, can you get me any breakfast?'

'Certainly, Master Graham. I have brought round a kettle, and I will make the water boil immediately. I suppose, sir' – this tentatively – 'you'll be going home today?'

'Home!' repeated the young man. 'Decidedly not. I'll never go home again till I return with some medal hung to my coat, or a leg or arm cut off. I've thought it all out, William. I'll go and enlist. There's a talk of war; and, living or dead, my father shall have reason to retract his opinion about my being a coward.'

'I am sure the admiral never thought you anything of the sort, sir,' said William. 'Why, you have the pluck of ten!'

'Not before him,' answered the young fellow sadly.

'You'll do nothing rash, Master Graham; you won't go 'listing, or aught of that sort, in your anger?'

'If I do not, what is to become of me?' asked the other. 'I cannot dig – to beg I am ashamed. Why, but for you, I should not have had a roof over my head last night.'

'Not much of a roof, I am afraid, sir.'

'Not much of a roof!' repeated the young man. 'Why, who could desire a better? What a capital room this is,' he went on, looking around the apartment, where William was now kindling a fire; 'one might dine twenty people here easily!'

'If you think so well of the place, Master Graham, you might stay here for a while, till you have made up your mind what you are going to do. The landlord won't make any objection, I am very sure.'

'Oh! nonsense; he would want a long rent for a house like this.'

'I dare say; *if he could get it*,' was William's significant answer.

'What do you mean? Won't the place let?'

'No, sir. I did not tell you last night, but there was a murder done here, and people are shy of the house ever since.'

'A murder! What sort of a murder? Who was murdered?'

'A woman, Master Graham – the landlord's sister; she lived here all alone, and was supposed to have money. Whether she had or not, she was found dead from a stab in her breast, and if there ever was any money, it must have been taken at the same time, for none ever was found in the house from that day to this.'

'Was that the reason your wife would not stop here?' asked the young man, leaning against the mantelshelf, and looking thoughtfully down on William.

'Yes, sir. She could not stand it any longer; she got that thin and nervous no one would have believed it possible; she never saw anything, but she said she heard footsteps and voices, and then when she walked through the hall, or up the staircase, someone always seemed to be following her. We put the children to sleep in that big room you had last night, and they declared they often saw an old woman sitting by the hearth. Nothing ever came my way,' finished William, with a laugh; 'I was always ready to go to sleep the minute my head touched the pillow.'

'Were not the murderers discovered?' asked Graham Coulton.

'No, sir; the landlord, Miss Tynan's brother, had always lain under the suspicion of it – quite wrongfully, I am very sure – but he will never clear himself now. It was known he came and asked her for help a day or two before the murder, and it was also known he was able within a week or two to weather whatever trouble had been harassing him. Then, you see, the money was never found; and, altogether, people scarce knew what to think.'

'Humph!' ejaculated Graham Coulton, and he took a few turns up and down the apartment. 'Could I go and see this landlord?'

'Surely, sir, if you had a hat,' answered William, with such a serious decorum that the young man burst out laughing.

'That is an obstacle, certainly,' he remarked, 'and I must make a note do instead. I have a pencil in my pocket, so here goes.'

Within half an hour from the dispatch of that note William was back again with a sovereign; the landlord's compliments, and he would be much obliged if Mr Coulton could 'step round'.

'You'll do nothing rash, sir,' entreated William.

'Why, man,' answered the young fellow, 'one may as well be picked off by a ghost as a bullet. What is there to be afraid of?'

William only shook his head. He did not think his young master was made of the stuff likely to remain alone in a haunted house and solve the mystery it assuredly contained by dint of his own unassisted endeavours. And yet when Graham Coulton came out of the landlord's house he looked more bright and gay than usual, and walked up the Lambeth road to the place where William awaited his return, humming an air as he paced along.

'We have settled the matter,' he said. 'And now if the dad wants his son for Christmas, it will trouble him to find him.'

'Don't say that, Master Graham, don't,' entreated the man, with a shiver; 'maybe after all it would have been better if you had never happened to chance upon Vauxhall Walk.'

'Don't croak, William,' answered the young man; 'if it was not the best day's work I ever did for myself I'm a Dutchman.'

During the whole of that forenoon and afternoon, Graham Coulton searched diligently for the missing treasure Mr Tynan assured him had never been discovered. Youth is confident and self-opinionated, and this fresh explorer felt satisfied that, though others had failed, he would be successful. On the second floor he found one door locked, but he did not pay much attention to that at the moment, as he believed if there was anything concealed it was more likely to be found in the lower than the upper part of the house. Late into the evening he pursued his researches in the kitchen and cellars and old-fashioned cupboards, of which the basement had an abundance.

It was nearly eleven, when, engaged in poking about amongst the empty bins of a wine cellar as large as a family vault, he suddenly felt a rush of cold air at his back. Moving, his candle was instantly extinguished, and in the very moment of being left in darkness he saw, standing in the doorway, a woman, resembling her who had haunted his dreams overnight.

He rushed with outstretched hands to seize her, but clutched only air. He relit his candle, and closely examined the basement, shutting off communication with the ground floor ere doing so. All in vain. Not a trace could he find of living creature – not a window was open – not a door unbolted.

'It is very odd,' he thought, as, after securely fastening the door at the top of the staircase, he searched the whole upper portion of the house, with the exception of the one room mentioned.

'I must get the key of that tomorrow,' he decided, standing gloomily with his back to the fire and his eyes wandering about the drawing-room, where he had once again taken up his abode.

Even as the thought passed through his mind, he saw standing in the open doorway a woman with white dishevelled hair, clad in mean garments, ragged and dirty. She lifted her hand and shook it at him with a menacing gesture, and then, just as he was darting towards her, a wonderful thing occurred.

From behind the great mirror there glided a second female figure, at the sight of which the first turned and fled, uttering piercing shrieks as the other followed her from storey to storey.

Sick almost with terror, Graham Coulton watched the dreadful pair as they fled upstairs past the locked room to the top of the house.

It was a few minutes before he recovered his self-possession. When he did so, and searched the upper apartments, he found them totally empty.

That night, ere lying down before the fire, he carefully locked and bolted the drawing-room door; before he did more he drew the heavy settle in front of it, so that if the lock were forced no entrance could be effected without considerable noise.

For some time he lay awake, then dropped into a deep sleep, from which he was awakened suddenly by a noise as if of something scuffling stealthily behind the wainscot. He raised himself on his elbow and listened, and, to his consternation, beheld seated at the opposite side of the hearth the same woman he had seen before in his dreams, lamenting over her gold.

The fire was not quite out, and at that moment shot up a last tongue of flame. By the light, transient as it was, he saw that the figure pressed a ghostly finger to its lips, and by the turn of its head and the attitude of its body seemed to be listening.

He listened also – indeed, he was too much frightened to do aught else; more and more distinct grew the sounds which had aroused him, a stealthy rustling coming nearer and nearer – up and up it seemed, behind the wainscot.

'It is rats,' thought the young man, though, indeed, his teeth were almost chattering in his head with fear. But then in a moment he saw what disabused him of that idea – *the gleam of a candle or lamp through a crack in the panelling*. He tried to rise, he strove to shout – all in vain; and, sinking down, remembered nothing more till he awoke to find the grey light of an early morning stealing through one of the shutters he had left partially unclosed.

For hours after his breakfast, which he scarcely touched, long after William had left him at mid-day, Graham Coulton, having in the morning made a long and close survey of the house, sat thinking before the fire, then, apparently having made up his mind, he put on the hat he had bought, and went out.

When he returned the evening shadows were darkening down, but the pavements were full of people going marketing, for it was Christmas Eve, and all who had money to spend seemed bent on shopping.

It was terribly dreary inside the old house that night. Through the deserted rooms Graham could feel that ghostly semblance was wandering mournfully. When he turned his back he knew she was flitting from the mirror to the fire, from the fire to the mirror; but he was not afraid of her now – he was far more afraid of another matter he had taken in hand that day.

The horror of the silent house grew and grew upon him. He could hear the beating of his own heart in the dead quietude which reigned from garret to cellar.

At last William came; but the young man said nothing to him of what was in his mind. He talked to him cheerfully and hopefully enough – wondered where his father would think he had got to, and hoped Mr Tynan might send him some Christmas pudding. Then the man said it was time for him to go, and, when Mr Coulton went downstairs to the hall-door, remarked the key was not in it.

'No,' was the answer, 'I took it out today, to oil it.'

'It wanted oiling,' agreed William, 'for it worked terribly stiff.' Having uttered which truism he departed.

Very slowly the young man retraced his way to the drawing-room, where he only paused to lock the door on the outside; then taking off his boots he went up to the top of the house, where, entering the front attic, he waited patiently in darkness and in silence.

It was a long time, or at least it seemed long to him, before he heard the same sound which had aroused him on the previous night – a stealthy rustling – then a rush of cold air – then cautious footsteps – then the quiet opening of a door below.

It did not take as long in action as it has required to tell. In a moment the young man was out on the landing and had closed a portion of the panelling on the wall which stood open; noiselessly he crept back to the attic window, unlatched it, and sprung a rattle, the sound of which echoed far and near through the deserted streets, then rushing down the stairs, he encountered a man who, darting past him, made for the landing above; but perceiving the way of escape closed, fled down again, to find Graham struggling desperately with his fellow.

'Give him the knife – come along,' he said savagely; and next instant Graham felt something like a hot iron through his shoulder, and then heard a thud, as one of the men, tripping in his rapid flight, fell from the top of the stairs to the bottom.

At the same moment there came a crash, as if the house was falling, and faint, sick, and bleeding, young Coulton lay insensible on the threshold of the room where Miss Tynan had been murdered.

When he recovered he was in the dining-room, and a doctor was examining his wound.

Near the door a policeman stiffly kept guard. The hall was full of people; all the misery and vagabondism the streets contain at that hour was crowding in to see what had happened.

Through the midst two men were being conveyed to the station-house; one, with his head dreadfully injured, on a stretcher, the other handcuffed, uttering frightful imprecations as he went.

After a time the house was cleared of the rabble, the police took possession of it, and Mr Tynan was sent for.

'What was that dreadful noise?' asked Graham feebly, now seated on the floor, with his back resting against the wall.

'I do not know. Was there a noise?' said Mr Tynan, humouring his fancy, as he thought.

'Yes, in the drawing-room, I think; the key is in my pocket.'

Still humouring the wounded lad, Mr Tynan took the key and ran upstairs.

When he unlocked the door, what a sight met his eyes! The mirror had fallen – it was lying all over the floor shivered into a thousand pieces; the console table had been borne down by its weight, and the marble slab was shattered as well. But this was not what chained his attention. Hundreds, thousands of gold pieces were scattered about, and an aperture behind the glass contained boxes filled with securities and deeds and bonds, the possession of which had cost his sister her life.

* * * * *

'Well, Graham, and what do you want?' asked Admiral Coulton that evening as his eldest born appeared before him, looking somewhat pale but otherwise unchanged.

'I want nothing,' was the answer, 'but to ask your forgiveness. William has told me all the story I never knew before; and, if you let me, I will try to make it up to you for the trouble you have had. I am provided for,' went on the young fellow, with a nervous laugh; 'I have made my fortune since I left you, and another man's fortune as well.'

'I think you are out of your senses,' said the Admiral shortly.

'No, sir, I have found them,' was the answer; 'and I mean to strive and make a better thing of my life than I should ever have done had I not gone to the Old House in Vauxhall Walk.'

'Vauxhall Walk! What is the lad talking about?'

'I will tell you, sir, if I may sit down,' was Graham Coulton's answer, and then he told his story.

Margaret Oliphant

THE OPEN DOOR

I TOOK the house of Brentwood on my return from India in 18—, for the temporary accommodation of my family, until I could find a permanent home for them. It had many advantages which made it peculiarly appropriate. It was within reach of Edinburgh, and my boy Roland, whose education had been considerably neglected, could go in and out to school, which was thought to be better for him than either leaving home altogether or staying there always with a tutor. The first of these expedients would have seemed preferable to me, the second commended itself to his mother. The doctor, like a judicious man, took the midway between. 'Put him on his pony, and let him ride into the High School every morning; it will do him all the good in the world,' Dr Simson said; 'and when it is bad weather there is the train.' His mother accepted the solution of the difficulty more easily than I could have hoped; and our pale-faced boy, who had never known anything more invigorating than Simla, began to encounter the brisk breezes of the North in the subdued severity of the month of May. Before the time of the vacation in July we had the satisfaction of seeing him begin to acquire something of the brown and ruddy complexion of his schoolfellows. The English system did not commend itself to Scotland in those days. There was no little Eton at Fettes; nor do I think, if there had been, that a genteel exotic of that class would have tempted either my wife or me. The lad was doubly precious to us, being the only one left us of many; and he was fragile in body we believed, and deeply sensitive in mind. To keep him at home, and yet to send him to school – to combine the advantages of the two systems – seemed to be everything that could be desired. The two girls also found at Brentwood everything they wanted. They were near enough to Edinburgh to have masters and lessons as many as they required for completing that never-ending education which the young people seem to require nowadays. Their mother married me when she was younger than Agatha, and I should like to see them improve upon their mother! I myself was then no more than twenty-five – an age at which I see the young fellows now groping about them, with no notion what they are going to do with their lives. However, I suppose every generation has a conceit of itself which elevates it, in its own opinion, above that which comes after it.

Brentwood stands on that fine and wealthy slope of country, one of the richest in Scotland, which lies between the Pentland Hills and the Firth. In clear weather you could see the blue gleam – like a bent bow, embracing the wealthy fields and scattered houses – of the great estuary on one side of you; and on the other the blue heights, not gigantic like those we had been used to, but just high enough for all the glories of the atmosphere, the play of clouds, and sweet reflections, which give to a hilly country an interest and a charm which nothing else can emulate. Edinburgh, with its two lesser heights – the Castle and the Calton Hill – its spires and towers piercing through the smoke, and Arthur's Seat lying crouched behind, like a guardian no longer very needful, taking his repose beside the well-beloved charge, which is now, so to speak, able to take care of itself without him – lay at our right hand. From the lawn and drawing-room windows we could see all these varieties of landscape. The colour was sometimes a little chilly, but sometimes, also, as animated and full of vicissitude as a drama. I was never tired of it. Its colour and freshness revived the eyes which had grown weary of arid plains and blazing skies. It was always cheery, and fresh, and full of repose.

The village of Brentwood lay almost under the house, on the other side of the deep little ravine, down which a stream – which ought to have been a lovely, wild, and frolicsome little river – flowed between its rocks and trees. The river, like so many in that district, had, however, in its earlier life been sacrificed to trade, and was grimy with paper-making. But this did not affect our pleasure in it so much as I have known it to affect other streams. Perhaps our water was more rapid – perhaps less clogged with dirt and refuse. Our side of the dell was charmingly *accidenté*, and clothed with fine trees, through which various paths wound down to the river-side and to the village bridge which crossed the stream. The village lay in the hollow, and climbed, with very prosaic houses, the other side. Village architecture does not flourish in Scotland. The blue slates and the grey stone are sworn foes to the picturesque; and though I do not, for my own part, dislike the interior of an old-fashioned pewed and galleried church, with its little family settlements on all sides, the square box outside, with its bit of a spire like a handle to lift it by, is not an improvement to the landscape. Still, a cluster of houses on differing elevations – with scraps of garden coming in between, a hedgerow with clothes laid out to dry, the opening of a street with its rural sociability, the women at their doors, the slow waggon lumbering along – gives a centre to the landscape. It was cheerful to look at, and convenient in a hundred ways. Within ourselves we had walks in plenty, the glen being always beautiful in all its phases, whether the woods were green in the spring or ruddy in the autumn. In the park which surrounded the house were the ruins of the former mansion of Brentwood, a much smaller and less important house than the solid Georgian edifice which we inhabited. The ruins were picturesque, however, and gave importance to the place. Even we, who were but temporary tenants, felt a vague pride in them, as if they somehow reflected a certain consequence upon ourselves. The old building had the remains of a tower, an indistinguishable mass of mason-work, overgrown with ivy, and the shells of walls attached to this were half filled up with soil. I had never examined it closely, I am ashamed to say. There was a large room, or what had been a large room, with the lower part of the windows still existing, on the principal floor, and underneath other windows, which were perfect, though half filled up with fallen soil, and waving with a wild growth of brambles and chance growths of all kinds. This was the oldest part of all. At a little distance were some very commonplace and disjointed fragments of the building, one of them suggesting a certain pathos by its very commonness and the complete wreck which it showed. This was the end of a low gable, a bit of grey wall, all encrusted with lichens, in which was a common doorway. Probably it had been a servants' entrance, a back-door, or opening into what are called 'the offices' in Scotland. No offices remained to be entered – pantry and kitchen had all been swept out of being; but there stood the doorway open and vacant, free to all the winds, to the rabbits, and every wild creature. It struck my eye, the first time I went to Brentwood, like a melancholy comment upon a life that was over. A door that led to nothing – closed once perhaps with anxious care, bolted and guarded, now void of any meaning. It impressed me, I remember, from the first; so perhaps it may be said that my mind was prepared to attach to it an importance, which nothing justified.

The summer was a very happy period of repose for us all. The warmth of Indian suns was still in our veins. It seemed to us that we could never have enough of the greenness, the dewiness, the freshness of the northern landscape. Even its mists were pleasant to us, taking all the fever out of us, and pouring in vigour and refreshment. In autumn we followed the fashion of the time, and went away for change which we did not in the least require. It was when the family had settled down for the winter, when the days were short and dark, and the rigorous reign of frost upon us, that the incidents occurred which alone could justify me in intruding upon the world my private affairs. These incidents were, however, of so curious a character, that I hope my inevitable references to my own family and pressing personal interests will meet with a general pardon.

I was absent in London when these events began. In London an old
Indian plunges back into the interests with which all his previous life has
been associated, and meets old friends at every step. I had been circulating
among some half-dozen of these – enjoying the return to my former life in
shadow, though I had been so thankful in substance to throw it aside –
and had missed some of my home letters, what with going down from
Friday to Monday to old Benbow's place in the country, and stopping on
the way back to dine and sleep at Sellar's and to take a look into Cross's
stables, which occupied another day. It is never safe to miss one's letters.
In this transitory life, as the Prayer-book says, how can one ever be certain
what is going to happen? All was well at home. I knew exactly (I thought)
what they would have to say to me: 'The weather has been so fine, that
Roland has not once gone by train, and he enjoys the ride beyond
anything.' 'Dear papa, be sure that you don't forget anything, but bring us
so-and-so and so-and-so' – a list as long as my arm. Dear girls and dearer
mother! I would not for the world have forgotten their commissions, or
lost their little letters, for all the Benbows and Crosses in the world.

But I was confident in my home-comfort and peacefulness. When I got
back to my club, however, three or four letters were lying for me, upon
some of which I noticed the 'immediate', 'urgent', which old-fashioned
people and anxious people still believe will influence the post-office and
quicken the speed of the mails. I was about to open one of these, when the
club porter brought me two telegrams, one of which, he said, had arrived
the night before. I opened, as was to be expected, the last first, and this
was what I read: 'Why don't you come or answer? For God's sake, come.
He is much worse.' This was a thunderbolt to fall upon a man's head who
had only one son, and he the light of his eyes! The other telegram, which
I opened with hands trembling so much that I lost time by my haste, was
to much the same purport: 'No better; doctor afraid of brain-fever. Calls
for you day and night. Let nothing detain you.' The first thing I did was to
look up the time-tables to see if there was any way of getting off sooner
than by the night-train, though I knew well enough there was not! and
then I read the letters, which furnished, alas! too clearly, all the details.
They told me that the boy had been pale for some time, with a scared
look. His mother had noticed it before I left home, but would not say
anything to alarm me. This look had increased day by day; and soon it was
observed that Roland came home at a wild gallop through the park, his
pony panting and in foam, himself 'as white as a sheet', but with the
perspiration streaming from his forehead. For a long time he had resisted
all questioning, but at length had developed such strange changes of
mood, showing a reluctance to go to school, a desire to be fetched in the

carriage at night – which was a ridiculous piece of luxury – an unwillingness to go out into the grounds, and nervous start at every sound, that his mother had insisted upon an explanation. When the boy – our boy Roland, who had never known what fear was – began to talk to her of voices he had heard in the park, and shadows that had appeared to him among the ruins, my wife promptly put him to bed and sent for Dr Simson – which, of course, was the only thing to do.

I hurried off that evening, as may be supposed, with an anxious heart. How I got through the hours before the starting of the train, I cannot tell. We must all be thankful for the quickness of the railway when in anxiety; but to have thrown myself into a post-chaise as soon as horses could be put to, would have been a relief. I got to Edinburgh very early in the blackness of the winter morning, and scarcely dared look the man in the face at whom I gasped 'What news?' My wife had sent the brougham for me, which I concluded, before the man spoke, was a bad sign. His answer was that stereotyped answer which leaves the imagination so wildly free – 'Just the same.' Just the same! What might that mean? The horses seemed to me to creep along the long dark country-road. As we dashed through the park, I thought I heard some one moaning among the trees, and clenched my fist at him (whoever he might be) with fury. Why had the fool of a woman at the gate allowed any one to come in to disturb the quiet of the place? If I had not been in such hot haste to get home, I think I should have stopped the carriage and got out to see what tramp it was that had made an entrance and chosen my grounds, of all places in the world – when my boy was ill! – to grumble and groan in. But I had no reason to complain of our slow pace here. The horses flew like lightning along the intervening path, and drew up at the door all panting, as if they had run a race. My wife stood waiting to receive me with a pale face, and a candle in her hand, which made her look paler still as the wind blew the flame about. 'He is sleeping,' she said in a whisper, as if her voice might wake him. And I replied, when I could find my voice, also in a whisper, as though the jingling of the horses' furniture and the sound of their hoofs must not have been more dangerous. I stood on the steps with her a moment, almost afraid to go in, now that I was here; and it seemed to me that I saw without observing, if I may say so, that the horses were unwilling to turn round, though their stables lay that way, or that the men were unwilling. These things occurred to me afterwards, though at the moment I was not capable of anything but to ask questions and to hear of the condition of the boy.

I looked at him from the door of his room, for we were afraid to go near, lest we should disturb that blessed sleep. It looked like actual sleep – not the lethargy into which my wife told me he would sometimes fall. She told me everything in the next room, which communicated with his, rising now and then and going to the door of communication; and in this there was much that was very startling and confusing to the mind. It appeared that ever since the winter began, since it was early dark and night had fallen before his return from school, he had been hearing voices among the ruins – at first only a groaning, he said, at which his pony was as much alarmed as he was, but by degrees a voice. The tears ran down my wife's cheeks as she described to me how he would start up in the night and cry out, 'Oh, mother, let me in! oh, mother, let me in!' with a pathos which rent her heart. And she sitting there all the time, only longing to do everything his heart could desire! But though she would try to soothe him, crying, 'You are at home, my darling. I am here. Don't you know me? Your mother is here,' he would only stare at her, and after a while spring up again with the same cry. At other times he would be quite reasonable, she said, asking eagerly when I was coming, but declaring that he must go with me as soon as I did so, 'to let them in'. 'The doctor thinks his nervous system must have received a shock,' my wife said. 'Oh, Henry, can it be that we have pushed him on too much with his work – a delicate boy like Roland? – and what is his work in comparison with his health? Even you would think little of honours or prizes if it hurt the boy's health.' Even I! as if I were an inhuman father sacrificing my child to my ambition. But I would not increase her trouble by taking any notice. After a while they persuaded me to lie down, to rest, and to eat – none of which things had been possible since I received their letters. The mere fact of being on the spot, of course, in itself was a great thing; and when I knew that I would be called in a moment, as soon as he was awake and wanted me, I felt capable, even in the dark, chill morning twilight, to snatch an hour or two's sleep. As it happened, I was so worn out with the strain of anxiety, and he so quieted and consoled by knowing I had come, that I was not disturbed till the afternoon, when the twilight had again settled down. There was just daylight enough to see his face when I went to him; and what a change in a fortnight! He was paler and more worn, I thought, than even in those dreadful days in the plains before we left India. His hair seemed to me to have grown long and lank; his eyes were like blazing lights projecting out of his white face. He got hold of my hand in a cold and tremulous clutch, and waved to everybody to go away. 'Go away – even mother,' he said – 'go away.' This went to her heart, for she did not like that even I should have more of the boy's confidence than herself; but my wife has never been a woman to think of herself, and she left us alone. 'Are they all gone?' he said, eagerly. 'They would not let me speak. The doctor treated me as if I were a fool. You know I am not a fool, papa.'

'Yes, yes my boy, I know; but you are ill, and quiet is so necessary. You are not only not a fool, Roland, but you are reasonable and understand. When you are ill you must deny yourself; you must not do everything that you might do being well.'

He waved his thin hand with a sort of indignation. 'Then, father, I am not ill,' he cried. 'Oh, I thought when you came you would not stop me – you would see the sense of it! What do you think is the matter with me, all of you? Simson is well enough, but he is only a doctor. What do you think is the matter with me? I am no more ill than you are. A doctor, of course, he thinks you are ill the moment he looks at you – that's what he's there for – and claps you into bed.'

'Which is the best place for you at present, my dear boy.'

'I made up my mind,' cried the little fellow, 'that I would stand it till you came home. I said to myself, I won't frighten mother and the girls. But now, father,' he cried, half jumping out of the bed, 'it's not illness – it's a secret.'

His eyes shone so wildly, his face was so swept with strong feeling, that my heart sank within me. It could be nothing but fever that did it, and fever had been so fatal. I got him into my arms to put him back into bed. 'Roland,' I said, humouring the poor child, which I knew was the only way, 'if you are going to tell me this secret to do any good, you know you must be quite quiet, and not excite yourself. If you excite yourself, I must not let you speak.'

'Yes, father,' said the boy. He was quiet directly, like a man, as if he quite understood. When I had laid him back on his pillow, he looked up at me with that grateful, sweet look with which children, when they are ill, break one's heart, the water coming into his eyes in his weakness. 'I was sure as soon as you were here you would know what to do,' he said.

'To be sure, my boy. Now keep quiet, and tell it all out like a man.' To think I was telling lies to my own child! for I did it only to humour him, thinking, poor little fellow, his brain was wrong.

'Yes, father. Father, there is some one in the park – some one that has been badly used.'

'Hush, my dear; you remember, there is to be no excitement. Well, who is this somebody, and who has been ill-using him? We will soon put a stop to that.'

'Ah,' cried Roland, 'but it is not so easy as you think. I don't know who it is. It is just a cry. Oh, if you could hear it! It gets into my head in my sleep. I heard it as clear as clear; and they think that I am dreaming – or raving perhaps,' the boy said, with a sort of disdainful smile.

This look of his perplexed me; it was less like fever than I thought. 'Are you quite sure you have not dreamt it, Roland?' I said.

'Dreamt? – that!' He was springing up again when he suddenly bethought himself, and lay down flat with the same sort of smile on his face. 'The pony heard it too,' he said 'She jumped as if she had been shot. If I had not grasped at the reins – for I was frightened, father—'

'No shame to you, my boy,' said I, though I scarcely knew why.

'If I hadn't held to her like a leech, she'd have pitched me over her head, and she never drew breath till we were at the door. Did the pony dream it?' he said, with a soft disdain, yet indulgence for my foolishness. Then he added slowly: 'It was only a cry the first time, and all the time before you went away. I wouldn't tell you, for it was so wretched to be frightened. I thought it might be a hare or a rabbit snared, and I went in the morning and looked, but there was nothing. It was after you went I heard it really first, and this is what he says.' He raised himself on his elbow close to me, and looked me in the face. '"Oh, mother, let me in! oh, mother, let me in!"' As he said the words a mist came over his face, the mouth quivered, the soft features all melted and changed, and when he had ended these pitiful words, dissolved in a shower of heavy tears.

Was it a hallucination? Was it the fever of the brain? Was it the disordered fancy caused by great bodily weakness? How could I tell? I thought it wisest to accept it as if it were all true.

'This is very touching, Roland,' I said.

'Oh, if you had just heard it, father! I said to myself, "if father heard it he would do something"; but mamma, you know, she's given over to Simson, and that fellow's a doctor, and never thinks of anything but clapping you into bed.'

'We must not blame Simson for being a doctor, Roland.'

'No, no,' said my boy, with delightful toleration and indulgence; 'oh, no; that's the good of him – that's what he's for; I know that. But you – you are different; you are just father: and you'll do something – directly, papa, directly – this very night.'

'Surely,' I said. 'No doubt, it is some little lost child.'

He gave me a sudden, swift look, investigating my face as though to see whether, after all, this was everything my eminence as 'father' came to – no more than that? Then he got hold of my shoulder, clutching it with his thin hand: 'Look here,' he said, with a quiver in his voice; 'suppose it wasn't – living at all!'

'My dear boy, how then could you have heard it?' I said.

He turned away from me, with a pettish exclamation – ' As if you didn't know better than that!'

'Do you want to tell me it is a ghost?' I said.

Roland withdrew his hand; his countenance assumed an aspect of great dignity and gravity; a slight quiver remained about his lips. 'Whatever it was – you always said we were not to call names. It was something – in trouble. Oh, father, in terrible trouble!'

'But, my boy,' I said – I was at my wits' end – 'if it was a child that was lost, or any poor human creature— But, Roland, what do you want me to do?'

'I should know if I was you,' said the child, eagerly. 'That is what I always said to myself – "Father will know." Oh, papa, papa, to have to face it night after night, in such terrible, terrible trouble! and never to be able to do it any good. I don't want to cry; it's like a baby, I know; but what can I do else? – out there all by itself in the ruin, and nobody to help it. I can't bear it, I can't bear it!' cried my generous boy. And in his weakness he burst out, after many attempts to restrain it, into a great childish fit of sobbing and tears.

I do not know that I ever was in a greater perplexity in my life; and afterwards, when I thought of it, there was something comic in it too. It is bad enough to find your child's mind possessed with the conviction that he has seen – or heard – a ghost. But that he should require you to go instantly and help that ghost, was the most bewildering experience that had ever come my way. I am a sober man myself, and not superstitious – at least any more than everybody is superstitious. Of course I do not believe in ghosts; but I don't deny, any more than other people, that there are stories which I cannot pretend to understand. My blood got a sort of chill in my veins at the idea that Roland should be a ghost-seer; for that generally means a hysterical temperament and weak health and all that men most hate and fear for their children. But that I should take up his ghost and right its wrongs, and save it from its trouble, was such a mission as was enough to confuse any man. I did my best to console my boy without giving any promise of this astonishing kind; but he was too sharp for me. He would have none of my caresses. With sobs breaking in at intervals upon his voice, and the rain-drops hanging on his eye-lids, he yet returned to the charge.

'It will be there now – it will be there all the night. Oh think, papa, think, if it was me! I can't rest for thinking of it. Don't!' he cried, putting away my hand – 'don't! You go and help it, and mother can take care of me.'

'But, Roland, what can I do?'

My boy opened his eyes, which were large with weakness and fever, and gave me a smile such, I think, as sick children only know the secret of. 'I was sure you would know as soon as you came. I always said – "Father will know"; and mother,' he cried, with a softening of repose upon his face, his limbs relaxing, his form sinking with a luxurious ease in his bed – 'mother can come and take care of me.'

I called her, and saw him turn to her with the complete dependence of a child, and then I went away and left them, as perplexed a man as any in Scotland. I must say, however, I had this consolation, that my mind was greatly eased about Roland. He might be under a hallucination, but his head was clear enough, and I did not think him so ill as everybody else did. The girls were astonished even at the ease with which I took it. 'How do you think he is?' they said in a breath, coming round me, laying hold of me. 'Not half so ill as I expected,' I said; 'not very bad at all.' 'Oh, papa, you are a darling,' cried Agatha, kissing me, and crying upon my shoulder; while little Jeanie, who was as pale as Roland, clasped both her arms around mine, and could not speak at all. I knew nothing about it, not half so much as Simson; but they believed in me; they had a feeling that all would go right now. God is very good to you when your children look to you like that. It makes one humble, not proud. I was not worthy of it; and then I recollected that I had to act the part of a father to Roland's ghost, which made me almost laugh, though I might just as well have cried. It was the strangest mission that ever was entrusted to mortal man.

It was then I remembered suddenly the looks of the men when they turned to take the brougham to the stables in the dark that morning: they had not liked it, and the horses had not liked it. I remembered that even in my anxiety about Roland I had heard them tearing along the avenue back to the stables, and had made a memorandum mentally that I must speak of it. It seemed to me that the best thing I could do was to go to the stables now and make a few inquiries. It is impossible to fathom the minds of rustics; there might be some devilry of practical joking, for anything I knew; or they might have some interest in getting up a bad reputation for the Brentwood avenue. It was getting dark by the time I went out, and nobody who knows the country will need to be told how black is the darkness of a November night under high laurel-bushes and yew-trees. I walked into the heart of the shrubberies two or three times, not seeing a step before me, till I came out upon the broader carriage-road, where the trees opened a little, and there was a faint grey glimmer of sky visible, under which the great limes and elms stood darkling like ghosts; but it grew black again as I approached the corner where the ruins lay. Both eyes and ears were on the alert, as may be supposed; but I could see nothing in the absolute gloom, and, so far as I can recollect, I heard nothing. Nevertheless, there came a strong impression upon me that somebody was

there. It is a sensation which most people have felt. I have seen when it
has been strong enough to awake me out of sleep, the sense of some one
looking at me. I suppose my imagination had been affected by Roland's
story; and the mystery of the darkness is always full of suggestions. I
stamped my feet violently on the gravel to rouse myself, and called out
sharply, 'Who's there?' Nobody answered, nor did I expect any one to
answer, but the impression had been made. I was so foolish that I did not
like to look back, but went sideways, keeping an eye on the gloom behind.
It was with great relief that I spied the light in the stables, making a sort of
oasis in the darkness. I walked very quickly into the midst of that lighted
and cheerful place, and thought the clank of the groom's pail one of the
pleasantest sounds I had ever heard. The coachman was the head of this
little colony, and it was to his house I went to pursue my investigations.
He was a native of the district, and had taken care of the place in the
absence of the family for years; it was impossible but that he must know
everything that was going on, and all the traditions of the place. The men,
I could see, eyed me anxiously when I thus appeared at such an hour
among them, and followed me with their eyes to Jarvis's house, where he
lived alone with his old wife, their children being all married and out in
the world. Mrs Jarvis met me with anxious questions. How was the poor
young gentleman? but the others knew, I could see by their faces, that not
even this was the foremost thing in my mind.

'Noises?' – ou ay, there'll be noises – the wind in the trees, and the water
soughing down the glen. As for tramps, Cornel, no, there's little o' that
kind of cattle about here; and Merran at the gate's a careful body.' Jarvis
moved about with some embarrassment from one leg to another as he
spoke. He kept in the shade, and did not look at me more than he could
help. Evidently his mind was perturbed, and he had reasons for keeping
his own counsel. His wife sat by, giving him a quick look now and then,
but saying nothing. The kitchen was very snug, and warm, and bright – as
different as could be from the chill and mystery of the night outside.

'I think you are trifling with me, Jarvis,' I said.

'Triflin', Cornel? no me. What would I trifle for? If the deevil himsel'
was in the auld hoose, I have no interest in't one way or another—'

'Sandy, hold your peace!' cried his wife imperatively.

'And what am I to hold my peace for, wi' the Cornel standing there
asking a' thae questions? I'm saying, if the deevil himsel'—'

'And I'm telling ye hold your peace!' cried the woman, in great
excitement. 'Dark November weather and lang nichts, and us that ken a'
we ken. How daur ye name – a name that shouldna be spoken?' She threw

down her stocking and got up, also in great agitation. 'I tell't ye you never could keep it. It's no a thing that will hide; and the haill toun kens as weel as you or me. Tell the Cornel straight out – or see, I'll do it. I dinna hold wi' your secrets; and a secret that the hiall toun kens!' She snapped her fingers with an air of large disdain. As for Jarvis, ruddy and big as he was, he shrank to nothing before this decided woman. He repeated to her two or three times her own adjuration, 'Hold your peace!' then, suddenly changing his tone, cried out, 'Tell him then, confound ye! I'll wash my hands o't. If a' the ghosts in Scotland were in the auld hoose, is that ony concern o' mine?'

After this I elicited without much difficulty the whole story. In the opinion of the Jarvises, and of everybody about, the certainty that the place was haunted was beyond all doubt. As Sandy and his wife warmed to the tale, one tripping up another in their eagerness to tell everything, it gradually developed as distinct a superstition as I ever heard, and not without poetry and pathos. How long it was since the voice had been heard first, nobody could tell with certainty. Jarvis's opinion was that his father, who had been coachman at Brentwood before him, had never heard anything about it, and that the whole thing had arisen within the last ten years, since the complete dismantling of the old house: which was a wonderfully modern date for a tale so well authenticated. According to these witnesses, and to several whom I questioned afterwards, and who were all in perfect agreement, it was only in the months of November and December that 'the visitation' occurred. During these months, the darkest of the year, scarcely a night passed without the recurrence of these inexplicable cries. Nothing, it was said, had ever been seen – at least nothing that could be identified. Some people, bolder or more imaginative than the others, had seen the darkness moving, Mrs Jarvis said, with unconscious poetry. It began when night fell and continued, at intervals, till day broke. Very often it was only an inarticulate cry and moaning, but sometimes the words which had taken possession of my poor boy's fancy had been distinctly audible – 'Oh, mother, let me in!' The Jarvises were not aware that there had ever been any investigation into it. The estate of Brentwood had lapsed into the hands of a distant branch of the family, who had lived but little there; and of the many people who had taken it, as I had done, few had remained through two Decembers. And nobody had taken the trouble to make a very close examination into the facts. 'No, no,' Jarvis said, shaking his head. 'No, no, Cornel. Wha wad set themsels up for a laughin'-stock to a' the country-side, making a wark about a ghost? Naebody believes in ghosts. It bid to be the wind in the trees, the last gentleman said, or some effec' o' the water wrastlin' among the rocks.

He said it was a' quite easy explained: but he gave up the hoose. And when you cam, Cornel, we were awfu' anxious you should never hear. What for should I have spoiled the bargain and hairmed the property for no-thing?'

'Do you call my child's life nothing?' I said in the trouble of the moment, unable to restrain myself. 'And instead of telling this all to me, you have told it to him – to a delicate boy, a child unable to sift evidence, or judge for himself, a tender-hearted young creature—'

I was walking about the room with an anger all the hotter that I felt it to be most likely quite unjust. My heart was full of bitterness against the stolid retainers of a family who were content to risk other people's children and comfort rather than let the house lie empty. If I had been warned I might have taken precautions, or left the place, or sent Roland away, a hundred things which now I could not do; and here I was with my boy in a brain-fever, and his life, the most precious life on earth, hanging in the balance, dependent on whether or not I could get to the reason of a commonplace ghost story! I paced about in high wrath, and seeing what I was to do; for, to take Roland away, even if he were able to travel, would not settle his agitated mind; and I feared even that a scientific explanation of refracted sound, or reverberation, or any other of the easy certainties with which we elder men are silenced, would have very little effect upon the boy.

'Cornel,' said Jarvis, solemnly, 'and *she'll* bear me witness – the young gentleman never heard a word from me – no, nor from either groom or gardener; I'll gie ye my word for that. In the first place, he's no a lad that invites ye to talk. There are some that are, and some that arena. Some will draw ye on, till ye've tellt them a' the clatter of the toun, and a' ye ken, and whiles mair. But Maister Roland, his mind's fu' of his books. He's aye civil and kind, and a fine lad; but no that sort. And ye see it's for a' our interest, Cornel, that you should stay at Brentwood. I took it upon me mysel' to pass the word – "No a syllable to Maister Roland, nor to the young leddies – no a syllable." The women-servants, that have little reason to be out at night, ken little or nothing about it. And some think it grand to have a ghost so long as they're no in the way of coming across it. If you had been tellt the story to begin with, maybe ye would have thought so yourself.'

This was true enough, though it did not throw any light upon my perplexity. If we had heard of it to start with, it is possible that all the family would have considered the possession of a ghost a distinct advantage. It is the fashion of the times. We never think what a risk it is to play with young imaginations, but cry out, in the fashionable jargon, 'A ghost – nothing else was wanted to make it perfect.' I should not have been above this myself. I should have smiled, of course, at the idea of the ghost at all, but then to feel that it was mine would have pleased my vanity. Oh, yes, I claim no exemption. The girls would have been delighted. I could fancy their eagerness, their interest, and excitement. No; if we had been told, it would have done no good – we should have made the bargain all the more eagerly, the fools that we are. 'And there has been no attempt to investigate it,' I said, 'to see what it really is?'

'Eh, Cornel,' said the coachman's wife, 'wha would investigate, as ye call it, a thing that nobody believes in? Ye would be the laughing-stock of a' the country-side, as my man says.'

'But you believe in it,' I said, turning upon her hastily. The woman was taken by surprise. She made a step backward out of my way.

'Lord, Cornel, how ye frighten a body! Me! – there's awful strange things in this world. An unlearned person doesna ken what to think. But the minister and the gentry they just laugh in your face. Inquire into the thing that is not! Na, na, we just let it be.'

'Come with me, Jarvis,' I said, hastily, 'and we'll make an attempt at least. Say nothing to the men or to anybody. I'll come back after dinner, and we'll make a serious attempt to see what it is, if it is anything. If I hear it – which I doubt – you may be sure I shall never rest till I make it out. Be ready for me about ten o'clock.'

'Me, Cornel!' Jarvis said, in a faint voice. I had not been looking at him in my own preoccupation, but when I did so, I found that the greatest change had come over the fat and ruddy coachman. 'Me, Cornel!' he repeated, wiping the perspiration from his brow. His ruddy face hung in flabby folds, his knees knocked together, his voice seemed half extinguished in his throat. Then he began to rub his hands and smile upon me in a deprecating, imbecile way. 'There's nothing I wouldna do to pleasure ye, Cornel,' taking a step further back. 'I'm sure *she* kens I've aye said I never had to do with a mair fair, weelspoken gentleman—' Here Jarvis came to a pause, again looking at me, rubbing his hands.

'Well?' I said.

'But eh, sir!' he went on, with the same imbecile yet insinuating smile, 'if ye'll reflect that I am no used to my feet. With a horse atween my legs, or the reins in my hand, I'm maybe nae worse than other men; but on fit, Cornel— It's no the – bogles; – but I've been cavalry, ya see,' with a little hoarse laugh, 'a' my life. To face a thing ye didna understan' – on your feet, Cornel—'

'Well, sir, if *I* do it,' said I tartly, 'why shouldn't you?'

'Eh, Cornel, there's an awfu' difference. In the first place, ye tramp about the haill country-side, and think naething of it; but a walk tires me mair than a hunard miles' drive; and then ye'e a gentleman, and do your ain pleasure; and you're no so auld as me; and it's for your ain bairn, ye see, Cornel; and then—'

'He believes in it, Cornel, and you dinna believe in it,' the woman said.

'Will you come with me?' I said, turning to her.

She jumped back, upsetting her chair in her bewilderment. 'Me!' with a scream, and then fell into a sort of hysterical laugh. 'I wouldna say but what I would go; but what would the folk say to hear of Cornel Mortimer with an auld silly woman at his heels?'

The suggestion made me laugh too, though I had little inclination for it. 'I'm sorry you have so little spirit, Jarvis,' I said. 'I must find some one else, I suppose.'

Jarvis, touched by this, began to remonstrate, but I cut him short. My butler was a soldier who had been with me in India, and was not supposed to fear anything – man or devil – certainly not the former; and I felt that I was losing time. The Jarvises were too thankful to get rid of me. They attended me to the door with the most anxious courtesies. Outside, the two grooms stood close by, a little confused by my sudden exit. I don't know if perhaps they had been listening – at least standing as near as possible, to catch any scrap of the conversation. I waved my hand to them as I went past, in answer to their salutations, and it was very apparent to me that they also were glad to see me go.

And it will be thought very strange, but it would be weak not to add, that I myself, though bent on the investigation I have spoken of, pledged to Roland to carry it out, and feeling that my boy's health, perhaps his life, depended on the result of my inquiry – I felt the most unaccountable reluctance to pass these ruins on my way home. My curiosity was intense; and yet it was all my mind could do to pull my body along. I dare say the scientific people would describe it the other way, and attribute my cowardice to the state of my stomach. I went on; but if I had followed my impulse, I should have turned and bolted. Everything in me seemed to cry out against it; my heart thumped, my pulses all began, like sledge-hammers, beating against my ears and every sensitive part. It was very dark, as I have said; the old house, with its shapeless tower, loomed a heavy mass through the darkness, which was only not entirely so solid as itself. On the other hand, the great dark cedars of which we were so proud seemed to fill up the night. My foot strayed out of the path in my confusion and the gloom together, and I brought myself up with a cry as I felt myself knock against something solid. What was it? The contact with hard stone and lime, and prickly bramblebushes, restored me a little to myself. 'Oh, it's only the old gable,' I said aloud, with a little laugh to reassure myself. The rough feeling of the stones reconciled me. As I groped about thus, I shook off my visionary folly. What so easily explained as that I should have strayed from the path in the darkness? This brought me back to common existence, as if I had been shaken by a wise hand out of all the silliness of superstition. How silly it was, after all! What did it matter which path I took? I laughed again, this time with better heart – when suddenly, in a moment, the blood was chilled in my veins, a shiver stole along my spine, my faculties seemed to forsake me. Close by me at my side, at my feet, there was a sigh. No, not a groan, not a moaning, not anything so tangible – a perfectly soft, faint, inarticulate sigh. I sprang back, and my heart stopped beating. Mistaken! no, mistake was impossible. I heard it as clearly as I hear myself speak; a long, soft, weary sigh, as if drawn to the utmost, and emptying out a load of sadness that filled the breast. To hear this in the solitude, in the dark, in the night (though it was still early), had an effect which I cannot describe. I feel it now – something cold creeping over me, up into my hair, and down to my feet, which refused to move. I cried out with a trembling voice, 'Who is there?' as I had done before – but there was no reply.

I got home – I don't quite know how; but in my mind there was no longer any indifference as to the thing, whatever it was, that haunted these ruins. My scepticism disappeared like a mist. I was as firmly determined that there was something as Roland was. I did not for a moment pretend to myself that it was possible I could be deceived; there were movements and noises which I understood all about, cracklings of small branches in the frost, and little rolls of gravel on the path, such as have a very eerie sound sometimes, and perplex you with wonder as to who has done it, *when there is no real mystery*; but I assure you all these little movements of nature don't affect you one bit *when there is something*. I understood *them*. I did not understand the sigh. That was not simple nature; there was meaning in it – feeling, the soul of a creature invisible. This is the thing that human nature trembles at – a creature invisible, yet with sensations, feelings, a power somehow of expressing itself. I had not the same sense of unwillingness to turn my back upon the scene of the mystery which I had experienced in going to the stables; but I almost ran home, impelled by eagerness to get everything done that had to be done in order to apply myself to finding it out. Bagley was in the hall as usual when I went in. He was always there in the afternoon, always with the appearance of perfect occupation, yet, so far as I know, never doing anything. The door was open, so that I hurried in without any pause, breathless; but the sight of his calm regard, as he came to help me off with my overcoat, subdued me in a moment. Anything out of the way, anything incomprehensible, faded to nothing in the presence of Bagley. You saw and wondered how *he* was made: the parting of his hair, the tie of his white neckcloth, the fit of his trousers, all perfect as works of art; but you could see how they were done, which makes all the difference. I flung myself upon him, so to speak, without waiting to note the extreme unlikeness of the man to anything of the kind I meant. 'Bagley,' I said, 'I want you to come out with me tonight to watch for—'

'Poachers, Colonel,' he said, a gleam of pleasure running all over him.

'No, Bagley; a great deal worse,' I cried.

'Yes, Colonel; at what hour, sir?' the man said; but then I had not told him what it was.

It was ten o'clock when we set out. All was perfectly quiet indoors. My wife was with Roland, who had been quite calm, she said, and who (though, no doubt, the fever must run its course) had been better since I came. I told Bagley to put on a thick greatcoat over his evening coat, and did the same myself – with strong boots; for the soil was like a sponge, or worse. Talking to him, I almost forgot what we were going to do. It was darker even than it had been before, and Bagley kept very close to me as we went along. I had a small lantern in my hand, which gave us a partial guidance. We had come to the corner where the path turns. On one side was the bowling-green, which the girls had taken possession of for their croquet-ground – a wonderful enclosure surrounded by high hedges of holly, three hundred years old and more; on the other, the ruins. Both were black as night; but before we got so far, there was a little opening in which we could just discern the trees and the lighter line of the road. I thought it best to pause there and take breath. 'Bagley,' I said, 'there is something about these ruins I don't understand. It is there I am going. Keep your eyes open and your wits about you. Be ready to pounce upon any stranger you see – anything, man or woman. Don't hurt, but seize – anything you see.' 'Colonel,' said Bagley, with a little tremor in his breath, 'they do say there's things there – as is neither man nor woman.' There was no time for words. 'Are you game to follow me, my man? that's the question,' I said. Bagley fell in without a word, and saluted. I knew then I had nothing to fear.

We went, so far as I could guess, exactly as I had come, when I heard that sigh. The darkness, however, was so complete that all marks, as of trees or paths, disappeared. One moment we felt our feet on the gravel, another sinking noiselessly into the slippery grass, that was all. I had shut up my lantern, not wishing to scare anyone, whoever it might be. Bagley followed, it seemed to me, exactly in my footsteps as I made my way, as I supposed, towards the mass of the ruined house. We seemed to take a long time groping along seeking this; the squash of the wet soil under our feet was the only thing that marked our progress. After a while I stood still to see, or rather feel, where we were. The darkness was very still, but no stiller than is usual in a winter's night. The sounds I have mentioned – the crackling of twigs, the roll of a pebble, the sound of some rustle in the dead leaves, or creeping creature on the grass – were audible when you listened, all mysterious enough when your mind is disengaged, but to me cheering now as signs of the livingness of nature, even in the death of the frost. As we stood still there came up from the trees in the glen the prolonged hoot of an owl. Bagley started with alarm, being in a state of general nervousness, and not knowing what he was afraid of. But to me the sound was encouraging and pleasant, being so comprehensible. 'An owl,' I said, under my breath. 'Y–es, Colonel,' said Bagley, his teeth chattering. We stood still about five minutes, while it broke into the still brooding of the air, the sound widening out in circles, dying upon the darkness. This sound, which is not a cheerful one, made me almost gay. It was natural, and relieved the tension of the mind. I moved on with new courage, my nervous excitement calming down.

When all at once, quite suddenly, close to us, at our feet, there broke out a cry. I made a spring backwards in the first moment of surprise and horror, and in doing so came sharply against the same rough masonry and brambles that had struck me before. This new sound came upwards from the ground – a low, moaning, wailing voice, full of suffering and pain. The contrast between it and the hoot of the owl was indescribable; the one with a wholesome wildness and naturalness that hurt nobody – the other a sound that made one's blood curdle, full of human misery. With a great deal of fumbling – for in spite of everything I could do to keep up my courage my hands shook – I managed to remove the slide of my lantern. The light leaped out like something living, and made the place visible in a moment. We were what would have been inside the ruined building had anything remained but the gable-wall which I have described. It was close to us, the vacant doorway in it going out straight into the blackness outside. The light showed the bit of wall, the ivy glistening upon it in clouds of dark green, the bramble-branches waving, and below, the open door – a door that led to nothing. It was from this the voice came which died out just as the light flashed upon this strange scene. There was a moment's silence, and then it broke forth again. The sound was so near, so penetrating, so pitiful, that, on the nervous start I gave, the light fell out of my hand. As I groped for it in the dark my hand was clutched by Bagley, who I think must have dropped upon his knees; but I was too much perturbed myself to think much of this. He clutched at me in the confusion of his terror, forgetting all his usual decorum. 'For God's sake, what is it, sir?' he gasped. If I yielded, there was evidently an end of both of us. 'I can't tell,' I said, 'any more than you; that's what we've got to find out: up, man, up!' I pulled him to his feet. 'Will you go round and examine the other side, or will you stay here with the lantern?' Bagley gasped at me with a face of horror. 'Can't we stay together, Colonel?' he said – his knees were trembling under him. I pushed him against the corner of the wall, and put the light into his hands. 'Stand fast till I come back; shake yourself together, man; let nothing pass you,' I said. The voice was within two or three feet of us, of that there could be no doubt.

I went myself to the other side of the wall, keeping close to it. The light shook in Bagley's hand, but tremulous though it was, shone out through the vacant door, one oblong block of light marking all the crumbling corners and hanging masses of foliage. Was that something dark huddled in a heap by the side of it? I pushed forward across the light in the doorway, and fell upon it with my hands; but it was only a juniper-bush growing close against the wall. Meanwhile, the sight of my figure crossing the doorway had brought Bagley's nervous excitement to a height: he flew at me, gripping my shoulder. 'I've got him, Colonel! I've got him!' he cried, with a voice of sudden exultation. He thought it was a man, and was at once relieved. But at that moment the voice burst forth again between us, at our feet – more close to us than any separate being could be. He dropped off from me, and fell against the wall, his jaw dropping as if he were dying. I suppose, at the same moment, he saw that it was me whom he had clutched. I, for my part, had scarcely more command of myself. I snatched the light out of his hand, and flashed it all about me wildly. Nothing – the juniper-bush which I thought I had never seen before, the heavy growth of the glistening ivy, the brambles waving. It was close to my ears now, crying, crying, pleading as if for life. Either I heard the same words Roland had heard, or else, in my excitement, his imagination got possession of mine. The voice went on, growing into distinct articulation, but wavering about, now from one point, now from another, as if the owner of it were moving slowly back and forward – 'Mother! mother!' and then an outburst of wailing. As my mind steadied, getting accustomed (as one's mind gets accustomed to anything), it seemed to me as if some uneasy, miserable creature was pacing up and down before a closed door. Sometimes – but that must have been excitement – I thought I heard a sound like knocking, and then another burst, 'Oh, mother! mother!' All this close, close to the space where I was standing with my lantern – now before me, now behind me: a creature restless, unhappy, moaning, crying, before the vacant doorway, which no one could either shut or open more.

'Do you hear it, Bagley? do you hear what it is saying?' I cried, stepping in through the doorway. He was lying against the wall – his eyes glazed, half dead with terror. He made a motion of his lips as if to answer me, but no sounds came; then lifted his hand with a curious imperative movement as if ordering me to be silent and listen. And how long I did so I cannot tell. It began to have an interest, an exciting hold upon me, which I could not describe. It seemed to call up visibly a scene any one could understand – a something shut out, restlessly wandering to and fro; sometimes the voice dropped, as if throwing itself down – sometimes wandered off a few paces, growing sharp and clear. 'Oh, mother, let me in! oh, mother, mother, let me in! oh, let me in!' every word was clear to me. No wonder the boy had gone wild with pity. I tried to steady my mind upon Roland, upon his conviction that I could do something, but my head swam with the excitement, even when I partially overcame the terror. At last the words died away, and there was a sound of sobs and moaning. I cried out, 'In the name of God who are you?' with a kind of feeling in my mind that to use the name of God was profane, seeing that I did not believe in ghosts or anything supernatural; but I did it all the same, and waited, my heart giving a leap of terror lest there should be a reply. Why this should have been I cannot tell, but I had a feeling that if there was an answer, it would be more than I could bear. But there was no answer; the moaning went on, and then, as if it had been real, the voice rose, a little higher again, the words recommenced, 'Oh, mother, let me in! oh, mother, let me in!' with an expression that was heart-breaking to hear.

As *if it had been real!* What do I mean by that? I suppose I got less alarmed as the thing went on. I began to recover the use of my senses – I seemed to explain it all to myself by saying that this had once happened, that it was a recollection of a real scene. Why there should have seemed something quite satisfactory and composing in this explanation I cannot tell, but so it was. I began to listen almost as if it had been a play, forgetting Bagley, who, I almost think, had fainted, leaning against the wall. I was startled out of this strange spectatorship that had fallen upon me by the sudden rush of something which made my heart jump once more, a large black figure in the doorway waving its arms. 'Come in! come in! come in!' it shouted out hoarsely at the top of a deep bass voice, and then poor Bagley fell down senseless across the threshold. He was less sophisticated than I – he had not been able to bear it any longer. I took him for something supernatural, as he took me, and it was some time before I awoke to the necessities of the moment. I remembered only after, that from the time I began to give my attention to the man, I heard the other voice no more. It was some time before I brought him to. It must have been a strange scene; the lantern making a luminous spot in the darkness, the man's white face lying on the black earth, I over him, doing what I could for him. Probably I should have been thought to be murdering him had any one seen us. When at last I succeeded in pouring a little brandy down his throat he sat up and looked about him wildly. 'What's up?' he said; then recognising me, tried to struggle to his feet with a faint 'Beg your pardon, Colonel.' I got him home as best I could, making him lean upon my arm. The great fellow was as weak as a child. Fortunately he did not for some time remember what had happened. From the time Bagley fell the voice had stopped, and all was still.

'You've got an epidemic in your house, Colonel,' Simson said to me next morning. 'What's the meaning of it all? Here's your butler raving about a voice. This will never do, you know; and so far as I can make out, you are in it too.'

'Yes, I am in it, doctor. I thought I had better speak to you. Of course you are treating Roland all right – but the boy is not raving, he is as sane as you or me. It's all true.'

'As sane as – I – or you. I never thought the boy insane. He's got cerebral excitement, fever. I don't know what you've got. There's something very queer about the look of your eyes.'

'Come,' said I, 'you can't put us all to bed, you know. You had better listen and hear the symptoms in full.'

The doctor shrugged his shoulders, but he listened to me patiently. He did not believe a word of the story, that was clear; but he heard it all from beginning to end. 'My dear fellow,' he said, 'the boy told me just the same. It's an epidemic. When one person falls a victim to this sort of thing, it's as safe as can be – there's always two or three.'

'Then how do you account for it?' I said.

'Oh, account for it! – that's a different matter; there's no accounting for the freaks our brains are subject to. If it's delusion; if it's some trick of the echoes or the winds – some phonetic disturbance or other—'

'Come with me tonight, and judge for yourself,' I said.

Upon this he laughed aloud, then said, 'That's not such a bad idea; but it would ruin me for ever if it were known that John Simson was ghost-hunting.'

'There it is,' said I; 'you dart down on us who are unlearned with your phonetic disturbances, but you daren't examine what the thing really is for fear of being laughed at. That's science!'

'It's not science – it's common sense,' said the doctor. 'The thing has delusion on the front of it. It is encouraging an unwholesome tendency even to examine. What good could come of it? Even if I am convinced, I shouldn't believe.'

'I should have said so yesterday; and I don't want you to be convinced or to believe,' said I. 'If you prove it to be a delusion, I shall be very much obliged to you for one. Come; somebody must go with me.'

'You are cool,' said the doctor. 'You've disabled this poor fellow of yours, and made him – on that point – a lunatic for life; and now you want to disable me. But for once, I'll do it. To save appearance, if you'll give me a bed, I'll come over after my last rounds.'

It was agreed that I should meet him at the gate, and that we should visit the scene of last night's occurrences before we came to the house, so that nobody might be the wiser. It was scarcely possible to hope that the cause of Bagley's sudden illness should not somehow steal into the knowledge of the servants at least, and it was better that all should be done as quietly as possible. The day seemed to me a very long one. I had to spend a certain part of it with Roland, which was a terrible ordeal for me – for what could I say to the boy? The improvement continued, but he was still in a very precarious state, and the trembling vehemence with which he turned to me when his mother left the room filled me with alarm. 'Father!' he said, quietly. 'Yes, my boy; I am giving my best attention to it – all is being done that I can do. I have not come to any conclusion – yet. I am neglecting nothing you said,' I cried. What I could not do was to give his active mind any encouragement to dwell upon the mystery. It was a hard predicament, for some satisfaction had to be given him. He looked at me very wistfully, with the great blue eyes which shone so large and brilliant out of his white and worn face. 'You must trust me,' I said. 'Yes, father. Father understands,' he said to himself, as if to soothe some inward doubt. I left him as soon as I could. He was about the most precious thing I had on earth, and his health my first thought; but yet somehow, in the excitement of this other subject, I put that aside, and preferred not to dwell upon Roland, which was the most curious part of it all.

That night at eleven I met Simson at the gate. He had come by train, and I let him in gently myself. I had been so much absorbed in the coming experiment that I passed the ruins in going to meet him, almost without thought, if you can understand that. I had my lantern; and he showed me a coil of taper which he had ready for use. 'There is nothing like light,' he said, in his scoffing tone. It was a very still night, scarcely a sound, but not so dark. We could keep the path without difficulty as we went along. As we approached the spot we could hear a low moaning, broken occasionally by a bitter cry. 'Perhaps that is your voice,' said the doctor; 'I thought it must be something of the kind. That's a poor brute caught in some of these infernal traps of yours; you'll find it among the bushes somewhere.' I said nothing. I felt no particular fear, but a triumphant satisfaction in what was to follow. I led him to the spot where Bagley and I had stood on the previous night. All was silent as a winter night could be – so silent that we heard far off the sound of the horses in the stables, the shutting of a window at the house. Simson lighted his taper and went peering about, poking into all the corners. We looked like two conspirators lying in wait for some unfortunate traveller; but not a sound broke the quiet. The moaning had stopped before we came up; a star or two shone over us in the sky, looking down as if surprised at our strange proceedings. Dr Simson did nothing but utter subdued laughs under his breath. 'I thought as much,' he said. 'It is just the same with tables and all other kinds of ghostly apparatus; a sceptic's presence stops everything. When I am present nothing ever comes off. How long do you think it will be necessary to stay here? Oh, I don't complain; only, when *you* are satisfied, I am – quite.'

I will not deny that I was disappointed beyond measure by this result. It made me look like a credulous fool. It gave the doctor such a pull over me as nothing else could. I should point all his morals for years to come, and his materialism, his scepticism, would be increased beyond endurance. 'It seems, indeed,' I said, 'that there is to be no—' 'Manifestation,' he said, laughing; 'that is what all the mediums say. No manifestations, in consequence of the presence of an unbeliever.' His laugh sounded very uncomfortable to me in the silence; and it was now near midnight. But that laugh seemed the signal; before it died away the moaning we had heard before was resumed. It started from some distance off, and came towards us, nearer and nearer, like some one walking along and moaning to himself. There could be no idea now that it was a hare caught in a trap. The approach was slow, like that of a weak person, with little halts and pauses. We heard it coming along the grass straight towards the vacant doorway. Simson had been a little startled by the first sound. He said hastily, 'That child has no business to be out so late.' But he felt, as well as I, that this was no child's voice. As it came nearer, he grew silent, and, going to the doorway with his taper, stood looking out towards the sound. The taper being unprotected blew about in the night air, though there was scarcely any wind. I threw the light of my lantern steady and white across the same space. It was a blaze of light in the midst of the blackness. A little icy thrill had gone over me at the first sound, but as it came close, I confess th t my only feeling was satisfaction. The scoffer could scoff no more. The light touched his own face, and showed a very perplexed c untenance. If he was afraid, he concealed it with great success, but he was perplexed. And then all that had happened on the previous night was enacted once more. It fell strangely upon me with a sense of repetition. Every cry, every sob seemed the same as before. I listened almost without any emotion at all in my own person, thinking of its effect upon Simson. He maintained a very bold front on the whole. All that coming and going of the voice was, if our ears could be trusted, exactly in front of the vacant, blank doorway, blazing full of light, which caught and shone in the glistening leaves of the great hollies at a little distance. Not a rabbit could have crossed the turf without being seen; but there was nothing. After a time, Simson, with a certain caution and bodily reluctance, as it seemed to me, went out with his roll of taper into this space. His figure showed against the holly in full outline. Just at this moment the voice sank, as was its custom, and seemed to fling itself down at the door. Simson recoiled violently, as if someone had come up against him, then turned, and held his taper low as if examining something. 'Do you see anybody?' I cried in a whisper, feeling the chill of nervous panic steal over me at this action. 'It's nothing but a – confounded juniper-bush,' he said. This I knew very well to be nonsense, for the juniper-bush was on the other side. He went about after this round and round, poking his taper everywhere, then returned to me on the inner side of the wall. He scoffed no longer; his face was contracted and pale. 'How long does this go on?' he whispered to me, like a man who does not wish to interrupt some one who is speaking. I had become too much perturbed myself to remark whether the successions and changes of the voice were the same as last night. It suddenly went out in the air almost as he was speaking, with a soft, reiterated sob dying away. If there had been anything to be seen, I should have said that the person was at that moment crouching on the ground close to the door.

We walked home very silent afterwards. It was only when we were in sight of the house that I said, 'What do you think of it?' 'I can't tell what to think of it,' he said, quickly. He took – though he was a very temperate man – not the claret I was going to offer him, but some brandy from the tray, and swallowed it almost undiluted. 'Mind you, I don't believe a word of it,' he said, when he had lighted his candle; 'but I can't tell what to think,' he turned round to add, when he was half-way upstairs.

All of this, however, did me no good with the solution of my problem. I was to help this weeping, sobbing thing, which was already to me as distinct a personality as anything I knew – or what should I say to Roland? It was on my heart that my boy would die if I could not find some way of helping this creature. You may be surprised that I should speak of it in this way. I did not know if it was man or woman; but I no more doubted that it was a soul in pain than I doubted my own being; and it was my business to soothe this pain – to deliver it, if that was possible. Was ever such a task given to an anxious father trembling for his only boy? I felt in my heart, fantastic as it may appear, that I must fulfil this somehow, or part with my child; and you may conceive that rather than do that I was ready to die. But even my dying would not have advanced me – unless by bringing me into the same world with that seeker at the door.

Next morning Simson was out before breakfast, and came in with evident signs of the damp grass on his boots, and a look of worry and weariness, which did not say much for the night he had passed. He improved a little after breakfast, and visited his two patients, for Bagley was still an invalid. I went out with him on his way to the train, to hear what he had to say about the boy. 'He is going on very well,' he said; 'there are no complications as yet. But mind you, that's not a boy to be trifled with, Mortimer. Not a word to him about last night.' I had to tell him then of my last interview with Roland, and of the impossible demand he had made upon me – by which, though he tried to laugh, he was much discomposed, as I could see. 'We must just perjure ourselves all round,' he said, 'and swear you exorcised it'; but the man was too kind-hearted to be satisfied with that. 'It's frightfully serious for you, Mortimer. I can't laugh as I should like to. I wish I saw a way out of it, for your sake. By the way,' he added shortly, 'didn't you notice that juniper-bush on the left-hand side?' 'There was one on the right hand of the door. I noticed you made that mistake last night.' 'Mistake!' he cried, with a curious low laugh, pulling up the collar of his coat as though he felt the cold – 'there's no juniper there this morning, left or right. Just go and see.' As he stepped into the train a few minutes after, he looked back upon me and beckoned me for a parting word. 'I'm coming back tonight,' he said.

I don't think I had any feeling about this as I turned away from that common bustle of the railway, which made my private preoccupations feel so strangely out of date. There had been a distinct satisfaction in my mind before that his scepticism had been so entirely defeated. But the more serious part of the matter pressed upon me now. I went straight from the railway to the manse, which stood on a little plateau on the side of the river opposite to the woods of Brentwood. The minister was one of a class which is not so common in Scotland as it used to be. He was a man of good family, well educated in the Scotch way, strong in philosophy, not so strong in Greek, strongest of all in experience – a man who had 'come across', in the course of his life, most people of note that had ever been in Scotland – and who was said to be very sound in doctrine, without infringing the toleration with which old men, who are good men, are generally endowed. He was old-fashioned; perhaps he did not think so much about the troublous problems of theology as many of the young men, nor ask himself any hard questions about the Confession of Faith – but he understood human nature, which is perhaps better. He received me with a cordial welcome. 'Come away, Colonel Mortimer,' he said; 'I'm all the more glad to see you, that I feel it's a good sign for the boy. He's doing well? – God be praised – and the Lord bless him and keep him. He has many a poor body's prayers – and that can do nobody harm.'

'He will need them all, Dr Moncrieff,' I said, 'and your counsel too.' And I told him the story – more than I had told Simson. The old clergyman listened to me with many suppressed exclamations, and at the end the water stood in his eyes.

'That's just beautiful,' he said. 'I do not mind to have heard anything like it; it's as fine as Burns when he wished deliverance to one – that is prayed for in no kirk. Ay, ay! so he would have you console the poor lost spirit? God bless the boy! There's something more than common in that, Colonel Mortimer. And also the faith of him in his father! – I would like to put that into a sermon.' Then the old gentleman gave me an alarmed look, and said, 'No, no; I was not meaning a sermon; but I must write it down for the *Children's Record*.' I saw the thought that passed through his mind. Either he thought, or he feared I would think, of a funeral sermon. You may believe this did not make me more cheerful.

I can scarcely say that Dr Moncrieff gave me any advice. How could anyone advise on such a subject? But he said, 'I think I'll come too. I'm an old man; I'm less liable to be frightened than those that are further off the world unseen. It behoves me to think of my own journey there. I've no cut-and-dry beliefs on the subject. I'll come too; and maybe at the moment the Lord will put into our heads what to do.'

This gave me a little comfort – more than Simson had given me. To be clear about the cause of it was not my grand desire. It was another thing that was in my mind – my boy. As for the poor soul at the open door, I had no more doubt, as I have said, of its existence than I had of my own. It was no ghost to me. I knew the creature, and it was in trouble. That was my feeling about it, as it was Roland's. To hear it first was a great shock to my nerves, but not now; a man will get accustomed to anything. But to do something for it was the great problem; how was I to be serviceable to a being that was invisible, that was mortal no longer? 'Maybe at the moment the Lord will put it into our heads.' This is very old-fashioned phraseology, and a week before, most likely, I should have smiled (though always with kindness) at Dr Moncrieff's credulity; but there was a great comfort, whether rational or otherwise I cannot say, in the mere sound of the words.

The road to the station and the village lay through the glen – not by the ruins; but though the sunshine and the fresh air, and the beauty of the trees, and the sound of the water were all very soothing to the spirits, my mind was so full of my own subject that I could not refrain from turning to the right hand as I got to the top of the glen, and going straight to the place which I may call the scene of all my thoughts. I was lying full in the sunshine, like all the rest of the world. The ruined gable looked due east, and in the present aspect of the sun the light streamed down through the doorway as our lantern had done, throwing a flood of light upon the damp grass beyond. There was a strange suggestion in the open door – so futile, a kind of emblem of vanity – all free around, so that you could go where you pleased, and yet that semblance of an enclosure – that way of entrance, unnecessary, leading to nothing. And why any creature should pray and weep to get in – to nothing: or be kept out – by nothing! You could not dwell upon it, or it made your brain go round. I remembered however, what Simson said about the juniper, with a little smile on my own mind as to the inaccuracy of recollection, which even a scientific man will be guilty of. I could see now the light of my lantern gleaming upon the wet glistening surface of the spiky leaves at the right hand – and he ready to go to the stake for it that it was the left! I went round to make sure. And then I saw what he had said. Right or left there was no juniper at all. I was confounded by this, though it was entirely a matter of detail: nothing at all: a bush of brambles waving, the grass growing up to the very walls. But after all, though it gave me a shock for a moment, what did that matter? There were marks as if a number of footsteps had been up and down in front of the door; but these might have been our steps; and all was bright, peaceful, and still. I poked about the other ruin – the larger ruins of the old house – for some time, as I had done before. There were marks upon the grass here and there, I could not call them footsteps, all about; but that told for nothing one way or another. I had examined the ruined rooms closely the first day. They were half filled up with soil and *débris*, withered brackens and bramble – no refuge for anyone there. It vexed me that Jarvis should see me coming from that spot when he came up to me for his orders. I don't know whether my nocturnal expeditions had got wind among the servants. But there was a significant look in his face. Something in it I felt was like my own sensation when Simson in the midst of his scepticism was struck dumb. Jarvis felt satisfied that his veracity had been put beyond question. I never spoke to a servant of mine in such a peremptory tone before. I sent him away 'with a flea in his lug', as the man described it afterwards. Interference of any kind was intolerable to me at such a moment.

But what was strangest of all was, that I could not face Roland. I did not go up to his room as I would have naturally done at once. This the girls could not understand. They saw there was some mystery in it. 'Mother has gone to lie down,' Agatha said; 'he had such a good night.' 'But he wants you so, papa!' cried little Jeanie, always with her two arms embracing mine in a pretty way she had. I was obliged to go at last – but what could I say? I could only kiss him, and tell him to keep still – that I was doing all I could. There is something mystical about the patience of a child. 'It will come all right won't it, father?' he said. 'God grant it may! I hope so, Roland,' 'Oh yes, it will come all right.' Perhaps he understood that in the midst of my anxiety I could not stay with him as I should have done otherwise. But the girls were more surprised than it is possible to describe. They looked at me with wondering eyes. 'If I were ill, papa, and you only stayed with me a moment, I should break my heart,' said Agatha. But the boy had a sympathetic feeling. He knew that of my own will I would not have done it. I shut myself up in the library, where I could not rest, but kept pacing up and down like a caged beast. What could I do? and if I could do nothing, what would become of my boy? These were the questions that, without ceasing, pursued each other through my mind.

Simson came out to dinner, and when the house was all still, and most of the servants in bed, we went out and met Dr Moncrieff, as we had appointed, at the head of the glen. Simson, for his part, was disposed to scoff at the doctor. 'If there are to be any spells, you know, I'll cut the whole concern,' he said. I did not make him any reply. I had not invited him; he could go or come as he pleased. He was very talkative, far more than suited my humour, as we went on. 'One thing is certain, you know, there must be some human agency,' he said. 'It is all bosh about apparitions. I never have investigated the laws of sound to any great extent, and there's a great deal in ventriloquism that we don't know much about.' 'If it's the same to you,' I said, 'I wish you'd keep all that to yourself, Simson. It doesn't suit my state of mind.' 'Oh, I hope I know how to respect idiosyncrasy,' he said. The very tone of his voice irritated me beyond measure. These scientific fellows, I wonder people put up with them as they do, when you have no mind for their cold-blooded confidence. Dr Moncrieff met us about eleven o'clock, the same time as on the previous night. He was a large man, with a venerable countenance and white hair – old, but in full vigour, and thinking less of a cold night walk than many a younger man. He had his lantern as I had. We were fully provided with means of lighting the place, and we were all of us resolute men. We had a rapid consultation as we went up, and the result was that we divided to different posts. Dr Moncrieff remained inside the wall – if you can call that inside where there was no wall but one. Simson placed himself on the side next the ruins, so as to intercept any communication with the old house, which was what his mind was fixed upon. I was posted on the other side. To say that nothing could come near without being seen was self-evident. It had been so also on the previous night. Now, with our three lights in the midst of the darkness, the whole place seemed illuminated. Dr Moncrieff's lantern, which was a large one, without any means of shutting up – an old-fashioned lantern with a pierced and ornamental top – shone steadily, the rays shooting out of it upward into the gloom. He placed it on the grass, where the middle of the room, if this had been a room, would have been. The usual effect of the light streaming out of the doorway was prevented by the illumination which Simson and I on either side supplied. With these differences, everything seemed as on the previous night.

And what occurred was exactly the same, with the same air of repetition, point for point, as I had formerly remarked. I declare that it seemed to me as if I were pushed against, put aside, by the owner of the voice as he paced up and down in his trouble – though these are perfectly futile words, seeing that the stream of light from my lantern, and that from Simson's taper, lay broad and clear, without a shadow, without the smallest break, across the entire breadth of the grass. I had ceased even to be alarmed, for my part. My heart was rent with pity and trouble – pity for the poor suffering human creature that moaned and pleaded so, and trouble for myself and my boy. God! if I could not find any help – and what help could I find? – Roland would die.

We were all perfectly still till the first outburst was exhausted, as I knew (by experience) it would be. Dr Moncrieff, to whom it was new, was quite motionless on the other side of the wall, as we were in our places. My heart had remained almost at its usual beating during the voice. I was used to it; it did not rouse all my pulses as it did at first. But just as it threw itself sobbing at the door (I cannot use other words), there suddenly came something which sent the blood coursing through my veins and my heart into my mouth. It was a voice inside the wall – the minister's well-known voice. I would have been prepared for it in any kind of adjuration, but I was not prepared for what I heard. It came out with a sort of stammering, as if too much moved for utterance. 'Willie, Willie! Oh, God preserve us! is it you?'

These simple words had an effect upon me that the voice of the invisible creature had ceased to have. I thought the old man, whom I had brought into this danger, had gone mad with terror. I made a dash round to the other side of the wall, half crazed myself with the thought. He was standing where I had left him, his shadow thrown vague and large upon the grass by the lantern which stood at his feet. I lifted my own light to see his face as I rushed forward. He was very pale, his eyes wet and glistening, his mouth quivering with parted lips. He neither saw nor heard me. We that had gone through this experience before, had crouched towards each other to get a little strength to bear it. But he was not even aware that I was there. His whole being seemed absorbed in anxiety and tenderness. He held out his hands, which trembled, but it seemed to me with eagerness, not fear. He went on speaking all the time. 'Willie, if it is you – and it's you, if it is not a delusion of Satan – Willie, lad! why come ye here frighting them that know you not? Why came ye not to me?'

He seemed to wait for an answer. When his voice ceased, his countenance, every line moving, continued to speak. Simson gave me another terrible shock, stealing into the open doorway with his light, as much awe-stricken, as wildly curious, as I. But the minister resumed, without seeing Simson, speaking to some one else. His voice took a tone of expostulation –

'Is this right to come here? Your mother's gone with your name on her lips. Do you think she would ever close her door on her own lad? Do ye think the Lord will close the door, ye faint-hearted creature? No! – I forbid ye! I forbid ye!' cried the old man. The sobbing voice had begun to resume its cries. He made a step forward, calling out the last words in a voice of command. 'I forbid ye! Cry out no more to man. Go home, ye wandering spirit! go home! Do you hear me? – me that christened ye, that have struggled with ye, that have wrestled for ye with the Lord!' Here the loud tones of his voice sank into tenderness. 'And her too, poor woman! poor woman; her you are calling upon. She's no here. You'll find her with the Lord. Go there and seek her, not here. Do you hear me, lad? go after her there. He'll let you in, though it's late. Man, take heart! if you will lie and sob and greet, let it be at heaven's gate, and no your poor mother's ruined door.'

He stopped to get his breath: and the voice had stopped, not as it had done before, when its time was exhausted and all its repetitions said, but with a sobbing catch in the breath as if overruled. Then the minister spoke again, 'Are you hearing me, Will? Oh, laddie, you've liked the beggarly elements all your days. Be done with them now. Go home to the Father – the Father! Are you hearing me?' Here the old man sank down upon his knees, his face raised upwards, his hands held up with a tremble in them, all white in the light in the midst of the darkness. I resisted as long as I could, although I cannot tell why – then I, too, dropped upon my knees.

Simson all the time stood in the doorway with an expression in his face such as words could not tell, his under lip drooped, his eyes wild, staring. It seemed to be to him, that image of blank ignorance and wonder, that we were praying. All the time the voice, with a low arrested sobbing, lay just where he was standing, as I thought.

'Lord,' the minister said – 'Lord, take him into Thy everlasting habitations. The mother he cries to is with Thee. Who can open to him but Thee? Lord, when is it too late for Thee, or what is too hard for Thee? Lord, let that woman there draw him inower! Let her draw him inower!'

I sprang forward to catch something in my arms that flung itself wildly within the door. The illusion was so strong, that I never paused till I felt my forehead graze against the wall and my hands clutch the ground – for there was nobody there to save from falling, as in my foolishness I thought. Simson held out his hand to me to help me up. He was trembling and cold, his lower lip hanging, his speech almost inarticulate. 'It's gone,' he said, stammering – 'it's gone!' We leant upon each other for a moment, trembling so much both of us that the whole scene trembled as if it were going to dissolve and disappear; and yet as long as I live I will never forget it – the shining of the strange lights, the blackness all round, the kneeling figure with all the whiteness of the light concentrated on its white venerable head and uplifted hands. A strange solemn stillness seemed to close all round us. By intervals a single syllable, 'Lord! Lord!' came from the old minister's lips. He saw none of us, nor thought of us. I never knew how long we stood, like sentinels guarding him at his prayers, holding our lights in a confused dazed way, not knowing what we did. But at last he rose from his knees, and standing up at his full height, raised his arms, as the Scotch manner is at the end of a religious service, and solemnly gave the apostolical benediction – to what? to the silent earth, the dark woods, the wide breathing atmosphere – for we were but spectators gasping an Amen!

It seemed to me that it must be the middle of the night, as we all walked back. It was in reality very late. Dr Moncrieff put his arm into mine. He walked slowly, with an air of exhaustion. It was as if we were coming from a death-bed. Something hushed and solemnised the very air. There was that sense of relief in it which there always is at the end of a death-struggle. And nature persistent, never daunted, came back in all of us, as we returned into the ways of life. We said nothing to each other, indeed, for a time; but when we got clear of the trees and reached the opening near the house, where we could see the sky, Dr Moncrieff himself was the first to speak. 'I must be going,' he said; 'it's very late, I'm afraid. I will go down the glen, as I came.'

'But not alone. I am going with you, doctor.'

'Well, I will not oppose it. I am an old man, and agitation wearies more than work. Yes; I'll be thankful of your arm. Tonight, Colonel, you've done me more good turns than one.'

I pressed his hand on my arm, not feeling able to speak. But Simson, who turned with us, and who had gone along all this time with his taper flaring, in entire unconsciousness, came to himself, apparently at the sound of our voices, and put out that wild little torch with a quick movement, as if of shame. 'Let me carry your lantern,' he said; 'it is heavy.' He recovered with a spring, and in a moment, from the awe-stricken spectator he had been, became himself sceptical and cynical. 'I should like to ask you a question,' he said. 'Do you believe in Purgatory, doctor? It's not in the tenets of the Church, so far as I know.'

'Sir,' said Dr Moncrieff, 'an old man like me is sometimes not very sure what he believes. There is just one thing I am certain of – and that is the loving-kindness of God.'

'But I thought that was in this life. I am no theologian—'

'Sir,' said the old man, again with a tremor in him which I could feel going over all his frame, 'if I saw a friend of mine within the gates of hell, I would not despair but his Father would take him by the hand still – if he cried like *yon*.'

'I allow it is very strange – very strange. I cannot see through it. That there must be human agency, I feel sure. Doctor, what made you decide upon the person and the name?'

The minister put out his hand with the impatience which a man might show if he were asked how he recognised his brother. 'Tuts!' he said, in familiar speech – then more solemnly, 'how should I not recognise a person that I know better – far better – than I know you?'

'Then you saw the man?'

Dr. Moncrieff made no reply. He moved his hand again with a little impatient movement, and walked on, leaning heavily on my arm. And we went on for a long time without another word, threading the dark paths, which were steep and slippery with the damp of the winter. The air was very still – not more than enough to make a faint sighing in the branches, which mingled with the sound of the water to which we were descending. When we spoke again, it was about indifferent matters – about the height of the river, and the recent rains. We parted with the minister at his own door, where his old housekeeper appeared in great perturbation, waiting for him. 'Eh, me, minister! the young gentleman will be worse?' she cried.

'Far from that – better. God bless him!' Dr Moncrieff said.

I think if Simson had begun again to me with his questions, I should have pitched him over the rocks as we returned up the glen; but he was silent, by a good inspiration. And the sky was clearer than it had been for many nights, shining high over the trees, with here and there a star faintly gleaming through the wilderness of dark and bare branches. The air, as I have said, was very soft in them, with a subdued and peaceful cadence. It was real, like every natural sound, and came to us like a hush of peace and relief. I thought there was a sound in it as of the breath of a sleeper, and it seemed clear to me that Roland must be sleeping, satisfied and calm. We went up to his room when we went in. There we found the complete hush of rest. My wife looked up out of a doze, and gave me a smile; 'I think he is a great deal better: but you are very late,' she said in a whisper, shading the light with her hand that the doctor might see his patient. The boy had got back something like his own colour. He woke as we stood all round his bed. His eyes had the happy half-awakened look of childhood, glad to shut again, yet pleased with the interruption and glimmer of the light. I stooped over him and kissed his forehead, which was moist and cool. 'All is well, Roland,' I said. He looked up at me with a glance of pleasure, and took my hand and laid his cheek upon it, and so went to sleep.

For some nights after, I watched among the ruins, spending all the dark hours up to midnight patrolling about the bit of wall which was associated with so many emotions; but I heard nothing, and saw nothing beyond the quiet course of nature: nor, so far as I am aware, has anything been heard again. Dr Moncrieff gave me the history of the youth, whom he never hesitated to name. I did not ask, as Simson did, how he recognised him. He had been a prodigal – weak, foolish, easily imposed upon, and 'led away', as people say. All that we had heard had passed actually in life, the Doctor said. The young man had come home thus a day or two after his mother died – who was no more than the housekeeper in the old house – and distracted with the news, had thrown himself down at the door and called upon her to let him in. The old man could scarcely speak of it for tears. To me it seemed as if – heaven help us, how little do we know about anything! – a scene like that might impress itself somehow upon the hidden heart of nature. I do not pretend to know how, but the repetition had struck me at the time as, in its terrible strangeness and incomprehensibility, almost mechanical – as if the unseen actor could not exceed or vary, but was bound to re-enact the whole. One thing that struck me, however, greatly, was the likeness between the old minister and my boy in the manner of regarding these strange phenomena. Dr Moncrieff was not terrified, as I had been myself, and all the rest of us. It was no 'ghost', as I fear we all vulgarly considered it, to him – but a poor creature whom he knew under these conditions, just as he had known him in the flesh, having no doubt of his identity. And to Roland it was the same. This spirit in pain – if it was a spirit – this voice out of the unseen – was a poor fellow-creature in misery, to be succoured and helped out of his trouble, to my boy. He spoke to me quite frankly about it when he got better. 'I knew father would find out some way,' he said. And this was when he was strong and well, and all idea that he would turn hysterical or become a seer of visions had happily passed away.

I must add one curious fact which does not seem to me to have any relation to the above, but which Simson made great use of, as the human agency which he was determined to find somehow. We had examined the ruins very closely at the time of these occurrences; but afterwards, when all was over, as we went casually about them one Sunday afternoon in the idleness of that unemployed day, Simson with his stick penetrated an old window which had been entirely blocked up with fallen soil. He jumped down into it in great excitement, and called me to follow. There we found a little hole – for it was more a hole than a room – entirely hidden under the ivy ruins, in which there was a quantity of straw laid in a corner, as if some one had made a bed there, and some remains of crusts about the floor. Some one had lodged there, and not very long before, he made out; and that this unknown being was the author of all the mysterious sounds we heard he is convinced. 'I told you it was human agency,' he said, triumphantly. He forgets, I suppose, how he and I stood with our lights seeing nothing, while the space between us was audibly traversed by something that could speak, and sob, and suffer. There is no argument with men of this kind. He is ready to get up a laugh against me on this slender ground. 'I was puzzled myself – I could not make it out – but I always felt convinced human agency was at the bottom of it. And here it is – and a clever fellow he must have been,' the doctor says.

Bagley left my service as soon as he got well. He assured me it was no want of respect; but he could not stand 'them kind of things', and the man was so shaken and ghastly that I was glad to give him a present and let him go. For my own part, I made a point of staying out the time, two years, for which I had taken Brentwood; but I did not renew my tenancy. By that time we had settled, and found ourselves a pleasant home of our own.

I must add that when the doctor defies me, I can always bring back gravity to his countenance, and a pause in his railing, when I remind him of the juniper-bush. To me that was a matter of little importance. I could believe it was mistaken. I did not care about it one way or other; but on his mind the effect was different. The miserable voice, the spirit in pain, he could think of as the result of ventriloquism, or reverberation, or – anything you please: an elaborate prolonged hoax executed somehow by the tramp that had found a lodging in the old tower. But the juniper-bush staggered him. Things have effects so different on the minds of different men.

Lanoe Falconer

CECILIA DE NOËL

CHAPTER I
ATHERLEY'S GOSPEL

'THERE is no revelation but that of science,' said Atherley.

It was after dinner in the drawing-room. From the cold of the early spring night, closed shutters and drawn curtains carefully protected us; shaded lamps and a wood fire diffused an exquisite twilight; we breathed a mild and even balmy atmosphere scented with hothouse flowers.

'And this revelation completely satisfies all reasonable desires,' he continued, surveying his small audience from the hearthrug where he stood; 'mind, I say all reasonable desires. If you have a healthy appetite for bread, you will get it and plenty of it, but if you have a sickly craving for manna, why then you will come badly off, that is all. This is the gospel of fact, not of fancy: of things as they actually are, you know, instead of as A dreamt they were, or B decided they ought to be, or C would like to have them. So this gospel is apt to look a little dull beside the highly coloured romances the churches have accustomed us to – as a modern plate-glass window might, compared with a stained-glass oriel in a mediæval cathedral. There is no doubt which is the prettier of the two. The question is, do you want pretty colour or do you want clear daylight?'

He paused, but neither of his listeners spoke. Lady Atherley was counting the stitches of her knitting; I was too tired; so he resumed: 'For my part, I prefer the daylight and the glass, without any daubing. What does science discover in the universe? Precision, accuracy, reliability – any amount of it; but as to pity, mercy, love! The fact is, that famous simile of the angel playing at chess was a mistake. Very smart, I grant you, but altogether misleading. Why! the orthodox quote it as much as the others – always a bad sign. It tickles these anthropomorphic fancies, which are at the bottom of all their creeds. Imagine yourself playing at chess, not with an angel, but with an automaton, an admirably constructed automaton whose mechanism can outwit your brains any day: calm and strong, if you like, but no more playing for love than the clock behind me is ticking for love; there you have a much clearer notion of existence. A much clearer notion, and a much more satisfactory notion too, I say. Fair play and no favour! What more can you ask, if you are fit to live?'

His kindling glance sought the farther end of the long drawing-room; had it fallen upon me instead, perhaps that last challenge might have been less assured; and yet how bravely it became the speaker, whose wide-browed head a no less admirable frame supported. Even the stiff evening uniform of his class could not conceal the grace of form which health and activity had moulded, working through highly favoured generations. There was latent force implied in every line of it, and, in the steady poise of look and mien, that perfect nervous balance which is the crown of strength.

'And with our creed, of course, we shift our moral code as well. The ten commandments, or at least the second table, we retain for obvious reasons, but the theological virtues must be got rid of as quickly as possible. Charity, for instance, is a mischievous quality – it is too indulgent to weakness, which is not to be indulged or encouraged, but stamped out. Hope is another pernicious quality leading to all kinds of preposterous expectations which never are, or can be, fulfilled; and as to faith, it is simply a vice. So far from taking anything on trust, you must refuse to accept any statement whatsoever till it is proved so plainly you can't help believing it whether you like it or not; just as a theorem in—'

'George,' said Lady Atherley, 'what is that noise?'

The question, timed as Lady Atherley's remarks so often were, came with something of a shock. Her husband, thus checked in full flight, seemed to reel for a moment, but quickly recovering himself, asked resignedly: 'What noise?'

'Such a strange noise, like the howling of a dog.'

'Probably it is the howling of a dog.'

'No, for it came from inside the house, and Tip sleeps outside now, in the saddle-room, I believe. It sounded in the servants' wing. Did you hear it, Mr Lyndsay?'

I confessed that I had not.

'Well, as I can offer no explanation,' said Atherley, 'perhaps I may be allowed to go on with what I was saying. Doubt, obstinate and almost invincible doubt, is the virtue we must now cultivate, just as—'

'Why, there it is again,' cried Lady Atherley.

Atherley instantly rang the bell near him, and while Lady Atherley continued to repeat that it was very strange, and that she could not imagine what it could be, he waited silently till his summons was answered by a footman.

'Charles, what is the meaning of that crying or howling which seems to come from your end of the house?'

'I think, Sir George,' said Charles, with the coldly impassive manner of a highly-trained servant – 'I think, Sir George, it must be Ann, the kitchen-maid, that you hear.'

'Indeed! and may I ask what Ann, the kitchen-maid, is supposed to be doing?'

'If you please, Sir George, she is in hysterics.'

'Oh! why?' exclaimed Lady Atherley plaintively.

'Because, my lady, Mrs Mallet has seen the ghost!'

'Because Mrs Mallet has seen the ghost!' repeated Atherley. 'Pray, what is Mrs Mallet herself doing under the circumstances?'

'She is having some brandy-and-water, Sir George.'

'Mrs Mallet is a sensible woman,' said Atherley heartily; 'Ann, the kitchen-maid, had better follow her example.'

'You may go, Charles,' said Lady Atherley; and, as the door closed behind him, exclaimed, 'I wish that horrid woman had never entered the house!'

'What horrid woman? Your too sympathetic kitchen-maid?'

'No, that – that Mrs Mallet.'

'Why are you angry with her? Because she has seen the ghost?'

'Yes, for I told her most particularly the very day I engaged her, after Mrs. Webb left us in that sudden way – I told her I never allowed the ghost to be mentioned.'

'And why, my dear, did you break your own excellent rule by mentioning it to her?'

'Because she had the impertinence to tell me, almost directly she came into the morning-room, that she knew all about the ghost; but I stopped her at once, and said that if ever she spoke of such a thing, especially to the other servants, I should be very much displeased; and now she goes and behaves in this way.'

'Where did you pick up this viper?'

'She comes from Quarley Beacon. There was no one in this stupid village who could cook at all, and Cecilia de Noël, who recommended her—'

'Cecilia de Noël!' repeated Atherley, with that long-drawn emphasis which suggests so much. 'My dear Jane, I must say that in taking a servant on Cissy's recommendation you did not display your usual sound common sense. I should as soon have thought of asking her to buy me a gun, knowing that she would carefully pick out the one least likely to shoot anything. Cissy is accustomed to look upon a servant as something to be waited on and taken care of. Her own household, as we all know, is composed chiefly of chronic invalids.'

'But I explained to Cecilia that I wanted somebody who was strong as well as a good cook; and I am sure there is nothing the matter with Mrs Mallet. She is as fat as possible, and as red! Besides, she has never been one of Cecilia's servants; she only goes there to help sometimes; and she says she is perfectly respectable.'

'Mrs Mallet says that Cissy is perfectly respectable?'

'No, George; it is not likely that I should allow a person in Mrs Mallet's position to speak disrespectfully to me about Cecilia. Cecilia said Mrs Mallet was perfectly respectable.'

'I should not think dear old Ciss exactly knew the meaning of the word.'

'Cecilia may be peculiar in many ways, but she is too much of a lady to send me any one who was not quite nice. I don't believe there is anything against Mrs Mallet's character. She cooks very well, you must allow that; you said only two days ago you never had tasted an omelette so nicely made in England.'

'Did she cook that omelette? Then I am sure she is perfectly respectable; and pray let her see as many ghosts as she cares to, especially if it leads to nothing worse than her taking a moderate quantity of brandy. Time to smoke, Lindy. I am off.'

I dragged myself up after my usual fashion, and was preparing to follow him, when Lady Atherley, directly he was gone, began:

'It is such a pity that clever people can never see things as others do. George always goes on in this way as if the ghost were of no consequence, but I always knew how it would be. Of course it is nice that George should come in for the place, as he might not have done if his uncle had married, and people said it would be delightful to live in such an old house, but there are a good many drawbacks, I can assure you. Sir Marmaduke lived abroad for years before he died, and everything has got into such a state. We have had to nearly refurnish the house; the bedrooms are not done yet. The servants' accommodation is very bad too, and there was no proper cooking-range in the kitchen. But the worst of all is the ghost. Directly I heard of it I knew we should have trouble with the servants; and we had not been here a month when our cook, who had lived with us for years, gave warning because the place was damp. At first she said it was the ghost, but when I told her not to talk such nonsense she said it was the damp. And then it is so awkward about visitors. What are we to do when the fishing season begins? I cannot get George to understand that some people have a great objection to anything of the kind, and are quite angry if you put them into a haunted room. And it is much worse than having only one haunted room, because we could make that into a bachelor's bedroom – I don't think they mind; or a linen cupboard, as they do at Wimbourne Castle; but this ghost seems to appear in all the rooms, and even in the halls and passages, so I cannot think what we are to do.'

I said it was extraordinary, and I meant it. That a ghost should venture into Atherley's neighbourhood was less amazing than that it should continue to exist in his wife's presence, so much more fatal than his eloquence to all but the tangible and the solid. Her orthodoxy is above suspicion, but after some hours of her society I am unable to contemplate any aspects of life save the comfortable and the uncomfortable: while the Universe itself appears to me only a gigantic apparatus especially designed to provide Lady Atherley and her class with cans of hot water at stated intervals, costly repasts elaborately served, and all other requisites of irreproachable civilisation.

But before I had time to say more, Atherley in his smoking-coat looked in to see if I was coming or not.

'Don't keep Mr Lyndsay up late, George,' said my kind hostess; 'he looks so tired.'

'You look dead beat,' he said later on, in his own particular and untidy den, as he carefully stuffed the bowl of his pipe. 'I think it would go better with you, old chap, if you did not hold yourself in quite so tight. I don't want you to rave or commit suicide in some untidy fashion, as the hero of a French novel does; but you are as well-behaved as a woman, without a woman's grand resources of hysterics and general unreasonableness all round. You always were a little too good for human nature's daily food. Your notions on some points are quite unwholesomely superfine. It would be a comfort to see you let out in some way. I wish you would have a real good fling for once.'

'I should have to pay too dear for it afterwards. My superfine habits are not a matter of choice only, you must remember.'

'Oh! – the women! Not the best of them is worth bothering about, let alone a shameless jilt.'

'You were always hard upon her, George. She jilted a cripple for a very fine specimen of the race. Some of your favourite physiologists would say she was quite right.'

'You never understood her, Lindy. It was not a case of jilting a cripple at all. She jilted three thousand a year and a small place for ten thousand a year and a big one.'

After all, it did hurt a little, which Atherley must have divined, for crossing the room on some pretext or another he let his strong hand rest, just for an instant, gently upon my shoulder, thus, after the manner of his race, mutely and concisely expressing affection and sympathy that might have swelled a canto.

'I shall be sorry,' he said presently, lying rather than sitting in the deep chair beside the fire, 'very sorry, if the ghost is going to make itself a nuisance.'

'What is the story of the ghost?'

'Story! God bless you, it has none to tell, sir; at least it never has told it, and no one else rightly knows it. It – I mean the ghost – is older than the family. We found it here when we came into the place about two hundred years ago, and it refused to be dislodged. It is rather uncertain in its habits. Sometimes it is not heard of for years; then all at once it reappears, generally, I may observe, when some imaginative female in the house is in love, or out of spirits, or bored in any other way. She sees it, and then, of course – the complaint being highly infectious – so do a lot more. One of the family started the theory it was the ghost of the portrait, or rather the unknown individual whose portrait hangs high up over the sideboard in the dining-room.'

'You don't mean the lady in green velvet with the snuff-box?'

'Certainly not; that is my own great-grand-aunt. I mean a square of black canvas with one round yellow spot in the middle and a dirty white smudge under the spot. There are members of this family – Aunt Eleanour, for instance – who tell me the yellow spot is a man's face and the dirty white smudge is an Elizabethan ruff. Then there is a picture of a man in armour in the oak room, which I don't believe is a portrait at all; but Aunt Henrietta swears it is, and of the ghost, too – as he was before he died, of course. And very interesting details both my aunts are ready to furnish concerning the two originals. It is extraordinary what an amount of information is always forthcoming about things of which nobody can know anything – as about the next world, for instance. The last time I went to church the preacher gave as minute an account of what our post-mortem experiences were to be as if he had gone through it all himself several times.'

'Well, does the ghost usually appear in a ruff or in armour?'

'It depends entirely upon who sees it – a ghost always does. Last night, for instance, I lay you odds it wore neither ruff nor armour, because Mrs Mallet is not likely to have heard of either the one or the other. Not that she saw the ghost – not she. What she saw was a bogie, not a ghost.'

'Why, what is the difference?'

'Immense! As big as that which separates the objective from the subjective. Any one can see a bogie. It is a real thing belonging to the external world. It may be a bright light, a white sheet, or a black shadow –

always at night, you know, or at least in the dusk, when you are apt to be a little mixed in your observations. The best example of a bogie was Sir Walter Scott's. It looked – in the twilight remember – exactly like Lord Byron, who had not long departed this life at the time Sir Walter saw it. Nine men out of ten would have gone off and sworn they had seen a ghost; why, religions have been founded on just such stuff: but Sir Walter, as sane a man as ever lived – though he did write poetry – kept his head clear and went up closer to his ghost, which proved on examination to be a waterproof.'

'A waterproof?'

'Or a railway rug – I forget which: the moral is the same.'

'Well, what is a ghost?'

'A ghost is nothing – an airy nothing manufactured by your own disordered senses of your own over-excited brain.'

'I beg to observe that I never saw a ghost in my life.'

'I am glad to hear it. It does you credit. If ever any one had an excuse for seeing a ghost it would be a man whose spine was jarred. But I meant nothing personal by the pronoun – only to give greater force to my remarks. The first person singular will do instead. The ghost belongs to the same lot, as the faces that make mouths at me when I have brain-fever, the reptiles that crawl about when I have an attack of the D.T., or – to take a more familiar example – the spots I see floating before my eyes when my liver is out of order. You will allow there is nothing supernatural in all that?'

'Certainly. Though, did not that pretty niece of Mrs Molyneux's say she used to see those spots floating before her eyes when a misfortune was impending?'

'I fancy she did, and true enough too, as such spots would very likely precede a bilious attack, which is misfortune enough while it lasts. But still, even Mrs Molyneux's niece, even Mrs Molyneux herself, would not say the fever faces, or the reptiles, or the spots, were supernatural. And in fact the ghost is, so far, more – more *recherché*, let us say, than the other things. It takes more than a bilious attack or a fever, or even D.T., to produce a ghost. It takes nothing less than a pretty high degree of nervous sensibility and excitable imagination. Now these two disorders have not been much developed yet by the masses, in spite of the school-boards: ergo, any apparition which leads to hysterics or brandy-and-water in the servants' hall is a bogie, not a ghost.'

He knocked the ashes out of his pipe, and added:

'And now, Lindy, as we don't want another ghost haunting the house, I will conduct you to by-by.'

It was a strange house, Weald Manor, designed, one might suppose, by some inveterate enemy of light. It lay at the foot of a steep hill which screened it from the morning sun, and the few windows which looked towards the rising day were so shaped as to admit but little of its brightness. At night it was even worse, at least in the halls and passages, for there, owing probably to the dark oak which lined both walls and floor, a generous supply of lamps did little more than illumine the surface of the darkness, leaving unfathomed and unexplained mysterious shadows that brooded in distant corners, or, towering giant-wise to the ceiling, loomed ominously overhead. Will-o'-the-wisp-like reflections from our lighted candles danced in the polished surface of panel and balustrade, as from the hall we went upstairs, I helping myself from step to step by Atherley's arm, as instinctively, as unconsciously almost, as he offered it. We stopped on the first landing. Before us rose the stairs leading to the gallery where Atherley's bedroom was: to our left ran 'the bachelor's passage', where I was lodged.

'Night, night,' were Atherley's parting words. 'Don't dream of flirts or ghosts, but sleep sound.'

Sleep sound! the kind words sounded like mockery. Sleep to me, always chary of her presence, was at best but a fair weather friend, instantly deserting me when pain or exhaustion made me crave the more for rest and forgetfulness; but I had something to do in the interim – a little *auto-da-fé* to perform, by which, with that faith in ceremonial, so deep laid in human nature, I meant once for all to lay the ghost that haunted me – the ghost of a delightful but irrevocable past, with which I had dallied too long.

Sitting before the wood-fire I slowly unfolded them: the three faintly-perfumed sheets with the gilt monogram above the pointed writing:

'Dear Mr Lyndsay,' ran the first, 'why did you not come over today? I was expecting you to appear all the afternoon. – Yours sincerely,   G.E.L.'

The second was dated four weeks later –

'You silly boy! I forbid you ever to write or talk of yourself in such a way again. You are not a cripple; and if you had ever had a mother or a sister, you would know how little women think of such things. How many more assurances do you expect from me? Do you wish me to propose to you again? No, if you won't have me, go. – Yours, in spite of yourself,   GLADYS'

The third – the third is too long to quote entire; besides, the substance is contained in this last sentence –

'So I think, my dear Mr Lyndsay, for your sake more than my own, our engagement had better be broken off.'

In this letter, dated six weeks ago, she had charged me to burn all that she had written to me, and as yet I had not done so, shrinking from the sharp unreasonable pain with which we bury the beloved dead. But the time of my mourning was accomplished. I tore the paper into fragments and dropped them into the flames.

It must have been the pang with which I watched them darken and shrivel that brought back the memory of another sharp stab. It was that day ten years ago, when I walked for the first time after my accident. Supported by a stick on one side, and by Atherley on the other, I crawled down the long gallery at home and halted before a high wide-open window to see the sunlit view of park and woods and distant downland. Then all at once, ridden by my groom, Charming went past with feet that verily danced upon the greensward, and quivering nostrils that rapturously inhaled the breath of spring and of morning. I said: 'George, I want *you* to have Charming.' And it made me smile, even in that bitter moment, to remember how indistinctly, how churlishly almost, Atherley accepted the gift, in his eager haste to get me out of sight and thought of it.

It was long before the last fluttering rags had vanished, transmuted into fiery dust. The clock on the landing had many times chanted its dirge since I had heard below the footsteps of the servants carrying away the lamps from the sitting-rooms and the hall. Later still came the far-off sound of Atherley's door closing behind him, like the final good night of the waking day. Over all the unconscious household had stolen that silence which is more than silence, that hush which seems to wait for something, that stillness of the night-watch which is kept alone. It was familiar enough to me, but tonight it had a new meaning; like the sunlight that shines when we are happy, or the rain that falls when we are weeping, it seemed, as if in sympathy, to be repeating and accenting what I could not so vividly have told in words. In my life, and for the second time, there was the same desolate pause, as if the dreary tale were finished and only the drearier epilogue remained to live through – the same sense of sad separation from the happy and the healthful.

I made a great effort to read, holding the book before me and compelling myself to follow the sentences, but that power of abstraction which can conquer pain does not belong to temperaments like mine. If only I could have slept, as men have been able to do upon the rack; but every hour that passed left me more awake, more alive, more supersensitive to suffering.

Early in the morning, long before the dawn, I must have been feverish, I think. My head and hands burned, the air of the room stifled me, I was losing my self-control.

I opened the window and leant out. The cool air revived me bodily, but to the fever of the spirit it brought no relief. To my heart, if not to my lips, sprang the old old cry for help which anguish has wrung from generation after generation. The agony of mine, I felt wildly, must pierce through sense, time, space, everything – even to the Living Heart of all, and bring thence some token of pity! For one instant my passion seemed to beat against the silent heavens, then to fall back bruised and bleeding.

Out of the darkness came not so much as a wind whisper or the twinkle of a star.

Was Atherley right after all?

CHAPTER II

THE STRANGER'S GOSPEL

FROM the short unsatisfying slumber which sometimes follows a night of insomnia I was awakened by the laughter and shouts of children. When I looked out I saw brooding above the hollow a still grey day, in whose light the woodlands of the park were all in sombre brown, and the trout stream between its sedgy banks glided dark and lustreless.

On the lawn, still wet with dew, and crossed by the shadows of the bare elms, Atherley's little sons, Harold and Denis, were playing with a very unlovely but much-beloved mongrel called Tip. They had bought him with their own pocket-money from a tinker who was ill-using him, and then claimed for him the hospitality of their parents; so, though Atherley often spoke of the dog as a disgrace to the household, he remained a member thereof, and received, from a family incapable of being uncivil, far less unkind, to an animal, as much attention as if he had been high-bred and beautiful – which indeed he plainly supposed himself to be.

When, about an hour later, after their daily custom, this almost inseparable trio fell into the breakfast-room as if the door had suddenly given way before them, the boys were able to revenge themselves for the rebuke this entrance provoked by the tidings they brought with them.

'I say, old Mallet is going,' cried Harold cheerfully, as he wriggled himself on to his chair. 'Denis, mind I want some of that egg-stuff.'

'Take your arms off the table, Harold,' said Lady Atherley. 'Pray, how do you know Mrs Mallet is going?'

'She said so herself. She said,' he went on, screwing up his nose and speaking in a falsetto to express the intensity of his scorn – 'she said she was afraid of the ghost.'

'I told you I did not allow that word to be mentioned.'

'I did not; it was old Mallet.'

'But, pray, what were you doing in old Mallet's domain?' asked Atherley.

'Cooking cabbage for Tip.'

'Hum! What with ghosts by night and boys by day, our cook seems to have a pleasant time of it; I shall be glad when Miss Jones's holidays are over. Castleman, is it true that Mrs. Mallet talks of leaving us because of the ghost?'

'I am sure I don't know, Sir George,' answered the old butler. 'She was going on about it very foolish this morning.'

'And how is the kitchen-maid?'

'Has not come down yet, Sir George; says her nerve is shook,' said Castleman, retiring with a plate to the sideboard; then added, with the freedom of an old servant, 'Bile, I should say.'

'Probably. We had better send for Doctor What's-his-name.'

'The usual doctor is away,' said Lady Atherley. 'There is a London doctor in his place. He is clever, Lady Sylvia said, but he gives himself airs.'

'Never mind what he gives himself if he gives his patients the right thing.'

'And after all we can manage very well without Ann, but what are we to do about Mrs Mallet? I always told you how it would be.'

'But, my dear, it is not my fault. You look as reproachfully at me as if it were my ghost which was causing all this disturbance instead of the ghost of a remote ancestor – predecessor, in fact.'

'No, but you will always talk just as if it was of no consequence.'

'I don't talk of the cook's going as being of no consequence. Far from it. But you must not let her go, that is all.'

'How can I prevent her going? I think you had better talk to her yourself.'

'I should like to meet her very much; would not you, Lindy? I should like to hear her story; it must be a blood-curdling one, to judge from its effect upon Ann. The only person I have yet met who pretended to have seen the ghost was Aunt Eleanour.'

'And what was it like, daddy?' asked Denis, much interested.

'She did not say, Den. She would never tell me anything about it.'

'Would she tell me?'

'I am afraid not. I don't think she would tell any one, except perhaps Mr Lyndsay. He has a way of worming things out of people.'

'Mr Lyndsay, how do you worm things out of people?'

'I don't know, Denis; you must ask your father.'

'First, by never asking any questions,' said Atherley promptly; 'and then by a curious way he has of looking as if he was listening attentively to what was said to him, instead of thinking, as most people do, what he shall say himself when he gets a chance of putting a word in.'

'But how could Aunt Eleanour see the ghost when there is not any such thing?' cried Harold.

'How indeed!' said his father, rising; 'that is just the puzzle. It will take you years to find it out. Lindy, look into the morning-room in about half an hour, and you will hear a tale whose lightest word will harrow up thy soul, etc., etc.'

As Lady Atherley kindly seconded this invitation I accepted it, though not with the consequences predicted. Anything less suggestive of the supernatural, or in every way less like the typical ghost-seer, was surely never produced than the round and rubicund little person I found in conversation with the Atherleys. Mrs Mallet was a brunette who might once have considered herself a beauty, to judge by the self-conscious and self-satisfied simper which the ghastliest recollections were unable to banish. As I entered I caught only the last words of Atherley's speech –

'— treating you well, Mrs Mallet?'

'Oh no, Sir George,' answered Mrs Mallet, standing very straight and stiff, with two plump red hands folded demurely before her; 'which I have not a word to say against any one, but have met, ever since I come here, with the greatest of kindness and respect. But the noises, sir, the noises of a night is more than I can bear.'

'Oh, they are only rats, Mrs Mallet.'

'No rats in this world ever made sech a noise, Sir George; which the very first night as I slep here, there come the most mysterioustest sounds as ever I hear, which I says to Hann, "Whatever are you a-doing?" which she woke up all of a suddent, as young people will, and said she never hear nor yet see nothing.'

'What was the noise like, Mrs Mallet?'

'Well, Sir George, I can only compare it to the dragging of heavy furniture, which I really thought at first it was her ladyship a-coming upstairs to waken me, took bad with burglars or a fire.'

'But, Mrs Mallet, I am sure you are too brave a woman to mind a little noise.'

'It is not only noises, Sir George. Last night—'

Mrs Mallet drew a long breath and closed her eyes.

'Yes, Mrs Mallet, pray go on; I am very curious to hear what did happen last night.'

'It makes the cold chills run over me to think of it. We was all gone to bed – leastways the maids and me, and Hann and me was but just got to my room when says she to me, "Oh la! whatever do you think?" says she; "I promised Ellen when she went out this afternoon as I would shut the windows in the pink bedroom at four o'clock, and never come to think of it till this minute," she says. "Oh dear," I says, "and them new chintzes will be entirely ruined with the damp. Why, what a good-for-nothing girl you are!" I says; "and what you thinks on half your time is more than I can tell." "Whatever shall I do?" she says, "for go along there at this time of night all by myself I dare not," says she. "Well," I says, "rather than you should go alone, I'll go along with you," I says, "for stay here by myself I would not," I says, "not if any one was to pay me hundreds." So we went down our stairs and along our passage to the door which you go into the gallery, Hann a-clutching hold of me and starting, which when we come into the gallery I was all of a tremble, and she shook so I said, "La! Hann, for goodness' sake do carry that candle straight, or you will grease the carpet shameful"; and come to the pink room I says, "Open the door." "La!" says she, "what if we was to see the ghost?" "Hold your silly nonsense this minute," I says, "and open the door," which she do, but stand right back for to let me go first, when, true as ever I am standing here, my lady, I see something white go by like a flash, and struck me cold in the face, and blew the candle out, and then come the fearfullest noise, which thunderclaps is nothing to it. Hann began a-screaming, and we ran as fast as ever we could till we come to the pantry, where Mr Castleman and the footman was. I thought I should ha' died: died I thought I should. My face was as white as that antimacassar.'

'How could you see your face, Mrs Mallet?' somewhat peevishly objected Lady Atherley.

But Mrs Mallet with great dignity retorted –

'Which I looked down my nose, and it were like a corpse's.'

'Very alarming,' said Atherley, 'but easily explained. Directly you opened the door there was, of course, a draught from the open window. The draught blew the candle out and knocked something over, probably a screen.'

'La' bless you, Sir George, it was more like paving-stones than screens a-falling.'

And indeed Mrs Mallet was so far right, that when, to settle the weighty question once for all, we adjourned in a body to the pink bedroom, we discovered that nothing less than the ceiling, or at least a portion of it, had fallen, and was lying in a heap of broken plaster upon the floor. However, the moral, as Atherley hastened to observe, was the same.

'You see, Mrs Mallet, this was what made the noise.'

Mrs Mallet made no reply, but it was evident she neither saw nor intended to see anything of the kind; and Atherley wisely substituted bribery for reasoning. But even with this he made little way till accidentally he mentioned the name of Mrs de Noël, when, as if it had been a name to conjure by, Mrs Mallet showed signs of softening.

'Yes, think of Mrs de Noël, Mrs Mallet; what will she say if you leave her cousin to starve?'

'I should not wish such a thing to happen for a moment,' said Mrs Mallet, as if this had been no figure of speech but the actual alternative, 'not to any relation of Mrs de Noël.'

And shortly after the debate ended with a cheerful 'Well, Mrs Mallet, you will give us another trial,' from Atherley.

'There,' he exclaimed, as we all three returned to the morning-room – 'there is as splendid an example of the manufacture of a bogie as you are ever likely to meet with. All the spiritual phenomena are produced much in the same way. Work yourself up into a great state of terror and excitement, in the first place; in the next, procure one companion, if not more, as credulous and excitable as yourself; go at a late hour and with a dim light to a place where you have been told you will see something supernatural; steadfastly and determinedly look out for it, and – you will have your reward. These are precisely the lines on which a spiritual séance is conducted, only instead of plaster, which is not always so obliging as to fall in the nick of time, you have a paid medium who supplies the material for your fancy to work upon. Mrs Mallet, you see, has discovered all this for herself – that woman is a born genius. Just think what she might have been and seen if she had lived in a sphere where neither cooking nor any other rational occupation interfered with her pursuit of the supernatural. Mrs Molyneux would be nowhere beside her.'

'I suppose she really does intend to stay,' said Lady Atherley.

'Of course she does. I always told you my powers of persuasion were irresistible.'

'But how annoying about the ceiling,' said Lady Atherley. 'Over the new carpet, too! What can make the plaster fall in this way?'

'It is the quality of the climate,' said Atherley. 'It is horribly destructive. If you would read the batch of letters now on my writing-table from tenant-farmers you would see what I mean: barns, roofs, gates, everything is falling to pieces and must immediately be repaired – at the landlord's expense, of course.'

'We must send for a plasterer,' said Lady Atherley, 'and then the doctor. Perhaps you would have time to go round his way, George.'

'No, I have no time to go anywhere but to Northside farm. Hunt has been waiting nearly half an hour for me, as it is. Lindy, would you like to come with me?'

'No, thank you, George; I too am a landowner, and I mean to look over my audit accounts today.'

'Don't compare yourself to a poor overworked underpaid landowner like me. You are one of the landlords they spout about in London parks on Sundays. You have nothing to do but sign receipts for your rents, paid in full and up to date.'

'Mr Lyndsay is an excellent landlord,' said Lady Atherley; 'and they tell me the new church and the schools he has built are charming.'

'Very mischievous things both,' said Atherley. 'Ta-ta.'

That afternoon, Atherley being still absent, and Lady Atherley having gone forth to pay a round of calls, the little boys undertook my entertainment. They were in rather a sober mood for them, having just forfeited four weeks' pocket-money towards expenses incurred by Tip in the dairy, where they had foolishly allowed him to enter; so they accepted very good-humouredly my objections to wading in the river or climbing trees, and took me instead for a walk to Beggar's Stile. We climbed up the steep carriage-drive to the lodge, passed through the big iron gates, turned sharply to the left, and went down the road which the park palings border and the elms behind them shade, past the little copse beyond the park, till we came to a tumble-down gate with a stile beside it in the hedgerow; and this was Beggar's Stile. It was just on the brow of the little hill which sloped gradually downward to the village beneath, and commanded a wide view of the broad shallow valley and of the rising ground beyond.

I was glad to sit down on the step of the stile.

'Are you tired already, Mr Lyndsay?' inquired Harold incredulously.

'Yes, a little.'

'I s'pose you are tired because you always have to pull your leg after you,' said Denis, turning upon me two large topaz-coloured eyes. 'Does it hurt you, Mr Lyndsay?'

'Mother told you not to talk about Mr Lyndsay's leg,' observed Harold sharply.

'No, she didn't; she said I was not to talk about the funny way he walked. She said—'

'Well, never mind, little man,' I interrupted. 'Is that Weald down there?'

'Yes,' cried Denis, maintaining his balance on the topmost bar but one of the gate with enviable ease. 'All these cottages and houses belong to Weald, and it is all daddy's on this side of the river down to where you see the white railings a long way down near the poplars, and that is the road we go to tea with Aunt Eleanour; and do you see a little blue speck on the hill over there? You could see if you had a tefelscope. Daddy showed me once; but you must shut your eye. That is Quarley Beacon, where Aunt Cissy lives.'

'No, she does not, stupid,' cried Harold, now suspended, head downwards, by one foot from the topmost rail of the gate. 'No one lives there. She lives in Quarley Manor, just behind.'

Denis replied indirectly to the discourteous tone of this speech by trying with the point of his own foot to dislodge that by which Harold maintained his remarkable position, and a scuffle ensued, wherein, though a non-combatant, I seemed likely to get the worst, when their attention was fortunately diverted by the sight of Tip sneaking off, and evidently with the vilest motives, towards the covert.

My memory was haunted that day by certain words spoken seven months ago by Atherley, and by me at the time very ungraciously received:

'Remember, if you do come a cropper, it will go hard with you, old man; you can't shoot or hunt or fish off the blues, like other men.'

No, nor could I work them off, as some might have done. I possessed no distinct talents, no marked vocation. If there was nothing behind and beyond all this, what an empty freak of destiny my life would have been – full, not even of sound and fury, but of dull commonplace suffering: a tale told by an idiot with a spice of malice in him.

Then the view before me made itself felt, as a gentle persistent sound might have done: a flat, almost featureless scene – a little village church with cottages and gardens clustering about it, straggling away from it, by copses and meadows in which winter had left only the tenderest shades of the saddest colours. The winding river brightened the dull picture with broken glints of silver, and the tawny hues of the foreground faded through soft gradations of violet and azure into a far distance of pearly grey. It is not the scenery men cross continents and oceans to admire, and yet it has a message of its own. I felt it that day when I was heart-weary, and was glad that in one corner of this restless world the little hills preach peace.

Meantime Tip had been recaptured, and when he, or rather the ground close beside him, had been beaten severely with sticks, and he himself upbraided in terms which left the censors hoarse, we went down again into the hollow. Then Lady Atherley returned and gave me tea; and afterwards, in the library, I worked at accounts till it was nearly too dark to write. No doubt on the high ground the sky was aflame with brilliant colour, of which only a dim reflection tinged the dreary view of sward and leafless trees, to which, for some mysterious reason, a gig crawling down the carriage-drive gave the last touch of desolation.

Just as I laid my pen aside the door opened, and Castleman introduced a stranger.

'If you will wait here, sir, I will find her ladyship.'

The newcomer was young and slight, with an erect carriage and a firm step. He had the finely-cut features and dull colouring which I associate with the high-pressure life of a busy town, so that I guessed who he was before his first words told me.

'No, thank you, I will not sit down; I expect to be called to my patient immediately.'

The thought of this said patient made me smile, and in explanation I told him from what she was supposed to be suffering.

'Well; it is less common than other forms of feverishness, but will probably yield to the same remedies,' was his only comment.

'You do not believe in ghosts?'

'Pardon me, I do, just as I believe in all symptoms. When my patient tells me he hears bells ringing in his ear, or feels the ground swaying under his feet, I believe him implicitly, though I know nothing of the kind is actually taking place. The ghost, so far, belongs to the same class as the other experiences, that it is a symptom – it may be of a very trifling, it may be of a very serious, disorder.'

The voice, the keen flash of the eye, impressed me. I recognised one of those alert intelligences, beside whose vivid flame the mental life of most men seems to smoulder. I wished to hear him speak again.

'Is this your view of all supernatural manifestations?'

'Of all so-called supernatural manifestations; I don't understand the word or the distinction. No event which has actually taken place can be supernatural. Since it belongs to the actual it must be governed by, it must be the outcome of, laws which everywhere govern the actual – everywhere and at all times. In fact, it must be natural, whatever we may think of it.'

'Then if a miracle could be proven, it would be no miracle to you?'

'Certainly not.'

'And it could convince you of nothing?'

'Neither me nor any one else who has outgrown his childhood, I should think. I have never been able to understand the outcry of the orthodox over their lost miracles. It makes their position neither better nor worse.

The miracles could never prove their creeds. How am I to recognise a divine messenger? He makes the furniture float about the room; he changes that coal into gold; he projects himself or his image here when he is a thousand miles away. Why, an emissary from the devil might do as much! It only proves – always supposing he really does these things instead of merely appearing to do so – it proves that he is better acquainted with natural laws than I am. What if he could kill me by an effort of the will? What if he could bring me to life again? It is always the same; he might still be morally my inferior; he might be a false prophet after all.'

He took out his watch and looked at it, by this simple action illustrating and reminding me of the difference between us – he talking to pass away the time, I thinking aloud the gnawing question at my heart.

'And you have no hope for anything beyond this?'

Something in my voice must have struck his ear, trained like every other organ of observation to quick and fine perception, for he looked at me more attentively, and it was in a gentler tone that he said –

'Surely, you do not mean for a life beyond this? One's best hope must be that the whole miserable business ends with death.'

'Have you found life so wretched?'

'I am not speaking from my own particular point of view. I am singularly, exceptionally, fortunate. I am healthy; I have tastes which I can gratify, work which I keenly enjoy. Whether the tastes are worth gratifying or the work worth doing I cannot say. At least they act as an anodyne to self-consciousness; they help me to forget the farce in which I play my part. Like Solomon, and all who have had the best of life, I call it vanity. What do you suppose it is to those – by far the largest number, remember – who have had the worst of it? To them it is not vanity, it is misery.'

'But they suffer under the invariable laws you speak of – laws working towards deliverance and happiness in the future.'

'The future? Yes, I know that form of consolation which seems to satisfy so many. To me it seems a hollow one. I have never yet been able to understand how any amount of ecstasy enjoyed by B a million years hence can make up for the torture A is suffering today. I suppose, dealing so much with individuals as I do, I am inclined to individualise like a woman. I think of units rather than of the mass. At this moment I have before me a patient now left suffering pain as acute as any the rack ever inflicted. How does it affect his case that centuries later such pain may be unknown?'

'Of course, the individual's one and only hope is a future existence. Then it may be all made up to him.'

'I see no reason to hope so. Either there is no God, and we shall still be at the mercy of the blind destiny we suffer under here; or there is a God, the God who looks on at this world and makes no sign! The sooner we escape from Him by annihilation the better.'

'Christians would tell you He had given a sign.'

'Yes; so they do in words and deny it in deeds. Nothing is sadder in the whole tragedy, or comedy, than these pitiable efforts to hide the truth, to gloss it over with fables which nobody in his heart of hearts believes – at least in these days. Why not face the worst like men? If we can't help being unhappy we can help being dishonest and cowardly. Existence is a misfortune. Let us frankly confess that it is, and make the best of it.'

He was not looking at his watch now; he was pacing the room. At last, he was in earnest, and had forgotten all accidents of time and place before the same enigma which perplexed myself.

'The best of it!' I re-echoed. 'Surely, under these circumstances, the best thing would be to commit suicide?'

'No,' he cried, stopping and turning sharply upon me. 'The worst, because the most cowardly; so long as you have strength, brains, money – anything with which you can do good.'

He looked past me through the window into the outer air, no longer faintly tinged, but dyed deep red by the light of the unseen but resplendent sunset, and added slowly, dejectedly, as if speaking to himself as much as to me –

'Yes, there is one thing worth living for – to help to make it all a little more bearable for the others.'

And then all at once, his face, so virile yet so delicate, so young and yet so sad, reminded me of one I had seen in an old picture – the face of an angel watching beside the dead Christ; and I cried –

'But are you certain He has made no sign; not hundreds of years ago, but in your own lifetime? not to saint or apostle, but to you, yourself? Has nothing which has happened to you, nothing you have ever seen or read or heard, tempted you to hope in something better?'

'Yes,' he said deliberately; 'I have had my weak moments. My conviction has wavered, not before religious teaching of any kind, however, nor before Nature, in which some people seem to find such promise; but I have met one or two women, and one man – all of them unknown, unremarkable people – whom the world never heard of, nor is likely to hear of, living uneventful obscure lives in out-of-the-way corners. For instance, there is a lady in this very neighbourhood, a relation of Sir George Atherley, I believe, Mrs de No—'

'Her ladyship would like to see you in the drawing-room, sir,' said Castleman, suddenly coming in.

The doctor bowed to me and immediately left the room.

CHAPTER III

MRS MOSTYN'S GOSPEL

'NO, they have not seen any more ghosts, sir,' replied Castleman scornfully next day, 'and never need have seen any. It is all along of this tea-drinking. We did not have this bother when the women took their beer regular. These teetotallers have done a lot of harm. They ought to be put down by Act of Parliament.'

And the kitchen-maid was better. Mrs Mallet, indeed, assured Lady Atherley that Hann was not long for this world, having turned just the same colour as the late Mr Mallet did on the eve of his death; but fortunately the patient herself, as well as the doctor, took a more hopeful view of the case.

'I can see Mrs Mallet is a horrible old croaker,' said Lady Atherley.

'Let her croak,' said Atherley, 'so long as she cooks as she did last night. That curry would have got her absolution for anything if your uncle had been here.'

'That reminds me, George, the ceiling of the spare room is not mended yet.'

'Why, I thought you sent to Whitford for a plasterer yesterday?'

'Yes, and he came; but Mrs Mallet has some extraordinary story about his falling into his bucket and spoiling his Sunday coat, and going home at once to change it. I can't make it out, but nothing is done to the ceiling.'

'I make it out,' said Atherley; 'I make out that he was a little the worse for drink. Have we not a plasterer in the village?'

'I think there is one. I fancy the Jacksons did not wish us to employ him, because he is a dissenter; but after all, giving him work is not the same as giving him presents.'

'No, indeed; nor do I see why, because he is a dissenter, I, who am only an infidel, am to put up with a hole in my ceiling.'

'Only, I don't know what his name is.'

'His name is Smart. Everybody in our village is called Smart — most inappropriately too.'

'No, George, the man the doctor told us about who is so dangerously ill is called Monk.'

'I am glad to hear it; but he doesn't belong to our parish, though he lives so close. He is actually in Rood Warren. His cottage is at the other side of the Common.'

'Then we can leave the wine and things as we go. And, George, while the boys are having tea with Aunt Eleanour, I think I shall drive on to Quarley Beacon and try and persuade Cecilia to come back and spend the night with us. I think we could manage to put her up in the little blue dressing-room. She is so good-natured; she won't mind its being so small.'

'Yes, do; I want Lyndsay to see her. And give my best love to Aunt Eleanour, and say that if she is going to send me any more tracts against Popery, I should be extremely obliged if she would prepay the postage sufficiently.'

'Oh no, George, I could not. It was only threepence.'

'Well, then, tell her it is no good sending any at all, because I have made up my mind to go over to Rome next July.'

'No, George; she might not like it, and I don't believe you are going to do anything of the kind. Oh, are you off already? I thought you would settle something about the plasterer.'

'No, no; I can't think of plasterers and repairs today. Even the galley-slave has his holiday – this is mine. I am going to see the hounds throw off at Rood Acre, and forget for one day that I have an inch of landed property in the world.'

'But, George, if the pink-room ceiling is not put right by Saturday, where shall we put Uncle Augustus?'

'Into the room just opposite to Lindy's.'

'What! that little room? In the bachelor's passage? A man of his age, and of his position!'

'I am sure it is large enough for anyone under a bishop. Besides, I don't think he is fussy about anything except his dinner.'

'It is not the way he is accustomed to be treated when he is on a visit, I can assure you. He is a person who is generally considered a great deal.'

'Well, I consider him a great deal. I consider him one of the finest old heathen I ever knew.'

Fortunately for their domestic peace, Lady Atherley usually misses the points of her husband's speeches, but there are some which jar upon her sense of the becoming, and this was one of them.

'I don't think,' she observed to me, the offender himself having escaped, 'that even if Uncle Augustus were not my uncle, a heathen is a proper name to call a clergyman, especially a canon – and one who is so looked up to in the Church. Have you ever heard him preach? But you must have heard about him, and about his sermons? I thought so. They are beautiful. When he preaches the church is crammed, and with the best people – in the season, when they are in town. And he has written a great many religious books too – sermons and hymns and manuals. There is a little book in red morocco you may have seen in my sitting-room – I know it was there a week ago – which he gave me, *The Life of Prayer*, with a short meditation and a hymn for every hour of the day – all composed by him. We don't see so much of him as I could wish. He is so grieved about George's views. He gave him some of his own sermons, but of course George would not look at them; and – so annoying – the last time he came I put the sermons, two beautiful large volumes of them, on the drawing-room table, and when we were all there after dinner George asked me quite loud what these smart books were, and where they came from. So altogether he has not come to see us for a long time; but as he happened to be staying with the Mountshires, I begged him to come over for a night or two; so you will hear him preach on Sunday.'

At lunch that day Lady Atherley proposed that I should accompany them to Woodcote. 'Do come, Mr Lyndsay,' said Denis. 'We shall have cakes for tea, and jam-sandwiches as well.'

'And there is an awfully jolly banister for sliding down,' added Harold, 'without any turns or landing, you know.'

I professed myself unable to resist such inducements. Indeed, I was almost glad to go. The recollection of Mrs Mostyn's cheerful face was as alluring to me that day as the thought of a glowing hearth might be to the beggar on the door-step. Here, at least, was one to whom life was a blessing; who partook of all it could bestow with an appetite as healthfully keen as her nephew's, but without his disinclination or disregard for anything besides.

The mild March day felt milder, the rooks cawed more cheerfully, and the spring flowers shone out more fearlessly around us when we had passed through the white gates of Woodcote – a favoured spot gently declining to the sunniest quarter, and sheltered from the north and north-east by barricades of elm-woods. The tiny domain was exquisitely ordered, as I love to see everything which appertains to women; and within the low white house, furnished after the simple and stiff fashion of a past generation, reigned the same dainty neatness, the same sunny cheerfulness, the native atmosphere of its chatelaine Mrs Mostyn – a white-haired old lady long past seventy, with the bloom of youth on her cheek, its vivacity in her step, and its sparkle in her eyes.

Hardly were the first greetings exchanged when the children opened the ball of conversation by inquiring eagerly when tea would be ready.

'How can you be so greedy?' said their mother. 'Why, you have only just finished your dinner.'

'We dined at half-past one, and it is nearly half-past three.'

'Poor darlings!' cried Mrs Mostyn, regarding them with the enraptured gaze of the true child-lover; 'their drive has made them hungry; and we cannot have tea very well before half-past four, because some old women from the village have come up to have tea, and the servants are busy attending to them. But I can tell you what you could do, dears. You know the way to the dairy; one of the maids is sure to be there; tell her to give you some cream. You will like that, won't you? Yes, you can go out by this door.'

'And remember to—'

Lady Atherley's exhortation remained unfinished, her sons having darted through the door-window like arrows from the bow.

'Since Miss Jones has been gone for her holiday the children are quite unmanageable,' she observed.

'Oh, it is such a good sign!' cried Mrs Mostyn heartily; 'it shows they are so thoroughly well. Mr Lyndsay, why have you chosen that uncomfortable chair? Come and sit over beside me, if you are not afraid of the fire. And now, Jane, my love, tell me how you are getting on at Weald.'

Then followed a long catalogue of accidents and disappointments, of faithlessness and incapacity, to which Mrs Mostyn supplied a running commentary of interjections sympathetic and consoling. There were, moreover, many changes for the worse since Sir Marmaduke had resided there: the shooting and the fishing had been alike neglected; the farmers were impoverished; the old places had changed hands.

'And a good many quite new people have come to live in small houses round Weald,' said Lady Atherley. 'They have left cards on us. Do you know what they are like?'

'Quite ladies and gentlemen, I believe, and nice enough as long as you don't get to know them too intimately; but they are always quarrelling.'

'About what?'

'About everything; but especially about church matters – decorations and anthems and other rubbish. What they want is less of the church and more of the Bible.'

'I believe Mr Jackson has a Bible-class every week.'

'But is it a Bible-class, or is it only called so? There is Mr Austyn at Rood Warren, a Romanist in disguise if ever there was one: he is by way of having a Bible-class, and one of our farmers' daughters attended it. "And what part of the Bible are you studying now?" I asked her. "We are studying early church history." "I don't know any such chapter in the

Bible as that," I said, and yet I know my Bible pretty well. She explained it was a continuation of the Acts of the Apostles. I said: "My dear child, don't you be misled by any jugglery of that kind; there is no continuation of the Bible; and as to what people call the early church, its doings and sayings are of no consequence at all. The one question we have to ask ourselves is this: "What does the Book say?" What is in the Book is God's word: what is not in the Book is only man's.'

The effect of this exposition on Lady Atherley was to make her ask eagerly whether the curate in charge at Rood Warren was one of the Austyns of Temple Leigh.

'I believe he is a nephew,' Mrs Mostyn admitted, quite gloomily for her. 'It is painful to see people of good standing going astray in this manner.'

'I was thinking it would be so convenient to get a young man over to dinner sometimes; and Rood Warren cannot be very far from us, for one of Mr Austyn's parishioners lives just at the end of Weald.'

'If you take my advice, my dearest Jane, you will not have anything to do with him. He is certain to be attractive – men of that sort always are; and there is no saying what he might do: perhaps gain an influence over George himself.'

'I don't think there need be any fear of that, for at dinner, you know, we need not have any religious discussions; I never will have them; they are almost as bad as politics, they make people so cross.'

Then she rose and explained her visit to Mrs de Noël.

'But, Mr Lyndsay,' said Mrs Mostyn, 'are you going to desert the old woman for the young one, or are you going to stay and see my gardens and have tea? That is right. Good-bye, my dearest Jane. Give my dear love to Cissy, and tell her to come over and see me – but I shall have a glimpse of her on your way back.'

'I hope Mrs de Noël may be persuaded to come back,' I said, as the carriage drove off, and we walked along a gravel path by lawns of velvet smoothness; 'I would so much like to meet her.'

'Have you never met her? Dear Cecilia! She is a sweet creature – the sweetest, I think, I ever met, though perhaps I ought not to say so of my own niece. She wants but one thing – the grace of God.'

We passed into a little wood, tapestried with ivy, carpeted with clustering primroses, and she continued –

'It is most mysterious. Both Cecilia and George, being left orphans so early, were brought up by my dear sister Henrietta. She was a believing Christian, and no children ever had greater religious advantages than these two. As soon as they could speak they learnt hymns or texts of

Scripture, and before they could read they knew whole chapters of the Bible by heart. George even now, I will say that for him, knows his Bible better than a good many clergymen. And the Sabbath, too. They were taught to reverence the Lord's day in a way children never are nowadays. All games and picture-books put away on Saturday night; regularly to church morning and afternoon, and in the evening Henrietta would talk to them and question them about the sermon. And after all, here is George who says he believes in nothing; and as to Cecilia, I never can make out what she does or does not believe. However, I am quite happy in my mind about them. I feel they are of the elect. I am as certain of their salvation as I am of my own.'

A sudden scampering of feet upon the gravel was followed by the appearance of the boys, rosy with exercise and excitement.

'Well, my darling boys, have you had your cream?'

'Oh yes, Aunt Eleanour,' cried Harold, 'and we have been into the farm-yard and seen the little pigs. Such jolly little beasts, Mr Lyndsay, and squeak so funnily when you pull their tails.'

'Oh, but I can't have my pigs unkindly treated.'

'Not unkindly, auntie,' cried Denis, swinging affectionately upon my arm; 'we only just tried to make their tails go straight, you know. And, Mr Lyndsay, there is such a dear little baby calf.'

'But I want to give apples to the horses,' cried Harold.

So we went to the fruit-house for apples, which Mrs Mostyn herself selected from an upper shelf, mounting a ladder with equal agility and grace; then to the stables, where these dainties were crunched by two very fat carriage-horses; then to the miniature farm-yard, and the tiny ivy-covered dairy beyond; and just as I was beginning to feel the first qualms of my besetting humiliation, fatigue, Mrs Mostyn led us round to the garden – a garden with high red walls, and a dial in the meeting-place of the flower-bordered paths; and we sat down in a rustic seat cosily fitted into one sunny corner, just behind a great bed of hyacinths in flower.

The children had but one regret: Tip had been left behind.

'But mamma would not let us bring him,' cried Harold in an aggrieved tone, 'because he will roll in the flower-beds.'

'Do you think it is nearly half-past four, Aunt Eleanour?' asked Denis.

'Very nearly, I should think. Suppose you were to go and see if they have brought the tea-kettle in; and if they have, call to me from the drawing-room window, and I will come.'

The tempered sunlight fell full upon the delicate hyacinth clusters – coral, snow-white, and faintest lilac – exhaling their exquisite odour, and the warm sweet air seemed to enwrap us tenderly. My spirits, heavy as lead, began to rise – strangely, irrationally. Sunlight has always for me a supersensuous beauty, while the colour and perfume of flowers move me as sound vibrations move the musician. Just then it was to me as if through Nature, from that which is behind Nature, there reached me a pitying, a comforting caress.

And in the same key were Mrs Mostyn's words when she next spoke.

'Mr Lyndsay, I am an old woman and you are very young, and my heart goes out to all young creatures in sorrow, especially to one who has no mother of his own, no, nor father even, to comfort him. I know what trouble you have had. Would you be offended if I said how deeply I felt for you?'

'Offended, Mrs Mostyn!'

'No. I see you understand me; you will not think me obtrusive when I say that I pray this great trial may be for your lasting good; may lead you to seek and to find salvation. The truth is brought home to us in many different ways, by many different instruments. My own eyes were opened by very extraordinary means.'

She was silent for a few instants, and then went on –

'When I was young, Mr Lyndsay, I lived for the world only. I went to church, of course, like other people, and said my prayers and called myself a Christian, but I did not know what the word meant. My sister Henrietta would often talk seriously to me, but it had no effect, and she was quite grieved over my hardened state; but my dear mother, a true saint, used to tell her to have no fear, that some day I should be sharply awakened to my soul's danger. But it was not till years after she was in heaven that her words came true.'

I looked at her and waited.

'We were still living at Weald Manor with my brother Marmaduke, and we had young people staying with us. They were all going – all but myself – to a ball at Carchester. I stayed at home because I had a slight cold, which made me feel tired and feverish, and disinclined to be dancing till early next morning. I went to bed early, and when I had sent away my maid I sat beside the fire for a little, thinking. You know the long gallery?'

'Yes.'

'My room was there; so I was quite alone, for the servants slept, just as they do now, in the opposite end of the house. But I had my dog with me, such a dear little thing, a black-and-tan terrier. He was lying asleep on the rug beside me. Well, all at once he got up and put his head on one side as if he heard something, and he began barking. I only said "Nonsense, Totty, lie down," and paid no more attention to him, till some moments afterwards he made a strange kind of noise as if he were trying to bark and was choked in some way. This made me look at him, and then I observed that he was trembling from head to foot, and staring in the strangest way at something behind me. I will honestly tell you he made me feel so uncomfortable I was afraid to look round; and still it was almost as bad to sit there and not look round, so at last I summoned up courage and turned my head. Then I saw it.'

'The ghost?'

'Yes.'

'What was it like?'

'It was like a shadow, only darker, and not lying against the wall as a shadow would do, but standing out from it in the air. It stood a little way from me in a corner of the room. It was in the shape of a man, with a ruff round his neck, and sleeves puffed out at the shoulders, as you often see in old pictures; but I don't remember much about that, for at the time I could think of nothing but the face.'

'And that—?'

'That was simply dreadful. I can't tell you what it was like. I could not have imagined it, if I had not seen it. It was the look – the look in its eyes. After all these years it makes me tremble when I think of it. But what I felt was not the same nervous feeling which made me afraid to turn round. It went much deeper – indeed it went deeper than anything in my life had ever gone before; it went right down to my soul, in fact, and made me feel I had a soul.'

She had turned quite pale.

'Yes, Mr Lyndsay, strange as it sounds, the mere sight of that face made me realise in an instant what I had read and heard thousands of times, and what my mother and Henrietta had told me over and over again about the utter nothingness of earthly aims and comforts – of what in an ordinary way is called life. I had heard very fine sermons preached about the same thing: "What is our life, it is even a vapour," and the "vain shadow" in which we walk. Have you ever thought how we can go on hearing and even repeating true and wise words without getting at their real sense, and, what is worse, without suspecting our own ignorance?'

'I know it well.'

'When Henrietta used to say that the whirl of worldly occupations and interests and amusements in which I was so engrossed did not deserve to be called life, and could never satisfy the eternal soul within me, it used to seem to me an exaggerated way of saying that the next world would be better than this one; but I saw the meaning of her words, I saw the truth of them, as I see these flowers before me, and feel the gravel under my feet: it came to me in a moment, the night these terrible eyes looked into mine.

The feeling did not last, but I have never forgotten it, and never shall. It was as if a veil were lifted for an instant, and I was standing outside of my life and looking back at it; and it seemed so poor and worthless and unreal – I can't explain myself properly.'

'And did the figure remain for any time?'

'I do not know. I think I must have fainted. They found me lying in a half-unconscious state in my chair when they came home. I was ill in bed for weeks with what the doctors call low fever. But neither the fever nor anything else could remove the impression that had been made. That terrible thing was a blessed messenger to me. My real conversion was not till years later, but the way was prepared by the great shock I then received, and which roused me to a sense of my danger.'

'What do you think the thing you saw was, Mrs Mostyn?'

'The ghost?'

'Yes.'

Slowly, thoughtfully, she answered me –

'I am certain it was a lost soul: nothing else could have worn that dreadful look.'

She paused for a few moments and then continued –

'Perhaps you are one of those who do not believe in the punishment of sin?'

'Who can disbelieve it, Mrs Mostyn? Call it what we like, it is a fact. It confronts us on every side. We might as well refuse to believe in death.'

'It is not that I meant! I was talking of punishment in the next world, Mr Lyndsay.'

'Well, there, too, no doubt it must continue, until the uttermost farthing is paid. I believe – at least I hope – that.'

She shook her head with a troubled expression.

'There is no paying that debt in the next world. It can only be paid here. Here, a free pardon is offered to us, and if we do not accept it, then— It is the fashion, even among believers, nowadays to avoid this awful subject. Preachers of the Gospel do not speak of it in the pulpit as they once did. It is considered too shocking for our modern notions. I have no patience with such weakness, such folly – worse than folly. It seems to me even more wrong to try and hide this terrible danger from ourselves and from others than to deny it altogether, as some poor deluded souls do. Mr Lyndsay, have you ever realised what the place of torment will be like?'

'Yes; once, Mrs Mostyn.'

'You were in pain?'

'I suppose it was pain,' I said.

For always, when anything revives this recollection, seared into my memory, the question rises: was it merely pain, physical pain, of which we all speak so easily and lightly? It lasted only ten minutes; ten minutes by the clock, that is. For me time was annihilated. There was no past or future, but only an intolerable present, in which mind and soul were blotted out, and all of sentient existence that remained was the animal consciousness of agony. I cannot share men's stoical contempt for a Gehenna, which is nothing worse.

'Mr Lyndsay, imagine pain, worse than any ever endured on earth going on and on, for ever!'

A bird, not a thrush, but one of the minor singers, lighting on a bough near us, trilled one simple but ecstatic phrase.

'Do you really and truly believe, Mrs Mostyn, that this will be the fate of any single being?'

'Of any single being? Do we not know that it is what will happen to the greatest number? For what does the Book say? "Many are called but few are chosen."'

Through the still, mild air, across the sun-steeped gardens, came the voices of the children –

'Aunt Eleanour! Aunt Eleanour!'

'Many are called,' she repeated, 'but few are chosen; and those who are not chosen shall be cast into everlasting fire.'

There was a pause. She turned to look at me, and, as if struck by something in my face, said gently, soothingly:

'Yes, it is a terrible thought, but only for the unregenerate. It has no terror for me. I trust it need have no terror for you. After all, how simple, how easy is the way of escape! You have only to believe.'

'And then?'

'And then you are safe, safe for evermore. Think of that. The foolish people who wish to explain away eternal punishment, forget that at the same time they explain away eternal happiness! You will be safe now, and after death you will be in heaven for evermore.'

'I shall be in heaven for evermore, and always there will be hell.'

'Yes.'

'Where the others will be?'

'What others? Only the wicked!'

'Aunt Eleanour! Aunt Eleanour!' called the children once more.

'I must go to them! But, Mr Lyndsay, think over what I have said.'

And I remained and obeyed her, and beheld, entire, distinct, the spectre that drives men to madness or despair – illimitable omnipotent Malice. In its shadow the colour of the flowers was quenched, and the music of the birds rang false. Yet it wore the consecration of time and authority! What if it were true?

'Mr Lyndsay,' said Denis at my elbow, 'Aunt Eleanour has sent me to fetch you to tea. Mr Lyndsay, do you hear? Why do you look so strange?'

He caught my hand anxiously as he spoke, and by that little human touch the spell was broken. The phantom vanished; and, looking into the child's eyes, I felt it was a lie.

CHAPTER IV

CANON VERNADE'S GOSPEL

THERE was no Mrs de Noël in the carriage when it returned; she had gone to London to stay with Mrs Donnithorne, whom Atherley spoke of as Aunt Henrietta, and was not expected home till Wednesday.

'I am sorry,' Lady Atherley observed, as we drove home through the dusk; 'I should like to have had her here when Uncle Augustus was with us. I would have asked Mrs Mostyn to dine with us, but I am not sure she and Uncle Augustus would get on. When her sister, Mrs Donnithorne, met Uncle Augustus and his wife at lunch at our house once, she said she thought no minister of the Gospel ought to allow his child to take part in worldly amusements or ceremonials. It was very awkward, because Uncle Augustus's eldest girl had been presented only the day before. And Aunt Clara, Uncle Augustus's wife, you know, who is rather quick, said it depended whether the minister of the Gospel was a gentleman or a shoe-black, because Mrs Donnithorne was attending a dissenting chapel then where the preacher was quite a common uneducated sort of person. And after that they would not talk to each other, and, altogether, I remember, it was very unpleasant. I do think it is such a pity,' cried Lady Atherley with real feeling, 'when people will take up these extreme religious views, as all the Atherleys do. I am sure it is quite a comfort to have someone like you in the house, Mr Lyndsay, who is not particular about religion.'

'If this is the best Aunt Eleanour has to show in the way of a ghost, she does well to keep so quiet about it,' was Atherley's comment on that part of the story which, by special permission, I repeated to him next day. 'I never heard a weaker ghost story. She explains the whole thing away as she tells it. She was, as she candidly admits, ill and feverish – sickening for a fever, in fact, when the most rational person's senses are apt to play them strange tricks. She is alone at the dead of night in a house she believes to be haunted; and then her dog – an odious little beast, I remember him well, always barking at something or nothing; – the dog suggests there is somebody near. She looks round into a dark part of the room, and naturally, inevitably – all things considered – sees a ghost. Did you say it wore a ruff and puffed sleeves?'

'So Mrs Mostyn said.'

'Of course, because, as I told you, Aunt Eleanour believed in the Elizabethan portrait theory. If it had been Aunt Henrietta, the ghost would have been in armour. Ghosts and all visitors from the other world obligingly correspond with the preconceived notions of the visionary. When a white robe and a halo were considered the proper celestial outfit, saints and angels always appeared with white robes and halos. In the same way, the African savage, who believes in a god with a crooked leg, always sees him in dreams, waking or asleep, with a crooked leg; and—'

Here we were interrupted by a great stir in the hall outside, and Lady Atherley looked in to explain that the carriage with Uncle Augustus was just coming down the drive.

Her manner reminded me of the full importance of this arrival, as well as of the unfortunate circumstance that, owing to the ill-timed absence of the dissenting plasterer, the Canon must be lodged in the little room opposite to my own.

However, when I went into the drawing-room, I found him accepting his niece's apologies and explanations with great good-humour. To me also he was especially gracious.

'I had the pleasure of dining at Lindesford, Mr Lyndsay, when you must have been in long clothes. I remember we had some of the finest trout I ever tasted. Are they still as good in your river?'

His voice, like himself, was massive and impressive; his bearing and manner inspired me with wistful admiration: what must life be to a man so self-confident, and so rightly self-confident?

'Is not Uncle Augustus a fine-looking man?' asked Lady Atherley, when he had left the room with Atherley. 'I cannot think why they do not make him a bishop; he would look so well in the robes. He ought to have had something when the last ministry was in, for Aunt Clara and Lord Lingford are cousins; but, unfortunately, the families were on bad terms because of a lawsuit.'

The morning after was bright and fair, so that sunlight mingled with the drowsy calm – Sunday in the country as we remember it, looking lovingly back from lands that are not English to the tenderer side of the Puritan Sabbath. But I missed my little *aubade* from the lawn, and not till breakfast-time did I behold my small friends, who then came into the breakfast-room, one on either side of their mother – two miniature sailors, exquisitely neat but visibly dejected. Behind walked Tip, demurely recognising the change in the atmosphere, but, undisturbed thereby, he at once, with his usual air of self-satisfied dignity, assumed his place in the largest arm-chair.

'The landau could take us all to church except you, George,' said Lady Atherley, looking thoughtfully into the fire as we waited for breakfast and the Canon. 'But I suppose you would prefer to walk?'

'Why should you suppose I am going to church, either walking or driving?'

'Well, I certainly hoped you would have gone today; as Uncle Augustus is going to preach it seems only polite to do so.'

'Well, I don't mind; I dare say it will do me no harm; and if it is understood I attend only out of consideration for my wife's uncle, then—'

He was interrupted by the entrance of the person in question.

Many times during breakfast Denis looked thoughtfully at his great-uncle, and at last inquired –

'Do you preach very long sermons, Uncle Augustus?'

'They are not generally considered so,' replied the Canon with some dignity.

'Denis, I have often told you not to ask questions,' said Lady Atherley.

'When I am grown up,' remarked Harold, 'I will be an atheist.'

'Do you know what an atheist is?' inquired his father.

'Yes, it is people who never go to Church.'

'But they go to lecture-rooms, which you would find worse.'

'But they don't have sermons.'

'Don't they? Hours long, especially when they bury each other.'

'Oh!' said Harold, evidently taken aback, and somewhat reconciled to the Church.

'When I am grown up,' said Denis, 'I mean to be the same church as Aunt Cissy.'

'And what may that be?' inquired the Canon.

Denis was silent and looked perplexed; but some time afterwards, when we were talking of other things, he called out, with the joy of one who has captured that elusive thing, a definition:

'In Aunt Cissy's church they climb trees and make toffee on Sundays.'

After which Lady Atherley seemed glad to take them both away with her.

It was perhaps this remark that led the Canon to ask, on the way to church –

'Is it true that Mrs de Noël attends a dissenting chapel?'

'No,' said Lady Atherley. 'But I know why people say so. She lent a field last year to the Methodists to have their camp-meeting in.'

'Oh! but that is a pity,' said the Canon. 'A very great pity – a person in her position encouraging dissent, especially when there is no real occasion for it. Clara's nephew, young Littlemore, did something of the kind last year, but then he was standing for the county; and though that hardly justifies it, it excuses, a little pandering to the multitude.'

'Cissy only let them have it once,' said Lady Atherley, as if making the best of it. 'And, indeed, I believe it rained so hard that day they were not able to have the meeting after all.'

Then the carriage stopped before the lych-gate, through which the fresh-faced school children were trooping; and while the bell clanged its last monotonous summons, we walked up between the village graves to the old church porch that older yews overshadow, where the village lads were loitering, as Sunday after Sunday their sleeping forefathers had loitered before them.

We worshipped that morning in a magnificent pew to one side of the chancel, and quite as large, from which we enjoyed a full view of clergy and congregation. The former consisted of the Canon, Mr Jackson, clergyman of the parish, and a young man I had not seen before. Not a large number had mustered to hear the Canon; the front seats were well filled by men and women in goodly apparel, but in the pews behind and in the side aisles there was a mere sprinkling of worshippers in the Sunday dress of country labourers. Our supplications were offered with as little ritualistic pageantry as Mrs Mostyn herself could have desired, though the choir probably sang oftener and better than she would have approved. In spite of their efforts it was as uninspiring a service as I have ever taken part in. This was not due, as might be suspected, to Atherley's presence, for his demeanour was irreproachable. His little sons, delighted at having him with them, carefully found his places for him in prayer and hymn-book, and kept watch that he did not lose them afterwards, so that he perforce assumed a really edifying degree of attention. Nor, indeed, did the rest of the congregation err in the direction of restlessness or wandering looks, but rather in the opposite extreme, insomuch that during the litany, when we were no longer supported by music, and had, most of us, assumed attitudes favourable to repose, we appeared one and all to succumb to it, especially towards the close, when, from the body of the church at least, only the aged clerk was heard to cry for mercy. But with the third service there came a change, which reminded me of how once in a foreign cathedral, when the procession filed by – the singing-men nudging each other, the standard-bearers giggling, and the English tourists craning to see the sight – the face of one white-haired old bishop beneath his canopy transformed for me a foolish piece of mummery into a prayer in action. So it was again, when the young stranger turned to us his pale clear-cut face, solemn with an awe as rapt as if he verily stood before the throne of Him he called upon, and felt Its glory beating on his face; then, by that one earnest and believing presence, all was transformed and redeemed; the old emblems recovered their first significance, the time-worn phrases glowed with life again, and we ourselves were altered – our very heaviness was pathetic: it was the lethargy of death itself, and our poor sleepy prayers the strain of manacled captives striving to be free.

The Canon's sermon did not maintain this high-strung mood, though why not it would be difficult to say. Like all his, it was eloquent, brilliant even, declaimed by a fine voice of wide compass, whose varying tones he used with the skill of a practised orator. The text was 'Our conversation is in Heaven', its theme the contrast between the man of this world, with his heart fixed upon its pomps, its vanities, its honours, and the believer indifferent to all these, esteeming them as dross merely compared to the heavenly treasure, the one thing needful. Certainly the utter worthlessness of the prizes for which men labour and so late take rest, barter their happiness, their peace, their honour, was never more scathingly depicted. I remember the organ-like bass of his note in passages which denounced the grovelling worship of earthly pre-eminence and riches, the clarion-like cry with which he concluded a stirring eulogy of the Christian's nobler service of things unseen.

'Brethren, as His kingdom is not of this world, so too our kingdom is not of this world.'

'I think you will admit, George,' said Lady Atherley, as we left the church, 'that you have had a good sermon today.'

'Yes, indeed,' heartily assented Atherley. 'It was excellent. Your uncle certainly knows his business, which is more than can be said of most preachers. It was a really splendid performance. But who on earth was he talking about – those wonderful people who don't care for money or success, or the best of everything generally? I never met any like them.'

'My dear George! How extraordinary you are! Any one could see, I should have thought, that he meant Christians.'

Atherley and the children walked home while we waited for the Canon, who stayed behind to exchange a few words in the vestry with his old schoolfellow, Mr Jackson.

As we drove home he made, aloud, some reflections, probably suggested by the difference between their positions.

'It really grieves me to see Jackson where he is at his age. He deserves a better living. He is an excellent fellow, and not without ability, but wanting, unfortunately, in tact and *savoir-faire*. He always had an unhappy knack of blurting out the truth in season and out of season. I did my best to get him a good living once – a first-rate living – in Sir John Marsh's gift; and I warned him before he went to lunch with Sir John to be careful what he said. "Sir John," I said, "is one of the old school; he thinks the Squire is pope of the parish, and you will have to humour him a little. He will talk a great deal of nonsense in this strain, and be careful not to contradict him, for he can't bear it." But Jackson did contradict him – flatly; he told me so himself, and, of course, Sir John would have nothing to say to him. "But he made such extravagant statements," said Jackson. "If I had kept quiet he would have thought I agreed with him." – "What did that matter?" I said. "Once you were vicar you could have shown him you didn't." – "The truth is," said Jackson, "I cannot sit by and hear black called white without protesting." That is Jackson all over! A man of that kind will never get on. And then, such an imprudent marriage – a woman without a penny!'

'I have never seen any one who wore such extraordinary bonnets,' said Lady Atherley.

'Who was that young man who bowed to the altar and crossed himself?' asked the Canon.

'I suppose that must be Mr Austyn, curate in charge at Rood Warren. He comes over to help Mr Jackson sometimes, I believe. George has met him; I have not. I want to get him over to dinner. He is a nephew of Mr Austyn of Temple Leigh.'

'Oh, that family!' said the Canon. 'I am sorry he has taken up such an extreme line. It is a great mistake. In the Church, preferment in these days always goes to the moderate men.'

'Rood Warren is not far from here,' said Lady Atherley, 'and he has a parishioner— Oh, that reminds me. Mr Lyndsay, would you be so kind as to look out and tell the coachman to drive round by Monk's? I want to leave some soup.'

'Monk, I presume, is a sick labourer?' said the Canon. 'I hope you are not as indiscriminate in your charities as most Ladies Bountiful.'

'Mr Jackson says this is a really deserving case. He knows all about him, though he really is in Mr Austyn's parish. Monk has never had anything from the parish, and been working hard all his life, and he is past seventy. He was breaking stones on the road a few weeks ago; but he caught a chill or something one very cold day, and has been laid up ever since. This is the house. Oh, Mr Lyndsay, you should not trouble to get out. As you are so kind, will you carry this in?'

The interior of the tiny thatched cottage was scrupulously clean and neat, as they nearly all are in the valley, but barer and more scantily furnished than most of them. No photographs or pictures decorated the white-washed walls, no scraps of carpet or matting hid the red-brick floor. The Monks were evidently of the poorest. An old piece of faded curtain had been hung from a rope between the chimney-piece and the door to shield the patient from the draught. He sat in a stiff wooden arm-chair near the fire, drawing his breath laboriously. 'He was better now,' said his wife, a nurse as old and as frail-looking as himself. 'Nights was the worst.' His shoulders were bent, his hair white with age, his withered features almost as coarse and as unshapely as the poor clothes he wore. The mask had been rough-hewn, to begin with; time and exposure had further defaced it. No gleam of intellectual life transpierced and illumined all. It was the face of an animal – ugly, ignorant, honest, patient. As I looked at it there came over me a rush of the pity I have so often felt for this suffering of age in poverty – so unpicturesque, so unwinning, to shallow sight so unpathetic – and I put out my hand and let it rest for a moment on his own, knotted with rheumatism, stained and seamed with toil. Then he looked up at me from under his shaggy brows with haggard, wistful eyes, and gasped: 'It's hard work, sir; it's hard work.' And I went out into the sunshine, feeling that I had heard the epitome of his life.

That night Mrs Mallet surpassed herself by her rendering of a *menu*, especially composed by Atherley for the delectation of their guest. Their pains were not wasted. The Canon's commendation of each course – and we talked of little else, I remember, from soup to dessert – was as discriminating as it was warm.

'I am glad you approve of our cook, Uncle,' said Lady Atherley in the drawing-room afterwards, 'for she is only a stop-gap. Our own cook left us quite suddenly the other day, and we had such difficulty in finding this one to take her place. No one can imagine how inconvenient it is to have a haunted house.'

'My dear Jane, you don't mean to tell me you are afraid of ghosts?'

'Oh no, Uncle.'

'And I am sure your husband is not?'

'No; but unfortunately cooks are.'

'Eh! what?'

Then Lady Atherley willingly repeated the story of her troubles.

'Preposterous! perfectly preposterous!' cried the Canon. 'The Education

Act in operation for all these years, and our lower orders still believe in bogies and hobgoblins! And yet it is hardly to be wondered at; their social superiors are not much wiser. The nonsense which is talked in society at present is perfectly incredible. Persons who are supposed to be in their right mind gravely relate to me such incidents that I could imagine myself transported to the Middle Ages. I hear of miraculous cures, of spirits summoned from the dead, of men and women floating in the air; and as to diabolic possession, it seems to have become as common as colds in the head.'

He had risen, and now addressed us from the hearthrug.

'Then Mrs Molyneux and others come and tell me about personal friends of their own who can foretell everything that is going to happen; who can read your inmost thoughts; who can compel others to do this and to do that, whether they like it or no; who, being themselves in one quarter of the globe, constantly appear to their acquaintances in another. "What!" I say. "They can be in two places at once, then! Certainly no conjurer can equal that!"

'And what do they say to that?' asked Atherley.

'Oh, they assure me the extraordinary beings who perform these marvels are not impostors, but very superior and religious characters. "If they are not impostors," I say, "then their right place is the lunatic asylum." "Oh but, Canon Vernade, you don't understand; it is only our Western ignorance which makes such things seem astonishing! Far more marvellous things are going on, and have been going on for centuries, in the East; for instance, in the Brotherhoods of – I forget – some unpronounceable name." "And how do you know they have?" I ask. "Oh, by their traditions, which have been handed on for generations." "That is very reliable information indeed," I say. "Pray, have you ever played a game of Russian scandal?" "Well; but, then, there are the sacred books. There can be no mistake about them, for they have been translated by learned European professors, who say the religious sentiments are perfectly beautiful." "Very possibly," I say. "But it does not follow that the historical statements are correct."

'I gave my ladies' Bible-class a serious lecture about it all the other day. I said: "Do, my dear ladies, get rid of these childish notions, these uncivilised hankerings after marvels and magic, which make you the dupe of one charlatan after another. Take up science, for a change; study natural philosophy; try and acquire accurate notions of the system under which we live; realise that we are not moving on the stage of a Christmas pantomime, but in a universe governed by fixed laws, in which the miraculous performances you describe to me never can, and never could, have taken place. And be sure of this, that any book and any teacher, however admirable their moral teaching, who tell you that two and two make anything but four, are not inspired, so far as arithmetic and common sense are concerned."'

'Hear, hear!' cried Atherley heartily.

The Canon's brow contracted a little.

'I need hardly explain,' he said, 'that what I said did not apply to revealed truth. Jane, my dear, as I must leave by an early train tomorrow, I think I shall say good night.'

I fell asleep that night early, and dreamt that I was sitting with Gladys in the frescoed dining-room of an old Italian palace. It was night, and through the open window came one long shaft of moonlight, that vanished in the aureole of the shaded lamp standing with wine and fruit upon the table between us. And I said in my dream –

'Oh, Gladys, will it be always like this, or must we part again?'

And she, smiling her slow soft smile, said: 'You may stay with me till the knock comes.'

'What knock, my darling?'

But even as I spoke I heard it, low and penetrating, and I stretched out my arms imploringly towards Gladys; but she only smiled, and the knock was repeated, and the whole scene dissolved around me, and I was sitting up in bed in semi-darkness, while somebody was tapping with a quick agitated touch at my door. I remembered then that I had forgotten to unlock it before I went to bed, and I rose at once and made haste to open it, not without a passing thrill of unpleasant conjecture as to what might be behind it. It was a tall figure in a long grey garment, who carried a lighted candle in his hand. For a moment, startled and stupefied as I was, I failed to recognise the livid face.

'Canon Vernade! You are ill?'

Too ill to speak, it would seem, for without a word he staggered forward and sank into a chair, letting the candle almost drop from his hand on to the table beside him; but when I put out my hand to ring the bell, he stayed me by a gesture. I looked at him, deadly pale, with blue shadows about the mouth and eyes, his head thrown helplessly back, and then I remembered some brandy I had in my dressing-bag. He took the glass from me and raised it to his lips with a trembling hand. I stood watching him, debating within myself whether I should disobey him by calling for help or not; but presently, to my great relief, I saw the stimulant take effect, and life come slowly surging back in colour to his cheeks, in strength to his whole prostrate frame. He straightened himself a little, and turned upon me a less distracted gaze than before.

'Mr Lyndsay, there is something horrible in this house.'

'Have you seen it?'

He shook his head.

'I saw nothing; it is what I felt.'

He shuddered.

I looked towards the grate. The fire had long been out, but the wood was still unconsumed, and I managed, inexpertly enough, to relight it. When a long blue flame sprang up, he drew his chair near the hearth and stretched towards the blaze his still tremulous hands.

'Mr Lyndsay,' he said, in a voice as strangely altered as his whole appearance, 'may I sit here a little – till it is light? I dread to go back to that room. But don't let me keep you up.'

I said, and in all honesty, that I had no inclination to sleep. I put on my dressing-gown, threw a rug over his knees, and took my place opposite to him on the other side of the fire; and thus we kept our strange vigil, while slowly above us broke the grim, cold dawn of early spring-time, which even the birds do not brighten with their babble.

Silently staring into the fire, he vouchsafed no further explanations, and I did not venture to ask for any; but I doubt if even such language as he could command would have been so full of horrible suggestion as that grey set face, and the terror-stricken gaze, which the growing light made every minute more distinct, more weird. What had so suddenly and so completely overthrown, not his own strength merely, but the defences of his faith? He groped amongst them still, for, from time to time, I heard him murmuring to himself familiar verses of prayer and psalm and gospel, as if he sought therewith to banish some haunting fear, to quiet some torturing suspicion. And at last, when the dull grey day had fully broken, he turned towards me, and cried in tones more heart-piercing than ever startled the great congregations in church or cathedral –

'What if it were all a delusion, and there be no Father, no Saviour?'

And the horror of the abyss into which he looked, flashing from his mind to my own, left me silent and helpless before him. Yet I longed to give him comfort; for, with the regal self-possession which had fallen from him, there had slipped from me too some undefined instinct of distrust and disapproval. All that I felt now was the sad tie of brotherhood which united us, poor human atoms, strong only in our capacity to suffer, tossed and driven, whitherward we knew not, in the purposeless play of soulless and unpitying forces.

Chapter V

AUSTYN'S GOSPEL

'HE did not see the ghost, you say; he only felt it? I should think he did –
on his chest. I never heard of a clearer case of nightmare. You must be
careful whom you tell the story to, old chap; for at the first go-off it sounds
as if it was not merely eating too much that was the matter. It was,
however, indigestion sure enough. No wonder! If a man of his age who
takes no exercise will eat three square meals a day, what else can he
expect? And Mallet is rather liberal with her cream.'

Atherley it was, of course, who propounded this simple interpretation
of the night's alarms, as he sat in his smoking-room reviewing his
trout-flies after an early breakfast we had taken with the Canon.

'You always account for the mechanism, but not for the effect. Why
should indigestion take that mental form?'

'Why, because indigestion constantly does in sleep, and out of it as
well, for that matter. A nightmare is not always a sense of oppression on
the chest only; it may be an overpowering dread of something you dream
you see. Indigestion can produce, waking or asleep, a very good imitation
of what is experienced in a blue funk. And there is another kind of dream
which is produced by fasting – that, I need hardly say, I have never
experienced. Indeed, I don't dream.'

'But the ghost – the ghost he almost saw.'

'The sinking horror produced the ghost, instead of *vice versa*, as you
might suppose. It is like a dream. In unpleasant dreams we fancy it is the
dream itself which makes us feel uncomfortable. It is just the other way
round. It is the discomfort that produces the dream. Have you ever dreamt
you were tramping through snow, and felt cold in consequence? I did the
other night. But I did not feel cold because I dreamt I was walking through
snow, but because I had not enough blankets on my bed; and because I
felt cold I dreamt about the snow. Don't you know the dream you make
up in a few moments about the knocking at the door when they call you in
the morning? And ghosts are only waking dreams.'

'I wonder if you ever had an illusion yourself – gave way to it, I mean.
You were in love once – twice,' I added hastily, in deference to Lady
Atherley.

'Only once,' said Atherley, calmly. 'Do you ever see her now, Lindy?
She has grown enormously fat. Certainly I have had my illusions, and I
don't object to them when they are pleasant and harmless – on the
contrary. Now, falling in love, if you don't fall too deep, is pleasant, and it

never lasts long enough to do much mischief. Marriage, of course, you will say, may be mischievous – only for the individual, it is useful for the race. What I object to is the deliberate culture of illusions which are not pleasant but distinctly depressing, like half your religious beliefs.'

'George,' said Lady Atherley, coming into the room at this instant; 'have you – oh, dear! what a state this room is in!'

'It is the housemaids. They never will leave things as I put them.'

'And it was only dusted and tidied an hour ago. Mr Lyndsay, did you ever see anything like it?'

I said, 'Never.'

'If Lindy has a fault in this world, it is that he is as pernickety, as my old nurse used to say – as pernickety as an old maid. The stiff formality of his room would give me the creeps, if anything could. The first thing I always want to do when I see it is to make hay in it.'

'It is what you always do do, before you have been an hour there,' I observed.

'Jane, in Heaven's name leave those things alone! Is this sort of thing all you came in for?'

'No; I really came in to ask if you had read Lucinda Molyneux's letter.'

'No, I have not; her writing is too bad for anything. Besides, I know exactly what she has got to say. She has at last found the religion which she has been looking for all her life, and she intends to be whatever it is for evermore.'

'That is not all. She wants to come and stay here for a few days.'

'What! Here? Now? Why, what – oh, I forgot the ghost! By Jove! You see, Jane, there are some advantages in having one on the premises when it procures you a visit from a social star like Mrs Molyneux. But where are you going to put her? Not in the bachelor's room, where your poor uncle made such a night of it? It wouldn't hold her dressing-bag, let alone herself.'

'Oh, but I hope the pink room will be ready. The plasterer from Whitford came out yesterday to apologise, and said he had been keeping his birthday.'

'Indeed! and how many times a year does he have a birthday?'

'I don't know, but he was quite sober; and he did the most of it yesterday and will finish it today, so it will be all right.'

'When is she coming, then?'

'Tomorrow. You would have seen that if you had read the letter. And there is a message for you in it, too.'

'Then find me the place, like an angel; I cannot wade through all these sheets of hieroglyphics. In the postscript? Let me see: "Tell Sir George I look forward to explaining to him the religious teaching which I have been studying for months." Months! Come; there must be something in a religion which Mrs Molyneux sticks to for months at a time – "studying for months under the guidance of its great apostle Baron Zinkersen—" What is this name? "The deeper I go into it all the more I feel in it that faith, satisfying to the reason as well as to the emotions, for which I have been searching all my life. It is certainly the religion of the future" – future underlined – "and I believe it will please even Sir George, for it so distinctly coincides with his own favourite theories." Favourite theories, indeed! I haven't any. My mind is as open as day to truth from any quarter. Only I distrust apostles with no vowels in their names ever since that one, two years ago, made off with the spoons.'

'No, George, he did not take any plate. It was money, and money Lucinda gave him herself for bringing her letters from her father.'

'Where was her father, then?' I inquired, much interested.

'Well, he was – a – he was dead,' answered Lady Atherley; 'and after some time a very low sort of person called upon Lucinda and said she wrote all the letters; but Lucinda could not get the money back without going to law, as some people wished her to do; but I am glad she did not, as I think the papers would have said very unpleasant things about it.'

'The apostle I liked best,' said Atherley, 'was the American one. I really admired old Stamps, and old Stamps admired me; for she knew I thoroughly understood what an unmitigated humbug she was. She had a fine sense of humour, too. How her eyes used to twinkle when I asked posers at her prayer-meetings!'

'Dreadful woman!' cried Lady Atherley. 'Lucinda brought her to lunch once. Such black nails, and she said she could make the plates and dishes fly about the room, but I said I would rather not. I am thankful she does not want to bring this baron with her.'

'I would not have him. I draw the line there, and also at spiritual séances. I am too old for them. Do you remember one I took you to at Mrs Molyneux's, Lindy, five years ago, when they raised poor old Professor Delaine, and he danced on the table and spelt bliss with one s? I was haunted for weeks afterwards by the dread that there might be a future life, in which we should make fools of ourselves in the same way. What is this?'

'It is the carriage just come back from the station. Mr Lyndsay and the little boys are going over to Rood Warren with a note for me. I hope you will see Mr Austyn, Mr Lyndsay, and persuade him to come over tomorrow.'

'What! To dine?' said Atherley. 'He won't come out to dinner in Lent.'

I thought so myself, but I was glad of the excuse to see again the delicate, austere face. As we drove along, I tried to define to myself the quality which marked it out from others. Not sweetness, not marked benevolence, but the repose of absolute spiritual conviction. Austyn's God can never be my God, and in his heaven I should find no rest; but, one among ten thousand, he believed in both, as the martyrs believed who perished in the flames, with a faith which would have stood the atheist's test; – 'We believe a thing, when we are prepared to act as if it were true.'

Rood Warren lay in a little hollow beside an armlet of the stream that waters all the valley. The hamlet consisted of a tiny church and a group of labourers' cottages, in one of which, presumably because there was no other habitation for him, the curate in charge made his home. An apple-faced old woman received me at the door, and hospitably invited me to wait within for Mr Austyn's return from morning service, which I did, while the carriage, with the little boys and Tip in it, drove up and down before the door. The room in which I waited, evidently the one sitting-room, was destitute of luxury or comfort as a monk's cell.

Profusion there was in one thing only – books. They indeed furnished the room, clothing the walls and covering the table; but ornaments there were none, not even sacred or symbolical, save, indeed, one large and beautifully-carved crucifix over a mantelpiece covered with letters and manuscripts. I have thought of this early home of Austyn's many a time as dignities have been literally thrust upon him by a world which since then has discovered his intellectual rank. He will end his days in a palace, and, one may confidently predict of him, remain as absolutely indifferent to his surroundings as in the little cottage at Rood Warren.

But he did not come, and presently his housekeeper came in with many apologies to explain he would not be back for hours, having started after service on a round of parish visiting instead of first returning home, as she had expected. She herself was plainly depressed by the fact. 'I did hope he would have come in for a bit of lunch first,' she said, sadly.

All I could do was to leave the note, to which late in the day came an answer, declining simply and directly on the ground that he did not dine out in Lent.

'I cannot see why,' observed Lady Atherley, as we sat together over the drawing-room fire after tea, 'because it is possible to have a very nice dinner without meat. I remember one we had abroad once at an hotel on Good Friday. There were sixteen courses, chiefly fish, no meat even in the soup, only cream and eggs and that sort of thing, all beautifully cooked with exquisite sauces. Even George said he would not mind fasting in that way. It would have been nice if he could have come to meet Mrs Molyneux tomorrow. I am sure they must be connected in some way, because Lord—'

And then my mind wandered whilst Lady Atherley entered into some genealogical calculations, for which she has nothing less than a genius. My attention was once again captured by the name de Noël, how introduced I know not, but it gave me an excuse for asking –

'Lady Atherley, what is Mrs de Noël like?'

'Cecilia? She is rather tall and rather fair, with brown hair. Not exactly pretty, but very ladylike-looking. I think she would be very good-looking if she thought more about her dress.'

'Is she clever?'

'No, not at all; and that is very strange, for the Atherleys are such a clever family, and she has quite the ways of a clever person, too; so odd, and so stupid about little things that any one can remember. I don't believe she could tell you, if you asked her, what relation her husband was to Lord Stowell.'

'She seems a great favourite.'

'Oh, no one could possibly help liking her. She is the most good-natured person; there is nothing she would not do to help one; she is a dear thing, but most odd, so very odd. I often think it is so fortunate that she married a sailor, because he is so much away from home.'

'Don't they get on, then?'

'Oh dear, yes; they are devoted to each other, and he thinks everything she does quite perfect. But then he is very different from most men; he thinks so little about eating, and he takes everything so easy; I don't think he cares what strange people Cecilia asks to the house.'

'Strange people!'

'Well; strange people to have on a visit. Invalids and – people that have nowhere else they could go to.'

'Do you mean poor people from the East End?'

'Oh no; some of them are quite rich. She had an idiot there with his mother once who was heir to a very large fortune in the Colonies somewhere; but of course nobody else would have had them, and I think it must have been very uncomfortable. And then once she actually had a woman who had taken to drinking. I did not see her, I am thankful to say.'

There was a little pause, and then Lady Atherley added –

'Cecilia has never been the same since her baby died. She used to have such a bright colour before that. He was not quite two years old, but she felt it dreadfully; and it was a great pity, for if he had lived he would have come in for all the Stowell property.'

The door opened.

'Why, George; how late you are, and – how wet! Is it raining?'

'Yes; hard.'

'Have you bought the ponies?'

'No; they won't do at all. But whom do you think I picked up on the way home? You will never guess. Your pet parson, Mr Austyn.'

'Mr Austyn!'

'Yes; I found him by the roadside not far from Monk's cottage, where he had been visiting, looking sadly at a spring-cart, which the owner thereof, one of the Rood Warren farmers, had managed to upset and damage considerably. He was giving Austyn a lift home when the spill took place. So, remembering your hankering and Lindy's for the society of this young Ritualist, I persuaded him that instead of tramping six miles through the wet he should come here and put up for the night with us; so, leaving the farmer free to get home on his pony, I clinched the matter by promising to send him back tomorrow in time for his eight o'clock service.'

'Oh dear! I wish I had known he was coming. I would have ordered a dinner he would like.'

'Judging by his appearance, I should say the dinner he would like will be easily provided.'

Atherley was right. Mr Austyn's dinner consisted of soup, bread, and water. He would not even touch the fish or the eggs elaborately prepared for his especial benefit. Yet he was far from being a skeleton at the feast, to whose immaterial side he contributed a good deal – not taking the lead in conversation, but readily following whosoever did, giving his opinions on one topic after another in the manner of a man well informed, cultured, thoughtful, original even, and at the same time with no warmer interest in all he spoke of than the inhabitant of another planet might have shown.

Atherley was impressed and even surprised to a degree unflattering to the rural clergy.

'This is indeed a *rara avis* of a country curate,' he confided to me after dinner, while Lady Atherley was unravelling with Austyn his connection with various families of her acquaintance. 'We shall hear of him in time to come, if, in the meanwhile, he does not starve himself to death. By the way, I lay you odds he sees the ghost. To begin with; he has heard of it – everybody has in this neighbourhood; and then St Anthony himself was never in a more favourable condition for spiritual visitations. Look at him; he is blue with asceticism. But he won't turn tail to the ghost; he'll hold his own. There's metal in him.'

This led me to ask Austyn, as we went down the bachelor's passage to our rooms, if he were afraid of ghosts.

'No; that is, I don't feel any fear now. Whether I should do so if face to face with one, is another question. This house has the reputation of being haunted, I believe. Have you seen the ghost yourself?'

'No, but I have seen others who did, or thought they did. Do you believe in ghosts?'

'I do not know that I have considered the subject sufficiently to say whether I do or not. I see no *prima facie* objection to their appearance. That it would be supernatural offers no difficulty to a Christian whose religion is founded on, and bound up with, the supernatural.'

'If you do see anything, I should like to know.'

I went away, wondering why he repelled as well as attracted me; what it was behind the almost awe-inspiring purity and earnestness I felt in him that left me with a chill sense of disappointment? The question was so perplexing and so interesting that I determined to follow it up next day, and ordered my servant to call me as early as Mr Austyn was wakened.

In the morning I had just finished dressing, but had not put out my candles, when a knock at the door was followed by the entrance of Austyn himself.

'I did not expect to find you up, Mr Lyndsay; I knocked gently, lest you should be asleep. In case you were not, I intended to come and tell you that I had seen the ghost.'

'Breakfast is ready,' said a servant at the door.

'Let me come down with you and hear about it,' I said.

We went down through staircase and hall, still plunged in darkness, to the dining-room, where lamps and fire burned brightly. Their glow falling on Austyn's face showed me how pale it was, and worn as if from watching.

Breakfast was set ready for him, but he refused to touch it.

'But tell me what you saw.'

'I must have slept two or three hours when I awoke with the feeling that there was someone besides myself in the room. I thought at first it was the remains of a dream and would quickly fade away; but it did not, it grew stronger. Then I raised myself in bed and looked round. The space between the sash of the window and the curtains – my shutters were not closed – allowed one narrow stream of moonlight to enter and lie across the floor. Near this, standing on the brink of it, as it were, and rising dark against it, was a shadowy figure. Nothing was clearly outlined but the face; *that* I saw only too distinctly. I rose and remained up for at least an hour before it vanished. I heard the clock outside strike the hour twice. I was not looking at it all this time – on the contrary, my hands were clasped across my closed eyes; but when from time to time I turned to see if it was gone, it was always there immovable, watchful. It reminded me of a wild beast waiting to spring, and I seemed to myself to be holding it at bay all the time with a great strain of the will, and, of course' – he hesitated for an instant, and then added – 'in virtue of a higher power.'

The reserve of all his school forbade him to say more, but I understood as well as if he had told me that he had been on his knees, praying all the time, and there rose before my mind a picture of the scene – moonlight, kneeling saint, and watching demon, which the leaf of some illustrated missal might have furnished.

The bronze timepiece over the fireplace struck half-past six.

'I wonder if the carriage is at the door,' said Austyn, rather anxiously. He went into the hall and looked out through the narrow windows. There was no carriage visible, and I deeply regretted the second interruption that must follow when it did come.

'Let us walk up the hill and on a little way together. The carriage will overtake us. My curiosity is not yet satisfied.'

'Then first, Mr Lyndsay, you must go back and drink some coffee; you are not strong as I am, or accustomed to go out fasting into the morning air.'

Outside in the shadow of the hill, where the fog lay thick and white, the gloom and the cold of the night still lingered, but as we climbed the hill we climbed, too, into the brightness of a sunny morning – brilliant, amber-tinted above the long blue shadows.

.   .   .   .   .

I had to speak first.

'Now tell me what the face was like.'

'I do not think I can. To begin with, I have a very indistinct remembrance of either the form or the colouring. Even at the time my impression of both was very vague; what so overwhelmed and transfixed my attention, to the exclusion of everything besides itself, was the look upon the face.'

'And that?'

'And that I literally cannot describe. I know no words that could depict it, no images that could suggest it; you might as well ask me to tell you what a new colour was like if I had seen it in my dreams, as some people declare they have done. I could convey some faint idea of it by describing its effect upon myself, but that, too, is very difficult – that was like nothing I have ever felt before. It was the realisation of much which I have affirmed all my life, and steadfastly believed as well, but only with what might be called a notional assent, as the blind man might believe that light is sweet, or one who had never experienced pain might believe it was something from which the senses shrink. Every day that I have recited the creed, and declared my belief in the Life Everlasting, I have by implication confessed my entire disbelief in any other. I knew that what seemed so solid is not solid, so real is not real; that the life of the flesh, of the senses, of things seen, is but the "stuff that dreams are made of" – "a dream within a dream", as one modern writer has called it; "the shadow of a dream", as another has it. But last night—'

He stood still, gazing straight before him, as if he saw something that I could not see.

'But last night,' I repeated, as we walked on again.

'Last night? I not only believed, I saw, I felt it with a sudden intuition conveyed to me in some inexplicable manner by the vision of that face. I felt the utter insignificance of what we name existence, and I perceived too behind it that which it conceals from us – the real Life, illimitable, unfathomable, the element of our true being, with its eternal possibilities of misery or joy.'

'And all this came to you through something of an evil nature?'

'Yes; it was like the effect of lightning on a pitch-dark night – the same vivid and lurid illumination of things unperceived before. It must be like the revelation of death, I should think, without, thank God, that fearful sense of the irrevocable which death must bring with it. Will you not rest here?'

For we had reached Beggar's Stile. But I was not tired for once, so keen, so life-giving was the air, sparkling with that fine elixir whereby morning braces us for the day's conflict. Below, through slowly-dissolving mists, the village showed as if it smiled, each little cottage hearth lifting its soft spiral of smoke to a zenith immeasurably deep, immaculately blue.

'But the ghost itself?' I said, looking up at him as we both rested our arms upon the gate. 'What do you think of that?'

'I am afraid there is no possible doubt what that was. Its face, as I tell you, was a revelation of evil – evil and its punishment. It was a lost soul.'

'Do you mean by a lost soul, a soul that is in never-ending torment?'

'Not in physical torment, certainly; that would be a very material interpretation of the doctrine. Besides, the Church has always recognised degree and difference in the punishment of the lost. This, however, they all have in common – eternal separation from the Divine Being.'

'Even if they repent and desire to be reunited to Him?'

'Certainly; that must be part of their suffering.'

'And yet you believe in a good God?'

'In what else could I believe, even without revelation? But goodness, divine goodness, is far from excluding severity and wrath, and even vengeance. Here the witness of science and of history is in accord with that of the Christian Church; their first manifestation of God is always of "one that is angry with us and threatens evil."'

The carriage had overtaken us and stopped now close to us. I rose to say good-bye. Austyn shook me by the hand and moved towards the carriage; then, as if checked by a sudden thought, returned upon his steps and stood before me, his earnest eyes fixed upon me as if the whole self-denying soul within him hungered to waken mine.

'I feel I must speak one word before I leave you, even if it be out of season. With the recollection of last night still so fresh, even the serious things of life seem trifles, far more its small conventionalities. Mr Lyndsay, your friend has made his choice, but you are dallying between belief and unbelief. Oh, do not dally long! We need no spirit from the dead to tell us life is short. Do we not feel it passing quicker and quicker every year? The one thing that is serious in all its shows and delusions is the question it puts to each one of us, and which we answer to our eternal loss or gain. Many different voices call to us in this age of false prophets, but one only threatens as well as invites. Would it not be only wise, prudent even, to give the preference to that? Mr Lyndsay, I beseech you, accept the teaching of the Church, which is one with that of conscience and of nature, and believe that there *is* a God, a Sovereign, a Lawgiver, a Judge.'

He was gone, and I still stood thinking of his words, and of his gaze while he spoke them.

The mists were all gone, now, leaving behind them in shimmering dewdrops an iridescent veil on mead and copse and garden; the river gleamed in diamond curves and loops, while in the covert near me the birds were singing as if from hearts that over-brimmed with joy.

And slowly, sadly, I repeated to myself the words – Sovereign, Lawgiver, Judge.

I was hungering for bread; I was given a stone.

Chapter VI

MRS MOLYNEUX'S GOSPEL

'THE room is all ready now,' said Lady Atherley, 'but Lucinda has never written to say what train she is coming by.'

'A good thing, too,' said Atherley; 'we shall not have to send for her. Those unlucky horses are worked off their legs already. Is that the carriage coming back from Rood Warren? Harold, run and stop it, and tell Marsh to drive round to the door before he goes to the stables. I may as well have a lift down to the other end of the village.'

'What do you want to do at the other end of the village?'

'I don't want to do anything, but my unlucky fate as a landowner compels me to go over and look at an eel-weir which has just burst. Lindy, come along with me, and cheer me up with one of your ghost stories. You are as good as a Christmas annual.'

'And on your way back,' said Lady Atherley, 'would you mind the carriage stopping to leave some brandy at Monk's? Mr Austyn told me last night he was so weak, and the doctor has ordered him brandy every hour.'

Atherley was disappointed with what he called my last edition of the ghost; he complained that it was little more definite than the Canon's.

'Your last two stories are too high-flown for my simple tastes. I want a good coherent description of the ghost himself, not the particular emotions he excited. I had expected better things from Austyn. Upon my word, as far as we have gone, old Aunt Eleanour's is the best. I think Austyn, with his mediæval turn of mind and his quite mediæval habit of living upon air, might have managed to raise something with horns and hoofs. It is a curious thing that in the dark ages the devil was always appearing to somebody. He doesn't make himself so cheap now. He has evidently more to do; but there is a fashion in ghosts as in other things, and that reminds me our ghost, from all we hear of it, is decidedly rococo. If you study the reports of societies that hunt the supernatural, you will find that the latest thing in ghosts is very quiet and commonplace. Rattling chains and blue lights, and even fancy dress, have quite gone out. And the people who see the ghosts are not even startled at first sight; they think it is a visitor, or a man come to wind the clocks. In fact, the chic thing for a ghost in these days is to be mistaken for a living person.'

'What puzzles me is that a sceptic like you can so easily swallow the astonishing coincidence of these different people all having imagined the ghost in the same house.'

'Why, the coincidence is not a bit more astonishing than several people in the same place having the same fever. Nothing in the world is so infectious as ghost-seeing. The oftener a ghost is seen, the oftener it will be seen. In this sort of thing particularly, one fool makes many. No, don't wait for me. Heaven only knows when I shall be released.'

The door of Monk's cottage was open, but no one was to be seen within, and no one answered to my knock, so, anxious to see him again, I groped my way up the dark ladder-like stairs to the room above. The first thing I saw was the bed where Monk himself was lying. They had drawn the sheet across his face: I saw what had happened. His wife was standing near, looking not so much grieved as stunned and tired. 'Would you like to see him, sir?' she asked, stretching out her withered hand to draw the sheet aside. I was glad afterwards I had not refused, as, but for fear of being ungracious, I would have done.

Since then I have seen death – 'in state' as it is called – invested with more than royal pomp, but I have never felt his presence so majestic as in that poor little garret. I know his seal may be painful, grotesque even: here it was wholly benign and beautiful. All discolorations had disappeared in an even pallor as of old ivory; all furrows of age and pain were smoothed away, and the rude peasant face was transfigured, glorified, by that smile of ineffable and triumphant repose.

Many times that day it rose before me, never more vividly than when, at dinner, Mrs Molyneux, in colours as brilliant as her complexion, and jewels as sparkling as her eyes, recounted in her silvery treble the latest flowers of fashionable gossip. I am always glad to be one of any audience which Mrs Molyneux addresses, not so much out of admiration for the discourse itself, as for the charm of gesture and intonation with which it is delivered. But the main question – the subject of Atherley's conversion – she did not approach till we were in the drawing-room, luxuriously established in deep and softly-cushioned chairs. Then, near the fire, but turned away from it so as to face us all, and in the prettiest of attitudes, she began, gracefully emphasising her more important points by movements of her spangled fan.

'I do not mention the name of the religion I wish to speak to you about, because – now I hope you won't be angry, but I am going to be quite horribly rude – because Sir George is certain to be so prejudiced against— oh yes, Sir George, you are; everybody is at first. Even I was, because it has been so horribly misrepresented by people who really know nothing about it. For instance, I have myself heard it said that it was only a kind of spiritualism. On the contrary, it is very much opposed to it, and has quite convinced me for one of the wickedness and danger of spiritualism.'

'Well, that is so much to its credit,' Atherley generously acknowledged.

'And then, people said it was very immoral. Far from that; it has a very high ethical standard indeed – a very moral aim. One of its chief objects is to establish a universal brotherhood amongst men of all nations and sects.'

'A what?' asked Atherley.

'A universal brotherhood.'

'My dear Mrs Molyneux, you don't mean to seriously offer that as a novelty. I never heard anything so hackneyed in my life. Why, it has been preached *ad nauseam* for centuries!'

'By the Christian Church, I suppose you mean. And pray how have they practised their preaching?'

'Oh, but excuse me; that is not the question. If your religion is as brand-new as you gave me to understand, there has been no time for practice. It must be all theory, and I hoped I was going to hear something original.'

'Oh really, Sir George, you are quite too naughty. How can I explain things if you are so flippant and impatient? In one sense, it is a very old religion; it is the truth which is in all religions, and some of its interesting doctrines were taught ages before Christianity was ever heard of, and proved, too, by miracles far far more wonderful than any in the New Testament. However, it is no good talking to you about that; what I really wanted you to understand is how infinitely superior it is to all other religions in its theological teaching. You know, Sir George, you are always finding fault with all the Christian Churches – and even with the Mahommedans too, for that matter – because they are so anthropomorphic, because they imply that God is a personal being. Very well, then, you cannot say that about this religion, because – this is what is so remarkable and elevated about it – it has nothing to do with God at all.'

'Nothing to do with what did you say?' asked Lady Atherley, diverted by this last remark from a long row of loops upon an ivory needle which she appeared to be counting.

'Nothing to do with God.'

'Do you know, Lucinda,' said Lady Atherley, 'if you would not mind, I fancy the coffee is just coming in, and perhaps it would be as well just to wait for a little, you know – just till the servants are out of the room? They might perhaps think it a little odd.'

'Yes,' said Atherley, 'and even unorthodox.'

Mrs Molyneux submitted to this interruption with the greatest sweetness and composure, and dilated on the beauty of the new chair-covers till Castleman and the footman had retired, when, with a coffee-cup instead of a fan in her exquisite hand, she took up the thread of her exposition.

'As I was saying, the distinction of this religion is that it has nothing to do with God. Of course it has other great advantages, which I will explain later, like its cultivation of a sixth sense, for instance—'

'Do you mean common sense?'

'Jane, what am I to do with Sir George? He is really incorrigible. How can I possibly explain things if you will not be serious?'

'I never was more serious in my life. Show me a religion which cultivates common sense, and I will embrace it at once.'

'It is just because I knew you would go on in this way that I do not attempt to say anything about the supernatural side of this religion, though it is very important and most extraordinary. I assure you, my dear Jane, the powers that people develop under it are really marvellous. I have friends who can see into another world as plainly as you can see this drawing-room, and talk as easily with spirits as I am talking with you.'

'Indeed!' said Lady Atherley politely, with her eyes fixed anxiously on something which had gone wrong with her knitting.

'Unfortunately, for that kind of thing you require to undergo such severe treatment; my health would not stand it; the London season itself is almost too much for me. It is a pity, for they all say I have great natural gifts that way, and I should have so loved to have taken it up; but to begin with, one must have no animal food and no stimulants, and the doctors always tell me I require a great deal of both.'

'Besides, *le jeu ne vaut pas la chandelle*,' said Atherley, 'if the spirits you are to converse with are anything like those we used to meet in your drawing-room.'

'That is not the same thing at all; those were only spooks.'

'Only what?'

'No, I will not explain; you only mean to make fun of it, and there is nothing to laugh at. What I am trying to show you is that side of the religion you will really approve – the unanthropomorphic side. It is not anything like atheism, you know, as some ill-natured people have said; it does not declare there is no God; it only declares that it is worse than useless to try and think of Him, far less pray to Him – because it is simply impossible. And that is quite scientific and philosophical, is it not? For all the great men are agreed now that the conditioned can know nothing of the unconditioned, and the finite can know nothing of the infinite. It is quite absurd to try, you know; and it is equally absurd to say anything about Him. You can't call Him Providence, because, as the universe is governed by fixed laws, there is nothing for him to provide; and we have no business to call Him Creator, because we don't really know that things were created. Besides,' said Mrs Molyneux, resuming her fan, which she furled and unfurled as she continued, 'I was reading in a delightful book the other day – I can't remember the author's name, but I think it begins with K or P. It explained so clearly that if the universe was created at all, it was created by the human mind. Then you can't call Him Father – it is quite blasphemous; and it is almost as bad to say He is merciful or loving, or anything of that kind, because mercy and love are only human attributes; and so is consciousness too, therefore we know He cannot be conscious; and I believe, according to the highest philosophical teaching, He has not any Being. So that altogether it is impossible, without being irreverent, to think of Him, far less speak to Him or of Him, because we cannot do so without ascribing to Him some conceivable quality – and He has not any. Indeed, even to speak of Him as *He* is not right; the pronoun is very anthropomorphic and misleading. So, when you come to consider all this carefully, it is quite evident – though it sounds rather strange at first – that the only way you can really honour and reverence God is by forgetting Him altogether.'

Here Mrs Molyneux paused, panting prettily for breath; but quickly recovering herself, proceeded: 'So in fact, it is just the same, practically speaking – remember I say only practically speaking – as if there were no God; and this religion—'

'Excuse me,' said Atherley; 'but if, as you have so forcibly explained to us, there is, practically speaking, no God, why should we hamper ourselves with any religion at all?'

'Why, to satisfy the universal craving after an ideal; the yearning for something beyond the sordid realities of animal existence and of daily life; to comfort, to elevate—'

'No, no, my dear Mrs Molyneux; pardon me, but the sooner we get rid of all this sort of rubbish the better. It is the indulgence they have given to such feelings that has made all the religions such a curse to the world. I don't believe, to begin with, that they are universal. I never experienced any such cravings and yearnings except when I was out of sorts; and I never met a thoroughly happy or healthy person who did. If people keep their bodies in good order and their minds well employed, they have no time for yearnings. It was bad enough when there was some pretext for them; when we imagined there was a God and a world which was better than this one. But now we know there is not the slightest ground for supposing anything of the kind, we had better have the courage of our opinions, and live up to them, or down to them. As to the word "ideal", it ought to be expunged from the vocabulary; I would like to make it penal to pronounce, or write, or print the word for a century. Why, we have been surfeited with the ideal by the Christian Churches; that's why we find the real so little to our taste. We've been so long fed upon sweet trash, we can't relish wholesome food. The cure for that is to take wholesome food or starve, not provide another sickly substitute. Pray, let us have no more religions. On the contrary, our first duty is to be as irreligious as possible – to believe in as little as we can, to trust in nobody but ourselves, to hope for nothing but the actual, to get rid of all high-flown notions of human beings and their destiny, and, above all, to avoid as poison the ideal, the sublime, the—'

His words were drowned at last in musical cries of indignation from Mrs Molyneux. I remember no more of the discussion, except that Atherley continued to reiterate his doctrine in different words, and Mrs Molyneux to denounce it with unabated fervour.

My thoughts wandered – I heard no more. I was tired and depressed, and felt grateful to Lady Atherley when, with invariable punctuality, at a quarter to eleven, she interrupted the symposium by rising and proposing that we should all go to bed.

My last distinct recollection of that evening is of Mrs Molyneux, with the folds of her gown in one hand, and a bedroom candlestick in the other, mounting the dark oak stairs, and calling out fervently as she went –

'Oh, how I pray that I may see the ghost!'

The night was stormy, and I could not sleep. The wind wailed fitfully outside the house, while within doors and windows rattled, and on the stairs and in the passages wandered strange and unaccountable noises, like stealthy footsteps or stifled voices. To this dreary accompaniment, as I lay awake in the darkness, I heard the lessons of the last few days repeated: witness after witness rose and gave his varying testimony; and when, before the discord and irony of it all, I bitterly repeated Pilate's question, the smile on that dead face would rise before me, and then I hoped again.

Between three and four the wind fell during a short space, and all responsive noises ceased. For a few minutes reigned absolute silence, then it was broken by two piercing cries – the cries of a woman in terror or in pain.

They disturbed even the sleepers, it was evident; for when I reached the end of my passage I heard opening doors, hurrying footsteps, and bells ringing violently in the gallery. After a little the stir was increased, presumably by servants arriving from the farther wing; but no one came my way till Atherley himself, in his dressing-gown, went hurriedly downstairs.

'Anything wrong?' I called as he passed me.

'Only Mrs Molyneux's prayer has been granted.'

'Of course she was bound to see it,' he said next day, as we sat together over a late breakfast. 'It would have been a miracle if she had not; but if I had known the interview was to be followed by such unpleasant consequences I shouldn't have asked her down. I was wandering about for hours looking for an imaginary bottle of sal-volatile Jane described as being in her sitting-room: and Jane herself was up till late – or rather early – this morning, trying to soothe Mrs Molyneux, who does not appear to have found the ghost quite such pleasant company as she expected. Oh yes, Jane is down; she breakfasted in her own room. I believe she is ordering dinner at this minute in the next room.'

Hardly had he said the words when outside, in the hall, resounded a prolonged and stentorian wail.

'What on earth is the matter now?' said Atherley, rising and making for the door. He opened it just in time for us to see Mrs Mallet go by – Mrs Mallet bathed in tears and weeping as I never have heard an adult weep before or since – in a manner which is graphically and literally described by the phrase 'roaring and crying'.

'Why, Mrs Mallet! What on earth is the matter?'

'Send for Mrs de Noël,' cried Mrs Mallet in tones necessarily raised to a high and piercing key by the sobs with which they were accompanied. 'Send for Mrs de Noël; send for that dear lady, and she will tell you whether a word has been said against my character till I come here, which I never wish to do, being frightened pretty nigh to death with what one told me and the other; and if you don't believe me, ask Mrs Stubbs as keeps the little sweet-shop near the church, if any one in the village will so much as come up the avenue after dark; and says to me, the very day I come here, "You have a nerve," she says; "I wouldn't sleep there if you was to pay me," she says; and I says, not wishing to speak against a family that was cousin to Mrs de Noël, "Noises is neither here nor there," I says, "and ghostisses keeps mostly to the gentry's wing," I says. And then to say as I put about that they was all over the house, and frighten the London lady's maid, which all I said was – and Hann can tell you that I speak the truth, for she was there – "some says one thing," says I, "and some says another, but I takes no notice of nothink." But put up with a deal, I have – more than ever I told a soul since I come here, which I promised Mrs de Noël when she asked me to oblige her; which the blue lights I have seen a many times, and tapping of coffin-nails on the wall, and never close my eyes for nights sometimes, but am entirely wore away, and my nerve that weak; and then to be so hurt in my feelings, and spoke to as I am not accustomed, but always treated everywhere I goes with the greatest of kindness and respect, which ask Mrs de Noël she will tell you, since ever I was a widow; but pack my things I will, and walk every step of the way, if it was pouring cats and dogs, I would, rather than stay another minute here to be so put upon; and send for Mrs de Noël if you don't believe me, and she will tell you the many high families she recommended me, and always give satisfaction. Send for Mrs de Noël—'

The swing door closed behind her, and the sounds of her grief and her reiterated appeals to Mrs de Noël died slowly away in the distance.

'What on earth have you been saying to her?' said Atherley to his wife, who had come out into the hall.

'Only that she behaved very badly indeed in speaking about the ghost to Mrs Molyneux's maid, who, of course, repeated it all directly and made Lucinda nervous. She is a most troublesome, mischievous old woman.'

'But she can cook. Pray what are we to do for dinner?'

'I am sure I don't know. I never knew anything so unlucky as it all is, and Lucinda looking so ill.'

'Well, you had better send for the doctor.'

'She won't hear of it. She says nobody could do her any good but Cecilia.'

'What! "Send for Mrs de Noël?" Poor Cissy! What do these excited females imagine she is going to do?'

'I don't know, but I do wish we could get her here.'

'But she is in London, is she not, with Aunt Henrietta?'

'Yes, and only comes home today.'

'Well, I will tell you what we might do if you want her badly. Telegraph to her to London and ask her to come straight on here.'

'I suppose she is sure to come?'

'Like a shot, if you say we are all ill.'

'No, that would frighten her. I will just say we want her particularly.'

'Yes, and say the carriage shall meet the 5.15 at Whitford station, and then she will feel bound to come. And as I shall not be back in time, send Lindy to meet her. It will do him good. He looks as if he had been sitting up all night with the ghost.'

It was a melancholy day. The wind was quieter, but the rain still fell. Indoors we were all in low spirits, not even excepting the little boys, much concerned about Tip, who was not his usual brisk and complacent self. His nose was hot, his little stump of a tail was limp, he hid himself under chairs and tables, whence he turned upon us sorrowful and beseeching eyes, and, most alarming symptom of all, refused sweet biscuits. During the afternoon he was confided to me by his little masters while they made an expedition to the stables, and I was sitting reading by the library fire with the invalid beside me when Lady Atherley came in to propose I should go into the drawing-room and talk to Mrs Molyneux, who had just come down.

'Did she ask to see me?'

'No; but when I proposed your going in, she did not say no.'

I did as I was asked to do, but with some misgivings. It was one of the few occasions when my misfortune became an advantage. No one, especially no woman, was likely to rebuff too sharply the intruder who dragged himself into her presence. So far from that, Mrs Molyneux, who was leaning against the mantelpiece and looking down listlessly into the fire, moved to welcome me with a smile and to offer me a hand startlingly cold. But after that she resumed her first attitude and made no attempt to converse – she, the most ready, the most voluble of women. Then followed an awkward pause, which I desperately broke by saying I was afraid she was not better.

'Better! I was not ill,' she answered, almost impatiently, and walked away towards the other side of the room. I understood that she wished to be alone, and was moving towards the door as quietly as possible when I was suddenly checked by her hand upon my elbow.

'Mr Lyndsay, why are you going? Was I rude? I did not mean to be. Forgive me; I am so miserable.'

'You could not be rude, I think, even if you wished to. It is I who am inconsiderate in intruding—'

'You are not intruding; please stay.'

'I would gladly stay if I could help you.'

'Can any one help me, I wonder?'

She went slowly back to the fire and sat down upon the fender-stool, and resting her chin upon her hand, and looking dreamily before her, repeated –

'Can any one help me, I wonder?'

I sat down on a chair near her and said –

'Do you think it would help you to talk of what has frightened you?'

'I don't think I can. I would tell you, Mr Lyndsay, if I could tell any one; for you know what it is to be weak and suffering; you are as sympathetic as a woman, and more merciful than some women. But part of the horror of it all is that I cannot explain it. Words seem to be no good, just because I have used them so easily and so meaninglessly all my life – just as words and nothing more.'

'Can you tell me what you saw?'

'A face, only a face, when I woke up suddenly. It looked as if it were painted on the darkness. But oh, the dreadfulness of it and what it brought with it! Do you remember the line, "Bring with you airs from heaven or blasts from hell"? Yes, it was in hell, because hell is not a great gulf, like Dante described, as I used to think; it is no place at all – it is something we make ourselves. I felt all this as I saw the face, for we ourselves are not what we think. Part of what I used to play with was true enough; it is all Mâyâ, a delusion, this sense-life – it is no life at all. The actual life is behind, under it all; it goes deep deep down, it stretches on, on – and yet it has nothing to do with space or time. I feel as if I were beating myself against a stone wall. My words can have no sense for you any more than they would have had for me yesterday.'

'But tell me, why should this discovery of this other life make you so miserable?'

'Oh, because it brings such a want with it. How can I explain? It is like a poor wretch stupefied with drink. Don't you know the poor creatures in the East End sometimes drink just that they may not feel how hungry and how cold they are? "They remember their misery no more." Is the life of the world and of outward things like that, if we live too much in it? I used to be so contented with it all – its pleasures, its little triumphs, even its gossip; and what I called my aspirations I satisfied with what was nothing more than phrases. And now I have found my real self, now I am awake, I want much more, and there is nothing – only a great silence, a great loneliness like that in the face. And the theories I talked about are no comfort any more; they are just what pretty speeches would be to a person in torture. Oh, Mr Lyndsay, I always feel that you are real, that you are good; tell me what you know. Is there nothing but this dark void beyond when life falls away from us?'

She lifted towards me a face quivering with excitement, and eyes that waited wild and famished for my answer – the answer I had not for her, and then indeed I tasted the full bitterness of the cup of unbelief.

'No,' she said presently, 'I knew it; no one can do me any good but Cecilia de Nöel.'

'And she believes?'

'It is not what she believes, it is what she is.'

She rested her head upon her hand and looked musingly towards the window, down which the drops were trickling, and said –

'Ever since I have known Cecilia I have always felt that if all the world failed this would be left. Not that I really imagined the world would fail me, but you know how one imagines things, how one asks oneself questions. If I was like this, if I was like that, what should I do? I used to say to myself, if the very worst happened to me, if I was ill of some loathsome disease from which everybody shrank away, or if my mind was unhinged and I was tempted with horrible temptations like I have read about, I would go to Cecilia. She would not turn from me; she would run to meet me as the father in the parable did, not because I was her friend but because I was in trouble. All who are in trouble are Cecilia's friends, and she feels to them just as other people feel towards their own children. And I could tell her everything, show her everything. Others feel the same; I have heard them say so – men as well as women. I know why – Cecilia's pity is so reverent, so pure. A great London doctor said to me once, "Remember, nothing is shocking or disgusting to a doctor." That is like Cecilia. No suffering could ever be disgusting or shocking to Cecilia, nor ridiculous, nor grotesque. The more humiliating it was, the more pitiful it would be to her. Anything that suffers is sacred to Cecilia. She would comfort, as if she went on her knees to one; and her touch on one's wounds, one's ugliest wounds, would be like,' – she hesitated and looked about her in quest of a comparison, then, pointing to a picture over the door, a picture of the Magdalene, kissing the bleeding feet upon the Cross, ended, 'like that.'

'Oh Mrs Molyneux,' I cried, 'if there be love like that in the world, then—'

The door opened and Castleman entered.

'If you please, sir, the carriage is at the door.'

Chapter VII

CECILIA'S GOSPEL

THE rain gradually ceased falling as we drove onward and upward to the station. It stood on high ground, overlooking a wide sweep of downland and fallow, bordered towards the west by close-set woodlands, purple that evening against a sky of limpid gold, which the storm-clouds discovered as they lifted.

I had not long to wait, for, punctual to its time, the train steamed into the station. From that part of the train to which I first looked, four or five passengers stepped out; not one of them certainly the lady that I waited for. Glancing from side to side I saw, standing at the far end of the platform, two women; one of them was tall; could this be Mrs de Noël? And yet no, I reflected as I went towards them, for she held a baby in her arms – a baby moreover swathed, not in white and laces, but in a tattered and discoloured shawl: while her companion, lifting out baskets and bundles from a third-class carriage, was poorly and evenly miserably clad. But again, as I drew nearer, I observed that the long fine hand which supported the child was delicately gloved, and that the cloak which swung back from the encircling arm was lined and bordered with very costly fur. This and something in the whole outline—

'Mrs de Noël?' I murmured inquiringly.

Then she turned towards me, and I saw her, as I often see her now in dreams, against that sunset background of aerial gold which the artist of circumstance had painted behind her, like a new Madonna, holding the child of poverty to her heart, pressing her cheek against its tiny head with a gesture whose exquisite tenderness, for at least that fleeting instant, seemed to bridge across the gulf which still yawns between Dives and Lazarus. So standing, she looked at me with two soft brown eyes, neither large nor beautiful, but in their outlook direct and simple as a child's. Remembering as I met them what Mrs Molyneux had said, I saw and comprehended as well what she meant. Benevolence is but faintly inscribed on the faces of most men, even of the better sort. 'I will love you, my neighbour,' we thereon decipher, 'when I have attended to my own business, in the first place; if you are lovable, or at least likeable, in the second.' But in the transparent gaze that Cecilia de Noël turned upon her fellows beamed love poured forth without stint and without condition. It was as if every man, woman, and child who approached her became instantly to her more interesting than herself, their defects more tolerable, their wants more imperative, their sorrows more moving than her own. In this lay the source of that mysterious charm so many have felt, so few have understood, and yielding to which even those least capable of appreciating her confessed that, whatever her conduct might be, she herself was irresistibly lovable. A kind of dream-like haze seemed to envelop us as I introduced myself, as she smiled upon me, as she resigned the child to its mother and bid them tenderly farewell; but the clear air of the real became distinct again when there stood suddenly before us a fat elderly female, whose countenance was flushed with mingled anxiety and displeasure.

'Law bless me, mem!' said the newcomer, 'I could not think wherever you could be. I have been looking up and down for you, all through the first-class carriages.'

'I am so sorry, Parkins,' said Mrs de Noël penitently; 'I ought to have let you know that I changed my carriage at Carchester. I wanted to nurse a baby whose mother was looking ill and tired. I saw them on the platform, and then they got into a third-class carriage, so I thought the best way would be to get in with them.'

'And where, if you please, mem,' inquired Parkins, in an icy tone and with a face stiffened by repressed displeasure – 'where do you think you have left your dressing-bag and humbrella?'

Mrs de Noël fixed her sweet eyes upon the speaker, as if striving to recollect the answer to this question, and then replied –

'She told me she lived quite near the station. I wish I had asked her how far. She is much too weak to walk any distance. I might have found a fly for her, might I not?'

Upon which Parkins gave a snort of irrepressible exasperation, and, evidently renouncing her mistress as beyond hope, forthwith departed in search of the missing property. I accompanied her, and, with the aid of the guard, we speedily found and secured both bag and umbrella, and, as the train steamed off, returned with these treasures to Mrs de Noël, still on the same spot and in the same attitude as we had left her, and all that she said was –

'It was so stupid, so forgetful, so just like me not to have asked her more about it. She had been ill; the journey itself was more than she could stand; and then to have to carry the baby! She said it was not far, but perhaps she only said that to please me. Poor people are so afraid of distressing one; they often make themselves out better off than they really are, don't they?'

I was embarrassed by this question, to which my own experience did not authorise me to answer yes; but I evaded the difficulty by consulting a porter, who fortunately knew the woman, and was able to assure us that her cottage was barely a stone's throw from the station. When I had conveyed to Mrs de Noël this information, which she received with an eager gratitude that the recovery of her bag and umbrella had failed to rouse, we left the station to go to the carriage, and then it was that, pausing suddenly, she cried out in dismay –

'Ah, you are hurt! you—'

She stopped abruptly; she had divined the truth, and her eyes grew softer with such tender pity as not yet had shone for me – motherless, sisterless – on any woman's face. As we drove home that evening she heard the story that never had been told before.

'You may have your faults, Cissy,' said Atherley, 'but I will say this for you – for smoothing people down when they have been rubbed the wrong way, you never had your equal.'

He lay back in a comfortable chair looking at his cousin, who, sitting on a low seat opposite the drawing-room fire, shaded her eyes from the glare with a little hand-screen.

'Mrs Molyneux, I hear, has gone to sleep,' he went on; 'and Mrs Mallet is unpacking her boxes. The only person who does not seem altogether happy is my old friend Parkins. When I inquired after her health a few minutes ago her manner to me was barely civil.'

'Poor Parkins is rather put out,' said Mrs de Noël in her slow gentle way. 'It is all my fault. I forgot to pack up the bodice of my best evening gown, and Parkins says it is the only one I look fit to be seen in.'

'But, my dear Cecilia,' said Lady Atherley, looking up from the work which she pursued beside a shaded lamp, 'why did not Parkins pack it up herself?'

'Oh, because she had some shopping of her own to do this forenoon, so she asked me to finish packing for her, and of course I said I would; and I promised to try and forget nothing; and then, after all, I went and left the bodice in a drawer. It is provoking! The fact is, James spoils me so when he is at home. He remembers everything for me, and when I do forget anything he never scolds me.'

'Ah, I expect he has a nice time of it,' said Atherley. 'However, it is not my fault. I warned him how it would be when he was engaged. I said: "I hope, for one thing, you can live on air, old chap, for you will get nothing more for dinner if you trust to Cissy to order it."'

'I don't believe you said anything of the kind,' observed Lady Atherley.

'No, dear Jane; of course he did not. He was very much pleased with our marriage. He said James was the only man he ever knew who was fit to marry me.'

'So he was,' agreed Atherley; 'the only man whose temper could stand all he would have to put up with. We had good proof of that even on the wedding-day, when you kept him kicking his heels for half an hour in the church while you were admiring the effect of your new finery in the glass.'

'What!' cried Lady Atherley incredulously.

'What really did happen, Jane,' said Mrs de Noël, 'was that when Edith Molyneux was trying on my wreath before a looking-glass over the fireplace, she unfortunately dropped it into the grate, and got it in such a mess. It took us a long time to get the black off, and some of the sprays were so spoiled, we had to take them out. And it was very unpleasant for Edith, as Aunt Henrietta was extremely angry, because the wreath was her present, you know, and it was very expensive; and as to Parkins, poor dear, she was so vexed she positively cried. She said I was the most trying lady she had ever waited upon. She often says so. I am afraid it is true.'

'Not a doubt of it,' said Atherley.

'Do not believe him, Cecilia,' said Lady Atherley: 'he thinks there is no one in the world like you.'

'Fortunately for the world,' said Atherley; 'any more of the sort would spoil it. But I am not going to stay here to be bullied by two women at once. Rather than that, I will go and write letters.'

He went, and soon afterwards Lady Atherley followed him.

Then the two little boys came in with Tip.

'We are not allowed to take him upstairs,' explained Harold, 'so we thought he might stay with you and Mr Lyndsay for a little, till Charles comes for him.'

'If you would let him lie upon your dress, Aunt Cissy,' suggested Denis; 'he would like that.'

Accordingly he was carefully settled on the outspread folds of the serge gown; and after the little boys had condoled with him in tones so melancholy that he was affected almost to tears, they went off to supper and to bed.

Silence followed, broken only by the ticking of the clock and the wailing of the wind outside. Mrs de Noël gazed into the fire with intent and unseeing eyes. Its warm red light softly illumined her whole face and figure, for in her abstraction she had let the hand-screen fall, and was stroking mechanically the little sleek head that nestled against her. Meantime I stared attentively at her, thinking I might do so without offence, seeing she had forgotten me and all else around her. Once, indeed, as if rising for a minute to the surface, with eyes that appeared to waken, she looked up and encountered my earnest gaze, but without shade of displeasure or discomfiture. She only smiled upon me, placidly as a sister might smile upon a brother, benignly as one might smile upon a child, and fell into her dream again. It was a wonderful look, especially from a woman, as unique in its complete unconsciousness as in its warm good-will; it was as soothing as the touch of her fine soft fingers must have been on Tip's hot head. I felt I could have curled myself up, as he did, at her feet and slept on – for ever. But, alas! the clock was checking the flying minutes and chanting the departing quarters, and presently the dressing-bell rang, Mrs de Noël stirred, gave a long sigh, and, plainly from the fullness of her heart and of the thoughts she had so long been following, said –

'Mr Lyndsay, is it not strange? So many people from the great world come and ask me if there is any God. Really good people, you know, so honourable, so generous, so self-sacrificing. It is just the same to me as if they should ask me whether the sun was shining, when all the time I saw the sunshine on their faces.'

'By the way,' said Atherley that night after dinner, when Mrs Molyneux was not present, 'where are you going to put Cissy tonight? Are you going to make a bachelor of her too?'

'Oh, such an uncomfortable arrangement!' said Lady Atherley. 'But Lucinda has set her heart on having Cecilia near her; so they have put up a little bed in the dressing-room for her.'

'Cissy is to keep the ghost at bay, is she?' said Atherley. 'I hope she may. I don't want another night as lively as the last.'

'Who else has seen the ghost?' asked Mrs de Noël, thoughtfully. 'Has Mr Lyndsay?'

'No, Lindy will never see the ghost; he is too much of a sceptic. Even if he saw it he would not believe in it, and there is nothing a ghost hates like that. But he has seen the people who saw the ghost, and he tells their several stories very well.'

'Would you tell me, Mr Lyndsay?' asked Mrs de Noël.

I could do nothing but obey her wish; still I secretly questioned the wisdom of doing so, especially when, as I went on, I observed stealing over her listening face the shadow of some disturbing thought.

'Well now, Cissy is thoroughly well frightened,' observed Atherley. 'Perhaps we had better go to bed.'

'It is no good saying so to Lucinda,' said Lady Atherley, as we all rose, 'because it only puts her out; but I shall always feel certain myself it was a mouse; because I remember in the house we had at Bournemouth two years ago there was a mouse in my room which often made such a noise knocking down the plaster inside the wall, it used to quite startle me.'

That night the storm finally subsided. When the morning came the rain fell no longer, the cry of the wind had ceased, and the cloud-curtain above us was growing lighter and softer as if penetrated and suffused by the growing sunshine behind it.

I was late for breakfast that day.

'Mr Lyndsay, Tip is all right again,' cried Denis at sight of me. 'Mrs Mallet says it was chicken bones he stole from the cat's dish.'

'Is that all?' observed Atherley sardonically; 'I thought he must have seen the ghost. By the bye, Cissy, did you see it?'

'Yes,' said Mrs de Noël simply, at which Atherley visibly started, and instantly began talking of something else.

Mrs Molyneux was to leave by an afternoon train, but, to the relief of everybody, it was discovered that Mrs Mallet had indefinitely postponed her departure. She remained in the mildest of humours and in the most philosophical of tempers, as I myself can testify; for, meeting her by accident in the hall, I was encouraged by the amiability of her simper to say that I hoped we should have no more trouble with the ghost, when she answered in words I have often since admiringly quoted –

'Perhaps not, sir, but I don't seem to care even if we do; for I had a dream last night, and a spirit seemed to whisper in my ear, "Don't be afraid; it is only a token of death."'

After Mrs Molyneux had started, with Mrs de Noël as her companion as far as the station, and all the rest of the party had gone out to sun themselves in the brightness of the afternoon, I worked through a long arrears of correspondence: and I was just finishing a letter, when Atherley, whom I supposed to be far distant, came into the library.

'I thought you had gone to pay calls with Lady Atherley?'

'Is it likely? Look here, Lindy, it is quite hot out of doors. Come, and let me tug you up the hill to meet Cissy coming home from the station, and then I promise you a rare treat.'

Certainly to meet Mrs de Noël anywhere might be so considered, but I did not ask if that was what he meant. It was milder; one felt it more at every step upward. The sun, low as it was, shone warmly as well as brilliantly between the clouds that he had thrust asunder and scattered in wild and beautiful disorder. It was one of those incredible days in early spring, balmy, tender, which our island summer cannot always match.

We went on till we reached Beggar's Stile.

'Sit down,' said Atherley, tossing on to the wet step a coat he carried over his arm. 'And there is a cigarette; you must smoke, if you please, or at least pretend to do so.'

'What does all this mean? What are you up to, George?'

'I am up to a delicate psychical investigation which requires the greatest care. The medium is made of such uncommon stuff; she has not a particle of brass in her composition. So she requires to be carefully isolated from all disturbing influences. I allow you to be present at the experiment, because discretion is one of your strongest points, and you always know when to hold your tongue. Besides, it will improve your mind. Cissy's story is certain to be odd, like herself, and will illustrate what I am always saying that— Here she is.'

He went forward to meet and to stop the carriage, out of which, at his suggestion, Mrs de Noël readily came down to join us.

'Do not get up, Mr Lyndsay,' she called out as she came towards us, 'or I will go away. I don't want to sit down.'

'Sit down, Lindy,' said Atherley sharply, 'Cissy likes tobacco in the open air.'

She rested her arms upon the gate and looked downwards.

'The dear dear old river! It makes me feel young again to look at it.'

'Cissy,' said Atherley, his arms on the gate, his eyes staring straight towards the opposite horizon, 'tell us about the ghost; were you frightened?'

There was a certain tension in the pause which followed. Would she tell us or not? I almost felt Atherley's rebound of satisfaction as well as my own at the sound of her voice. It was uncertain and faint at first, but by degrees grew firm again, as timidity was lost in the interest of what she told:

'Last night I sat up with Mrs Molyneux, holding her hand till she fell asleep, and that was very late, and then I went to the dressing-room, where I was to sleep; and as I undressed, I thought over what Mr Lyndsay had told us about the ghost; and the more I thought, the more sad and strange it seemed that not one of those who saw it, not even Aunt Eleanour, who is so kind and thoughtful, had had one pitying thought for it. And we who heard about it were just the same, for it seemed to us quite natural and even right that everybody should shrink away from it because it was so horrible; though that should only make them the more kind; just as we feel we must be more tender and loving to any one who is deformed, and the more shocking his deformity the more tender and loving. And what, I thought, if this poor spirit had come by any chance to ask for something; if it were in pain and longed for relief, or sinful and longed for forgiveness? How dreadful then that other beings should turn from it, instead of going to meet it and comfort it – so dreadful that I almost wished that I might see it, and have the strength to speak to it! And it came into my head that this might happen, for often and often when I have been very anxious to serve some one, the wish has been granted in a quite wonderful way. So when I said my prayers, I asked especially that if it should appear to me, I might have strength to forget all selfish fear and try only to know what it wanted. And as I prayed the foolish shrinking dread we have of such things seemed to fade away; just as when I have prayed for those towards whom I felt cold or unforgiving, the hardness has all melted away into love towards them. And after that came to me that lovely feeling which we all have sometimes – in church, or when we are praying alone, or more often in the open air, on beautiful summer days when it is warm and still; as if one's heart were beating and overflowing with love towards everything in this world and in all the worlds; as if the very grasses and the stones were dear, but dearest of all, the creatures that still suffer, so that to wipe away their tears forever, one feels that one would die – oh die so gladly! And always as if this were something not our own, but part of that wonderful great Love above us, about us, everywhere, clasping us all so tenderly and safely!'

Here her voice trembled and failed; she waited a little and then went on, 'Ah, I am too stupid to say rightly what I mean, but you who are clever will understand.

'It was so sweet that I knelt on, drinking it in for a long time; not praying, you know, but just resting, and feeling as if I were in heaven, till all at once, I cannot explain why, I moved and looked round. It was there at the other end of the room. It was . . . – much worse than I had dreaded it would be; as if it looked out of some great horror deeper than I could understand. The loving feeling was gone, and I was afraid – so much afraid, I only wanted to get out of sight of it. And I think I would have gone, but it stretched out its hands to me as if it were asking for something, and then, of course, I could not go. So, though I was trembling a little, I went nearer and looked into its face. And after that I was not afraid any more, I was too sorry for it; its poor poor eyes were so full of anguish. I cried: "Oh, why do you look at me like that? Tell me what I shall do."

'And directly I spoke I heard it moan. Oh, George, oh, Mr Lyndsay, how can I tell you what that moaning was like! Do you know how a little change in the face of some one you love, or a little tremble in his voice, can make you see quite clearly what nobody, not even the great poets, had been able to show you before?

'George, do you remember the day that grandmother died, when they all broke down and cried a little at dinner, all except Uncle Marmaduke? He sat up looking so white and stern at the end of the table. And I, foolish little child, thought he was not so grieved as the others – that he did not love his mother so much. But next day, quite by chance, I heard him, all alone, sobbing over her coffin. I remember standing outside the door and listening, and each sob went through my heart with a little stab, and I knew for the first time what sorrow was. But even his sobs were not so pitiful as the moans of that poor spirit. While I listened I learnt that in another world there may be worse for us to bear than even here – sorrow more hopeless, more lonely. For the strange thing was, the moaning seemed to come from so far far away; not only from somewhere millions and millions of miles away, but – this is the strangest of all – as if it came to me from time long since past, ages and ages ago. I know this sounds like nonsense, but indeed I am trying to put into words the weary long distance that seemed to stretch between us, like one I never should be able to cross. At last it spoke to me in a whisper which I could only just hear; at least it was more like a whisper than anything else I can think of, and it seemed to come like the moaning from far far away. It thanked me so meekly for looking at it and speaking to it. It told me that by sins committed against others when it was on earth it had broken the bond between itself and all other creatures. While it was what we call alive, it did not feel this, for the senses confuse us and hide many things from the good, and so still more from the wicked; but when it died and lost the body by which it seemed to be kept near to other beings, it found itself imprisoned in the most dreadful loneliness – loneliness which no one in this world can even imagine. Even the pain of solitary confinement, so it told me, which drives men mad, is only like a shadow or type of this loneliness of spirits. Others there might be, but it knew nothing of them – nothing besides this great empty darkness everywhere except the place it had once lived in, and the people who were moving about it; and even those it could only perceive dimly as if looking through a mist, and always so unutterably away from them all. I am not giving its own words, you know, George, because I cannot remember them. I am not certain it did speak to me; the thoughts seemed to pass in some strange way into my mind; I cannot explain how, for the still far-away voice did not really speak. Sometimes, it told me, the loneliness became agony, and it longed for a word or a sign from some other being, just as Dives longed for the drop of cold water; and at such times it was able to make the living people see it. But that, alas! was useless, for it only alarmed them so much that the bravest and most benevolent rushed away in terror or would not let it come near them. But still it went on showing itself to one after another, always hoping that some one would take pity on it and speak to it, for it felt that if comfort ever came to it, it must be through a living soul, and it knew of none save those in this world and in this place. And I said: "Why did you not turn for help to God?"

'Then it gave a terrible answer: it said, "What is God?"

'And when I heard these words there came over me a wild kind of pity, such as I used to feel when I saw my little child struggling for breath when he was ill, and I held out my arms to this poor lonely thing, but it shrank back, crying:

'"Speak to me, but do not touch me, brave human creature. I am all death, and if you come too near me the Death in me may kill the life in you."

'But I said: "No Death can kill the life in me, even though it kill my body. Dear fellow-spirit, I cannot tell you what I know; but let me take you in my arms; rest for an instant on my heart, and perhaps I may make you feel what I feel all around us."

'And as I spoke I threw my arms around the shadowy form and strained it to my breast. And I felt as if I were pressing to me only air, but air colder than any ice, so that my heart seemed to stop beating, and I could hardly breathe. But I still clasped it closer and closer, and as I grew colder it seemed to grow less chill.

'And at last it spoke, and the whisper was not far away, but near. It said:

'"It is enough; now I know what God is!"

'After that I remember nothing more, till I woke up and found myself lying on the floor beside the bed. It was morning, and the spirit was not there: but I have a strong feeling that I have been able to help it, and that it will trouble you no more.

'Surely it is late! I must go at once. I promised to have tea with the children.'

. . . . .

Neither of us spoke; neither of us stirred; when the sound of her light footfall was heard no more, there was complete silence. Below, the mists had gathered so thickly that now they spread across the valley one dead white sea of vapour in which village and woods and stream were all buried

– all except the little church spire, that, still unsubmerged, pointed triumphantly to the sky; and what a sky! For that which yesterday had steeped us in cold and darkness, now, piled even to the zenith in mountainous cloud-masses, was dyed, every crest and summit of it, in crimson fire, pouring from a great fount of colour, where, to the west, the heavens opened to show that wonder-world whence saints and singers have drawn their loveliest images of the Rest to come.

But perhaps I saw all things irradiated by the light which had risen upon my darkness – the light that never was on land or sea, but shines reflected in the human face.

'George, I am waiting for your interpretation.'

'It is very simple, Lindy,' he said.

But there was a tone in his voice I had heard once – and only once – before, when, through the first terrible hours that followed my accident, he sat patiently beside me in the darkened room, holding my hot hand in his broad cool palm.

'It is very simple. It is the most easily explained of all the accounts. It was a dream from beginning to end. She fell asleep praying, thinking, as she says; what was more natural or inevitable than that she should dream of the ghost? And it all confirms what I say: that visions are composed by the person who sees them. Nothing could be more characteristic of Cissy than the story she has just told us.'

'And let it be a dream,' I said. 'It is of no consequence, for the dreamer remains, breathing and walking on this solid earth. I have touched her hand, I have looked into her face. Thank God! she is no vision, the woman who could dream this dream! George, how do you explain the miracle of her existence?'

But Atherley was silent.

Louisa Baldwin

MANY WATERS CANNOT QUENCH LOVE

DID I not know my old friend John Horton to be as truthful as he is devoid of imagination, I should have believed that he was romancing or dreaming when he told me of a circumstance that happened to him some thirty years ago. He was at that time a bachelor, living in London and practising as a solicitor in Bedford Row. He was not a strong man, though neither nervous nor excitable, and as I said before singularly unimaginative.

If Horton told you a fact, you might be certain that it had occurred in the precise manner he stated. If he told it you a hundred times, he would not vary it in the repetition. This literal and conscientious habit of mind, made his testimony of value, and when he told me a fact that I should have disbelieved from any other man, from my friend I was obliged to accept it as truth.

It was during the long vacation in the autumn of 1857, that Horton determined to take a few weeks' holiday in the country. He was such an inveterate Londoner he had not been able to tear himself away from town for more than a few days at a time for many years past. But at length he felt the necessity for quiet and pure air, only he would not go far to seek them. It was easier then than it is now to find a lodging that would meet his requirements, a place in the country yet close to the town, and it was near Wandsworth that Horton found what he sought, rooms for a single gentleman in an old farm-house. He read the advertisement of the lodgings in the paper at luncheon, and went that very afternoon to see if they answered to the tempting description given. He had some little difficulty in finding Maitland's Farm. It was not easy to find his way through country lanes that to his town eyes looked precisely alike, and with nothing to indicate whether he had taken a right or wrong turning. The railway now runs shrieking over what were then green fields, lanes have been transformed into gas-lighted streets, and Maitland's Farm, the old red brick house standing in its high walled garden, has been pulled down long ago. The last time Horton went to look at the old place it was changed beyond recognition, and the orchard in which he gathered pears and apples during his stay at the farm, was now the site of a public house and a dissenting chapel.

It was on a hot afternoon early in September when Horton opened the big iron gates and walked up the path bordered with dahlias and hollyhocks leading to the front door, and rang for admittance at Maitland's Farm. The bell echoed in a distant part of the empty house and died away into silence, but no one came to answer its summons. As Horton stood waiting he took the opportunity of thoroughly examining the outside of the house. Though it was called a farm it had not been built for one originally. It was a substantial, four-storey brick house of Queen Anne's period, with five tall sash windows on each floor, and dormer windows in the tiled roof. The front door was approached by a shallow flight of stone steps, and above the fan-light projected a penthouse of solidly carved woodwork. On either side were brackets of wrought iron, supporting extinguishers that had quenched the torch of many a late returning reveller a century ago. Only the windows to right and left of the door had blinds or curtains, or betrayed any sign of habitation. 'Those are the rooms to be let, I wonder which is the bedroom,' thought my friend as he rang the bell for the second time. Presently he heard within the sound of approaching footsteps, there was a great drawing of bolts and after a final struggle with the rusty lock, the door was opened by an old woman of severe and cheerless aspect. Horton was the first to speak.

'I have called to see the rooms advertised to be let in this house.' The old woman eyed him from head to foot without making any reply, then opening the door wider, nodded to him to enter. He did so and found himself in a large paved hall lighted from the fan-light over the door, and by a high narrow window facing him at the top of a short flight of oak stairs. The air was musty and damp as that of an old church.

'A hall this size should have a fire in it,' said Horton, glancing at the empty rusty grate.

'Farmers and folks that work out of doors keep themselves warm without fires,' said the old woman sharply.

'This house was never built for a farm, why is it called one?' inquired Horton of his taciturn guide as she opened the door of the sitting-room.

'Because it was one,' was the blunt reply. 'When I was a girl it was the Manor House, and may be called that again for all I know, but thirty years since, a man named Maitland took it on a lease and farmed the land, and folks forgot the old name, and called it Maitland's Farm.'

'When did Maitland leave?'

'About two months ago.'

'Why did he go away from a nice place like this?'

'You are fond of asking questions,' remarked the old woman drily. 'He went for two good reasons, his lease was up, and his family was a big one. Nine children he had, from a girl of two-and-twenty down to a little lad of four years old. His wife and him thought it best to take 'em out to Australia, where there's room for all. They were glad to go, all but the eldest, Esther, and she nearly broke her heart over it. But then she had to leave her sweetheart behind her. He's a young man on a dairy farm near here, and though he's to follow her out and marry her in twelve months, she did nothing but mourn, same as if she was leaving him altogether.'

'Ah, indeed!' said Horton, who could not readily enter into details about people whom he did not know. 'So this is the sitting-room; it's large and airy, and has as much furniture in it as a man needs by himself. Now show me the bedroom, if you please.'

'Follow me upstairs, sir,' and the old woman preceded him slowly up the oak staircase, and opened the door of the back room on the first floor.

'Then the bedroom that you let is not over the sitting-room?'

'No, the front room is mine, and the room next to it is my son's. He's out all day at his work, but he sleeps here, and mostly keeps me company of an evening. I'm alone here all day looking after the place, and if you take the rooms I shall cook for you and wait on you myself.'

Horton liked the look of the bedroom. It was large and airy, with little furniture in it beyond a bed and a chest of drawers. But it was delicately clean, and silent as the grave. How a tired man might sleep here! The walls were decorated with old prints in black frames of the 'Rake's Progress' and 'Marriage à la Mode', and above the high carved mantelpiece hung an engraving of the famous portrait of Charles the First, on a prancing brown horse.

'Those things were on the walls when the Maitlands took the place, and they had to leave 'em where they found 'em,' said the old woman. 'And they found that sword too,' she added, pointing to a rusty cutlass that hung from a nail by the head of the bed; 'but I think they'd have done no great harm if they'd sold it for old iron.'

Horton took down the weapon and examined it. It was an ordinary cutlass, such as was worn by the marines in George the Third's reign, not old enough to be of antiquarian interest, nor of sufficient beauty of workmanship to make it of artistic value. He replaced it, and stepped to the windows and looked into the garden below. It was bounded by a high wall enclosing a row of poplars, and beyond lay the open country, visible for miles in the clear air, a sight to rest and fascinate the eye of a Londoner.

Horton made his bargain with the old woman whom the landlord had put into the house as caretaker, pending his decision about the disposition of the property. She was allowed to take a lodger for her own profit, and as soon as Mrs Belt found that the stranger agreed to her terms, she assured him that everything should be comfortably arranged for his reception by the following Wednesday.

Horton arrived at Maitland's Farm on the evening of the appointed day. A stormy autumnal sunset was casting an angry glow on the windows of the house, the rising wind filled the air with mournful sounds, and the poplars swayed against a background of lurid sky.

Mrs Belt was expecting her lodger, and promptly opened the door, candle in hand, when she heard the wheels stopping at the gate. The driver of the fly carried Horton's portmanteau into the hall, was paid his fare, and drove away thinking the darkening lanes more cheerful than the glimpse he had had of the inside of Maitland's Farm.

Horton was thoroughly pleased with his country quarters. The intense quiet of the almost empty house, that might have made another man melancholy, soothed and rested him. In the day time he wandered about the country, or amused himself in the garden and orchard, and he spent the long evenings alone, reading and smoking in his sitting-room. Mrs Belt brought in supper at nine o'clock, and usually stayed to have a chat with her lodger, and many a long story she related of her neighbours, and the Maitland family, while she waited upon him at his evening meal.

On several occasions she told him that Esther Maitland's sweetheart, Michael Winn, had come to talk with her about the Maitlands, or to bring her a newspaper containing tidings that their ship had reached some point on its long voyage in safety.

'You see the *Petrel* is a sailing vessel, sir, and there's no saying how long she'll take getting to Australia. The last news Michael had, she'd got as far as some islands with an outlandish name, and he's had a letter from Esther posted at a place called Madeira. And now he gives himself no peace till he can hear that the ship's safe as far as – somewhere, I think he said, in Africa.'

'It would be the Cape, Mrs Belt.'

'That's the name, sir, the Cape, and he werrits all the time for fear of storms and shipwrecks. But I tell him the world's a wide place, and the sea wider than all, and very likely when the chimney pots is flying about our heads in a gale here, the *Petrel*'s lying becalmed somewhere. And then he takes up my thought and turns it against me. "Yes," he says, "and when it's a dead calm here on shore, the ship may be sinking in a storm, and my Esther being drowned."'

'Michael Winn must be a very nervous young man.'

'That's where it is, sir, and I tell him when he follows the Maitlands it's a good job that he leaves no one behind him that'll werrit after him, the same as he's werrited after Esther.'

It was the middle of October, and Horton had been a month at the farm. The weather was now cold and wet, and he began to think it was time he returned to his snug London home, for the autumn rain made everything at Maitland's Farm damp and mouldy. It had blown half a gale all day, and the rain had fallen in torrents, keeping him a prisoner indoors. But he occupied himself in writing letters, and reading some legal documents his clerk had brought out to him, and the time passed rapidly. Indeed the evening flew by so quickly he had no idea it was nine o'clock, when Mrs Belt entered the room to lay the cloth for supper.

'It's stopped raining now, sir,' she said, as she poked the fire into a cheerful blaze, 'and a good job too, for Michael Winn brings me word the Wandle's risen fearful since morning, and it's out in places more than it's been for years. But there's a full moon tonight, so no one need walk into the water unless they've a mind to.'

Horton's head was too full of a knotty legal point to pay much heed to Mrs Belt, and the old woman, seeing that he was not in a mood for conversation, said nothing further. At half-past ten she brought her lodger some spirits and hot water, and his bedroom candle, and wished him good night. Horton sat reading for some time, and then made an entry in his diary concerning a day of which there was absolutely nothing to record, lighted his candle, and went upstairs. I am familiar with the precise order of each trifling circumstance. My friend has so often told me the events of that night, and never with the slightest addition or omission in the telling. It was his habit, the last thing at night, to draw up the blinds. He looked out of the window, and though the moon was at the full, the clouds had not yet dispersed, and her light was fitful and obscure. It was twenty minutes to twelve as he extinguished the candle by his bedside. Everything was propitious for rest. He was weary, and the house profoundly silent. The rain had stopped, the wind fallen to a sigh, and it seemed to him that as soon as his head pressed the pillow he sank into a dreamless slumber.

Shortly after two o'clock Horton awoke suddenly, passing instantaneously from deep sleep to the possession of every faculty in a heightened degree, and with an insupportable sense of fear weighing upon him like a thousand nightmares. He started up and looked around him. The perspiration poured from his brow, and his heart beat to suffocation. He was convinced that he had been waked by some strange and terrible noise, that had thrilled through the depths of sleep, and he dreaded the repetition of it inexpressibly. The room was flooded with moonlight streaming through the narrow windows, lying like sheets of molten silver on the floor, and the poplars in the garden cast tremulous shadows on the ceiling.

Then Horton heard through the silence of the house a sound that was not the moan of the wind, nor the rustling of trees, nor any sound he had heard before. Clear and distinct, as though it were in the room with him, he heard a voice of weeping and lamentation, with more than human sorrow in the cry, so that it seemed to him as though he listened to the mourning of a lost soul. He leaped up, struck a match, and lighted the candle, and seizing the cutlass that hung by the bed, unlocked the door, and opened it to listen.

So far as all ordinary sounds were concerned, the house was silent as death, and the moonlight streamed through the staircase window in a flood of pale light. But the unearthly sound of weeping, thrilling through heart and soul, came from the hall below, and Horton walked downstairs to the landing at the top of the first flight. There, on the lowest step, a woman was seated with bowed head, her face hidden in her hands, rocking to and fro in extremity of grief. The moonlight fell full on her, and he saw that she was only partly clothed, and her dark hair lay in confusion on her bare shoulders.

'Who are you, and what is the matter with you?' said Horton, and his trembling voice echoed in the silent house. But she neither stirred nor spoke, nor abated her weeping. Slowly he descended the moon-lit staircase till there were but four steps between him and the woman. A mortal fear was growing upon him.

'Speak! if you are a living being!' he cried. The figure rose to its full height, turned and faced him for a moment that seemed an eternity, and rushed full on the point of the cutlass Horton involuntarily presented. As the impalpable form glided up the blade of the weapon, a cold wave seemed to break over him, and he fell in a dead faint on the stairs.

How long he remained insensible he could not tell. When he came to himself and opened his eyes, the moon had set, and he groped his way in darkness to his room, where the candle had burnt itself out.

When Horton came down to breakfast, he looked as though he had been ill for a month, and his hands trembled like a drunkard's. At any other time Mrs Belt would have been struck by his appearance, but this morning she was too much excited by some bad news she had heard, to notice whether her lodger was looking well or ill. Horton asked her how she had slept, for if she had not heard the terrible sounds that waked him, it still seemed impossible she should not have heard his heavy fall on the stairs. Mrs Belt replied, with some astonishment at her lodger's concern for her welfare, that she had never had a better night, it was so quiet after the wind fell.

'But did your son think the house was quiet, did he sleep too?' asked Horton with feverish eagerness.

Mrs Belt was yearning to impart her bad news to her lodger, and remarking that she had something else to do than ask folks how they slept o' nights, she said a neighbour had just told her that Michael Winn had fallen into the Wandle during the night – no one knew how – and was drowned, and they were carrying his body home then.

'What a terrible blow for his sweetheart,' said Horton, greatly shocked.

'Aye! there's a pretty piece of news to send her, when she's expecting to see poor Michael himself soon.'

'Mrs Belt, have you any portrait of Esther Maitland you could show me? I've heard the girl's name so often I'm curious to know what she is like.' And the old woman retired to hunt among her treasures for a small photograph on glass, that Esther had given her before she went away. Presently Mrs Belt returned, polishing the picture with her apron.

'It's but a poor affair, sir, taken in a caravan on the Common, yet it's like the girl, it's very like.'

It was a miserable production, a cheap and early effort in photography, and Horton rose from the table with the picture in his hand to examine it at the window. And there, surrounded by the thin brass frame, he recognised the face of all faces that had dismayed him, the face he beheld in the vision of the preceding night. He suppressed a groan, and turned from the window with a face so white, that, as he handed the picture back to Mrs Belt, she said, 'You're not feeling well this morning, sir.'

'No, I'm feeling very ill. I must get back to town today to be near to my own doctor. You shall be no loser by my leaving you so suddenly, but if I am going to be ill, I am best in my own home.' For Horton could not have stayed another night at Maitland's Farm to save his life.

He was at his office in Bedford Row by noon, and his clerks thought that he looked ten years older for his visit to the country.

A little more than three weeks after Horton returned to town, when his nerves were beginning to recover their accustomed tone, his attention was unexpectedly recalled to the abhorrent subject of the apparition he had seen. He read in his daily paper that the mail from the Cape had brought news of the wreck of the sailing vessel *Petrel* bound for Australia, with loss of all on board, in a violent storm off the coast, shortly before the steamer left for England. By a careful comparison of dates, allowing for the variation of time, the conviction was forced upon John Horton that the ill-fated ship foundered at the very hour in which he beheld the wraith of Esther Maitland. She and her lover, divided by thousands of miles, both perished by drowning at the same time – Michael Winn in the little river at home, and Esther Maitland in the depths of a distant ocean.

Violet Hunt

THE PRAYER

I

'It is but giving over of a game,
That must be lost.' – PHILASTER

'COME, Mrs Arne – come, my dear, you must not give way like this! You can't stand it – you really can't! Let Miss Kate take you away – now do!' urged the nurse, with her most motherly of intonations.

'Yes, Alice, Mrs Joyce is right. Come away – do come away – you are only making yourself ill. It is all over; you can do nothing! Oh, oh, do come away!' implored Mrs Arne's sister, shivering with excitement and nervousness.

A few moments ago Dr Graham had relinquished his hold on the pulse of Edward Arne with the hopeless movement of the eyebrows that meant – the end.

The nurse had made the little gesture of resignation that was possibly a matter of form with her. The young sister-in-law had hidden her face in her hands. The wife had screamed a scream that had turned them all hot and cold – and flung herself on the bed over her dead husband. There she lay; her cries were terrible, her sobs shook her whole body.

The three gazed at her pityingly, not knowing what to do next. The nurse, folding her hands, looked towards the doctor for directions, and the doctor drummed with his fingers on the bed-post. The young girl timidly stroked the shoulder that heaved and writhed under her touch.

'Go away! Go away!' her sister reiterated continually, in a voice hoarse with fatigue and passion.

'Leave her alone, Miss Kate,' whispered the nurse at last; 'she will work it off best herself, perhaps.'

She turned down the lamp as if to draw a veil over the scene. Mrs Arne raised herself on her elbow, showing a face stained with tears and purple with emotion.

'What! Not gone?' she said harshly. 'Go away, Kate, go away! It is my house. I don't want you, I want no one – I want to speak to my husband. Will you go away – all of you. Give me an hour, half-an-hour – five minutes!'

She stretched out her arms imploringly to the doctor.

'Well . . .' said he, almost to himself.

He signed to the two women to withdraw, and followed them out into the passage. 'Go and get something to eat,' he said peremptorily, 'while you can. We shall have trouble with her presently. I'll wait in the dressing-room.'

He glanced at the twisting figure on the bed, shrugged his shoulders, and passed into the adjoining room, without, however, closing the door of communication. Sitting down in an arm-chair drawn up to the fire, he stretched himself and closed his eyes. The professional aspects of the case of Edward Arne rose up before him in all its interesting forms of complication . . .

It was just this professional attitude that Mrs Arne unconsciously resented both in the doctor and in the nurse. Through all their kindness she had realised and resented their scientific interest in her husband, for to them he had been no more than a curious and complicated case; and now that the blow had fallen, she regarded them both in the light of executioners. Her one desire, expressed with all the shameless sincerity of blind and thoughtless misery, was to be free of their hateful presence and alone – alone with her dead!

She was weary of the doctor's subdued manly tones – of the nurse's commonplace motherliness, too habitually adapted to the needs of all to be appreciated by the individual – of the childish consolation of the young sister, who had never loved, never been married, did not know what sorrow was! Their expressions of sympathy struck her like blows, the touch of their hands on her body, as they tried to raise her, stung her in every nerve.

With a sigh of relief she buried her head in the pillow, pressed her body more closely against that of her husband, and lay motionless.

Her sobs ceased.

The lamp went out with a gurgle. The fire leaped up, and died. She raised her head and stared about her helplessly, then sinking down again she put her lips to the ear of the dead man.

'Edward – dear Edward!' she whispered, 'why have you left me? Darling, why have you left me? I can't stay behind – you know I can't. I am too young to be left. It is only a year since you married me. I never thought it was only for a year. "Till death us do part!" Yes, I know that's in it, but nobody ever thinks of that! I never thought of living without you! I meant to die with you . . .

'No – no – I can't die – I must not – till my baby is born. You will never see it. Don't you want to see it? Don't you? Oh, Edward, speak! Say something, darling, one word – one little word! Edward! Edward! are you there? Answer me for God's sake, answer me!

'Darling, I am so tired of waiting. Oh, think, dearest. There is so little time. They only gave me half-an-hour. In half-an-hour they will come and take you away from me – take you where I can't come to you – with all my love I can't come to you! I know the place – I saw it once. A great lonely place full of graves, and little stunted trees dripping with dirty London rain . . . and gas-lamps flaring all round . . . but quite, quite dark where the grave is . . . a long grey stone just like the rest. How could you stay there? – all alone – all alone – without me?

'Do you remember, Edward, what we once said – that whichever of us died first should come back to watch over the other, in the spirit? I promised you, and you promised me. What children we were! Death is not what we thought. It comforted us to say that then.

'Now, it's nothing – nothing – worse than nothing! I don't want your spirit – I can't see it – or feel it – I want you, you, your eyes that looked at me, your mouth that kissed me—'

She raised his arms and clasped them round her neck, and lay there very still, murmuring, 'Oh, hold me, hold me! Love me if you can. Am I hateful? This is me! These are your arms . . .'

The doctor in the next room moved in his chair. The noise awoke her from her dream of contentment, and she unwound the dead arm from her neck, and, holding it up by the wrist, considered it ruefully.

'Yes, I can put it round me, but I have to hold it there. It is quite cold – it doesn't care. Ah, my dear, you don't care! You are dead. I kiss you, but you don't kiss me. Edward! Edward! Oh, for heaven's sake kiss me once. Just once!

'No, no, that won't do – that's not enough! that's nothing! worse than nothing! I want you back, you, all you . . . What shall I do? . . . I often pray . . . Oh, if there be a God in heaven, and if He ever answered a prayer, let Him answer mine – my only prayer. I'll never ask another – and give you back to me! As you were – as I loved you – as I adored you! He must listen. He must! My God, my God, he's mine – he's my husband, he's my lover – give him back to me!'

'Left alone for half-an-hour or more with the corpse! It's not right!'

The muttered expression of the nurse's revolted sense of professional decency came from the head of the staircase, where she had been waiting for the last few minutes. The doctor joined her.

'Hush, Mrs Joyce! I'll go to her now.'

The door creaked on its hinges as he gently pushed it open and went in.

'What's that? What's that?' screamed Mrs Arne. 'Doctor! Doctor! Don't touch me! Either I am dead or he is alive!'

'Do you want to kill yourself, Mrs Arne?' said Dr Graham, with calculated sternness, coming forward; 'come away!'

'Not dead! Not dead!' she murmured.

'He is dead, I assure you. Dead and cold an hour ago! Feel!' He took hold of her, as she lay face downwards, and in so doing he touched the dead man's cheek – it was not cold! Instinctively his finger sought a pulse.

'Stop! Wait!' he cried in his intense excitement. 'My dear Mrs Arne, control yourself!'

But Mrs Arne had fainted, and fallen heavily off the bed on the other side. Her sister, hastily summoned, attended to her, while the man they had all given over for dead was, with faint gasps and sighs and reluctant moans, pulled, as it were, hustled and dragged back over the threshold of life.

II

'Why do you always wear black, Alice?' asked Esther Graham. 'You are not in mourning that I know of.'

She was Dr Graham's only daughter and Mrs Arne's only friend. She sat with Mrs Arne in the dreary drawing-room of the house in Chelsea. She had come to tea. She was the only person who ever did come to tea there.

She was brusque, kind, and blunt, and had a talent for making inappropriate remarks. Six years ago Mrs Arne had been a widow for an hour! Her husband had succumbed to an apparently mortal illness, and for the space of an hour had lain dead. When suddenly and inexplicably he had revived from his trance, the shock, combined with six weeks' nursing, had nearly killed his wife. All this Esther had heard from her father. She herself had only come to know Mrs Arne after her child was born, and all the tragic circumstances of her husband's illness put aside, and it was hoped forgotten. And when her idle question received no answer from the pale absent woman who sat opposite, with listless lack-lustre eyes fixed on the green and blue flames dancing in the fire, she hoped it had passed unnoticed. She waited for five minutes for Mrs Arne to resume the conversation, then her natural impatience got the better of her.

'Do say something, Alice!' she implored.

'Esther, I beg your pardon!' said Mrs Arne. 'I was thinking.'

'What were you thinking of?'

'I don't know.'

'No, of course you don't. People who sit and stare into the fire never do think, really. They are only brooding and making themselves ill, and that is what you are doing. You mope, you take no interest in anything, you never go out – I am sure you have not been out of doors today?'

'No – yes – I believe not. It is so cold.'

'You are sure to feel the cold if you sit in the house all day, and sure to get ill! Just look at yourself!'

Mrs Arne rose and looked at herself in the Italian mirror over the chimney-piece. It reflected faithfully enough her even pallor, her dark hair and eyes, the sweeping length of her eyelashes, the sharp curves of her nostrils, and the delicate arch of her eyebrows, that formed a thin sharp black line, so clear as to seem almost unnatural.

'Yes, I do look ill,' she said with conviction.

'No wonder. You choose to bury yourself alive.'

'Sometimes I do feel as if I lived in a grave. I look up at the ceiling and fancy it is my coffin-lid.'

'Don't please talk like that!' expostulated Miss Graham, pointing to Mrs Arne's little girl. 'If only for Dolly's sake, I think you should not give way to such morbid fancies. It isn't good for her to see you like this always.'

'Oh, Esther,' the other exclaimed, stung into something like vivacity, 'don't reproach me! I hope I am a good mother to my child!'

'Yes, dear, you are a model mother – and model wife too. Father says the way you look after your husband is something wonderful, but don't you think for your own sake you might try to be a little gayer? You encourage these moods, don't you? What is it? Is it the house?'

She glanced around her – at the high ceiling, at the heavy damask *portières*, the tall cabinets of china, the dim oak panelling – it reminded her of a neglected museum. Her eye travelled into the farthest corners, where the faint filmy dusk was already gathering, lit only by the bewildering cross-lights of the glass panels of cabinet doors – to the tall narrow windows – then back again to the woman in her mourning dress, cowering by the fire. She said sharply –

'You should go out more.'

'I do not like to – leave my husband.'

'Oh, I know that he is delicate and all that, but still, does he never permit you to leave him? Does he never go out by himself?'

'Not often!'

'And you have no pets! It is very odd of you. I simply can't imagine a house without animals.'

'We did have a dog once,' answered Mrs Arne plaintively, 'but it howled so we had to give it away. It would not go near Edward . . . But please don't imagine that I am dull! I have my child.' She laid her hand on the flaxen head at her knee.

Miss Graham rose, frowning.

'Ah, you are too bad!' she exclaimed. 'You are like a widow exactly, with one child, stroking its orphan head and saying, "Poor fatherless darling."'

Voices were heard outside. Miss Graham stopped talking quite suddenly, and sought her veil and gloves on the mantelpiece.

'You need not go, Esther,' said Mrs Arne. 'It is only my husband.'

'Oh, but it is getting late,' said the other, crumpling up her gloves in her muff, and shuffling her feet nervously.

'Come!' said her hostess, with a bitter smile, 'put your gloves on properly – if you must go – but it is quite early still.'

'Please don't go, Miss Graham,' put in the child.

'I must. Go and meet your papa, like a good girl.'

'I don't want to.'

'You mustn't talk like that, Dolly,' said the doctor's daughter absently, still looking towards the door. Mrs Arne rose and fastened the clasps of the big fur-cloak for her friend. The wife's white, sad, oppressed face came very close to the girl's cheerful one, as she murmured in a low voice –

'You don't like my husband, Esther? I can't help noticing it. Why don't you?'

'Nonsense!' retorted the other, with the emphasis of one who is repelling an overtrue accusation. 'I do, only—'

'Only what?'

'Well, dear, it is foolish of me, of course, but I am – a little afraid of him.'

'Afraid of Edward!' said his wife slowly. 'Why should you be?'

'Well, dear – you see – I – I suppose women can't help being a little afraid of their friends' husbands – they can spoil their friendships with their wives in a moment, if they choose to disapprove of them. I really must go! Good-bye, child; give me a kiss! Don't ring, Alice. Please don't! I can open the door for myself—'

'Why should you?' said Mrs Arne. 'Edward is in the hall; I heard him speaking to Foster.'

'No; he has gone into his study. Good-bye, you apathetic creature!' She gave Mrs Arne a brief kiss and dashed out of the room. The voices outside had ceased, and she had reasonable hopes of reaching the door without being intercepted by Mrs Arne's husband. But he met her on the stairs. Mrs Arne, listening intently from her seat by the fire, heard her exchange a few shy sentences with him, the sound of which died away as they went downstairs together. A few moments after, Edward Arne came into the room and dropped into the chair just vacated by his wife's visitor.

He crossed his legs and said nothing. Neither did she.

His nearness had the effect of making the woman look at once several years older. Where she was pale he was well-coloured; the network of little filmy wrinkles that, on a close inspection, covered her face, had no parallel on his smooth skin. He was handsome; soft, well-groomed flakes of auburn hair lay over his forehead, and his steely blue eyes shone equally, a contrast to the sombre fire of hers, and the masses of dark crinkly hair that shaded her brow. The deep lines of permanent discontent furrowed that brow as she sat with her chin propped on her hands, and her elbows resting on her knees. Neither spoke. When the hands of the clock over Mrs Arne's head pointed to seven, the white-aproned figure of the nurse appeared in the doorway, and the little girl rose and kissed her mother very tenderly.

Mrs Arne's forehead contracted. Looking uneasily at her husband, she said to the child tentatively, yet boldly, as one grasps the nettle, 'Say good night to your father!'

The child obeyed, saying 'Good night' indifferently in her father's direction.

'Kiss him!'

'No, please – please not.'

Her mother looked down on her curiously, sadly . . .

'You are a naughty, spoilt child!' she said, but without conviction. 'Excuse her, Edward.'

He did not seem to have heard.

'Well, if you don't care— ' said his wife bitterly. 'Come, child!' She caught the little girl by the hand and left the room.

At the door she half turned and looked fixedly at her husband. It was a strange ambiguous gaze; in it passion and dislike were strangely combined. Then she shivered and closed the door softly after her.

The man in the arm-chair sat with no perceptible change of attitude, his unspeculative eyes fixed on the fire, his hands clasped idly in front of him. The pose was obviously habitual. The servant brought lights and closed the shutters, drew the curtains, and made up the fire noisily, without, however, eliciting any reproof from his master.

Edward Arne was an ideal master, as far as Foster was concerned. He kept cases of cigars, but never smoked them, although the supply had often to be renewed. He did not care what he ate or drank, although he kept as good a cellar as most gentlemen – Foster knew that. He never interfered, he counted for nothing, he gave no trouble. Foster had no intention of ever leaving such an easy place. True, his master was not cordial; he very seldom addressed him or seemed to know whether he was there, but then neither did he grumble if the fire in the study was allowed to go out, or interfere with Foster's liberty in any way. He had a better place of it than Annette, Mrs Arne's maid, who would be called up in the middle of the night to bathe her mistress's forehead with eau-de-Cologne, or made to brush her long hair for hours together to soothe her. Naturally enough Foster and Annette compared notes as to their respective situations, and drew unflattering parallels between this capricious wife and model husband.

III

Miss Graham was not a demonstrative woman. On her return home she somewhat startled her father, as he sat by his study table, deeply interested in his diagnosis book, by the sudden violence of her embrace.

'Why this excitement?' he asked, smiling and turning round. He was a young-looking man for his age; his thin wiry figure and clear colour belied the evidence of his hair, tinged with grey, and the tired wrinkles that gave value to the acuteness and brilliancy of the eyes they surrounded.

'I don't know!' she replied, 'only you are so nice and alive somehow. I always feel like this when I come back from seeing the Arnes.'

'Then don't go to see the Arnes.'

'I'm so fond of her, father, and she will never come here to me, as you know. Or else nothing would induce me to enter her tomb of a house, and talk to that walking funeral of a husband of hers. I managed to get away today without having to shake hands with him. I always try to avoid it. But, father, I do wish you would go and see Alice.'

'Is she ill?'

'Well, not exactly ill, I suppose, but her eyes make me quite uncomfortable, and she says such odd things! I don't know if it is you or the clergyman she wants, but she is all wrong somehow! She never goes out except to church; she never pays a call, or has any one to call on her! Nobody ever asks the Arnes to dinner, and I'm sure I don't blame them – the sight of that man at one's table would spoil any party – and they never entertain. She is always alone. Day after day I go in and find her sitting over the fire, with that same brooding expression. I shouldn't be surprised in the least if she were to go mad some day. Father, what is it? What is the tragedy of the house? There is one, I am convinced. And yet, though I have been the intimate friend of that woman for years, I know no more about her than the man in the street.'

'She keeps her skeleton safe in the cupboard,' said Dr Graham. 'I respect her for that. And please don't talk nonsense about tragedies. Alice Arne is only morbid – the malady of the age. And she is a very religious woman.'

'I wonder if she complains of her odious husband to Mr Bligh. She is always going to his services.'

'Odious?'

'Yes, odious!' Miss Graham shuddered. 'I cannot stand him! I cannot bear the touch of his cold froggy hands, and the sight of his fishy eyes! That inane smile of his simply makes me shrivel up. Father, honestly, do you like him yourself?'

'My dear, I hardly know him! It is his wife I have known ever since she was a child, and I a boy at college. Her father was my tutor. I never knew her husband till six years ago, when she called me in to attend him in a very serious illness. I suppose she never speaks of it? No? A very odd affair. For the life of me I cannot tell how he managed to recover. You needn't tell people, for it affects my reputation, but I didn't save him! Indeed I have never been able to account for it. The man was given over for dead!'

'He might as well be dead for all the good he is,' said Esther scornfully. 'I have never heard him say more than a couple of sentences in my life.'

'Yet he was an exceedingly brilliant young man; one of the best men of his year at Oxford – a good deal run after – poor Alice was wild to marry him!'

'In love with that spiritless creature? He is like a house with someone dead in it, and all the blinds down!'

'Come, Esther, don't be morbid – not to say silly! You are very hard on the poor man! What's wrong with him? He is the ordinary, common-place, cold-blooded specimen of humanity, a little stupid, a little selfish – people who have gone through a serious illness like that are apt to be – but on the whole, a good husband, a good father, a good citizen—'

'Yes, and his wife is afraid of him, and his child hates him!' exclaimed Esther.

'Nonsense!' said Dr Graham sharply. 'The child is spoilt. Only children are apt to be – and the mother wants a change or a tonic of some kind. I'll go and talk to her when I have time. Go along and dress. Have you forgotten that George Graham is coming to dinner?'

After she had gone the doctor made a note on the corner of his blotting-pad, 'Mem.: to go and see Mrs Arne,' and dismissed the subject of the memorandum entirely from his mind.

George Graham was the doctor's nephew, a tall, weedy, cumbrous young man, full of fads and fallacies, with a gentle manner that somehow inspired confidence. He was several years younger than Esther, who loved to listen to his semi-scientific, semi-romantic stories of things met with in the course of his profession. 'Oh, I come across very queer things!' he would say mysteriously. 'There's a queer little widow—!'

'Tell me about your little widow?' asked Esther that day after dinner, when, her father having gone back to his study, she and her cousin sat together as usual.

He laughed.

'You like to hear of my professional experiences? Well, she certainly interested me,' he said thoughtfully. 'She is an odd psychological study in her way. I wish I could come across her again.'

'Where did you come across her, and what is her name?'

'I don't know her name, I don't want to; she is not a personage to me, only a case. I hardly know her face even. I have never seen it except in the twilight. But I gathered that she lived somewhere in Chelsea, for she came out on to the Embankment with only a kind of lacy thing over her head; she can't live far off, I fancy.'

Esther became instantly attentive. 'Go on,' she said.

'It was three weeks ago,' said George Graham. 'I was coming along the Embankment about ten o'clock. I walked through that little grove, you know, just between Cheyne Walk and the river, and I heard in there someone sobbing very bitterly. I looked and saw a woman sitting on a seat, with her head in her hands, crying. I was most awfully sorry, of course, and I thought I could perhaps do something for her, get her a glass of water, or salts, or something. I took her for a woman of the people – it was quite dark, you know. So I asked her very politely if I could do anything for her, and then I noticed her hands – they were quite white and covered with diamonds.'

'You were sorry you spoke, I suppose,' said Esther.

'She raised her head and said – I believe she laughed – "Are you going to tell me to move on?"'

'She thought you were a policeman?'

'Probably – if she thought at all – but she was in a semi-dazed condition. I told her to wait till I came back, and dashed round the corner to the chemist's and bought a bottle of salts. She thanked me, and made a little effort to rise and go away. She seemed very weak. I told her I was a medical man, I started in and talked to her.'

'And she to you?'

'Yes, quite straight. Don't you know that women always treat a doctor as if he were one step removed from their father confessor – not human –

not in the same category as themselves? It is not complimentary to one as a man, but one hears a good deal one would not otherwise hear. She ended by telling me all about herself – in a veiled way, of course. It soothed her – relieved her – she seemed not to have had an outlet for years!'

'To a mere stranger!'

'To a doctor. And she did not know what she was saying half the time. She was hysterical, of course. Heavens! what nonsense she talked! She spoke of herself as a person somehow haunted, cursed by some malign fate, a victim of some fearful spiritual catastrophe, don't you know? I let her run on. She was convinced of the reality of a sort of "doom" that she had fancied had befallen her. It was quite pathetic. Then it got rather chilly – she shivered – I suggested her going in. She shrank back; she said, "If you only knew what a relief it is, how much less miserable I am out here! I can breathe; I can live – it is my only glimpse of the world that is alive – I live in a grave – oh, let me stay!" She seemed positively afraid to go home.'

'Perhaps someone bullied her at home.'

'I suppose so, but then – she had no husband. He died, she told me, years ago. She had adored him, she said—'

'Is she pretty?'

'Pretty! Well, I hardly noticed. Let me see! Oh, yes, I suppose she was pretty – no, now I think of it, she would be too worn and faded to be what you call pretty.'

Esther smiled.

'Well, we sat there together for quite an hour, then the clock of Chelsea church struck eleven, and she got up and said "Good-bye," holding out her hand quite naturally, as if our meeting and conversation had been nothing out of the common. There was a sound like a dead leaf trailing across the walk and she was gone.'

'Didn't you ask if you should see her again?'

'That would have been a mean advantage to take.'

'You might have offered to see her home.'

'I saw she did not mean me to.'

'She was a lady, you say,' pondered Esther. 'How was she dressed?'

'Oh, all right, like a lady – in black – mourning, I suppose. She has dark crinkly hair, and her eyebrows are very thin and arched – I noticed that in the dusk.'

'Does this photograph remind you of her?' asked Esther suddenly, taking him to the mantelpiece.

'Rather!'

'Alice! Oh, it couldn't be – she is not a widow, her husband is alive – has your friend any children?'

'Yes, one, she mentioned it.'

'How old?'

'Six years old, I think she said. She talks of the "responsibility of bringing up an orphan".'

'George, what time is it?' Esther asked suddenly.

'About nine o'clock.'

'Would you mind coming out with me?'

'I should like it. Where shall we go?'

'To St Adhelm's! It is close by here. There is a special late service tonight, and Mrs Arne is sure to be there.'

'Oh, Esther – curiosity!'

'No, not mere curiosity. Don't you see if it is my Mrs Arne who talked to you like this, it is very serious? I have thought her ill for a long time; but as ill as that—'

At St Adhelm's Church, Esther Graham pointed out a woman who was kneeling beside a pillar in an attitude of intense devotion and abandonment. She rose from her knees, and turned her rapt face up towards the pulpit whence the Reverend Ralph Bligh was holding his impassioned discourse. George Graham touched his cousin on the shoulder, and motioned to her to leave her place on the outermost rank of worshippers.

'That is the woman!' said he.

IV

'Mem.: to go and see Mrs Arne.' The doctor came across this note in his blotting-pad one day six weeks later. His daughter was out of town. He had heard nothing of the Arnes since her departure. He had promised to go and see her. He was a little conscience-stricken. Yet another week elapsed before he found time to call upon the daughter of his old tutor.

At the corner of Tite Street he met Mrs Arne's husband, and stopped. A doctor's professional kindliness of manner is, or ought to be, independent of his personal likings and dislikings, and there was a pleasant cordiality about his greeting which should have provoked a corresponding fervour on the part of Edward Arne.

'How are you, Arne?' Graham said. 'I was on my way to call on your wife.'

'Ah – yes!' said Edward Arne, with the ascending inflection of polite acquiescence. A ray of blue from his eyes rested transitorily on the doctor's face, and in that short moment the latter noted its intolerable vacuity, and for the first time in his life he felt a sharp pang of sympathy for the wife of such a husband.

'I suppose you are off to your club? – er – good bye!' he wound up abruptly. With the best will in the world he somehow found it almost impossible to carry on a conversation with Edward Arne, who raised his hand to his hat-brim in token of salutation, smiled sweetly, and walked on.

'He really is extraordinarily good-looking,' reflected the doctor, as he watched him down the street and safely over the crossing with a certain degree of solicitude for which he could not exactly account. 'And yet one feels one's vitality ebbing out at the finger-ends as one talks to him. I shall begin to believe in Esther's absurd fancies about him soon. Ah, there's the little girl!' he exclaimed, as he turned into Cheyne Walk and caught sight of her with her nurse, making violent demonstrations to attract his attention. 'She is alive, at any rate. How is your mother, Dolly?' he asked.

'Quite well, thank you,' was the child's reply. She added, 'She's crying. She sent me away because I looked at her. So I did. Her cheeks are quite red.'

'Run away – run away and play!' said the doctor nervously. He ascended the steps of the house, and rang the bell very gently and neatly.

'Not at— ' began Foster, with the intonation of polite falsehood, but stopped on seeing the doctor, who, with his daughter, was a privileged person. 'Mrs Arne will see you, Sir.'

'Mrs Arne is not alone?' he said interrogatively.

'Yes, Sir, quite alone. I have just taken tea in.'

Dr Graham's doubts were prompted by the low murmur as of a voice, or voices, which came to him through the open door of the room at the head of the stairs. He paused and listened while Foster stood by, merely remarking, 'Mrs Arne do talk to herself sometimes, Sir.'

It was Mrs Arne's voice – the doctor recognised it now. It was not the voice of a sane or healthy woman. He at once mentally removed his visit from the category of a morning call, and prepared for a semi-professional inquiry.

'Don't announce me,' he said to Foster, and quietly entered the back drawing-room, which was separated by a heavy tapestry *portière* from the room where Mrs Arne sat, with an open book on the table before her, from which she had been apparently reading aloud. Her hands were now clasped tightly over her face, and when, presently, she removed them and began feverishly to turn page after page of her book, the crimson of her cheeks was seamed with white where her fingers had impressed themselves.

The doctor wondered if she saw him, for though her eyes were fixed in his direction, there was no apprehension in them. She went on reading, and it was the text, mingled with passionate interjection and fragmentary utterances, of the Burial Service that met his ears.

'"For as in Adam all die!" All die! It says all! For he must reign . . . The last enemy that shall be destroyed is Death. What shall they do if the dead rise not at all! . . . I die daily . . .! Daily! No, no, better get it over . . . dead and buried . . . out of sight, out of mind . . . under a stone. Dead men don't come back . . . Go on! Get it over. I want to hear the earth rattle on the coffin, and then I shall know it is done. "Flesh and blood cannot inherit!" Oh, what did I do? What have I done? Why did I wish it so fervently? Why did I pray for it so earnestly? God gave me my wish—'

'Alice! Alice!' groaned the doctor.

She looked up. '"When this corruptible shall have put on incorruption—" "Dust to dust, ashes to ashes, earth to earth—" Yes, that is it. "After death, though worms destroy this body—"'

She flung the book aside and sobbed.

'That is what I was afraid of. My God! My God! Down there – in the dark – for ever and ever and ever! I could not bear to think of it! My Edward! And so I interfered . . . and prayed . . . and prayed till . . . Oh! I am punished. Flesh and blood could not inherit! I kept him there – I would not let him go . . . I kept him . . . I prayed . . . I denied him Christian burial . . . Oh, how could I know . . .'

'Good heavens, Alice!' said Graham, coming sensibly forward, 'what does this mean? I have heard of schoolgirls going through the marriage service by themselves, but the burial service—'

He laid down his hat and went on severely, 'What have you to do with such things? Your child is flourishing – your husband alive and here—'

'And who kept him here?' interrupted Alice Arne fiercely, accepting the fact of his appearance without comment.

'You did,' he answered quickly, 'with your care and tenderness. I believe the warmth of your body, as you lay beside him for that half-hour, maintained the vital heat during that extraordinary suspension of the heart's action, which made us all give him up for dead. You were his best doctor, and brought him back to us.'

'Yes, it was I – it was I – you need not tell me it was I!'

'Come, be thankful!' he said cheerfully. 'Put that book away, and give me some tea, I'm very cold.'

'Oh, Dr Graham, how thoughtless of me!' said Mrs Arne, rallying at the slight imputation on her politeness he had purposely made. She tottered to the bell and rang it before he could anticipate her.

'Another cup,' she said quite calmly to Foster, who answered it. Then she sat down quivering all over with the suddenness of the constraint put upon her.

'Yes, sit down and tell me all about it,' said Dr Graham good-humouredly, at the same time observing her with the closeness he gave to difficult cases.

'There is nothing to tell,' she said simply, shaking her head, and futilely altering the position of the tea-cups on the tray. 'It all happened years ago. Nothing can be done now. Will you have sugar?'

He drank his tea and made conversation. He talked to her of some Dante lectures she was attending; of some details connected with her child's Kindergarten classes. These subjects did not interest her. There was a subject she wished to discuss, he could see that a question trembled on her tongue, and tried to lead up to it.

She introduced it herself, quite quietly, over a second cup. 'Sugar, Dr Graham? I forget. Dr Graham, tell me, do you believe that prayers – wicked unreasonable prayers – are granted?'

He helped himself to another slice of bread and butter before answering.

'Well,' he said slowly, 'it seems hard to believe that every fool who has a voice to pray with, and a brain where to conceive idiotic requests with, should be permitted to interfere with the economy of the universe. As a rule, if people were long-sighted enough to see the result of their petitions, I fancy very few of us would venture to interfere.'

Mrs Arne groaned.

She was a good Churchwoman, Graham knew, and he did not wish to sap her faith in any way, so he said no more, but inwardly wondered if a too rigid interpretation of some of the religious dogmas of the Vicar of St Adhelm's, her spiritual adviser, was not the clue to her distress. Then she put another question –

'Eh! What?' he said. 'Do I believe in ghosts? I will believe you if you will tell me you have seen one.'

'You know, Doctor,' she went on, 'I was always afraid of ghosts – of spirits – things unseen. I couldn't ever read about them. I could not bear the idea of some one in the room with me that I could not see. There was a text that always frightened me that hung up in my room: "Thou, God, seest me!" It frightened me when I was a child, whether I had been doing wrong or not. But now,' shuddering, 'I think there are worse things than ghosts.'

'Well, now, what sort of things?' he asked good-humouredly. 'Astral bodies— ?'

She leaned forward and laid her hot hand on his.

'Oh, Doctor, tell me, if a spirit – without the body we know it by – is terrible, what of a body' – her voice sank to a whisper, 'a body – senseless – lonely – stranded on this earth – without a spirit?'

She was watching his face anxiously. He was divided between a morbid inclination to laugh and the feeling of intense discomfort provoked by this wretched scene. He longed to give the conversation a more cheerful turn, yet did not wish to offend her by changing it too abruptly.

'I have heard of people not being able to keep body and soul together,' he replied at last, 'but I am not aware that practically such a division of forces has ever been achieved. And if we could only accept the theory of the de-spiritualised body, what a number of antipathetic people now wandering about in the world it would account for!'

The piteous gaze of her eyes seemed to seek to ward off the blow of his misplaced jocularity. He left his seat and sat down on the couch beside her.

'Poor child! poor girl! you are ill, you are over-excited. What is it? Tell me,' he asked her as tenderly as the father she had lost in early life might have done. Her head sank on his shoulder.

'Are you unhappy?' he asked her gently.

'Yes!'

'You are too much alone. Get your mother or your sister to come and stay with you.'

'They won't come,' she wailed. 'They say the house is like a grave. Edward has made himself a study in the basement. It's an impossible room – but he has moved all his things in, and I can't – I won't go to him there . . .'

'You're wrong. For it's only a fad,' said Graham, 'he'll tire of it. And you must see more people somehow. It's a pity my daughter is away. Had you any visitors today?'

'Not a soul has crossed the threshold for eighteen days.'

'We must change all that,' said the doctor vaguely. 'Meantime you must cheer up. Why, you have no need to think of ghosts and graves – no need to be melancholy – you have your husband and your child—'

'I have my child – yes.'

The doctor took hold of Mrs Arne by the shoulder and held her a little away from him. He thought he had found the cause of her trouble – a more commonplace one than he had supposed.

'I have known you, Alice, since you were a child,' he said gravely. 'Answer me! You love your husband, don't you?'

'Yes.' It was as if she were answering futile prefatory questions in the witness-box. Yet he saw by the intense excitement in her eyes that he had come to the point she feared, and yet desired to bring forward.

'And he loves you?'

She was silent.

'Well, then, if you love each other, what more can you want? Why do you say you have only your child in that absurd way?'

She was still silent, and he gave her a little shake.

'Tell me, have you and he had any difference lately? Is there any – coldness – any – temporary estrangement between you?'

He was hardly prepared for the burst of foolish laughter that proceeded from the demure Mrs Arne as she rose and confronted him, all the blood in her body seeming for the moment to rush to her usually pale cheeks.

'Coldness! Temporary estrangement! If that were all! Oh, is every one blind but me? There is all the world between us! – all the difference between this world and the next!'

She sat down again beside the doctor and whispered in his ear, and her words were like a breath of hot wind from some Gehenna of the soul.

'Oh, Doctor, I have borne it for six years, and I must speak. No other woman could bear what I have borne, and yet be alive! And I loved him so; you don't know how I loved him! That was it – that was my crime—'

'Crime?' repeated the doctor.

'Yes, crime! It was impious, don't you see? But I have been punished. Oh, Doctor, you don't know what my life is! Listen! Listen! I must tell you. To live with a— At first before I guessed when I used to put my arms round him, and he merely submitted – and then it dawned on me what I was kissing! It is enough to turn a living woman into stone – for I am living, though sometimes I forget it. Yes, I am a live woman, though I live in a grave. Think what it is! – to wonder every night if you will be alive in the morning, to lie down every night in an open grave – to smell death in every corner – every room – to breathe death – to touch it . . .'

The *portière* in front of the door shook, a hoopstick parted it, a round white clad bundle supported on a pair of mottled red legs peeped in, pushing a hoop in front of her. The child made no noise. Mrs Arne seemed to have heard her, however. She slewed round violently as she sat on the sofa beside Dr Graham, leaving her hot hands clasped in his.

'You ask Dolly,' she exclaimed. 'She knows it, too – she feels it.'

'No, no, Alice, this won't do!' the doctor adjured her very low. Then he raised his voice and ordered the child from the room. He had managed to lift Mrs Arne's feet and laid her full length on the sofa by the time the maid reappeared. She had fainted.

He pulled down her eyelids and satisfied himself as to certain facts he had up till now dimly apprehended. When Mrs Arne's maid returned, he gave her mistress over to her care and proceeded to Edward Arne's new study in the basement.

'Morphia!' he muttered to himself, as he stumbled and faltered through gaslit passages, where furtive servants eyed him and scuttled to their burrows.

'What is he burying himself down here for?' he thought. 'Is it to get out of her way? They *are* a nervous pair of them!'

Arne was sunk in a large arm-chair drawn up before the fire. There was no other light, except a faint reflection from the gas-lamp in the road, striking down past the iron bars of the window that was sunk below the level of the street. The room was comfortless and empty, there was little furniture in it except a large bookcase at Arne's right hand and a table with a Tantalus on it standing some way off. There was a faded portrait in pastel of Alice Arne over the mantelpiece, and beside it, a poor pendant, a pen and ink sketch of the master of the house. They were quite discrepant, in size and medium, but they appeared to look at each other with the stolid attentiveness of newly married people.

'Seedy, Arne?' Graham said.

'Rather, today. Poke the fire for me, will you?'

'I've known you quite seven years,' said the doctor cheerfully, 'so I presume I can do that . . . There, now! . . . And I'll presume further— What have we got here?'

He took a small bottle smartly out of Edward Arne's fingers and raised his eyebrows. Edward Arne had rendered it up agreeably; he did not seem upset or annoyed.

'Morphia. It isn't a habit. I only got hold of the stuff yesterday – found it about the house. Alice was very jumpy all day, and communicated her nerves to me, I suppose. I've none as a rule, but do you know, Graham, I seem to be getting them – feel things a good deal more than I did, and want to talk about them.'

'What, are you growing a soul?' said the doctor carelessly, lighting a cigarette.

'Heaven forbid!' Arne answered equably. 'I've done very well without it all these years. But I'm fond of old Alice, you know, in my own way. When I was a young man, I was quite different. I took things hardly and got excited about them. Yes, excited. I was wild about Alice, wild! Yes, by Jove! though she has forgotten all about it.'

'Not that, but still it's natural she should long for some little demonstration of affection now and then . . . and she'd be awfully distressed if she saw you fooling with a bottle of morphia! You know, Arne, after that narrow squeak you had of it six years ago, Alice and I have a good right to consider that your life belongs to us!'

Edward Arne settled in his chair and replied, rather fretfully –

'All very well, but you didn't manage to do the job thoroughly. You didn't turn me out lively enough to please Alice. She's annoyed because when I take her in my arms, I don't hold her tight enough. I'm too quiet, too languid! . . . Hang it all, Graham, I believe she'd like me to stand for Parliament! . . . Why can't she let me just go along my own way? Surely a man who's come through an illness like mine can be let off parlour tricks? All this worry – it culminated the other day when I said I wanted to colonise a room down here, and did, with a spurt that took it out of me horribly, – all this worry, I say, seeing her upset and so on, keeps me low, and so I feel as if I wanted to take drugs to soothe me.'

'Soothe!' said Graham. 'This stuff is more than soothing if you take enough of it. I'll send you something more like what you want, and I'll take this away, by your leave.'

'I really can't argue!' replied Arne . . . 'If you see Alice, tell her you find me fairly comfortable and don't put her off this room. I really like it best. She can come and see me here, I keep a good fire, tell her . . . I feel as if I wanted to sleep . . . ' he added brusquely.

'You have been indulging already,' said Graham softly. Arne had begun to doze off. His cushion had sagged down, the doctor stooped to rearrange it, carelessly laying the little phial for the moment in a crease of the rug covering the man's knees.

Mrs Arne in her mourning dress was crossing the hall as he came to the top of the basement steps and pushed open the swing door. She was giving some orders to Foster, the butler, who disappeared as the doctor advanced.

'You're about again,' he said, 'good girl!'

'Too silly of me,' she said, 'to be hysterical! After all these years! One should be able to keep one's own counsel. But it is over now, I promise I will never speak of it again.'

'We frightened poor Dolly dreadfully. I had to order her out like a regiment of soldiers.'

'Yes, I know. I'm going to her now.'

On his suggestion that she should look in on her husband first she looked askance.

'Down there!'

'Yes, that's his fancy. Let him be. He is a good deal depressed about himself and you. He notices a great deal more than you think. He isn't quite as apathetic as you describe him to be . . . Come here!' He led her into the unlit dining-room a little way. 'You expect too much, my dear. You do really! You make too many demands on the vitality you saved.'

'What did one save him for?' she asked fiercely. She continued more quietly, 'I know. I am going to be different.'

'Not you,' said Graham fondly. He was very partial to Alice Arne in spite of her silliness. 'You'll worry about Edward till the end of the chapter. I know you. And' – he turned her round by the shoulder so that she fronted the light in the hall – 'you elusive thing, let me have a good look at you . . . Hum! Your eyes, they're a bit starey . . .'

He let her go again with a sigh of impotence. Something must be done . . . soon . . . he must think . . . He got hold of his coat and began to get into it . . .

Mrs Arne smiled, buttoned a button for him and then opened the front door, like a good hostess, a very little way. With a quick flirt of his hat he was gone, and she heard the clap of his brougham door and the order 'Home'.

'Been saying good-bye to that thief Graham?' said her husband gently, when she entered his room, her pale eyes staring a little, her thin hand busy at the front of her dress . . .

'Thief? Why? One moment! Where's your switch?'

She found it and turned on a blaze of light from which her husband seemed to shrink.

'Well, he carried off my drops. Afraid of my poisoning myself, I suppose?'

'Or acquiring the morphia habit,' said his wife in a dull level voice, 'as I have.'

She paused. He made no comment. Then, picking up the little phial Dr Graham had left in the crease of the rug, she spoke –

'You are the thief, Edward, as it happens, this is mine.'

'Is it? I found it knocking about: I didn't know it was yours. Well, will you give me some?'

'I will, if you like.'

'Well, dear, decide. You know I am in your hands and Graham's. He was rubbing that into me today.'

'Poor lamb!' she said derisively; 'I'd not allow my doctor, or my wife either, to dictate to me whether I should put an end to myself, or not.'

'Ah, but you've got a spirit, you see!' Arne yawned. 'However, let me have a go at the stuff and then you put it on top of the wardrobe or a shelf, where I shall know it is, but never reach out to get it, I promise you.'

'No, you wouldn't reach out a hand to keep yourself alive, let alone kill yourself,' said she. 'That is you all over, Edward.'

'And don't you see that is why I did die,' he said, with earnestness unexpected by her. 'And then, unfortunately, you and Graham bustled up and wouldn't let Nature take its course . . . I rather wish you hadn't been so officious.'

'And let you stay dead,' said she carelessly. 'But at the time I cared for you so much that I should have had to kill myself, or commit suttee like a Bengali widow. Ah, well!'

She reached out for a glass half-full of water that stood on the low ledge of a bookcase close by the arm of his chair . . . 'Will this glass do? What's in it? Only water? How much morphia shall I give you? An overdose?'

'I don't care if you do, and that's a fact.'

'It was a joke, Edward,' she said piteously.

'No joke to me. This fag end of life I've clawed hold of, doesn't interest me. And I'm bound to be interested in what I'm doing or I'm no good. I'm no earthly good now. I don't enjoy life, I've nothing to enjoy it with – in here – ' he struck his breast. 'It's like a dull party one goes to by accident. All I want to do is to get into a cab and go home.'

His wife stood over him with the half-full glass in one hand and the little bottle in the other. Her eyes dilated . . . her chest heaved . . .

'Edward!' she breathed. 'Was it all so useless?'

'Was what useless? Yes, as I was telling you, I go as one in a dream – a bad, bad dream, like the dreams I used to have when I overworked at college. I was brilliant, Alice, brilliant, do you hear? At some cost, I expect! Now I hate people – my fellow creatures. I've left them. They come and go, jostling me, and pushing me, on the pavements as I go along, avoiding them. Do you know where they should be, really, in relation to me?'

He rose a little in his seat – she stepped nervously aside, made as if to put down the bottle and the glass she was holding, then thought better of it and continued to extend them mechanically.

'They should be over my head. I've already left them and their petty nonsense of living. They mean nothing to me, no more than if they were ghosts walking. Or perhaps, it's I who am a ghost to them? . . . You don't understand it. It's because I suppose you have no imagination. You just know what you want and do your best to get it. You blurt out your blessed petition to your Deity and the idea that you're irrelevant never enters your head, soft, persistent, High Church thing that you are! . . .'

Alice Arne smiled, and balanced the objects she was holding. He motioned her to pour out the liquid from one to the other, but she took no heed; she was listening with all her ears. It was the nearest approach to the language of compliment, to anything in the way of loverlike personalities that she had heard fall from his lips since his illness. He went on, becoming as it were lukewarm to his subject –

'But the worst of it is that once break the cord that links you to humanity – it can't be mended. Man doesn't live by bread alone . . . or lives to disappoint you. What am I to you, without my own poor personality? . . . Don't stare so, Alice! I haven't talked so much or so intimately for ages, have I? Let me try and have it out . . . Are you in any sort of hurry?'

'No, Edward.'

'Pour that stuff out and have done . . . Well, Alice, it's a queer feeling, I tell you. One goes about with one's looks on the ground, like a man who eyes the bed he is going to lie down in, and longs for. Alice, the crust of the earth seems a barrier between me and my own place. I want to scratch the boardings with my nails and shriek something like this: "Let me get down to you all, there where I belong!" It's a horrible sensation, like a vampire reversed! . . .'

'Is that why you insisted on having this room in the basement?' she asked breathlessly.

'Yes, I can't bear being upstairs, somehow. Here, with these barred windows and stone-cold floors . . . I can see the people's feet walking above there in the street . . . one has some sort of illusion . . .'

'Oh!' She shivered and her eyes travelled like those of a caged creature round the bare room and fluttered when they rested on the sombre windows imperiously barred. She dropped her gaze to the stone flags that showed beyond the oasis of Turkey carpet on which Arne's chair stood . . . Then to the door, the door that she had closed on entering. It had heavy bolts, but they were not drawn against her, though by the look of her eyes it seemed she half imagined they were . . .

She made a step forward and moved her hands slightly. She looked down on them and what they held . . . then changed the relative positions of the two objects and held the bottle over the glass . . .

'Yes, come along!' her husband said. 'Are you going to be all day giving it me?'

With a jerk, she poured the liquid out into a glass and handed it to him. She looked away – towards the door . . .

'Ah, your way of escape!' said he, following her eyes. Then he drank, painstakingly.

The empty bottle fell out of her hands. She wrung them, murmuring –

'Oh, if I had only known!'

'Known what? That I should go near to cursing you for bringing me back?'

He fixed his cold eyes on her, as the liquid passed slowly over his tongue . . .

' – Or that you would end by taking back the gift you gave?'

Mary Cholmondeley

LET LOOSE

The dead abide with us! Though stark and cold
Earth seems to grip them, they are with us still.

SOME years ago I took up architecture, and made a tour through Holland, studying the buildings of that interesting country. I was not then aware that it is not enough to take up art. Art must take you up, too. I never doubted but that my passing enthusiasm for her would be returned. When I discovered that she was a stern mistress, who did not immediately respond to my attentions, I naturally transferred them to another shrine. There are other things in the world besides art. I am now a landscape gardener.

But at the time of which I write I was engaged in a violent flirtation with architecture. I had one companion on this expedition, who has since become one of the leading architects of the day. He was a thin, determined-looking man with a screwed-up face and heavy jaw, slow of speech, and absorbed in his work to a degree which I quickly found tiresome. He was possessed of a certain quiet power of overcoming obstacles which I have rarely seen equalled. He has since become my brother-in-law, so I ought to know; for my parents did not like him much and opposed the marriage, and my sister did not like him at all, and refused him over and over again; but, nevertheless, he eventually married her.

I have thought since that one of his reasons for choosing me as his travelling companion on this occasion was because he was getting up steam for what he subsequently termed 'an alliance with my family', but the idea never entered my head at the time. A more careless man as to dress I have rarely met, and yet, in all the heat of July in Holland, I noticed that he never appeared without a high, starched collar, which had not even fashion to commend it at that time.

I often chaffed him about his splendid collars, and asked him why he wore them, but without eliciting any response. One evening, as we were walking back to our lodgings in Middeburg, I attacked him for about the thirtieth time on the subject.

'Why on earth do you wear them?' I said.

'You have, I believe, asked me that question many times,' he replied, in his slow, precise utterance; 'but always on occasions when I was occupied. I am now at leisure, and I will tell you.'

And he did.

I have put down what he said, as nearly in his own words as I can remember them.

Ten years ago, I was asked to read a paper on English Frescoes at the Institute of British Architects. I was determined to make the paper as good as I could, down to the slightest details, and I consulted many books on the subject, and studied every fresco I could find. My father, who had been an architect, had left me, at his death, all his papers and note-books on the subject of architecture. I searched them diligently, and found in one of them a slight unfinished sketch of nearly fifty years ago that specially interested me. Underneath was noted, in his clear, small hand – *Frescoed east wall of crypt. Parish Church. Wet Waste-on-the-Wolds, Yorkshire (via Pickering)*.

The sketch had such a fascination for me that I decided to go there and see the fresco for myself. I had only a very vague idea as to where Wet Waste-on-the-Wolds was, but I was ambitious for the success of my paper; it was hot in London, and I set off on my long journey not without a certain degree of pleasure, with my dog Brian, a large nondescript brindled creature, as my only companion.

I reached Pickering, in Yorkshire, in the course of the afternoon, and then began a series of experiments on local lines which ended, after several hours, in my finding myself deposited at a little out-of-the-world station within nine or ten miles of Wet Waste. As no conveyance of any kind was to be had, I shouldered my portmanteau, and set out on a long white road that stretched away into the distance over the bare, treeless wold. I must have walked for several hours, over a waste of moorland patched with heather, when a doctor passed me, and gave me a lift to within a mile of my destination. The mile was a long one, and it was quite dark by the time I saw the feeble glimmer of lights in front of me, and found that I had reached Wet Waste. I had considerable difficulty in getting any one to take me in; but at last I persuaded the owner of the public-house to give me a bed, and, quite tired out, I got into it as soon as possible, for fear he should change his mind, and fell asleep to the sound of a little stream below my window.

I was up early next morning, and inquired directly after breakfast the way to the clergyman's house, which I found was close at hand. At Wet Waste everything was close at hand. The whole village seemed composed of a straggling row of one-storeyed grey stone houses, the same colour as the stone walls that separated the few fields enclosed from the surrounding waste, and as the little bridges over the beck that ran down one side of the grey wide street. Everything was grey. The church, the low tower of which I could see at a little distance, seemed to have been built of the same stone; so was the parsonage when I came up to it, accompanied on my way by a mob of rough, uncouth children, who eyed me and Brian with half-defiant curiosity.

The clergyman was at home, and after a short delay I was admitted. Leaving Brian in charge of my drawing materials, I followed the servant into a low panelled room, in which, at a latticed window, a very old man was sitting. The morning light fell on his white head bent low over a litter of papers and books.

'Mr er – ?' he said, looking up slowly, with one finger keeping his place in a book.

'Blake.'

'Blake,' he repeated after me, and was silent.

I told him that I was an architect; that I had come to study a fresco in the crypt of his church, and asked for the keys.

'The crypt,' he said, pushing up his spectacles and peering hard at me. 'The crypt has been closed for thirty years. Ever since—' and he stopped short.

'I should be much obliged for the keys,' I said again.

He shook his head.

'No,' he said. 'No one goes in there now.'

'It is a pity,' I remarked, 'for I have come a long way with that one object'; and I told him about the paper I had been asked to read, and the trouble I was taking with it.

He became interested. 'Ah!' he said, laying down his pen, and removing his finger from the page before him, 'I can understand that. I also was young once, and fired with ambition. The lines have fallen to me in somewhat lonely places, and for forty years I have held the cure of souls in this place, where, truly, I have seen but little of the world, though I myself may be not unknown in the paths of literature. Possibly you may have read a pamphlet, written by myself, on the Syrian version of the Three Authentic Epistles of Ignatius?'

'Sir,' I said, 'I am ashamed to confess that I have not time to read even the most celebrated books. My one object in life is my art. *Ars longa, vita brevis*, you know.'

'You are right, my son,' said the old man, evidently disappointed, but looking at me kindly. 'There are diversities of gifts, and if the

Lord has entrusted you with a talent, look to it. Lay it not up in a napkin.'

I said I would not do so if he would lend me the keys of the crypt. He seemed startled by my recurrence to the subject and looked undecided.

'Why not?' he murmured to himself. 'The youth appears a good youth. And superstition! What is it but distrust in God!'

He got up slowly, and taking a large bunch of keys out of his pocket, opened with one of them an oak cupboard in the corner of the room.

'They should be here,' he muttered, peering in; 'but the dust of many years deceives the eye. See, my son, if among these parchments there be two keys; one of iron and very large, and the other steel, and of a long thin appearance.'

I went eagerly to help him, and presently found in a back drawer two keys tied together, which he recognised at once.

'Those are they,' he said. 'The long one opens the first door at the bottom of the steps which go down against the outside wall of the church hard by the sword graven in the wall. The second opens (but it is hard of opening and of shutting) the iron door within the passage leading to the crypt itself. My son, is it necessary to your treatise that you should enter this crypt?'

I replied that it was absolutely necessary.

'Then take them,' he said, 'and in the evening you will bring them to me again.'

I said I might want to go several days running, and asked if he would not allow me to keep them till I had finished my work; but on that point he was firm.

'Likewise,' he added, 'be careful that you lock the first door at the foot of the steps before you unlock the second, and lock the second also while you are within. Furthermore, when you come out lock the iron inner door as well as the wooden one.'

I promised I would do so, and, after thanking him, hurried away, delighted at my success in obtaining the keys. Finding Brian and my sketching materials waiting for me in the porch, I eluded the vigilance of my escort of children by taking the narrow private path between the parsonage and the church which was close at hand, standing in a quadrangle of ancient yews.

The church itself was interesting, and I noticed that it must have arisen out of the ruins of a previous building, judging from the number of fragments of stone caps and arches, bearing traces of very early carving, now built into the walls. There were incised crosses, too, in some places, and one especially caught my attention, being flanked by a large sword. It was in trying to get a nearer look at this that I stumbled, and, looking down, saw at my feet a flight of narrow stone steps green with moss and mildew. Evidently this was the entrance to the crypt. I at once descended the steps, taking care of my footing, for they were damp and slippery in the extreme. Brian accompanied me, as nothing would induce him to remain behind. By the time I had reached the bottom of the stairs, I found myself almost in darkness, and I had to strike a light before I could find the keyhole and the proper key to fit into it. The door, which was of wood, opened inwards fairly easily, although an accumulation of mould and rubbish on the ground outside showed it had not been used for many years. Having got through it, which was not altogether an easy matter, as nothing would induce it to open more than about eighteen inches, I carefully locked it behind me, although I should have preferred to leave it open, as there is to some minds an unpleasant feeling in being locked in anywhere, in case of a sudden exit seeming advisable.

I kept my candle alight with some difficulty, and after groping my way down a low and of course exceedingly dank passage, came to another door. A toad was squatting against it, who looked as if he had been sitting there about a hundred years. As I lowered the candle to the floor, he gazed at the light with unblinking eyes, and then retreated slowly into a crevice in the wall, leaving against the door a small cavity in the dry mud which had gradually silted up round his person. I noticed that this door was of iron, and had a long bolt, which, however, was broken. Without delay, I fitted the second key into the lock, and pushing the door open after considerable difficulty, I felt the cold breath of the crypt upon my face. I must own I experienced a momentary regret at locking the second door again as soon as I was well inside, but I felt it my duty to do so. Then, leaving the key in the lock, I seized my candle and looked round. I was standing in a low vaulted chamber with groined roof, cut out of the solid rock. It was difficult to see where the crypt ended, as further light thrown on any point only showed other rough archways or openings, cut in the rock, which had probably served at one time for family vaults. A peculiarity of the Wet Waste crypt, which I had not noticed in other places of that description, was the tasteful arrangement of skulls and bones which were packed about four feet high on either side. The skulls were symmetrically built up to within a few inches of the top of the low archway on my left, and the shin bones were arranged in the same manner on my right. *But the fresco!* I looked round for it in vain. Perceiving at the further end of the crypt a very low and very massive archway, the entrance to which was not filled up with bones, I passed under it, and found myself in a second smaller chamber. Holding my candle above my head, the first object its light fell upon was – the fresco, and at a glance I saw that it was unique. Setting down some of my things with a trembling hand on a rough stone shelf hard by, which had evidently been a credence table, I examined the work more closely. It was a reredos over what had probably been the altar at the time the priests were proscribed. The fresco belonged to the earliest part of the fifteenth century, and was so perfectly preserved that I could almost trace the limits of each day's work in the plaster, as the artist had dashed it on and smoothed it out with his trowel. The subject was the Ascension, gloriously treated. I can hardly describe my elation as I stood and looked at it, and reflected that this magnificent specimen of English fresco painting would be made known to the world by myself. Recollecting myself at last, I opened my sketching bag, and, lighting all the candles I had brought with me, set to work.

Brian walked about near me, and though I was not otherwise than glad of his company in my rather lonely position, I wished several times I had left him behind. He seemed restless, and even the sight of so many bones appeared to exercise no soothing effect upon him. At last, however, after repeated commands, he lay down, watchful but motionless, on the stone floor.

I must have worked for several hours, and I was pausing to rest my eyes and hands, when I noticed for the first time the intense stillness that surrounded me. No sound from *me* reached the outer world. The church clock which had clanged out so loud and ponderously as I went down the steps, had not since sent the faintest whisper of its iron tongue down to me below. All was silent as the grave. This *was* the grave. Those who had come here had indeed gone down into silence. I repeated the words to myself, or rather they repeated themselves to me.

Gone down into silence.

I was awakened from my reverie by a faint sound. I sat still and listened. Bats occasionally frequent vaults and underground places.

The sound continued, a faint, stealthy, rather unpleasant sound. I do not know what kinds of sounds bats make, whether pleasant or otherwise. Suddenly there was a noise as of something falling, a momentary pause – and then – an almost imperceptible but distant jangle as of a key.

I had left the key in the lock after I had turned it, and I now regretted having done so. I got up, took one of the candles, and went back into the larger crypt – for though I trust I am not so effeminate as to be rendered nervous by hearing a noise for which I cannot instantly account; still, on occasions of this kind, I must honestly say I should prefer that they did not occur. As I came towards the iron door, there was another distinct (I had almost said hurried) sound. The impression on my mind was one of great haste. When I reached the door, and held the candle near the lock to take out the key, I perceived that the other one, which hung by a short string to its fellow, was vibrating slightly. I should have preferred not to find it vibrating, as there seemed no occasion for such a course; but I put them both into my pocket, and turned to go back to my work. As I turned, I saw on the ground what had occasioned the louder noise I had heard, namely, a skull which had evidently just slipped from its place on the top of one of the walls of bones, and had rolled almost to my feet. There, disclosing a few more inches of the top of an archway behind, was the place from which it had been dislodged. I stooped to pick it up, but fearing to displace any more skulls by meddling with the pile, and not liking to gather up its scattered teeth, I let it lie, and went back to my work, in which I was soon so completely absorbed that I was only roused at last by my candles beginning to burn low and go out one after another.

Then, with a sigh of regret, for I had not nearly finished, I turned to go. Poor Brian, who had never quite reconciled himself to the place, was beside himself with delight. As I opened the iron door he pushed past me, and a moment later I heard him whining and scratching, and I had almost added, beating, against the wooden one. I locked the iron door, and hurried down the passage as quickly as I could, and almost before I had got the other one ajar there seemed to be a rush past me into the open air, and Brian was bounding up the steps and out of sight. As I stopped to take out the key, I felt quite deserted and left behind. When I came out once more into the sunlight, there was a vague sensation all about me in the air of exultant freedom.

It was already late in the afternoon, and after I had sauntered back to the parsonage to give up the keys, I persuaded the people of the public-house to let me join in the family meal, which was spread out in the kitchen. The inhabitants of Wet Waste were primitive people, with the frank, unabashed manner that flourishes still in lonely places, especially in the wilds of Yorkshire; but I had no idea that in these days of penny posts and cheap newspapers such entire ignorance of the outer world could have existed in any corner, however remote, of Great Britain.

When I took one of the neighbour's children on my knee – a pretty little girl with the palest aureole of flaxen hair I had ever seen – and began to draw pictures for her of the birds and beasts of other countries, I was instantly surrounded by a crowd of children, and even grown-up people, while others came to their doorways and looked on from a distance, calling to each other in the strident unknown tongue which I have since discovered goes by the name of 'Broad Yorkshire'.

The following morning, as I came out of my room, I perceived that something was amiss in the village. A buzz of voices reached me as I passed the bar, and in the next house I could hear through the open window a high-pitched wail of lamentation.

The woman who brought me my breakfast was in tears, and in answer to my questions, told me that the neighbour's child, the little girl whom I had taken on my knee the evening before, had died in the night.

I felt sorry for the general grief that the little creature's death seemed to arouse, and the uncontrolled wailing of the poor mother took my appetite away.

I hurried off early to my work, calling on my way for the keys, and with Brian for my companion descended once more into the crypt, and drew and measured with an absorption that gave me no time that day to listen for sounds real or fancied. Brian, too, on this occasion seemed quite content, and slept peacefully beside me on the stone floor. When I had worked as long as I could, I put away my books with regret that even then I had not quite finished, as I had hoped to do. It would be necessary to come again for a short time on the morrow. When I returned the keys late that afternoon, the old clergyman met me at the door, and asked me to come in and have tea with him.

'And has the work prospered?' he asked, as we sat down in the long, low room, into which I had just been ushered, and where he seemed to live entirely.

I told him it had, and showed it to him.

'You have seen the original, of course?' I said.

'Once,' he replied, gazing fixedly at it. He evidently did not care to be communicative, so I turned the conversation to the age of the church.

'All here is old,' he said. 'When I was young, forty years ago, and came here because I had no means of mine own, and was much moved to marry at that time, I felt oppressed that all was so old; and that this place was so far removed from the world, for which I had at times longings grievous to be borne; but I had chosen my lot, and with it I was forced to be content. My son, marry not in youth, for love, which truly in that season is a mighty power, turns away the heart from study, and young children break the back of ambition. Neither marry in middle life, when a woman is seen to be but a woman and her talk a weariness, so you will not be burdened with a wife in your old age.'

I had my own views on the subject of marriage, for I am of opinion that a well-chosen companion of domestic tastes and docile and devoted temperament may be of material assistance to a professional man. But, my opinons once formulated, it is not of moment to me to discuss them with others, so I changed the subject, and asked if the neighbouring villages were as antiquated as Wet Waste.

'Yes, all about here is old,' he repeated. 'The paved road leading to Dyke Fens is an ancient pack road, made even in the time of the Romans. Dyke Fens, which is very near here, a matter of but four or five miles, is likewise old, and forgotten by the world. The Reformation never reached it. It stopped here. And at Dyke Fens they still have a priest and a bell, and bow down before the saints. It is a damnable heresy, and weekly I expound it as such to my people, showing them true doctrines; and I have heard that this same priest has so far yielded himself to the Evil One that he has preached against me as withholding gospel truths from my flock; but I take no heed of it, neither of his pamphlet touching the Clementine Homilies, in which he vainly contradicts that which I have plainly set forth and proven beyond doubt, concerning the word *Asaph*.'

The old man was fairly off on his favourite subject, and it was some time before I could get away. As it was, he followed me to the door, and I only escaped because the old clerk hobbled up at that moment, and claimed his attention.

The following morning I went for the keys for the third and last time. I had decided to leave early the next day. I was tired of Wet Waste, and a certain gloom seemed to my fancy to be gathering over the place. There was a sensation of trouble in the air, as if, although the day was bright and clear, a storm were coming.

This morning, to my astonishment, the keys were refused to me when I asked for them. I did not, however, take the refusal as final – I make it a rule never to take a refusal as final – and after a short delay I was shown into the room where, as usual, the clergyman was sitting, or rather, on this occasion, was walking up and down.

'My son,' he said with vehemence, 'I know wherefore you have come, but it is of no avail. I cannot lend the keys again.'

I replied that, on the contrary, I hoped he would give them to me at once.

'It is impossible,' he repeated. 'I did wrong, exceeding wrong. I will never part with them again.'

'Why not?'

He hesitated, and then said slowly:

'The old clerk, Abraham Kelly, died last night.' He paused, and then went on: 'The doctor has just been here to tell me of that which is a mystery to him. I do not wish the people of the place to know it, and only to me he has mentioned it, but he has discovered plainly on the throat of the old man, and also, but more faintly on the child's, marks as of strangulation. None but he has observed it, and he is at a loss how to account for it. I, alas! can account for it but in one way, but in one way!'

I did not see what all this had to do with the crypt, but to humour the old man, I asked what that way was.

'It is a long story, and, haply, to a stranger it may appear but foolishness, but I will even tell it; for I perceive that unless I furnish a reason for withholding the keys, you will not cease to entreat me for them.

'I told you at first when you inquired of me concerning the crypt, that it had been closed these thirty years, and so it was. Thirty years ago a certain Sir Roger Despard departed this life, even the Lord of the manor of Wet Waste and Dyke Fens, the last of his family, which is now, thank the Lord, extinct. He was a man of a vile life, neither fearing God nor regarding man, nor having compassion on innocence, and the Lord appeared to have given him over to the tormentors even in this world, for he suffered many things of his vices, more especially from drunkenness, in which seasons, and they were many, he was as one possessed by seven devils, being an abomination to his household and a root of bitterness to all, both high and low.

'And, at last, the cup of his iniquity being full to the brim, he came to die, and I went to exhort him on his death-bed; for I heard that terror had come upon him, and that evil imaginations encompassed him so thick on every side, that few of them that were with him could abide in his presence. But when I saw him I perceived that there was no place of repentance left for him, and he scoffed at me and my superstition, even as he lay dying, and swore there was no God and no angel, and all were damned even as he was. And the next day, towards evening, the pains of death came upon him, and he raved the more exceedingly, inasmuch as he said he was being strangled by the Evil One. Now on his table was his hunting knife, and with his last strength he crept and laid hold upon it, no man withstanding him, and swore a great oath that if he went down to burn in hell, he would leave one of his hands behind on earth, and that it would never rest until it had drawn blood from the throat of another and strangled him, even as he himself was being strangled. And he cut off his own right hand at the wrist, and no man dared go near him to stop him, and the blood went through the floor, even down to the ceiling of the room below, and thereupon he died.

'And they called me in the night, and told me of his oath, and I counselled that no man should speak of it, and I took the dead hand, which none had ventured to touch, and I laid it beside him in his coffin; for I thought it better he should take it with him, so that he might have it, if haply some day after much tribulation he should perchance be moved to stretch forth his hands towards God. But the story got spread about, and the people were affrighted, so, when he came to be buried in the place of his fathers, he being the last of his family, and the crypt likewise full, I had it closed, and kept the keys myself, and suffered no man to enter therein any more; for truly he was a man of an evil life, and the devil is not yet wholly overcome, nor cast chained into the lake of fire. So in time the story died out, for in thirty years much is forgotten. And when you came and asked me for the keys, I was at the first minded to withhold them; but I thought it was a vain superstition, and I perceived that you do but ask a second time for what is first refused; so I let you have them, seeing it was not an idle curiosity, but a desire to improve the talent committed to you, that led you to require them.'

The old man stopped, and I remained silent, wondering what would be the best way to get them just once more.

'Surely, sir,' I said at last, 'one so cultivated and deeply read as yourself cannot be biased by an idle superstition.'

'I trust not,' he replied, 'and yet – it is a strange thing that since the crypt was opened two people have died, and the mark is plain upon the throat of the old man and visible on the young child. No blood was drawn, but the second time the grip was stronger than the first. The third time, perchance—'

'Superstition such as that,' I said with authority, 'is an entire want of faith in God. You once said so yourself.'

I took a high moral tone which is often efficacious with conscientious, humble-minded people.

He agreed, and accused himself of not having faith as a grain of mustard seed; but even when I had got him so far as that, I had a severe struggle for the keys. It was only when I finally explained to him that if any malign influence *had* been let loose the first day, at any rate, it was out now for good or evil, and no further going or coming of mine could make any difference, that I finally gained my point. I was young, and he was old; and, being much shaken by what had occurred, he gave way at last, and I wrested the keys from him.

I will not deny that I went down the steps that day with a vague, indefinable repugnance, which was only accentuated by the closing of the two doors behind me. I remembered then, for the first time, the faint jangling of the key and other sounds which I had noticed the first day, and how one of the skulls had fallen. I went to the place where it still lay. I have already said these walls of skulls were built up so high as to be within a few inches of the top of the low archways that led into more distant portions of the vault. The displacement of the skull in question had left a small hole just large enough for me to put my hand through. I noticed for the first time, over the archway above it, a carved coat-of-arms, and the name, now almost obliterated, of Despard. This, no doubt, was the Despard vault. I could not resist moving a few more skulls and looking in, holding my candle as near the aperture as I could. The vault was full. Piled high, one upon another, were old coffins, and remnants of coffins, and strewn bones. I attribute my present determination to be cremated to the painful impression produced on me by this spectacle. The coffin nearest the archway alone was intact, save for a large crack across the lid. I could not get a ray from my candle to fall on the brass plates, but I felt no doubt this was the coffin of the wicked Sir Roger. I put back the skulls, including the one which had rolled down, and carefully finished my work. I was not there much more than an hour, but I was glad to get away.

If I could have left Wet Waste at once I should have done so, for I had a totally unreasonable longing to leave the place; but I found that only one train stopped during the day at the station from which I had come, and that it would not be possible to be in time for it that day.

Accordingly I submitted to the inevitable, and wandered about with Brian for the remainder of the afternoon and until late in the evening, sketching and smoking. The day was oppressively hot, and even after the sun had set across the burnt stretches of the wolds, it seemed to grow very little cooler. Not a breath stirred. In the evening, when I was tired of loitering in the lanes, I went up to my own room, and after contemplating afresh my finished study of the fresco, I suddenly set to work to write the part of my paper bearing upon it. As a rule, I write with difficulty, but that evening words came to me with winged speed, and with them a hovering impression that I must make haste, that I was much pressed for time. I wrote and wrote, until my candles guttered out and left me trying to finish by the moonlight, which, until I endeavoured to write by it, seemed as clear as day.

I had to put away my MS., and, feeling it was too early to go to bed, for the church clock was just counting out ten, I sat down by the open window and leaned out to try and catch a breath of air. It was a night of exceptional beauty; and as I looked out my nervous haste and hurry of mind were allayed. The moon, a perfect circle, was – if so poetic an expression be permissible – as it were, sailing across a calm sky. Every detail of the little village was as clearly illuminated by its beams as if it were broad day; so, also, was the adjacent church with its primeval yews, while even the wolds beyond were dimly indicated, as if through tracing paper.

I sat a long time leaning against the window-sill. The heat was still intense. I am not, as a rule, easily elated or readily cast down; but as I sat that night in the lonely village on the moors, with Brian's head against my knee, how, or why, I know not, a great depression gradually came upon me.

My mind went back to the crypt and the countless dead who had been laid there. The sight of the goal to which all human life, and strength, and beauty, travel in the end, had not affected me at the time, but now the very air about me seemed heavy with death.

What was the good, I asked myself, of working and toiling, and grinding down my heart and youth in the mill of long and strenuous effort, seeing that in the grave folly and talent, idleness and labour lie together, and are alike forgotten? Labour seemed to stretch before me till my heart ached to think of it, to stretch before me even to the end of life, and then came, as the recompense of my labour – the grave. Even if I succeeded, if, after wearing my life threadbare with toil, I succeeded, what remained to me in the end? The grave. A little sooner, while the hands and eyes were still strong to labour, or a little later, when all power and vision had been taken from them; sooner or later only – *the grave*.

I do not apologise for the excessively morbid tenor of these reflections, as I hold that they were caused by the lunar effects which I have endeavoured to transcribe. The moon in its various quarterings has always exerted a marked influence on what I may call the sub-dominant, namely, the poetic side of my nature.

I roused myself at last, when the moon came to look in upon me where I sat, and, leaving the window open, I pulled myself together and went to bed.

I fell asleep almost immediately, but I do not fancy I could have been asleep very long when I was wakened by Brian. He was growling in a low, muffled tone, as he sometimes did in his sleep, when his nose was buried in his rug. I called out to him to shut up; and as he did not do so, turned in bed to find my match box or something to throw at him. The moonlight was still in the room, and as I looked at him I saw him raise his head and evidently wake up. I admonished him, and was just on the point of falling asleep when he began to growl again in a low, savage manner that waked me most effectually. Presently he shook himself and got up, and began prowling about the room. I sat up in bed and called to him, but he paid no attention. Suddenly I saw him stop short in the moonlight; he showed his teeth, and crouched down, his eyes following something in the air. I looked at him in horror. Was he going mad? His eyes were glaring, and his head moved slightly as if he were following the rapid movements of an enemy. Then, with a furious snarl, he suddenly sprang from the ground, and rushed in great leaps across the room towards me, dashing himself against the furniture, his eyes rolling, snatching and tearing wildly in the air with his teeth. I saw he had gone mad. I leaped out of bed, and rushing at him, caught him by the throat. The moon had gone behind a cloud; but in the darkness I felt him turn upon me, felt him rise up, and his teeth close in my throat. I was being strangled. With all the strength of despair, I kept my grip of his neck, and, dragging him across the room, tried to crush in his head against the iron rail of my bedstead. It was my only chance. I felt the blood running down my neck. I was suffocating. After one moment of frightful struggle, I beat his head against the bar and heard his skull give way. I felt him give one strong shudder, a groan, and then I fainted away.

When I came to myself I was lying on the floor, surrounded by the people of the house, my reddened hands still clutching Brian's throat. Someone was holding a candle towards me, and the draught from the window made it flare and waver. I looked at Brian. He was stone dead. The blood from his battered head was trickling slowly over my hands. His great jaw was fixed in something that – in the uncertain light – I could not see.

They turned the light a little.

'Oh, God!' I shrieked. 'There! Look! Look!'

'He's off his head,' said some one, and I fainted again.

I was ill for about a fortnight without regaining consciousness, a waste of time of which even now I cannot think without poignant regret. When I did recover consciousness, I found I was being carefully nursed by the old clergyman and the people of the house. I have often heard the unkindness of the world in general inveighed against, but for my part I can honestly say that I have received many more kindnesses than I have time to repay. Country people especially are remarkably attentive to strangers in illness.

I could not rest until I had seen the doctor who attended me, and had received his assurance that I should be equal to reading my paper on the appointed day. This pressing anxiety removed, I told him of what I had seen before I fainted the second time. He listened attentively, and then assured me, in a manner that was intended to be soothing, that I was suffering from an hallucination, due, no doubt, to the shock of my dog's sudden madness.

'Did you see the dog after it was dead?' I asked.

He said he did. The whole jaw was covered with blood and foam; the teeth certainly seemed convulsively fixed, but the case being evidently one of extraordinarily virulent hydrophobia, owing to the intense heat, he had had the body buried immediately.

My companion stopped speaking as we reached our lodgings, and went upstairs. Then, lighting a candle, he slowly turned down his collar.

'You see I have the marks still,' he said, 'but I have no fear of dying of hydrophobia. I am told such peculiar scars could not have been made by the teeth of a dog. If you look closely you see the pressure of the five fingers. That is the reason why I wear high collars.'

Ella D'Arcy

THE VILLA LUCIENNE

MADAME Koetlegon told the story, and told it so well that her audience seemed to know the sombre alley, the neglected garden, the shuttered house, as intimately as though they had visited it themselves, seemed to feel a faint reverberation of the incommunicable thrill which she had felt – which the surly guardian, the torn rag of lace, the closed pavilion had made her feel. And yet, as you will see, there is in reality no story at all; it is merely an account of how, when in the Riviera two winters ago, she went with some friends to look over a furnished villa, which one of them thought of taking.

It was afternoon when we started on our expedition, Madame de M—, Cécile her widowed daughter-in-law, and I. Cécile's little girl Renée, the nurse, and Médor, the boarhound of which poor Guy had been so inordinately fond, dawdled after us up the steep and sunny road.

The December day was deliciously blue and warm. Cécile took off her furs and carried them over her arm. We only put down our sunshades when a screen of olive-trees on the left interposed their grey-green foliage between us and the sunshine.

Up in these trees barefooted men armed with bamboos were beating the branches to knock down the fruit; and three generations of women, grandmothers, wives, and children, knelt in the grass, gathering up the little purplish olives into baskets. All these paused to follow us with black persistent eyes, as we passed by; but the men went on working, unmoved. The tap-tapping, swish-swishing, of their light sticks against the boughs played a characteristically southern accompaniment to our desultory talk.

We were reasonably happy, pleasantly exhilarated by the beauty of the weather and the scene. Renée and Médor, with shrill laughter and deep-mouthed joy-notes, played together the whole way. And when the garden wall, which now replaced the olive-trees upon our right, gave place to a couple of iron gates standing open upon a broad straight drive, and we, looking up between the overarching palm-trees and cocoanuts, saw a white, elegant, sun-bathed house at the end, Cécile jumped to the conclusion that here was the Villa Lucienne, and that nowhere else could she find a house which on the face of it would suit her better.

But the woman who came to greet us, the jocund, brown-faced young woman, with the superb abundance of bosom beneath her crossed neckerchief of orange-coloured wool, told us no; this was the Villa Soleil (appropriate name!) and belonged to Monsieur Morgera, the deputy, who was now in Paris. The Villa Lucienne was higher up; she pointed vaguely behind her through the house; a long walk round by the road. But if these ladies did not mind a path which was a trifle damp perhaps, owing to Monday's rain, they would find themselves in five minutes at the Villa, for the two houses in reality were not more than a stone's throw apart.

She conducted us across a spacious garden golden with sunshine, lyric with bird-song, brilliant with flowers, where eucalyptus, mimosa, and tea-roses interwove their strong and subtle perfumes through the air, to an angle in a remote laurel hedge. Here she stooped to pull aside some ancient pine-boughs which ineffectually closed the entrance to a dark and trellised walk. Peering up at it, it seemed to stretch away interminably into green gloom, the ground rising a little all the while, and the steepness of the ascent being modified every here and there by a couple of rotting wooden steps.

We were to go up this alley, our guide told us, and we would be sure to find Laurent at the top. Laurent, she explained to us, was the gardener who lived at the Villa Lucienne and showed it to visitors. But there were not many who came, although it had been to let an immense time, ever since the death of old Madame Gray, and that had occurred before she, the speaker, had come south with the Morgeras. We were to explain to Laurent that we had been sent up from the Villa Soleil, and then it would be all right. For he sometimes used the alley himself, as it gave him a short cut into Antibes; but the passage had been blocked up many years ago, to prevent the Morgera children running into it.

Oh, Madame was very kind, it was no trouble at all, and of course if these ladies liked they could return by the alley also; but once they found themselves at the Villa they would be close to the upper road, which they would probably prefer. Then came her cordial voice calling after Cécile, 'Madame had best put on her furs again, it is cold in there.'

It was cold and damp too, with the damp coldness of places where sun and wind never penetrate. It was so narrow that we had to walk in single file. The walls on either hand, the low roof above our heads, were formed of trellised woodwork dropping into complete decay. But roof and walls might have been removed altogether, and the tunnel nevertheless would still have retained its shape; for the creepers which overgrew it had with time developed gnarled trunks and branches, which formed a second natural tunnelling outside. Through the broken places in the woodwork we could see the thick, inextricably twisted stems; and beyond again was a tangled matting of greenery, that suffered no drop of sunlight to trickle through. The ground was covered with lichens, deathstools, and a spongy moss exuding water beneath the foot, and one had the consciousness that the whole place, floor, walls, and roof, must creep with the repulsive, slimy, running life, which pullulates in dark and solitary places.

The change from the gay and scented garden to this dull alley, heavy with the smells of moisture and decay, was curiously depressing. We followed each other in silence; first Cécile; then Renée clinging to her nurse's hand, with Médor pressing close against them; Madame de M— next; and I brought up the rear.

You would have pronounced it impossible to find in any southern garden so sombre a place, but that, after all, it is only in the south that such extraordinary contrasts of gaiety and gloom ever present themselves.

The sudden tearing away of a portion of one of the wooden steps beneath my tread startled us all, and the circular scatter of an immense colony of woodlice that had formed its habitat in the crevices of the wood, filled me with shivering disgust. I was exceedingly glad when we emerged from the tunnel upon daylight again and the Villa.

Upon daylight, but not upon sunlight, for the small garden in which we found ourselves was ringed round by the compact tops of the umbrella-pines which climbed the hill on every side. The site had been chosen, of course, on account of the magnificent view which we knew must be obtainable from the Villa windows, though from where we stood we could see nothing but the dark trees, the wild garden, the overshadowed house. And we saw none of these things very distinctly, for our attention was focussed on a man standing there in the middle of the garden, knee-deep in the grass, evidently awaiting us.

He was a short, thick-set peasant, dressed in the immensely wide blue velveteen trousers, the broad crimson sash, and the flannel shirt, open at the throat, which are customary in these parts. He was strong-necked as a bull, dark as a mulatto, and his curling, grizzled hair was thickly matted over his head and face and breast. He wore a flat knitted cap, and held the inevitable cigarette between his lips, but he made no attempt to remove one or the other at our approach. He stood stolid, silent, his hands thrust deep into his pockets, staring at us, and shifting from one to another his suspicious and truculent little eyes.

So far as I was concerned, and though the Villa had proved a palace, I should have preferred abandoning the quest at once to going over it in his company; but Cécile addressed him with intrepid politeness.

'We had been permitted to come up from the Villa Soleil. We understood that the Villa Lucienne was to let furnished; if so, might we look over it?'

From his heavy, expressionless expression, one might have supposed that the very last thing he expected or desired was to find a tenant for the Villa, and I thought with relief that he was going to refuse Cécile's request. But, after a longish pause:

'Yes, you can see it,' he said, grudgingly, and turned from us, to disappear into the lower part of the house.

We looked into each other's disconcerted faces, then round the grey and shadowy garden: a garden long since gone to ruin, with paths and flower-beds inextricably mingled, with docks and nettles choking up the rose-trees run wild, with wind-planted weeds growing from the stone vases on the terrace, with grasses pushing between the marble steps leading up to the hall door.

In the middle of the lawn a terra-cotta faun, tumbled from his pedestal, grinned sardonically up from amidst the tangled greenery, and Madame de M— began to quote:

> 'Un vieux faune en terre-cuite
> Rit au centre des boulingrins,
> Présageant sans doute une fuite
> De ces instants sereins
> Qui m'ont conduit et t'ont conduit . . .'

The Villa itself was as dilapidated, as mournful-looking as the garden. The ground-floor alone gave signs of occupation, in a checked shirt spread out upon a window-ledge to dry, in a worn besom, an earthenware pipkin, and a pewter jug, ranged against the wall. But the upper part, with the yellow plaster crumbling from the walls, the grey painted persiennes all monotonously closed, said with a thousand voices it was never opened, never entered, had not been lived in for years.

Our surly gardener reappeared, carrying some keys. He led the way up the steps. We exchanged mute questions; all desire to inspect the Villa was gone. But Cécile is a woman of character: she devoted herself.

'I'll just run up and see what it is like,' she said; 'it's not worth while you should tire yourself too, Mamma. You, all, wait here.'

We stood at the foot of the steps; Laurent was already at the top. Cécile began to mount lightly towards him, but before she was half-way she turned, and to our surprise, 'I wish you would come up, all of you,' she said, and stopped there until we joined her.

Laurent fitted a key to the door, and it opened with a shriek of rusty hinges. As he followed us, pulling it to behind him, we found ourselves in total darkness. I assure you I went through a bad quarter of a minute. Then we heard the turning of a handle, an inner door was opened, and in the semi-daylight of closed shutters we saw the man's squat figure going from us down a long, old-fashioned, vacant drawing-room towards two windows at the further end.

At the same instant Renée burst into tears:

'Oh, I don't like it. Oh, I'm frightened!' she sobbed.

'Little goosie!' said her grandmother, 'see, it's quite light now!' for Laurent had pushed back the persiennes, and a magical panorama had sprung into view: the whole range of the mountains behind Nice, their snow-caps suffused with a heavenly rose colour by the setting sun.

But Renée only clutched tighter at Madame de M—'s gown, and wept:

'Oh, I don't like it, Bonnemaman! She is looking at me still. I want to go home!'

'No one is looking at you,' her grandmother told her: 'talk to your friend Médor. He'll take care of you.'

But Renée whispered:

'He wouldn't come in; he's frightened too.'

And, listening, we heard the dog's impatient and complaining bark calling to us from the garden.

Cécile sent Renée and the nurse to join him, and while Laurent let them out, we stepped on to the terrace, and for a moment our hearts were eased by the incomparable beauty of the view, for, raised now above the tree-tops, we looked over the admirable bay, the illimitable sky; we feasted our eyes upon unimaginable colour, upon matchless form. We were almost prepared to declare that the possession of the Villa was a piece of good fortune not to be let slip, when we heard a step behind us, and turned to see Laurent surveying us morosely from the window threshold, and again to experience the oppression of his ungenial personality.

Under his guidance we now inspected the century-old furniture, the faded silks, the tarnished gilt, the ragged brocades which had once embellished the room. The oval mirrors were dim with mildew, the parquet floor might have been a mere piece of grey drugget, so thick was the overlying dust. Curtains, yellowish, ropey, of undeterminable material, hung forlornly where once they had draped windows and doors. Originally they may have been of rose satin, for there were traces of rose colour still on the walls and the ceiling, painted in gay southern fashion with loves and doves, festoons of flowers, and knots of ribbons. But these paintings were all fragmentary, indistinct, seeming to lose sequence and outline the more diligently you tried to decipher them.

Yet you could not fail to see that when first furnished the room must have been charming and coquettish. I wondered for whom it had been thus arranged, why it had been thus abandoned. For there grew upon me, I cannot tell you why, the curious conviction that the last inhabitant of the room having casually left it, had, from some unexpected obstacle, never again returned. They were but the merest trifles that created this idea: the tiny heap of brown ash which lay on a marble guéridon, the few withered twigs in the vase beside it, speaking of the last rose plucked from the garden; the big berceuse chair drawn out beside the sculptured mantelpiece which seemed to retain the impression of the last occupant; and in the dark recesses of the unclosed hearth the smouldering heat which my fancy detected in the half-charred logs of wood.

The other rooms in the Villa resembled the *salon*; each time our surly guide opened the shutters we saw a repetition of the ancient furniture, of the faded decoration; everything dust-covered and time-decayed. Nor in these other rooms was any sign of former occupation to be seen, until, caught upon the girandole of a pier-glass, a long ragged fragment of lace took my eye; an exquisitely fine and cobwebby piece of lace, as though caught and torn from some gala shawl or flounce, as the wearer had hurried by.

It was odd perhaps to see this piece of lace caught thus, but not odd enough surely to account for the strange emotion which seized hold of me: an overwhelming pity, succeeded by an overwhelming fear. I had had a momentary intention to point the lace out to the others, but a glance at Laurent froze the words on my lips. Never in my life have I experienced such a paralysing fear. I was filled with an intense desire to get away from the man and from the Villa.

But Madade de M—, looking from the window, had noticed a pavilion standing isolated in the garden. She inquired if it were to be let with the house. He gave a surly assent. Then she supposed we could visit it. No, said the man, that was impossible. Cécile pointed out it was only right that tenants should see the whole of the premises for which they would have to pay, but he refused this time with so much rudeness, his little brutish eyes narrowed with so much malignancy, that the panic which I had just experienced now seized the others, and it was a *sauve-qui-peut*.

We gathered up Renée, nurse, and Médor in our hasty passage through the garden, and found our way unguided to the gate upon the upper road.

At once at large beneath the serene evening sky, winding slowly westward down the olive-bordered ways: 'What an odious old ruffian!' said one; 'What an eerie, uncanny place!' said another. We compared notes. We found that each of us had been conscious of the same immense, the same inexplicable sense of fear.

Cécile, the least nervous of women, had felt it the first. It had laid hold of her when going up the steps to the door, and it had been so real a terror, she explained to us, that if we had not joined her she would have turned back. Nothing could have induced her to enter the Villa alone.

Madame de M—'s account was that her mind had been more or less troubled from the first moment of entering the garden, but that when the man refused us access to the pavilion, it had been suddenly invaded by a most intolerable sense of wrong. Being very imaginative (poor Guy undoubtedly derived his extraordinary gifts from her), Madame de M— was convinced that the gardener had murdered some one and buried the body inside the pavilion.

But for me it was not so much the personality of the man – although I admitted he was unprepossessing enough – as the Villa itself which inspired fear. Fear seemed to exude from the walls, to dim the mirrors with its clammy breath, to stir shudderingly among the tattered draperies, to impregnate the whole atmosphere as with an essence, a gas, a contagious disease. You fought it off for a shorter or longer time, according to your powers of resistance, but you were bound to succumb to it at last. The oppressive and invisible fumes had laid hold of us one after the other, and the incident of the closed pavilion had raised our terrors to a ludicrous pitch.

Nurse's experiences, which she gave us a day or two later, supported this view. For she told us that when Renée began to cry, and she took her hand to lead her out, all at once she felt quite nervous and uncomfortable too, as though the little one's trouble had passed by touch into her.

'And what is very strange,' said she, 'when we reached the garden, there was Médor, his forepaws planted firmly on the ground, his whole body rigid, and his hair bristling all along his backbone from end to end.'

Nurse was convinced that both the child and the dog had seen something which we others could not see.

This reminded us of a word of Renée's, a very curious word:

'I don't like it, *she* is looking at me still,' – and Cécile undertook to question her.

'You remember, Renée, when mother took you the other day to look over the pretty Villa—'

Renée opened wide apprehensive eyes.

'Why did you cry?'

'I was frightened at the lady,' she whispered.

'The lady . . . where was the lady?' Cécile asked her.

'She was in the drawing-room, sitting in the big chair.'

'Was she an old lady like grandmamma, or a young lady like mother?'

'She was like Bonnemaman,' said Renée, and her little mouth began to quiver.

'And what did she do?'

'She got up and began to – to come—'

But here Renée again burst into tears. And as she is a very nervous, a very excitable child, we had to drop the subject.

But what it all meant, whether there was anything in the history of the house or of its guardian which could account for our sensations, we never knew. We made inquiries, of course, concerning Laurent and the Villa Lucienne, but we learned very little, and that little was so vague, so remote, so irrelevant, that it does not seem worth while repeating.

The indisputable fact is the overwhelming fear which the adventure awoke in each and all of us; and this effect is impossible to describe, being just the crystallisation of one of those subtle, unformulated emotions in which only poor Guy himself could have hoped to succeed.

Gertrude Atherton

THE STRIDING PLACE

GERTRUDE Atherton was inspired to write this story during her tour of the Yorkshire Dales in the early 1890s. In her autobiography she writes:

'I made it a practice wherever I went to read the local chronicle, and that of this district was particularly interesting because of the famous river Wharfe, a narrow turbulent stream with a dark history. It roared along through the woods between high and gloomy banks, and at one point was so narrow that an active man could leap across; but a slip meant death. "The Striding Place" was immediately in front of a ledge in midstream beneath which was a suction so powerful that no man who fell in could escape it. He disappeared under the ledge with the speed of light, to be flung out later, mangled and unrecognisable, into the boiling waters beyond.

> "This striding place is called the Strid;
>   A name which it took of yore.
> A thousand years hath it borne that name,
>   And it shall a thousand more."

Wordsworth had been inspired to write a poem on "The Boy of Egremond", a venturesome heir of these ancestral acres who had been done to death in the Strid, and I read it in the local history.

I haunted that spot, fascinated, and consumed with a desire to write a gruesome story of the Strid, but could think of nothing. I anathematised my imagination, which, it seemed to me, should have been jarred into immediate action. One night I determined to try an experiment. Just before dropping off to sleep I ordered my mind to conceive that story and have it formulated when I awoke. And the moment I opened my eyes, there it was. I wrote it out before leaving the bed. It was called "The Striding Place", and eventually published in the London Speaker. I sent it first to the Yellow Book, but it was declined by the editor (Henry Harland) on the ground that it was "far too gruesome". It seems to me the best short story I ever wrote, and it was even more of a triumph to appear in the Speaker.'

THE STRIDING PLACE

WEIGALL, continental and detached, tired early of grouse-shooting. To stand propped against a sod fence while his host's workmen routed up the birds with long poles and drove them towards the waiting guns, made him feel himself a parody on the ancestors who had roamed the moors and forests of this West Riding of Yorkshire in hot pursuit of game worth the killing. But when in England in August he always accepted whatever proffered for the season, and invited his host to shoot pheasants on his estates in the South. The amusements of life, he argued, should be accepted with the same philosophy as its ills.

It had been a bad day. A heavy rain had made the moor so spongy that it fairly sprang beneath the feet. Whether or not the grouse had haunts of their own, wherein they were immune from rheumatism, the bag had been small. The women, too, were an unusually dull lot, with the exception of a new-minded *débutante* who bothered Weigall at dinner by demanding the verbal restoration of the vague paintings on the vaulted roof above them.

But it was no one of these things that sat on Weigall's mind as, when the other men went up to bed, he let himself out of the castle and sauntered down to the river. His intimate friend, the companion of his boyhood, the chum of his college days, his fellow-traveller in many lands, the man for whom he possessed stronger affection than for all men, had mysteriously disappeared two days ago, and his track might have sprung to the upper air for all trace he had left behind him. He had been a guest on the adjoining estate during the past week, shooting with the fervour of the true sportsman, making love in the intervals to Adeline Cavan, and apparently in the best of spirits. As far as was known, there was nothing to lower his mental mercury, for his rent-roll was a large one, Miss Cavan blushed whenever he looked at her, and, being one of the best shots in England, he was never happier than in August. The suicide theory was preposterous, all agreed, and there was as little reason to believe him murdered. Nevertheless, he had walked out of March Abbey two nights ago without hat or overcoat, and had not been seen since.

The country was being patrolled night and day. A hundred keepers and working men were beating the woods and poking the bogs on the moors, but as yet not so much as a handkerchief had been found.

Weigall did not believe for a moment that Wyatt Gifford was dead, and although it was impossible not to be affected by the general uneasiness, he was disposed to be more angry than frightened. At Cambridge Gifford had been an incorrigible practical joker, and by no means had outgrown the habit; it would be like him to cut across the country in his evening clothes, board a cattle train, and amuse himself touching up the picture of the sensation in West Riding.

However, Weigall's affection for his friend was too deep to companion with tranquillity in the present state of doubt, and, instead of going to bed early with the other men, he determined to walk until ready for sleep. He went down to the river and followed the path through the woods. There was no moon, but the stars sprinkled their cold light upon the pretty belt of water flowing placidly past wood and ruin, between green masses of overhanging rocks or sloping banks tangled with tree and shrub, leaping occasionally over stones with the harsh notes of an angry scold, to recover its equanimity the moment the way was clear again.

It was very dark in the depths where Weigall trod. He smiled as he recalled a remark of Gifford's: 'An English wood is like a good many other things in life – very promising at a distance, but a hollow mockery when you get within. You see daylight on both sides, and the sun freckles the very bracken. Our woods need the night to make them seem what they ought to be – what they once were, before our ancestors' descendants demanded so much more money, in these so much more various days.'

Weigall strolled along, smoking, and thinking of his friend, his pranks – many of which had done more credit to his imagination than this – and recalling conversations that had lasted the night through. Just before the end of the London season they had walked the streets one hot night after a party, discussing the various theories of the soul's destiny. That afternoon they had met at the coffin of a college friend whose mind had been a blank for the past three years. Some months previously they had called at the asylum to see him. His expression had been senile, his face imprinted with the record of debauchery. In death the face was placid, intelligent, without ignoble lineation – the face of the man they had known at college. Weigall and Gifford had had no time to comment there, and the afternoon and evening were full; but, coming forth from the house of festivity together, they had reverted almost at once to the topic.

'I cherish the theory,' Gifford had said, 'that the soul sometimes lingers in the body after death. During madness, of course, it is an impotent prisoner, albeit a conscious one. Fancy its agony, and its horror! What more natural than that, when the life-spark goes out, the tortured soul should take possession of the vacant skull and triumph once more for a few hours while old friends look their last? It has had time to repent while compelled to crouch and behold the result of its work, and it has shrived itself into a state of comparative purity. If I had my way, I should stay inside my bones until the coffin had gone into its niche, that I might obviate for my poor old comrade the tragic impersonality of death. And I should like to see justice done to it, as it were – to see it lowered among its ancestors with the ceremony and solemnity that are its due. I am afraid that if I dissevered myself too quickly, I should yield to curiosity and hasten to investigate the mysteries of space.'

'You believe in the soul as an independent entity, then – that it and the vital principle are not one and the same?'

'Absolutely. The body and soul are twins, life comrades – sometimes friends, sometimes enemies, but always loyal in the last instance. Some day, when I am tired of the world, I shall go to India and become a mahatma, solely for the pleasure of receiving proof during life of this independent relationship.'

'Suppose you were not sealed up properly, and returned after one of your astral flights to find your earthly part unfit for habitation? It is an experiment I don't think I should care to try, unless even juggling with soul and flesh had palled.'

'That would not be an uninteresting predicament. I should rather enjoy experimenting with broken machinery.'

The high wild roar of water smote suddenly on Weigall's ear and checked his memories. He left the wood and walked out on the huge slippery stones which nearly close the River Wharfe at this point, and watched the waters boil down into the narrow pass with their furious untiring energy. The black quiet of the woods rose high on either side. The stars seemed colder and whiter just above. On either hand the perspective of the river might have run into a rayless cavern. There was no lonelier spot in England, nor one which had the right to claim so many ghosts, if ghosts there were.

Weigall was not a coward, but he recalled uncomfortably the tales of those that had been done to death in the Strid.[1] Wordsworth's Boy of Egremond had been disposed of by the practical Whitaker; but countless others, more venturesome than wise, had gone down into that narrow boiling course, never to appear in the still pool a few yards beyond. Below the great rocks which form the walls of the Strid was believed to be a natural vault, on to whose shelves the dead were drawn. The spot had an ugly fascination. Weigall stood, visioning skeletons, uncoffined and green, the home of the eyeless things which had devoured all that had covered and filled that rattling symbol of man's mortality; then fell to wondering if any one had attempted to leap the Strid of late. It was covered with slime; he had never seen it look so treacherous.

[1] 'This striding-place is called the "Strid",
A name which it took of yore;
A thousand years hath it borne the name,
And it shall a thousand more.'

He shuddered and turned away, impelled, despite his manhood, to flee the spot. As he did so, something tossing in the foam below the fall – something as white, yet independent of it – caught his eye and arrested his step. Then he saw that it was describing a contrary motion to the rushing water – an upward backward motion. Weigall stood rigid, breathless; he fancied he heard the crackling of his hair. Was that a hand? It thrust itself still higher above the boiling foam, turned sidewise, and four frantic fingers were distinctly visible against the black rock beyond.

Weigall's superstitious terror left him. A man was there, struggling to free himself from the suction beneath the Strid, swept down, doubtless, but a moment before his arrival, perhaps as he stood with his back to the current.

He stepped as close to the edge as he dared. The hand doubled as if in imprecation, shaking savagely in the face of that force which leaves its creatures to immutable law; then spread wide again, clutching, expanding, crying for help as audibly as the human voice.

Weigall dashed to the nearest tree, dragged and twisted off a branch with his strong arms, and returned as swiftly to the Strid. The hand was in the same place, still gesticulating as wildly; the body was undoubtedly caught in the rocks below, perhaps already half-way along one of those hideous shelves. Weigall let himself down upon a lower rock, braced his shoulder against the mass beside him, then, leaning out over the water, thrust the branch into the hand. The fingers clutched it convulsively. Weigall tugged powerfully, his own feet dragged perilously near the edge. For a moment he produced no impression, then an arm shot above the waters.

The blood sprang to Weigall's head; he was choked with the impression that the Strid had him in her roaring hold, and he saw nothing. Then the mist cleared. The hand and arm were nearer, although the rest of the body was still concealed by the foam. Weigall peered out with distended eyes. The meagre light revealed in the cuffs links of a peculiar device. The fingers clutching the branch were as familiar.

Weigall forgot the slippery stones, the terrible death if he stepped too far. He pulled with passionate will and muscle. Memories flung themselves into the hot light of his brain, trooping rapidly upon each other's heels, as in the thought of the drowning. Most of the pleasures of his life, good and bad, were identified in some way with this friend. Scenes of college days, of travel, where they had deliberately sought adventure and stood between one another and death upon more occasions than one, of hours of delightful companionship among the treasures of art, and others in the pursuit of pleasure, flashed like the changing particles of a kaleidoscope. Weigall had loved several women; but he would have flouted in these moments the thought that he had ever loved any woman as he loved Wyatt Gifford. There were so many charming women in the world, and in the thirty-two years of his life he had never known another man to whom he had cared to give his intimate friendship.

He threw himself on his face. His wrists were cracking, the skin was torn from his hands. The fingers still gripped the stick. There was life in them yet.

Suddenly something gave way. The hand swung about, tearing the branch from Weigall's grasp. The body had been liberated and flung outward, though still submerged by the foam and spray.

Weigall scrambled to his feet and sprang along the rocks, knowing that the danger from suction was over and that Gifford must be carried straight to the quiet pool. Gifford was a fish in the water and could live under it longer than most men. If he survived this, it would not be the first time that his pluck and science had saved him from drowning.

Weigall reached the pool. A man in his evening clothes floated on it, his face turned towards a projecting rock over which his arm had fallen, upholding the body. The hand that had held the branch hung limply over the rock, its white reflection visible in the black water. Weigall plunged into the shallow pool, lifted Gifford in his arms and returned to the bank. He laid the body down and threw off his coat that he might be the freer to practise the methods of resuscitation. He was glad of the moment's respite. The valiant life in the man might have been exhausted in that last struggle. He had not dared to look at his face, to put his ear to the heart. The hesitation lasted but a moment. There was no time to lose.

He turned to his prostrate friend. As he did so, something strange and disagreeable smote his senses. For a half-moment he did not appreciate its nature. Then his teeth clacked together, his feet, his outstretched arms pointed towards the woods. But he sprang to the side of the man and bent down and peered into his face. There was no face.

Willa Cather

THE AFFAIR AT GROVER STATION

I HEARD this story sitting on the rear platform of an accommodation freight that crawled along through the brown, sun-dried wilderness between Grover Station and Cheyenne. The narrator was 'Terrapin' Rodgers, who had been a classmate of mine at Princeton, and who was then cashier in the B— railroad office at Cheyenne. Rodgers was an Albany boy, but after his father failed in business, his uncle got 'Terrapin' a position on a Western railroad, and he left college and disappeared completely from our little world, and it was not until I was sent West, by the University with a party of geologists who were digging for fossils in the region about Sterling, Colorado, that I saw him again. On this particular occasion Rodgers had been down at Sterling to spend Sunday with me, and I accompanied him when he returned to Cheyenne.

When the train pulled out of Grover Station, we were sitting smoking on the rear platform, watching the pale yellow disc of the moon that was just rising and that drenched the naked, grey plains in a soft lemon-coloured light. The telegraph poles scored the sky like a musical staff as they flashed by, and the stars, seen between the wires, looked like the notes of some erratic symphony. The stillness of the night and the loneliness and barrenness of the plains were conducive to an uncanny train of thought. We had just left Grover Station behind us, and the murder of the station agent at Grover, which had occurred the previous winter, was still the subject of much conjecturing and theorising all along that line of railroad. Rodgers had been an intimate friend of the murdered agent, and it was said that he knew more about the affair than any other living man, but with that peculiar reticence which at college had won him the soubriquet 'Terrapin', he had kept what he knew to himself, and even the most accomplished reporter on the *New York Journal*, who had travelled half-way across the continent for the express purpose of pumping Rodgers, had given him up as impossible. But I had known Rodgers a long time, and since I had been grubbing in the chalk about Sterling, we had fallen into a habit of exchanging confidences, for it is good to see an old face in a strange land. So, as the little red station house at Grover faded into the distance, I asked him point blank what he knew about the murder of Lawrence O'Toole. Rodgers took a long pull at his black-briar pipe as he answered me.

'Well, yes. I could tell you something about it, but the question is how much you'd believe, and whether you could restrain yourself from reporting it to the Society for Psychical Research. I never told the story but once, and then it was to the Division Superintendent, and when I finished the old gentleman asked if I were a drinking man, and remarking that a fertile imagination was not a desirable quality in a railroad employee, said it would be just as well if the story went no further. You see it's a gruesome tale, and someway we don't like to be reminded that there are more things in heaven and earth than our systems of philosophy can grapple with. However, I should rather like to tell the story to a man who would look at it objectively and leave it in the domain of pure incident where it belongs. It would unburden my mind, and I'd like to get a scientific man's opinion on the yarn. But I suppose I'd better begin at the beginning, with the dance which preceded the tragedy, just as such things follow each other in a play. I notice that Destiny, who is a good deal of an artist in her way, frequently falls back upon that elementary principle of contrast to make things interesting for us.

'It was the thirty-first of December, the morning of the incoming Governor's inaugural ball, and I got down to the office early, for I had a heavy day's work ahead of me, and I was going to the dance and wanted to close up by six o'clock. I had scarcely unlocked the door when I heard someone calling Cheyenne on the wire, and hurried over to the instrument to see what was wanted. It was Lawrence O'Toole, at Grover, and he said he was coming up for the ball on the extra, due in Cheyenne at nine o'clock that night. He wanted me to go up to see Miss Masterson and ask her if she could go with him. He had had some trouble in getting leave of absence, as the last regular train for Cheyenne then left Grover at 5:45 in the afternoon, and as there was an east-bound going through Grover at 7:30, the dispatcher didn't want him array, in case there should be orders for the 7:30 train. So Larry had made no arrangement with Miss Masterson, as he was uncertain about getting up until he was notified about the extra.

'I telephoned Miss Masterson and delivered Larry's message. She replied that she had made an arrangement to go to the dance with Mr Freymark, but added laughingly that no other arrangement held when Larry could come.

'About noon Freymark dropped in at the office, and I suspected he'd got his time from Miss Masterson. While he was hanging around, Larry called me up to tell me that Helen's flowers would be up from Denver on the Union Pacific passenger at five, and he asked me to have them sent up to her promptly and to call for her that evening in case the extra should be late. Freymark, of course, listened to the message, and when the sounder stopped, he smiled in a slow, disagreeable way, and saying, "Thank you. That's all I wanted to know." left the office.

'Lawrence O'Toole had been my predecessor in the cashier's office at Cheyenne, and he needs a little explanation now that he is under ground, though when he was in the world of living men, he explained himself better than any man I have ever met, East or West. I've knocked about a good deal since I cut loose from Princeton, and I've found that there are a great many good fellows in the world, but I've not found many better than Larry. I think I can say, without stretching a point, that he was the most popular man on the Division. He had a faculty of making everyone like him that amounted to a sort of genius. When he first went to working on the road, he was the agent's assistant down at Sterling, a mere kid fresh from Ireland, without a dollar in his pocket, and no sort of backing in the world but his quick wit and handsome face. It was a face that served him as a sight draft, good in all banks.

'Freymark was cashier at the Cheyenne office then, but he had been up to some dirty work with the company, and when it fell in the line of Larry's duty to expose him, he did so without hesitating. Eventually Freymark was discharged, and Larry was made cashier in his place. There was, after that, naturally, little love lost between them, and to make matters worse, Helen Masterson took a fancy to Larry, and Freymark had begun to consider himself pretty solid in that direction. I doubt whether Miss Masterson ever really liked the blackguard, but he was a queer fish, and she was a queer girl and she found him interesting.

'Old John J. Masterson, her father, had been United States Senator from Wyoming, and Helen had been educated at Wellesley and had lived in Washington a good deal. She found Cheyenne dull and had got into the Washington way of tolerating anything but stupidity, and Freymark certainly was not stupid. He passed as an Alsatian Jew, but he had lived a good deal in Paris and had been pretty much all over the world, and spoke the more general European languages fluently. He was a wiry, sallow, unwholesome looking man, slight and meagerly built, and he looked as though he had been dried through and through by the blistering heat of the tropics. His movements were as lithe and agile as those of a cat, and invested with a certain unusual, stealthy grace. His eyes were small and black as bright jet beads; his hair very thick and coarse and straight, black with a sort of purple lustre to it, and he always wore it correctly parted in the middle and brushed smoothly about his ears. He had a pair of the most impudent red lips that closed over white, regular teeth. His hands, of which he took the greatest care, were the yellow, wrinkled hands of an old man, and shrivelled at the finger tips, though I don't think he could have been much over thirty. The long and short of it is that the fellow was uncanny. You somehow felt that there was that in his present, or in his past, or in his destiny which isolated him from other men. He dressed in excellent taste, was always accommodating, with the most polished manners and an address extravagantly deferential. He went into cattle after he lost his job with the company and had an interest in a ranch ten miles out, though he spent most of his time in Cheyenne at the Capitol card rooms. He had an insatiable passion for gambling, and he was one of the few men who make it pay.

'About a week before the dance, Larry's cousin, Harry Burns, who was a reporter on the London *Times*, stopped in Cheyenne on his way to 'Frisco, and Larry came up to meet him. We took Burns up to the club, and I noticed that he acted rather queerly when Freymark came in. Burns went down to Grover to spend a day with Larry, and on Saturday Larry wired me to come down and spend Sunday with him, as he had important news for me.

'I went, and the gist of his information was that Freymark, then going by another name, had figured in a particularly ugly London scandal that happened to be in Burns' beat, and his record had been exposed. He was, indeed, from Paris, but there was not a drop of Jewish blood in his veins, and he dated from farther back than Israel. His father was a French soldier who, during his service in the East, had bought a Chinese slave girl, had become attached to her, and married her, and after her death had brought her child back to Europe with him. He had entered the civil service and held several subordinate offices in the capital, where his son was educated. The boy, socially ambitious and extremely sensitive about his Asiatic blood, after having been blackballed at a club, had left and lived by an exceedingly questionable traffic in London, assuming a Jewish patronymic to account for his Oriental complexion and traits of feature. That explained everything. That explained why Freymark's hands were those of a centenarian. In his veins crept the sluggish amphibious blood of a race that was already old when Jacob tended the flocks of Laban upon the hills of Padan-Aram, a race that was in its mort cloth before Europe's swaddling clothes were made.

'Of course, the question at once came up as to what ought to be done with Burns' information. Cheyenne clubs are not exclusive, but a

Chinaman who had been engaged in Freymark's peculiarly unsavoury traffic would be disbarred in almost any region outside of Whitechapel. One thing was sure: Miss Masterson must be informed of the matter at once.

'"On second thought," said Larry, "I guess I'd better tell her myself. It will have to be done easy like, not to hurt her self-respect too much. Like as not I'll go off my head the first time I see him and call him rat-eater to his face."

'Well to get back to the day of the dance, I was wondering whether Larry would stay over to tell Miss Masterson about it the next day, for of course he couldn't spring such a thing on a girl at a party.

'That evening I dressed early and went down to the station at nine to meet Larry. The extra came in, but no Larry. I saw Connelly, the conductor, and asked him if he had seen anything of O'Toole, but he said he hadn't, that the station at Grover was open when he came through, but that he found no train orders and couldn't raise anyone, so he supposed O'Toole had come up on 153. I went back to the office and called Grover, but got no answer. Then I sat down at the instrument and called for fifteen minutes straight. I wanted to go then and hunt up the conductor on 153, the passenger that went through Grover at 5:30 in the afternoon, and ask him what he knew about Larry, but it was then 9:45 and I knew Miss Masterson would be waiting, so I jumped into the carriage and told the driver to make up time. On my way to the Mastersons' I did some tall thinking. I could find no explanation for O'Toole's non-appearance, but the business of the moment was to invent one for Miss Masterson that would neither alarm nor offend her. I couldn't exactly tell her he wasn't coming, for he might show up yet, so I decided to say the extra was late, and I didn't know when it would be in.

'Miss Masterson had been an exceptionally beautiful girl to begin with, and life had done a great deal for her. Fond as I was of Larry, I used to wonder whether a girl who had led such a full and independent existence would ever find the courage to face life with a railroad man who was so near the bottom of a ladder that is so long and steep.

'She came down the stairs in one of her Paris gowns that are as meat and drink to Cheyenne society reporters, with her arms full of American Beauty roses and her eyes and cheeks glowing. I noticed the roses then, though I didn't know that they were the boy's last message to the woman he loved. She paused half-way down the stairs and looked at me, and then over my head into the drawing-room, and then her eyes questioned mine. I bungled at my explanation and she thanked me for coming, but she couldn't hide her disappointment, and scarcely glanced at herself in the mirror as I put her wrap about her shoulders.

'It was not a cheerful ride down to the Capitol. Miss Masterson did her duty by me bravely, but I found it difficult to be even decently attentive to what she was saying. Once arrived at Representative Hall, where the dance was held, the strain was relieved, for the fellows all pounced on her for dances, and there were friends of hers there from Helena and Laramie, and my responsibility was practically at an end. Don't expect me to tell you what a Wyoming inaugural ball is like. I'm not good at that sort of thing, and this dance is merely incidental to my story. Dance followed dance, and still no Larry. The dances I had with Miss Masterson were torture. She began to question and cross-question me, and when I got tangled up in my lies, she became indignant. Freymark was late in arriving. It must have been after midnight when he appeared, correct and smiling, having driven up from his ranch. He was effusively gay and insisted upon shaking hands with me, though I never willingly touched those clammy hands of his. He was constantly dangling about Miss Masterson, who made rather a point of being gracious to him. I couldn't much blame her under the circumstances, but it irritated me, and I'm not ashamed to say that I rather spied on them. When they were on the balcony I heard him say:

'"You see I've forgiven this morning entirely."

'She answered him rather coolly:

'"Ah, but you are constitutionally forgiving. However, I'll be fair and forgive too. It's more comfortable."

'Then he said in a slow, insinuating tone, and I could fairly see him thrust out those impudent red lips of his as he said it: "If I can teach you to forgive, I wonder whether I could not also teach you to forget? I almost think I could. At any rate I shall make you remember this night.

> *Rappelles-toi lorsque les destinées*
> *M'auront de toi pour jamas séparé."*

'As they came in, I saw him slip one of Larry's red roses into his pocket.

'It was not until near the end of the dance that the clock of destiny sounded the first stroke of the tragedy. I remember how gay the scene was, so gay that I had almost forgotten my anxiety in the music, flowers and laughter. The orchestra was playing a waltz, drawing the strains out long and sweet like the notes of a flute, and Freymark was dancing with Helen. I was not dancing myself then, and suddenly noticed some confusion among the waiters who stood watching by one of the doors, and Larry's black dog, Duke, all foam at the mouth, shot in the side and bleeding, dashed in through the door and eluding the caterer's men, ran half the length of the hall and threw himself at Freymark's feet, uttering a howl piteous enough to herald any sort of calamity. Freymark, who had not seen him before, turned with an exclamation of rage and a face absolutely livid and kicked the wounded brute half-way across the slippery floor. There was something fiendishly brutal and horrible in the episode, it was the breaking out of the barbarian blood through his mask of European civilisation, a jet of black mud that spurted up from some nameless pest hole of filthy heathen cities. The music stopped, people began moving about in a confused mass, and I saw Helen's eyes seeking mine appealingly. I hurried to her, and by the time I reached her Freymark had disappeared.

'"Get the carriage and take care of Duke," she said, and her voice trembled like that of one shivering with cold.

'When we were in the carriage, she spread one of the robes on her knee, and I lifted the dog up to her, and she took him in her arms, comforting him.

'"Where is Larry, and what does all this mean?" she asked. "You can't put me off any longer, for I danced with a man who came up on the extra."

'Then I made a clean breast of it, and told her what I knew, which was little enough.

'"Do you think he is ill?" she asked.

'I replied, "I don't know what to think. I'm all at sea," – For since the appearance of the dog I was genuinely alarmed.

'She was silent for a long time, but when the rays of the electric street lights flashed at intervals into the carriage, I could see that she was leaning back with her eyes closed and the dog's nose against her throat. At last she said with a note of entreaty in her voice, "Can't you think of anything?" I saw that she was thoroughly frightened and told her that it would probably all end in a joke, and that I would telephone her as soon as I heard from Larry, and would more than likely have something amusing to tell her.

'It was snowing hard when we reached the Senator's, and when we got out of the carriage she gave Duke tenderly over to me and I remember how she dragged on my arm and how played out and exhausted she seemed.

'"You really must not worry at all," I said. "You know how uncertain railroad men are. It's sure to be better at the next inaugural ball; we'll all be dancing together then."

'"The next inaugural ball," she said as we went up the steps, putting out her hand to catch the snow-flakes. – "That seems a long way off."

'I got down to the office late next morning, and before I had time to try Grover, the dispatcher at Holyoke called me up to ask whether Larry were still in Cheyenne. He couldn't raise Grover, he said, and he wanted to give Larry train orders for 151, the east-bound passenger. When he heard what I had to say, he told me I had better go down to Grover on 151 myself, as the storm threatened to tie up all the trains and we might look for trouble.

'I had the veterinary surgeon fix up Duke's side, and I put him in the express car, and boarded the 151 with a mighty cold, uncomfortable sensation in the region of my diaphragm.

'It had snowed all night long, and the storm had developed into a blizzard, and the passenger had difficulty in making any headway at all.

'When we got into Grover I thought it was the most desolate spot I had ever looked on, and as the train pulled out, leaving me there, I felt like sending a message of farewell to the world. You know what Grover is, a red box of a station, section house barricaded by coal sheds and a little group of dwellings at the end of everything, with the desert running out on every side to the sky line. The houses and the station were covered with a coating of snow that clung to them like a wet plaster, and the siding was one deep snow drift, banked against the station door. The plain was a wide, white ocean of swirling, drifting snow, that beat and broke like the thrash of the waves in the merciless wind that swept, with nothing to break it, from the Rockies to the Missouri.

'When I opened the station door, the snow fell in upon the floor, and Duke sat down by the empty, fireless stove and began to howl and whine in a heart-breaking fashion. Larry's sleeping room upstairs was empty. Downstairs, everything was in order, and all the station work had been done up. Apparently the last thing Larry had done was to bill out a car of wool from the Oasis sheep ranch for Dewey, Gould & Co., Boston. The car had gone out on 153, the east-bound that left Grover at seven o'clock the night before, so he must have been there at that time. I copied the bill in the copy book, and went over to the section house to make inquiries.

'The section boss was getting ready to go out to look after his track. He said he had seen O'Toole at 5:30, when the west-bound passenger went through, and, not having seen him since, supposed he was still in Cheyenne. I went over to Larry's boarding house, and the woman said he must be in Cheyenne, as he had eaten his supper at five o'clock the night before, so that he would have time to get his station work done and dress. The little girl, she said, had gone over at five to tell him that supper was ready. I questioned the child carefully. She said there was another man, a stranger, in the station with Larry when she went in and that though she didn't hear anything they said, and Larry was sitting with his chair tilted back and his feet on the stove, she somehow had thought they were quarrelling. The stranger, she said, was standing; he had a fur coat on and his eyes snapped like he was mad, and she was afraid of him. I asked her if she could recall anything else about him, and she said, "Yes, he had very red lips." When I heard that, my heart grew cold as a snow lump, and when I went out the wind seemed to go clear through me. It was evident enough that Freymark had gone down there to make trouble, had quarrelled with Larry and had boarded either the 5:30 passenger or the extra, and got the conductor to let him off at his ranch, and accounted for his late appearance at the dance.

'It was five o'clock then, but the 5:30 train was two hours late, so there was nothing to do but sit down and wait for the conductor, who had gone out on the seven o'clock east-bound the night before, and who must have seen Larry when he picked up the car of wool. It was growing dark by that time. The sky was a dull lead colour, and the snow had drifted about the little town until it was almost buried, and was still coming down so fast that you could scarcely see your hand before you.

'I was never so glad to hear anything as that whistle, when old 153 came lumbering and groaning in through the snow. I ran out on the platform to meet her, and her headlight looked like the face of an old friend. I caught the conductor's arm the minute he stepped off the train, but he wouldn't talk until he got in by the fire. He said he hadn't seen O'Toole at all the night before, but he had found the bill for the wool car on the table, with a note from Larry asking him to take the car out on the Q.T., and he had concluded that Larry had gone up to Cheyenne on the 5:30. I wired the Cheyenne office and managed to catch the express clerk who had gone through on the extra the night before. He wired me saying that he had not seen Larry board the extra, but that his dog had crept into his usual place in the express car, and he had supposed Larry was in the coach. He had seen Freymark get on at Grover, and the train had slowed up a trifle at his ranch to let him off, for Freymark stood in with some of the boys and sent his cattle shipments our way.

'When the night fairly closed down on me, I began to wonder how a gay, expansive fellow like O'Toole had ever stood six months at Grover. The snow had let up by that time, and the stars were beginning to glitter cold and bright through the hurrying clouds. I put on my ulster and went outside. I began a minute tour of inspection, I went through empty freight cars run down by the siding, searched the coal houses and primitive cellar, examining them carefully, and calling O'Toole's name. Duke at my heels dragged himself painfully about, but seemed as much at sea as I, and betrayed the nervous suspense and alertness of a bird dog that has lost his game.

'I went back to the office and took the big station lamp upstairs to make a more careful examination of Larry's sleeping room. The suit of clothes that he usually wore at his work was hanging on the wall. His shaving things were lying about, and I recognised the silver-backed military hair brushes that Miss Masterson had given him at Christmas time, lying on his chiffonier. The upper drawer was open and a pair of white kid gloves was lying on the corner. A white string tie hung across his pipe rack, it was crumpled and had evidently proved unsatisfactory when he tied it. On the chiffonier lay several clean handkerchiefs with holes in them, where he had unfolded them and thrown them by in a hasty search for a whole one. A black silk muffler hung on the chair back, and a top hat was set awry on the head of a plaster cast of Parnell, Larry's hero. His dress suit was missing, so there was no doubt that he had dressed for the party. His overcoat lay on his trunk and his dancing shoes were on the floor, at the foot of the bed beside his everyday ones. I knew that his pumps were a little tight, he had joked about them when I was down the Sunday before the dance, but he had only one pair, and he couldn't have got another in Grover if he had tried himself. That set me to thinking. He was a dainty fellow about his shoes and I knew his collection pretty well. I went to his closet and found them all there. Even granting him a prejudice against overcoats, I couldn't conceive of his going out in that stinging weather without shoes. I noticed that a surgeon's case, such as are carried on passenger trains, and which Larry had once appropriated in Cheyenne, was open, and that the roll of medicated cotton had been pulled out and recently used. Each discovery I made served only to add to my perplexity. Granted that Freymark had been there, and granted that he had played the boy an ugly trick, he could not have spirited him away without the knowledge of the train crew.

'"Duke, old doggy," I said to the poor spaniel who was sniffing and whining about the bed, "you haven't done your duty. You must have seen what went on between your master and that clam-blooded Asiatic, and you ought to be able to give me a tip of some sort."

'I decided to go to bed and make a fresh start on the ugly business in the morning. The bed looked as though someone had been lying on it, so I started to beat it up a little before I got in. I took off the pillow and as I pulled up the mattress, on the edge of the ticking at the head of the bed, I saw a dark red stain about the size of my hand. I felt the cold sweat come out on me, and my hands were dangerously unsteady, as I carried the lamp over and set it down on the chair by the bed. But Duke was too quick for me, he had seen that stain and leaping on the bed began sniffing it, and whining like a dog that is being whipped to death. I bent down and felt it with my fingers. It was dry but the colour and stiffness were unmistakeably those of coagulated blood. I caught up my coat and vest and ran down stairs with Duke yelping at my heels. My first impulse was to go and call someone, but from the platform not a single light was visible, and I knew the section men had been in bed for hours. I remembered then, that Larry was often annoyed by haemorrhages at the nose in that high altitude, but even that did not altogether quiet my nerves, and I realised that sleeping in that bed was quite out of the question.

'Larry always kept a supply of brandy and soda on hand, so I made myself a stiff drink and filled the stove and locked the door, turned down the lamp and lay down on the operator's table. I had often slept there when I was night operator. At first it was impossible to sleep, for Duke kept starting up and limping to the door and scratching at it, yelping nervously. He kept this up until I was thoroughly unstrung, and though I'm ordinarily cool enough, there wasn't money enough in Wyoming to have bribed me to open that door. I felt cold all over every time I went near it, and I even drew the big rusty bolt that was never used, and it seemed to me that it groaned heavily as I drew it, or perhaps it was the wind outside that groaned. As for Duke, I threatened to put him out, and boxed his ears until I hurt his feelings, and he lay down in front of the door with his muzzle between his paws and his eyes shining like live coals and riveted on the crack under the door. The situation was gruesome enough, but the liquor had made me drowsy and at last I fell asleep.

'It must have been about three o'clock in the morning that I was awakened by the crying of the dog, a whimper low, continuous and pitiful, and indescribably human. While I was blinking my eyes in an effort to get thoroughly awake, I heard another sound, the grating sound of chalk on a wooden black board, or of a soft pencil on a slate. I turned my head to the right, and saw a man standing with his back to me, chalking something on the bulletin board. At a glance I recognised the broad, high shoulders and the handsome head of my friend. Yet there was that about the figure which kept me from calling his name or from moving a muscle where I lay. He finished his writing and dropped the chalk, and I distinctly heard its click as it fell. He made a gesture as though he were dusting his fingers, and then turned facing me, holding his left hand in front of his mouth. I saw him clearly in the soft light of the station lamp. He wore his dress clothes, and began moving towards the door silently as a shadow in his black stocking feet. There was about his movements an indescribable stiffness, as though his limbs had been frozen. His face was chalky white, his hair seemed damp and was plastered down close about his temples. His eyes were colourless jellies, dull as lead, and staring straight before him. When he reached the door, he lowered the hand he held before his mouth to lift the latch. His face was turned squarely towards me, and the lower jaw had fallen and was set rigidly upon his collar, the mouth was wide open and was *stuffed full of white cotton!* Then I knew it was a dead man's face I looked upon.

'The door opened, and that stiff black figure in stockings walked as noiselessly as a cat out into the night. I think I went quite mad then. I dimly remember that I rushed out upon the siding and ran up and down screaming, "Larry, Larry!" until the wind seemed to echo my call. The stars were out in myriads, and the snow glistened in their light, but I could see nothing but the wide, white plain, not even a dark shadow anywhere. When at last I found myself back in the station, I saw Duke lying before the door and dropped on my knees beside him, calling him by name. But Duke was past calling back. Master and dog had gone together, and I dragged him into the corner and covered his face, for his eyes were colourless and soft, like the eyes of that horrible face, once so beloved.

'The black board? O, I didn't forget that. I had chalked the time of the accommodation on it the night before, from sheer force of habit, for it isn't customary to mark the time of trains in unimportant stations like Grover. My writing had been rubbed out by a moist hand, for I could see the finger marks clearly, and in place of it was written in blue chalk simply,

C.B. & Q. 26387

'I sat there drinking brandy and muttering to myself before that black board until those blue letters danced up and down, like magic lantern pictures when you jiggle the slides. I drank until the sweat poured off me like rain and my teeth chattered, and I turned sick at the stomach. At last an idea flashed upon me. I snatched the way bill off the hook. The car of wool that had left Grover for Boston the night before was numbered 26387.

'I must have got through the rest of the night somehow, for when the sun came up red and angry over the white plains, the section boss found me sitting by the stove, the lamp burning full blaze, the brandy bottle empty beside me, and with but one idea in my head, that box car 26387 must be stopped and opened as soon as possible, and that somehow it would explain.

'I figured that we could easily catch it in Omaha, and wired the freight agent there to go through it carefully and report anything unusual. That night I got a wire from the agent stating that the body of a man had been found under a woolsack at one end of the car with a fan and an invitation to the inaugural ball at Cheyenne in the pocket of his dress coat. I wired him not to disturb the body until I arrived, and started for Omaha. Before I left Grover the Cheyenne office wired me that Freymark had left town, going west over the Union Pacific. The company detectives never found him.

'The matter was clear enough then. Being a railroad man, he had hidden the body and sealed up the car and billed it out, leaving a note for the conductor. Since he was of a race without conscience or sensibilities, and since his past was more infamous than his birth, he had boarded the extra and had gone to the ball and danced with Miss Masterson with blood undried upon his hands.

'When I saw Larry O'Toole again, he was lying stiff and stark in the undertakers' rooms in Omaha. He was clad in his dress clothes, with black stockings on his feet, as I had seen him forty-eight hours before. Helen Masterson's fan was in his pocket. His mouth was wide open and stuffed full of white cotton.

'He had been shot in the mouth, the bullet lodging between the third and fourth vertebrae. The haemorrhage had been very slight and had been checked by the cotton. The quarrel had taken place about five in the afternoon. After supper Larry had dressed, all but his shoes, and had lain down to snatch a wink of sleep, trusting to the whistle of the extra to waken him. Freymark had gone back and shot him while he was asleep, afterwards placing his body in the wool car, which, but for my telegram, would not have been opened for weeks.

'That's the whole story. There is nothing more to tell except one detail that I did not mention to the superintendent. When I said good-bye to the boy before the undertaker and coroner took charge of the body, I lifted his right hand to take off a ring that Miss Masterson had given him and the ends of the fingers were covered with blue chalk.'

Mary E. Wilkins (Freeman)

THE VACANT LOT

WHEN it became generally known in Townsend Centre that the Townsends were going to move to the city, there was great excitement and dismay. For the Townsends to move was about equivalent to the town's moving. The Townsend ancestors had founded the village a hundred years ago. The first Townsend had kept a wayside hostelry for man and beast, known as the 'Sign of the Leopard'. The sign-board, on which the leopard was painted a bright blue, was still extant, and prominently so, being nailed over the present Townsend's front door. This Townsend, by name David, kept the village store. There had been no tavern since the railroad was built through Townsend Centre in his father's day. Therefore the family, being ousted by the march of progress from their chosen employment, took up with a general country store as being the next thing to a country tavern, the principal difference consisting in the fact that all the guests were transients, never requiring bedchambers, securing their rest on the tops of sugar and flour barrels and codfish boxes, and their refreshment from stray nibblings at the stock in trade, to the profitless deplenishment of raisins and loaf sugar and crackers and cheese.

The flitting of the Townsends from the home of their ancestors was due to a sudden access of wealth from the death of a relative and the desire of Mrs Townsend to secure better advantages for her son George, sixteen years old, in the way of education, and for her daughter Adrianna, ten years older, better matrimonial opportunities. However, the last inducement for leaving Townsend Centre was not openly stated, only ingeniously surmised by the neighbours.

'Sarah Townsend don't think there's anybody in Townsend Centre fit for her Adrianna to marry, and so she's goin' to take her to Boston to see if she can't pick up somebody there,' they said. Then they wondered what Abel Lyons would do. He had been a humble suitor for Adrianna for years, but her mother had not approved, and Adrianna, who was dutiful, had repulsed him delicately and rather sadly. He was the only lover whom she had ever had, and she felt sorry and grateful; she was a plain, awkward girl, and had a patient recognition of the fact.

But her mother was ambitious, more so than her father, who was rather pugnaciously satisfied with what he had, and not easily disposed to change. However, he yielded to his wife and consented to sell out his business and purchase a house in Boston and move there.

David Townsend was curiously unlike the line of ancestors from whom he had come. He had either retrograded or advanced, as one might look at it. His moral character was certainly better, but he had not the fiery spirit and eager grasp at advantage which had distinguished them. Indeed, the old Townsends, though prominent and respected as men of property and influence, had reputations not above suspicions. There was more than one dark whisper regarding them handed down from mother to son in the village, and especially was this true of the first Townsend, he who built the tavern bearing the Sign of the Blue Leopard. His portrait, a hideous effort of contemporary art, hung in the garret of David Townsend's home. There was many a tale of wild roistering, if no worse, in that old roadhouse, and high stakes, and quarrelling in cups, and blows, and money gotten in evil fashion, and the matter hushed up with a high hand for inquirers by the imperious Townsends who terrorised everybody. David Townsend terrorised nobody. He had gotten his little competence from his store by honest methods – the exchanging of sterling goods and true weights for country produce and country shillings. He was sober and reliable, with intense self-respect and a decided talent for the management of money. It was principally for this reason that he took great delight in his sudden wealth by legacy. He had thereby greater opportunities for the exercise of his native shrewdness in a bargain. This he evinced in his purchase of a house in Boston.

One day in spring the old Townsend house was shut up, the Blue Leopard was taken carefully down from his lair over the front door, the family chattels were loaded on the train, and the Townsends departed. It was a sad and eventful day for Townsend Centre. A man from Barre had rented the store – David had decided at the last not to sell – and the old familiars congregated in melancholy fashion and talked over the situation. An enormous pride over their departed townsman became evident. They paraded him, flaunting him like a banner in the eyes of the new man. 'David is awful smart,' they said; 'there won't nobody get the better of him in the city if he has lived in Townsend Centre all his life. He's got his eyes open. Know what he paid for his house in Boston? Well, sir, that house cost twenty-five thousand dollars, and David he bought it for five. Yes, sir, he did.'

'Must have been some out about it,' remarked the new man, scowling over his counter. He was beginning to feel his disparaging situation.

'Not an out, sir. David he made sure on't. Catch him gettin' bit. Everythin' was in apple-pie order, hot an' cold water and all, and in one of the best locations of the city – real high-up street. David he said the rent in that street was never under a thousand. Yes, sir, David he got a bargain – five thousand dollars for a twenty-five-thousand-dollar house.'

'Some out about it!' growled the new man over the counter.

However, as his fellow townsmen and allies stated, there seemed to be no doubt about the desirableness of the city house which David Townsend had purchased and the fact that he had secured it for an absurdly low price. The whole family were at first suspicious. It was ascertained that the house had cost a round sum only a few years ago; it was in perfect repair; nothing whatever was amiss with plumbing, furnace, anything. There was not even a soap factory within smelling distance, as Mrs Townsend had vaguely surmised. She was sure that she had heard of houses being undesirable for such reasons, but there was no soap factory. They all sniffed and peeked; when the first rainfall came they looked at the ceiling, confidently expecting to see dark spots where the leaks had commenced, but there were none. They were forced to confess that their suspicions were allayed, that the house was perfect, even overshadowed with the mystery of a lower price than it was worth. That, however, was an additional perfection in the opinion of the Townsends, who had their share of New England thrift. They had lived just one month in their new house, and were happy, although at times somewhat lonely from missing the society of Townsend Centre, when the trouble began. The Townsends, although they lived in a fine house in a genteel, almost fashionable, part of the city, were true to their antecedents and kept, as they had been accustomed, only one maid. She was the daughter of a farmer on the outskirts of their native village, was middle-aged, and had lived with them for the last ten years. One pleasant Monday morning she rose early and did the family washing before breakfast, which had been prepared by Mrs Townsend and Adrianna, as was their habit on washing-days. The family were seated at the breakfast table in their basement dining-room, and this maid, whose name was Cordelia, was hanging out the clothes in the vacant lot. This vacant lot seemed a valuable one, being on a corner. It was rather singular that it had not been built upon. The Townsends had wondered at it and agreed that they would have preferred their own house to be there. They had, however, utilised it as far as possible with their innocent, rural disregard of property rights in unoccupied land.

'We might just as well hang out our washing in that vacant lot,' Mrs Townsend had told Cordelia the first Monday of their stay in the house.

'Our little yard ain't half big enough for all our clothes, and it is sunnier there, too.'

So Cordelia had hung out the wash there for four Mondays, and this was the fifth. The breakfast was about half finished – they had reached the buckwheat cakes – when this maid came rushing into the dining-room and stood regarding them, speechless, with a countenance indicative of the utmost horror. She was deadly pale. He hands, sodden with soapsuds, hung twitching at her sides in the folds of her calico gown; her very hair, which was light and sparse, seemed to bristle with fear. All the Townsends turned and looked at her. David and George rose with a half-defined idea of burglars.

'Cordelia Battles, what is the matter?' cried Mrs Townsend. Adrianna gasped for breath and turned as white as the maid. 'What is the matter?' repeated Mrs Townsend, but the maid was unable to speak. Mrs Townsend, who could be peremptory, sprang up, ran to the frightened woman and shook her violently. 'Cordelia Battles, you speak,' said she, 'and not stand there staring that way, as if you were struck dumb! What is the matter with you?'

Then Cordelia spoke in a fainting voice.

'There's – somebody else – hanging out clothes – in the vacant lot,' she gasped, and clutched at a chair for support.

'Who?' cried Mrs Townsend, rousing to indignation, for already she had assumed a proprietorship in the vacant lot. 'Is it the folks in the next house? I'd like to know what right they have! We are next to that vacant lot.'

'I – dunno – who it is,' gasped Cordelia.

'Why, we've seen that girl next door go to mass every morning,' said Mrs Townsend. 'She's got a fiery red head. Seems as if you might know her by this time, Cordelia.'

'It ain't that girl,' gasped Cordelia. Then she added in a horror-stricken voice, 'I couldn't see who 'twas.'

They all stared.

'Why couldn't you see?' demanded her mistress. 'Are you struck blind?'

'No, ma'am.'

'Then why couldn't you see?'

'All I could see was— ' Cordelia hesitated, with an expression of the utmost horror.

'Go on,' said Mrs Townsend, impatiently.

'All I could see was the shadow of somebody, very slim, hanging out the clothes, and— '

'What?'

'I could see the shadows of the things flappin' on their line.'

'You couldn't see the clothes?'

'Only the shadow on the ground.'

'What kind of clothes were they?'

'Queer,' replied Cordelia, with a shudder.

'If I didn't know you so well, I should think you had been drinking,' said Mrs Townsend. 'Now, Cordelia Battles, I'm going out in that vacant lot and see myself what you're talking about.'

'I can't go,' gasped the woman.

With that Mrs Townsend and all the others, except Adrianna, who remained to tremble with the maid, sallied forth into the vacant lot. They had to go out the area gate into the street to reach it. It was nothing unusual in the way of vacant lots. One large poplar tree, the relic of the old forest which had once flourished there, twinkled in one corner; for the rest, it was overgrown with coarse weeds and a few dusty flowers. The Townsends stood just inside the rude board fence which divided the lot from the street and stared with wonder and horror, for Cordelia had told the truth. They all saw what she had described – the shadow of an exceedingly slim woman moving along the ground with up-stretched arms, the shadows of strange, nondescript garments flapping from a shadowy line, but when they looked up for the substance of the shadows nothing was to be seen except the clear, blue October air.

'My goodness!' gasped Mrs Townsend. Her face assumed a strange gathering of wrath in the midst of her terror. Suddenly she made a determined move forward, although her husband strove to hold her back.

'You let me be,' said she. She moved forward. Then she recoiled and gave a loud shriek. 'The wet sheet flapped in my face,' she cried. 'Take me away, take me away!' Then she fainted. Between them they got her back to the house. 'It was awful,' she moaned when she came to herself, with the family all around her where she lay on the dining-room floor. 'Oh, David, what do you suppose it is?'

'Nothing at all,' replied David Townsend stoutly. He was remarkable for courage and staunch belief in actualities. He was now denying to himself that he had seen anything unusual.

'Oh, there was,' moaned his wife.

'I saw something,' said George, in a sullen, boyish bass.

The maid sobbed convulsively and so did Adrianna for sympathy.

'We won't talk any about it,' said David. 'Here, Jane, you drink this hot tea – it will do you good; and Cordelia, you hang out the clothes in our own yard. George, you go and put up the line for her.'

'The line is out there,' said George, with a jerk of his shoulder.

'Are you afraid?'

'No, I ain't,' replied the boy resentfully, and went out with a pale face.

After that Cordelia hung the Townsend wash in the yard of their own house, standing always with her back to the vacant lot. As for David Townsend, he spent a good deal of his time in the lot watching the shadows, but he came to no explanation, although he strove to satisfy himself with many.

'I guess the shadows come from the smoke from our chimneys, or else the poplar tree,' he said.

'Why do the shadows come on Monday mornings, and no other?' demanded his wife.

David was silent.

Very soon new mysteries arose. One day Cordelia rang the dinner-bell at their usual dinner hour, the same as in Townsend Centre, high noon, and the family assembled. With amazement Adrianna looked at the dishes on the table.

'Why, that's queer!' she said.

'What's queer?' asked her mother.

Cordelia stopped short as she was about setting a tumbler of water beside a plate, and the water slopped over.

'Why,' said Adrianna, her face paling, 'I – thought there was boiled dinner. I – smelt cabbage cooking.'

'I knew there would be something else come up,' gasped Cordelia, leaning hard on the back of Adrianna's chair.

'What do you mean?' asked Mrs Townsend sharply, but her own face began to assume the shocked pallor which it was so easy nowadays for all their faces to assume at the merest suggestion of anything out of the common.

'I smelt cabbage cooking all the morning up in my room,' Adrianna said faintly, 'and here's codfish and potatoes for dinner.'

The Townsends all looked at one another. David rose with an exclamation and rushed out of the room. The others waited tremblingly. When he came back his face was lowering.

'What did you—' Mrs Townsend asked hesitatingly.

'There's some smell of cabbage out there,' he admitted reluctantly. Then he looked at her with a challenge. 'It comes from the next house,' he said. 'Blows over our house.'

'Our house is higher.'

'I don't care; you can never account for such things.'

'Cordelia,' said Mrs Townsend, 'you go over to the next house and you ask if they've got cabbage for dinner.'

Cordelia switched out of the room, her mouth set hard. She came back promptly.

'Says they never have cabbage,' she announced with gloomy triumph and a conclusive glance at Mr Townsend. 'Their girl was real sassy.'

'Oh, father, let's move away; let's sell the house,' cried Adrianna in a panic-stricken tone.

'If you think I'm going to sell a house that I got as cheap as this one because we smell cabbage in a vacant lot, you're mistaken,' replied David firmly.

'It isn't the cabbage alone,' said Mrs Townsend.

'And a few shadows,' added David. 'I am tired of such nonsense. I thought you had more sense, Jane.'

'One of the boys at school asked me if we lived in the house next to the vacant lot on Wells Street and whistled when I said "Yes",' remarked George.

'Let him whistle,' said Mr Townsend.

After a few hours the family, stimulated by Mr Townsend's calm, common sense, agreed that it was exceedingly foolish to be disturbed by a mysterious odour of cabbage. They even laughed at themselves.

'I suppose we have got so nervous over those shadows hanging out clothes that we notice every little thing,' conceded Mrs Townsend.

'You will find out some day that that is no more to be regarded than the cabbage,' said her husband.

'You can't account for that wet sheet hitting my face,' said Mrs Townsend, doubtfully.

'You imagined it.'

'I *felt* it.'

That afternoon things went on as usual in the household until nearly four o'clock. Adrianna went downtown to do some shopping. Mrs Townsend sat sewing beside the bay window in her room, which was a front one in the third storey. George had not got home. Mr Townsend was writing a letter in the library. Cordelia was busy in the basement; the twilight, which was coming earlier and earlier every night, was beginning to gather, when suddenly there was a loud crash which shook the house from its foundations. Even the dishes on the sideboard rattled, and the glasses rang like bells. The pictures on the walls of Mrs Townsend's room swung out from the walls. But that was not all: every looking-glass in the house cracked simultaneously – as nearly as they could judge – from top to bottom, then shivered into fragments over the floors. Mrs Townsend was too frightened to scream. She sat huddled in her chair, gasping for breath, her eyes, rolling from side to side in incredulous terror, turned towards the street. She saw a great black group of people crossing it just in front of the vacant lot. There was something inexpressibly strange and gloomy about this moving group; there was an effect of sweeping, wavings and foldings of sable draperies and gleams of deadly white faces; then they passed. She twisted her head to see, and they disappeared in the vacant lot. Mr Townsend came hurrying into the room; he was pale, and looked at once angry and alarmed.

'Did you fall?' he asked inconsequently, as if his wife, who was small, could have produced such a manifestation by a fall.

'Oh, David, what is it?' whispered Mrs Townsend.

'Darned if I know!' said David.

'Don't swear. It's too awful. Oh, see the looking-glass, David!'

'I see it. The one over the library mantel is broken, too.'

'Oh, it is a sign of death!'

Cordelia's feet were heard as she staggered on the stairs. She almost fell into the room. She reeled over to Mr Townsend and clutched his arm. He cast a sidewise glance, half furious, half commiserating at her.

'Well, what is it all about?' he asked.

'I don't know. What is it? Oh, what is it? The looking-glass in the kitchen is broken. All over the floor. Oh, oh! What is it?'

'I don't know any more than you do. I didn't do it.'

'Lookin'-glasses broken is a sign of death in the house,' said Cordelia. 'If it's me, I hope I'm ready; but I'd rather die than be so scared as I've been lately.'

Mr Townsend shook himself loose and eyed the two trembling women with gathering resolution.

'Now, look here, both of you,' he said. 'This is nonsense. You'll die sure enough of fright if you keep on this way. I was a fool myself to be startled. Everything it is is an earthquake.'

'Oh, David!' gasped his wife, not much reassured.

'It is nothing but an earthquake,' persisted Mr Townsend. 'It acted just like that. Things are always broken on the walls, and the middle of the room isn't affected. I've read about it.'

Suddenly Mrs Townsend gave a loud shriek and pointed.

'How do you account for that,' she cried, 'if it's an earthquake? Oh, oh, oh!'

She was on the verge of hysterics. Her husband held her firmly by the arm as his eyes followed the direction of her rigid pointing finger. Cordelia looked also, her eyes seeming converged to a bright point of fear. On the floor in front of the broken looking-glass lay a mass of black stuff in a gruesome long ridge.

'It's something you dropped there,' almost shouted Mr Townsend.

'It ain't. Oh!'

Mr Townsend dropped his wife's arm and took one stride towards the object. It was a very long crepe veil. He lifted it, and it floated out from his arm as if imbued with electricity.

'It's yours,' he said to his wife.

'Oh, David, I never had one. You know, oh, you know I – shouldn't – unless you died. How came it there?'

'I'm darned if I know,' said David, regarding it. He was deadly pale, but still resentful rather than afraid.

'Don't hold it; don't!'

'I'd like to know what in thunder all this means?' said David. He gave the thing an angry toss and it fell on the floor in exactly the same long heap as before.

Cordelia began to weep with racking sobs. Mrs Townsend reached out and caught her husband's hand with ice-cold fingers.

'What's got into this house, anyhow?' he growled.

'You'll have to sell it. Oh, David, we can't live here.'

'As for my selling a house I paid only five thousand for when it's worth twenty-five, for any such nonsense as this, I won't!'

David gave one stride towards the black veil, but it rose from the floor and moved away before him across the room at exactly the same height as if suspended from a woman's head. He pursued it, clutching vainly, all around the room, then he swung himself on his heel with an exclamation and the thing fell to the floor again in the long heap. Then were heard hurrying feet on the stairs and Adrianna burst into the room. She ran straight to her father and clutched his arm; she tried to speak, but she chattered unintelligibly; her face was blue. Her father shook her violently.

'Adrianna, do have more sense!' he cried.

'Oh, David, how can you talk so?' sobbed her mother.

'I can't help it. I'm mad!' said he with emphasis. 'What has got into this house and you all, anyhow?'

'What is it, Adrianna, poor child,' asked her mother. 'Only look what has happened here.'

'It's an earthquake,' said her father staunchly; 'nothing to be afraid of.'

'How do you account for *that*?' said Mrs Townsend in an awful voice, pointing to the veil.

Adrianna did not look – she was too engrossed with her own terrors. She began to speak in a breathless voice.

'I – was – coming – by the vacant lot,' she panted, 'and – I – I – had my new hat in a paper bag and – a parcel of blue ribbon, and – I saw a crowd, an awful – oh! a whole crowd of people with white faces, as if – they were dressed all in black.'

'Where are they now?'

'I don't know. Oh!' Adrianna sank gasping feebly into a chair.

'Get her some water, David,' sobbed her mother.

David rushed with an impatient exclamation out of the room and returned with a glass of water which he held to his daughter's lips.

'Here, drink this!' he said roughly.

'Oh, David, how can you speak so?' sobbed his wife.

'I can't help it. I'm mad clean through,' said David.

Then there was a hard bound upstairs, and George entered. He was very white, but he grinned at them with an appearance of unconcern.

'Hullo!' he said in a shaking voice, which he tried to control. 'What on earth's to pay in that vacant lot now?'

'Well, what is it?' demanded his father.

'Oh, nothing, only – well, there are lights over it exactly as if there was a house there, just about where the windows would be. It looked as if you could walk right in, but when you look close there are those old dried-up weeds rattling away on the ground the same as ever. I looked at it and couldn't believe my eyes. A woman saw it, too. She came along just as I did. She gave one look, then she screeched and ran. I waited for some one else, but nobody came.'

Mr Townsend rushed out of the room.

'I dare say it'll be gone when he gets there,' began George, then he stared round the room. 'What's to pay here?' he cried.

'Oh, George, the whole house shook all at once, and all the looking-glasses broke,' wailed his mother, and Adrianna and Cordelia joined.

George whistled with pale lips. Then Mr Townsend entered.

'Well,' asked George, 'see anything?'

'I don't want to talk,' said his father. 'I've stood just about enough.'

'We've got to sell and go back to Townsend Centre,' cried his wife in a wild voice. 'Oh, David, say you'll go back.'

'I won't go back for any such nonsense as this, and sell a twenty-five-thousand-dollar house for five thousand,' said he firmly.

But that very night his resolution was shaken. The whole family watched together in the dining-room. They were all afraid to go to bed – that is, all except possibly Mr Townsend. Mrs Townsend declared firmly that she for one would leave that awful house and go back to Townsend Centre whether he came or not, unless they all stayed together and watched, and Mr Townsend yielded. They chose the dining-room for the reason that it was nearer the street should they wish to make their egress hurriedly, and they took up their station around the dining-table on which Cordelia had placed a luncheon.

'It looks exactly as if we were watching with a corpse,' she said in a horror-stricken whisper.

'Hold your tongue if you can't talk sense,' said Mr Townsend.

The dining-room was very large, finished in oak, with a dark blue paper above the wainscoting. The old sign of the tavern, the Blue Leopard, hung over the mantelshelf. Mr Townsend had insisted on hanging it there. He had a curious pride in it. The family sat together until after midnight and nothing unusual happened. Mrs Townsend began to nod; Mr Townsend read the paper ostentatiously. Adrianna and Cordelia stared with roving eyes about the room, then at each other as if comparing notes on terror. George had a book which he studied furtively. All at once Adrianna gave a startled exclamation and Cordelia echoed her. George whistled faintly. Mrs Townsend awoke with a start and Mr Townsend's paper rattled to the floor.

'Look!' gasped Adrianna.

The sign of the Blue Leopard over the shelf glowed as if a lantern hung over it. The radiance was thrown from above. It grew brighter and brighter as they watched. The Blue Leopard seemed to crouch and spring with life. Then the door into the front hall opened – the outer door, which had been carefully locked. It squeaked and they all recognised it. They sat staring. Mr Townsend was as transfixed as the rest. They heard the outer door shut, then the door into the room swung open and slowly that awful black group of people which they had seen in the afternoon entered. The Townsends with one accord rose and huddled together in a far corner; they all held to each other and stared. The people, their faces gleaming with a whiteness of death, their black robes waving and folding, crossed the room. They were a trifle above mortal height, or seemed so to the terrified eyes which saw them. They reached the mantelshelf where the sign-board hung, then a black-draped long arm was seen to rise and make a motion, as if plying a knocker. Then the whole company passed out of sight, as if through the wall, and the room was as before. Mrs Townsend was shaking in a nervous chill, Adrianna was almost fainting, Cordelia was in hysterics. David Townsend stood glaring in a curious way at the sign of the Blue Leopard. George stared at him with a look of horror. There was something in his father's face which made him forget everything else. At last he touched his arm timidly.

'Father,' he whispered.

David turned and regarded him with a look of rage and fury, then his face cleared; he passed his hand over his forehead.

'Good Lord! What *did* come to me?' he muttered.

'You looked like that awful picture of old Tom Townsend in the garret in Townsend Centre, father,' whimpered the boy, shuddering.

'Should think I might look like 'most any old cuss after such a darned work as this,' growled David, but his face was white. 'Go and pour out some hot tea for your mother,' he ordered the boy sharply. He himself shook Cordelia violently. 'Stop such actions!' he shouted in her ears, and shook her again. 'Ain't you a church member?' he demanded; 'what be you afraid of? You ain't done nothin' wrong, have ye?'

Then Cordelia quoted Scripture in a burst of sobs and laughter.

'Behold, I was shapen in iniquity; and in sin did my mother conceive me,' she cried out. 'If I ain't done wrong, mebbe them that's come before me did, and when the Evil One and the Powers of Darkness is abroad I'm liable, I'm liable!' Then she laughed loud and long and shrill.

'If you don't hush up,' said David, but still with that white terror and horror on his own face, 'I'll bundle you out in that vacant lot whether or no. I mean it.'

Then Cordelia was quiet, after one wild roll of her eyes at him. The colour was returning to Adrianna's cheeks; her mother was drinking hot tea in spasmodic gulps.

'It's after midnight,' she gasped, 'and I don't believe they'll come again tonight. Do you, David?'

'No, I don't,' said David conclusively.

'Oh, David, we mustn't stay another night in this awful house.'

'We won't. Tomorrow we'll pack off bag and baggage to Townsend Centre, if it takes all the fire department to move us,' said David.

Adrianna smiled in the midst of her terror. She thought of Abel Lyons.

The next day Mr Townsend went to the real estate agent who had sold him the house.

'It's no use,' he said, 'I can't stand it. Sell the house for what you can get. I'll give it away rather than keep it.'

Then he added a few strong words as to his opinion of parties who sold him such an establishment. But the agent pleaded innocent for the most part.

'I'll own I suspected something wrong when the owner, who pledged me to secrecy as to his name, told me to sell that place for what I could get, and did not limit me. I had never heard anything, but I began to suspect something was wrong. Then I made a few inquiries and found out that there was a rumour in the neighbourhood that there was something out of the usual about that vacant lot. I had wondered myself why it wasn't built upon. There was a story about its being undertaken once, and the contract made, and the contractor dying; then another man took it and one of the workmen was killed on his way to dig the cellar, and the others struck. I didn't pay much attention to it. I never believed much in that sort of thing anyhow, and then, too, I couldn't find out that there had ever been anything wrong about the house itself, except as the people who had lived there were said to have seen and heard queer things in the vacant lot, so I thought you might be able to get along, especially as you didn't look like a man who was timid, and the house was such a bargain as I never handled before. But this you tell me is beyond belief.'

'Do you know the names of the people who formerly owned the vacant lot?' asked Mr Townsend.

'I don't know for certain,' replied the agent, 'for the original owners flourished long before your or my day, but I do know that the lot goes by the name of the old Gaston lot. What's the matter? Are you ill?'

'No; it is nothing,' replied Mr Townsend. 'Get what you can for the house; perhaps another family might not be as troubled as we have been.'

'I hope you are not going to leave the city?' said the agent, urbanely.

'I am going back to Townsend Centre as fast as steam can carry me after we get packed up and out of that cursed house,' replied Mr David Townsend.

He did not tell the agent nor any of his family what had caused him to start when told the name of the former owners of the lot. He remembered all at once the story of a ghastly murder which had taken place in the Blue Leopard. The victim's name was Gaston and the murderer had never been discovered.

Isabella Banks

HAUNTED!

And so, it is said, you are haunted!
  My friend, we are haunted all;
And every homestead holds a ghost
  That ever has held a pall.

Do you think that the empty cradle
  Has never a ghost within?
Or the unused nursery table
  Hears never a ghostly din?

Think you there is never a patter
  Of unseen feet on the floor?
Or that never a voiceless clamour
  Floats in through the garden door?

Is there ever a maid or widow
  Whose love lies under a stone,
Who holds not a ghost to her aching heart,
  To cherish and call her own?

Is there ever a grey-haired beauty
  Looks not in her glass to see –
No time-worn face – but the phantom form
  Of the belle she was wont to be?

Was there ever a wretch abandoned,
  A waif from the hour of birth,
Whose unknown mother was not to him
  A ghost on the dreary earth?

Could there ever be man or woman,
  Facing through lane or street,
Who could not extend an open hand
  Some shadowy friend to greet?

Could there ever be man or woman
   So lonely and loveless through life,
Was never haunted by kith or kin,
   Spirit of peace or strife?

Could there ever be human being
   With heart so narrow and small
That never a ghost could hide therein,
   To waken at Memory's call?

There are some with vision beclouded
   Who see not all that they might;
And some, of a finer essence born,
   Who see with the inner sight.

To these the past hath its phantoms,
   More real than solid earth;
And to these death does not mean decay,
   But only another birth.

NOTES ON THE AUTHORS

Gertrude Franklin Atherton (1857–1948) née Horn, was an independent and forceful American novelist, who in the early stages of her writing career was branded as a member of 'the erotic school'. She is especially noted for her novels *The Conqueror* (1902), based on the life of Alexander Hamilton, and *Black Oxen* (1923) which deals with the rejuvenation of a New York social celebrity by means of a glandular operation. 'The Striding Place', one of her best short stories, was first published in *The Speaker* magazine, in 1896. Her supernatural fiction has often been favourably compared to that of both Edith Wharton and Henry James. Her last book, published in her ninetieth year, was on her native city, *My San Francisco* (1947). Benjamin Franklin was her great-granduncle.

Louisa Baldwin (1845–1925) was one of the well-known Macdonald sisters (daughters of a Wesleyan minister), several of whom made marriages of note. Her eldest sister Alice was the mother of Rudyard Kipling, and Georgiana and Agnes married the artists Sir Edward Burne-Jones and Sir Edward Poynter respectively. Louisa herself married the ironmaster and MP Alfred Baldwin, and she lived long enough to see her only son Stanley become Prime Minister. She was a prolific writer of fiction, poetry, and children's tales, and like many other Victorian women of the time (some of the best are found elsewhere in this anthology), she penned several excellent ghost stories for the *Argosy*, *Cornhill*, and other magazines. The best of them were collected into a volume entitled *The Shadow on the Blind* (1895), and dedicated to her nephew Rudyard Kipling.

Isabella Banks (1821–1897) née Varley, known to her reading public as 'Mrs G. Linnaeus Banks', wrote several popular and controversial novels, of which the best known is *The Manchester Man* (1876). She was a firm believer in the supernatural, and collected many ghost stories (all based on fact) from her family and friends, published together in *Through the Night* (1882). Mrs Banks was also an accomplished poet, and 'Haunted!' is taken from her volume of verse *Ripples and Breakers* (1898).

Mary Elizabeth Braddon (1835–1915) became a scandalous success at the age of twenty-five with *Lady Audley's Secret* (1862), followed in 1863 with *Aurora Floyd*. A sensation novelist, often compared to Wilkie Collins, for many years Miss Braddon edited two popular magazines, *Belgravia* and *Temple Bar*, in which several of her novels first appeared. She published over eighty novels and numerous short stories. Among her excellent ghost stories, the best two are 'Eveline's Visitant' (a stalwart of many anthologies) and the short tale reprinted here, 'The Cold Embrace'. They both appeared originally in one of her earlier works, *Ralph the Bailiff and Other Tales* (1867).

Charlotte Brontë (1816–1855), the author of *Jane Eyre*, began writing poems and fantasy stories at the age of twelve, and several of these pieces were rediscovered and published many years after her death. 'Napoleon and the Spectre' was one of a number of fragments preserved by her widower, the Rev. Arthur Bell Nichols. Extracts appeared in *Poet-Lore* (Autumn 1897), and its first separate edition was printed for private circulation by Clement Shorter in February 1919, limited to only twenty-five copies. The story was later published for a wider audience in the Brontë collection of juvenilia, *The Twelve Adventurers* (1925). It was originally written in 1833, nearly thirty years after the mysterious death of French general Charles Pichegru, who Charlotte Brontë apparently believed had been strangled at the instigation of Napoleon – hence the identity of the ghost, 'Piche', which returns to haunt the French Emperor.

Rhoda Broughton (1840–1920). 'In the late nineteenth century' (wrote Michael Sadleir) 'the name "Rhoda Broughton" on a title-page, or as a symbol of conversation of witty but alarming pungency, was almost a national institution.' Her earlier novels horrified the censorious mid-Victorians and provoked anonymous reviewers to abuse; but they were eagerly devoured by those whom the moralists claimed to protect and the reviewers to influence. Her best-known works are *Cometh up as a Flower* (dedicated to her uncle, J. Sheridan Le Fanu), *Not Wisely but Too Well*, *Goodbye Sweetheart*, *Nancy*, and *Belinda*. Her collected uncanny tales appeared first as *Tales for Christmas Eve* in 1873, and later as *Twilight Stories* in 1879.

Willa Cather (1876–1947) was one of America's greatest novelists. Her earliest writings consisted chiefly of poems (*April Twilights*, 1903) and short stories (*The Troll Garden*, 1905), but her first novel, *Alexander's Bridge*, was not published until 1912. She went on to publish twelve novels, including *My Antonia* (1918), *A Lost Lady* (1923), *My Mortal Enemy* (1926), and *Death Comes for the Archbishop* (1927). 'The Affair at Grover Station' was first published in *The Library* (16 June and 23 June, 1900).

Mary Cholmondeley (1859–1925) has suffered from unjust neglect in recent years. A semi-invalid throughout her life, the book which made her famous was *Red Pottage* (1899), an attack on middle-class hypocrisy. The little-known tale 'Let Loose' originally appeared in *Temple Bar* magazine (April 1890), and was reprinted in the American edition of *Moth and Rust* (1902) – but not in the British edition. It has been favourably compared to F.G. Loring's classic supernatural tale 'The Tomb of Sarah' (1900).

Mrs Catherine Crowe (1790–1872), née Stevens, retains a unique place in mid-nineteenth-century literature through her major compilations of supernatural lore – in her own words 'probably the best storehouses of ghost stories in the English language' – *The Night Side of Nature* (1848), *Light and Darkness* (1850; concentrating more on crime and villainy), and the celebrated *Ghosts and Family Legends* (1858). 'Round the Fire' ('Seventh Evening') is taken from the third collection. All these books enjoyed great popularity among Victorian readers, and *The Night Side of Nature* is still in print today. All the stories were ostensibly true, first-hand narratives, but related, as most fictional tales of the era, with dialogue.

Ella D'Arcy (1857–1937) was one of the select *fin-de-siècle* group associated with the celebrated *Yellow Book* in the mid-1890s, with Wilde, Beardsley, Beerbohm, Dowson, and Henry James. She wrote many fine short stories, collected in *Monochromes*, *The Bishop's Dilemma*, and *Modern Instances*. 'The Villa Lucienne', her delicate ghost story set on the Riviera, first appeared in Volume X of *The Yellow Book* in 1896, and was reprinted in *Modern Instances* (1898).

Amelia Ann Blandford Edwards (1831–1892) is now best remembered for her invaluable work in creating the Egypt Exploration Fund, and her excellent travel books *A Thousand Miles Up the Nile* (1877) and *Untrodden Peaks and Unfrequented Valleys* (1873). She was also a gifted novelist and short story writer, with over a dozen fine ghost stories to her credit. Only a few of these, notably 'The Phantom Coach', have been reprinted with any regularity; one of her finest, but lesser known, tales is 'The Story of Salome'. This first appeared (anonymously) in the *Tinsleys* Christmas Annual entitled *Storm-Bound* (1872), and was reprinted in her collection *Monsieur Maurice* (1873).

'Lanoe Falconer' (pseudonym of Mary Elizabeth Hawker, 1848–1908) achieved great success with her first novella, *Mademoiselle Ixe* (1890), which was translated into many foreign languages. It was quickly followed by *Cecilia de Noël* and *The Hotel d'Angleterre*, both first published in 1891. A promising career was cut short by illness, although she completed one final volume, *Old Hampshire Vignettes*, which appeared shortly before her death.

Elizabeth Gaskell (1810–1865), née Stevenson, is best known for her novels *Cranford*, *North and South*, and *Mary Barton*. It was while *Cranford* was appearing serially (and anonymously) from 1851 to 1853 in *Household Words* magazine that the editor Charles Dickens asked Mrs Gaskell to write a ghost story for the first special Christmas issue in December 1852. This was 'The Old Nurse's Story', her most powerful and best-known tale in the genre. The best collection of her Gothic stories is *Mrs Gaskell's Tales of Mystery and Horror*, edited by Michael Ashley (1978).

Violet Hunt (1862–1942), daughter of the painter Alfred William Hunt, became in her late teens a member of the 'Rossetti Circle'. During her long literary life she numbered among her intimate friends Henry James, W.H. Hudson, D.H. Lawrence, Joseph Conrad, Rebecca West, Ford Madox Ford, and other famous names of the Edwardian era. Among her many novels are *A Hard Woman*, *The Wife of Altamont*, *The Workaday Woman*, and *The Last Ditch*. One leading critic wrote: 'She tells her stories clearly and vigorously, and invests them with a valiant significance.' Her outstanding volumes of short stories are *Tales of the Uneasy* (1911) and *More Tales of the Uneasy* (1925). 'The Prayer' was first published under the title 'The Story of a Ghost' in the Christmas Number of *Chapman's Magazine of Fiction* (December 1895).

'Vernon Lee' (pseudonym of Violet Paget, 1856–1935) is highly respected by *cognoscenti* for her brilliant tales of the supernatural. In the opinion of Montague Summers, 'even Le Fanu and M.R. James cannot be ranked above the genius of this lady'. The majority of her short stories were written in the earlier part of her career, during the last two decades of the Victorian era, and were later collected in three volumes: *Hauntings* (1890), *Pope Jacynth* (1904), and *For Maurice* (1927). 'Winthrop's Adventure', one of her finest stories, dates from 1881, and is taken from the third collection.

Rosa Mulholland (1841–1921) was a noted Irish writer whose many novels depicting Irish peasant life are now largely forgotten. Early in her career she received much encouragement from Charles Dickens who printed many of her tales in his magazine *All the Year Round*, including 'Not to Be Taken at Bed-Time', which appeared in the 1865 Christmas Number (alongside Dickens's own 'To Be Taken with a Grain of Salt'). Other supernatural stories can be found in her collection, *The Haunted Organist of Hurly Burly* (1891), which includes the title story. 'The Ghost at the Rath', and 'The Ghost of Wildwood Chase'. Later she became the wife and biographer of the noted Irish Celtic scholar Sir John T. Gilbert.

Dinah Maria Mulock (1826–1887) is best remembered for her novel *John Halifax, Gentleman* (1856), an immense success both in Britain and America. She was a prolific writer of novels, fairy-tales, essays, poems, and short stories. The latter are now very rarely anthologised and deserve to be revived. Her neglected little classic ghost story "The Last House in C— Street" first appeared in *Fraser's Magazine*, August 1856; and was published a year later in her collection *Nothing New*. Dinah Mulock became Mrs Craik in 1864, the same year she was awarded a Civil List Pension – which she put aside for authors less fortunate and successful than herself.

Mrs Margaret Oliphant (1828–1897), a prolific novelist, biographer, and historian, was the author of that brilliant series of novels of English provincial life, 'The Carlingford Chronicles'. She was also one of the greatest writers of ghost stories this country has ever produced. 'Who has ever achieved the same variety of literary work with anything like the same level of excellence?' declared one of the many appreciative tributes after she died. According to her *Autobiography and Letters*, the idea of 'The Open Door' was first suggested to her by part of the grounds belonging to Colinton House, near Edinburgh, where William Blackwood (her publisher) was then residing. This story, which originally appeared in *Blackwoods Magazine* (January 1882), is generally considered to be one of the best ghost stories ever written.

Charlotte Riddell (1832–1906) née Cowan, was a very popular established Victorian novelist. Like several of her contemporaries, she wrote many fine ghost stories (often for Christmas Annuals), and several of these were collected into *Weird Stories* (1882), *Idle Tales* (1888), and *The Banshee's Warning* (1894). Her biographer S.M. Ellis (writing in 1931) declared that *Weird Stories* (from which the following is taken) 'comprise some of the best ghost tales ever written'. Her stories about 'uncomfortable houses' (notably 'Old Mrs Jones', 'Walnut Tree House', 'Nut Bush Farm', and 'The Old House in Vauxhall Walk') are now highly regarded as classics of the genre.

Mary Eleanor Wilkins (1852–1930) was an American author who wrote with sympathy and realism about New England village life. Apart from many novels, she wrote more than two hundred short stories including several classics of the supernatural. The best of these appeared in *The Wind in the Rose-bush* (1903). Her later works appeared under her married name, Mary E. Wilkins Freeman. The American Academy of Arts and Letters awarded her the Howells medal for fiction in 1926.

Mrs Henry Wood (1814–1887) née Ellen Price, achieved her first great success with *East Lynne* (1861), and by the time of her death she had reached sales of five million copies from her various popular works. Ghosts and the supernatural often featured in her short stories, but they were never collected into a single volume. Many of them can be found in her much loved *'Johnny Ludlow'* series of which the *Spectator* wrote: 'We regard these stories as almost perfect of their kind.' And the *Daily Telegraph* added: 'Fresh, clear, simple, strong in purpose and in execution, these stories have won admiration as true works of inventive art.'

Other Books of Interest from Virago

THE VIRAGO BOOK OF GHOST STORIES: THE TWENTIETH CENTURY

'Space is inadequate for the celebration of volume one of *The Virago Book of Ghost Stories*' – *Observer*

This marvellous collection of twentieth-century tales – many from the 1920s and 1930s, the heyday of the ghost story – includes work by some thirty women writers. All of them demonstrate a subtle power to delight and chill at the same time as they explore those ghostly margins of the supernatural which are part of private experience as well as of popular tradition.

Absorbing, entertaining, deliciously unnerving, the collection is an important addition to women's literary heritage. It is also an irresistible read for those with a taste for being spooked.

Stories by: Cynthia Asquith, Enid Bagnold, Elizabeth Bowen, Angela Carter, E. M. Delafield, Winifred Holtby, Elizabeth Jane Howard, Sara Maitland, E. Nesbit, Elizabeth Taylor, Lisa St Aubin de Terán, Mary Webb, Fay Weldon, Edith Wharton, and many more.

THE VIRAGO BOOK OF FAIRY TALES

Edited and introduced by Angela Carter
Illustrated by Corinna Sargood

'A winner, full of various peoples, wicked and funny and bizarre' – *A. S. Byatt, Independent*

Fairy tales are a shorthand way of describing the marvellous narratives that have been passed down through the generations by word of mouth. We don't know the names of the people who made up the stories, but there's a mythical figure, 'Mother Goose', who knows *all* the stories. *The Virago Book of Fairy Tales* contains the pick of Mother Goose's feathers. Lyrical tales, bloody tales, hilariously funny, ripely bawdy, stories that show the dark and the light side of life – from Europe, the Arctic, the USA, Africa, in the Middle East and Asia.

With a deft and magical touch, Angela Carter has put together a collection of wonderful, little-known stories, featuring startling heroines. Be they brave, good, silly, cruel, awesomely clever or unfortunate, they are always centre stage, as large as life, even larger.

Once upon a time fairy tales weren't meant just for children, and neither is *The Virago Book of Fairy Tales*. It's a grown-up book decorated with equally grown-up pictures – and teenagers will love it too.

THE SECOND VIRAGO BOOK OF FAIRY TALES

Edited by Angela Carter
Introduced by Marina Warner
Illustrated by Corinna Sargood

'Her imagination was one of the most dazzling this century
. . . for her, fantasy always turns back its eyes to stare hard
at reality, never losing sight of material conditions' – *Marina
Warner*

'*Trumps Grimm*' claimed the *Observer* on the publication of
the first volume of *The Virago Book of Fairy Tales*. Such was
the delight in Angela Carter's pick of Mother Goose's
feathers that she compiled a second volume, once again
embracing the wicked, the funny and the bizarre from the
Arctic to Asia.

This treasure trove, perfectly complemented by the
bewitching drawings of Corinna Sargood, brims with pretty
maids and old crones, crafty women and bad girls,
enchantresses and midwives, rascal aunts and odd sisters.
The Second Virago Book of Fairy Tales is a fabulous
celebration of strong minds, low cunning, black arts and
dirty tricks – and a wonderful gift to us all, as could only
have been collected by the unique Angela Carter.